For Joe.

This (and everything) is for you.

HarperTeen is an imprint of HarperCollins Publishers.

Dark Room Etiquette

Library of Congress Control Number: 2022932404
ISBN 978-0-06-305173-7

Typography by Chris Kwon
22 23 24 25 26   PC/LSCH   10 9 8 7 6 5 4 3 2 1
❖
First Edition

DARK ROOM ETIQUETTE

ROBIN ROE

An Imprint of HarperCollinsPublishers

PROLOGUE

I'm having coffee with my statue friend.

"This isn't bad, right?" I say. "Maybe not as nice as a *Caffè Americano* . . ."

My friend doesn't laugh. He's never really had the best sense of humor.

With a sigh, I lower the paper cup back onto the table. Straight ahead of me there's an old-fashioned television, the kind with one of those fish-eye screens, and in it I can see the entire room: dilapidated wood paneling, a shiny silver door, an ancient paisley sofa, and me—at a round table right in the center. If I stay perfectly still, my reflection looks like stone.

I wave. A blurry hand waves back.

Yep. This is what becomes of a person with too much free time— they talk to themselves and befriend their own reflection.

Shaking myself out of it, I quit pretending my cup of water is coffee and grab a paintbrush. I'm determined to complete a self-portrait today, or at least a passable human. I study my face in the screen, but it's got a fun-house-mirror effect, so my drawing turns out wavy and featureless, like a shadow with green eyes.

Maybe I should just stick to what I'm good at.

I dip my brush into the water, slosh it around to clean it, then plunge it into the well of blue paint, and start covering the shadow-boy in choppy ocean strokes. I'm so focused I barely notice when the silver door slides open behind me.

My eyes find the TV screen again, and for a second it looks like a statue father is standing in the threshold. But then he moves, ruining the illusion by stepping into the room and setting his thermos on the table next to my watercolors. When I look up at him, he ruffles my hair with a big hand that smells like motor oil.

"Been doing this all day?" he asks, unfastening the top button of his flannel shirt.

"Yessir, pretty much."

Smiling, he squeezes my shoulder and holds up a brown paper sack.

"Is *that* . . ." I edit my tone, asking as carefully as I can, "Is that my surprise?"

His cheerful expression evaporates, making it clear I didn't ask carefully enough. "What's the problem? You don't even know what it is."

"It's just when you said *surprise* this morning . . . I thought . . ."

"You wanna go outside."

I don't answer, which is the same as a yes.

Looking bone-weary now, he drops the sack onto the table and takes a heavy seat in the empty chair across from me. "You know it's not safe."

"Just for a few minutes." I'm trying not to whine, which sucks because I'm failing miserably. "I bet no one would even see me."

"We can't take that kind of chance."

"But—"

"I told you *no*."

I glare at the tabletop. I can't help it.

"Are you gonna sulk now?"

"I'm not."

"Then change your face."

Sometimes that order feels impossible, like he might as well be telling me to shapeshift. But I concentrate, make my eyebrows relax and my lips go slack. I'm rearranging all my cells, creating the face of a boy who is sorry.

He taps the side of the bag with two fingers. "You don't care about this?"

"Yessir, I do. I just want—"

"Enough," he snaps. "You can't always get what you want. Now gimme your foot."

I take an invisible breath, and then I empty my eyes.

Turning in my seat, I stretch out my leg. I keep my face blank as his fingers slide behind the shackle to touch my skin. He takes the key ring from his pocket, shuffles though the many keys, and unlocks the cuff. Now that my foot is free, I rub my ankle where the flesh is a little raw.

He's still watching me—I can feel it—so I sneak in a hidden breath, fill my face with gratitude, and say, "Thank you."

ONE

"Slow down."

I let out an aggravated huff and check my speedometer. I'm not going *that* fast, and even if I were, in what world is it even remotely okay for Lex to order me around in my own car?

Deciding not to answer, I slant a smile at Bria, who's euphoric in the bucket seat beside me, like we're on our way to a party instead of the first day of junior year.

She crosses her long legs, her brown hair cascading over her shoulders as she adjusts the black-framed glasses she wears purely for aesthetic purposes. She likes to do this thing where she rips the glasses off her face and stuns you with her beauty. It's funny because there isn't much of a difference, but either way she's striking, like an all-American girl at a photo shoot.

"Aren't you excited?" she says.

Luke sticks his wild blond head in between us. "*I'm* excited!"

"We can tell," I say, teasing. "You're wearing your best *Star Wars* shirt and everything."

He nods cheerfully, then returns to his position of cuddling Lex in the back seat.

"Can you believe it, Saye?" Bria clutches my arm. "We're finally eligible for court!"

"Court?"

"*Homecoming* court! Of course I can't be queen yet, not until we're seniors. But princess!"

"You're already a princess," I tell her, and she flutters her long lashes—the ones she had installed last week, strand by perfect strand. Her glossy red lips move fast as she tells me about this year's theme and how we have to color-coordinate our outfits because *we'll remember that night FOREVER and EVER!*

I honestly don't know how she can get excited about another school dance. Nothing ever happens. Just the same bad music and sexually-repressed principals making sure no one dances close enough to enjoy themselves.

"We have six weeks," I remind her.

Her hazel eyes bulge. "You're right! There's so much to do!"

"What do you need to do besides buy a dress?"

"Trust me. A lot." She pats my shoulder like my ignorance is charming.

"Well, I have to plan the entire after-party."

"But you have a team of people helping you with that."

"He *does?*" Lex pipes up from the back seat.

Bria nods at her, then says to me, "I bet you'll get prince, Saye."

I grimace. King sounds cool, I *guess*, but the king's kid? Not so much.

"Yeah, probably," I agree, glancing in the rearview mirror just in time to catch Lex rolling her eyes.

Bria pivots to the back seat. "Hey, Lex, have you picked out your dress?"

"I'm not sure I have a date yet," Lex answers, and right on cue Luke assures her that she most definitely has a date, but he has to figure out how to ask her in the most perfect way. Another glance to the mirror, and I catch the pair of them smiling into each other's eyes like it's going to be their wedding day.

"What about you?" Bria curls her fingers over my thigh. "Are you going to ask me in a *romantic* way?"

Before I have to answer that, Lex says, "We're going to get pulled over if you don't slow down."

"Saye . . ." Luke's voice drifts to the front of the convertible. "Maybe you should."

Meeting his eyes in the mirror, I scowl. We've been best friends since preschool, and he's never given me shit about anything—not till Lex moved here this summer. She breezed into that Fourth of July celebration on the Square, all sophisticated and runway-pretty with her perfect cheekbones and mermaid hair, and somehow she gravitated to *Luke* of all people. And it's cool that he has a girl-friend. Seriously, good for him. But I don't know why it has to be a girl who's constantly giving me death glares.

"It's *fine*," I snap. "We're not going to get pulled over."

And that's when I hear the shriek of a siren.

"Oh my God! I told you!" Lex is clearly about to lose it, and Luke starts murmuring that everything's going to be okay as I pull onto the shoulder.

With a bored sigh, Bria checks her cell phone. "I hope this doesn't make us late. I have a Student Government meeting before school."

"It won't." I give her a quick kiss. "Everything's cool."

There's a loud thud behind me, and I turn to find an enormous cop knocking his baton against my tinted window. As soon as I press the button to lower it, he pokes his upper body inside, reminding me of the time I went on a drive-through safari with my third-grade class and a moose stuck his head into our bus.

"Do you have any idea how fast you were going?" Moose Cop growls.

"I have some idea, yes."

He looks dumfounded for a second—and then pissed. When I don't start quaking, he lowers his sunglasses to scowl at me more directly in a way that I guess is supposed to be intimidating.

It's not.

We lock eyes until his gaze strays to my hyper-red Aston Martin, and to me again with an expression I'm used to. He's *jealous*.

"License and registration."

I hand them over and see the exact moment he recognizes my name. *Sayers Wayte.*

A multitude of expressions cross his face all at once, then he returns my cards. "I'm gonna let you off with a warning. But you need to watch your speed."

And he stalks off.

As I merge back onto the road, Lex asks, slow and astounded, "What just happened?"

Bria gives her a meaningful smile. "You've got a lot to learn about this town."

7

✛ ✛ ✛

We're a block from school when Bria cranks the windows down and the music up. Clusters of kids turn to stare as I zip past the bronzed lion at the main entrance and into a spot at the front of the student parking lot.

I kill the engine, climb out, and immediately, a bunch of friends surround my car. Everyone has the chemical smell of new clothes and too much hair product. Bria's in her element, gliding from person to person, while I hang back with Luke and Lex, where I'm forced to watch them whisper into each other's ears.

I must be making a face because Luke's forehead wrinkles in concern. "Aww. Are you feeling left out?" He asks this without a trace of sarcasm as he slings an arm over my shoulder.

Immediately, I try to squirm out of reach—it's next to impossible to look cool when someone's sympathetically cuddling you. Luke smiles like I'm being funny, but he removes his arm. I've just struck a more respectable pose when Garrett makes his way over, wearing a plain white tee with rolled-up sleeves like a 1950s greaser. His heavy black eyebrows are mid-glower, and he's clearly about as excited to be here as I am.

"Hey." He presses his big fist into mine. "You taking that weight training class this year?"

"Uh. No." I can't imagine using public gym equipment covered in some stranger's sweat. "You?"

"Yeah. I'm benching three hundred now."

I also can't imagine having to sit beside Garrett, trying to lift as much as he can. Once upon a time we were both average-height boys just shy of average weight, but he keeps hitting the growth spurt lottery, while my height's been stubbornly in check for months.

"Hey, Lex!" Bria calls out. "If you want to join the SGA, we should probably go."

Luke relinquishes his tight hold on Lex's hand, then watches the girls disappear into the school with the pitiful eyes of a puppy someone left out in the rain.

"So . . ." Garrett says to him. "You and the new girl?"

Luke's immediately on guard. "Yeah?"

"Just surprised."

"Why?"

Garrett shrugs. "She's so full of herself. All she talks about is New York like she's too good for anyone in Texas."

A knowing smile spreads across Luke's face. "You mean she shot you down."

"She *wishes*. I'm with Marissa." Garrett's eyes are hooded, but I spot the irritation flashing in them, and I let out a groan. We've been at school for less than thirty minutes, and he and Luke are already getting into it. "Does Lex know you're Luke *Bi*walker?"

If Luke's bothered by being called that, he doesn't let it show. "Garrett, you do realize this is the twenty-first century, right?" He flings out his arms as if he'd like to hug the whole world. "Sexuality is fluid!"

"Yeah, maybe for you. All's I'm saying is Lex thinks she's better than everybody."

The enormous grin hasn't budged from Luke's face. "No. She

doesn't. She just has very particular tastes."

Amused, I pat his back. "Yep, she has a thing for skinny kids who like Yoda. Honestly, Luke, she may be your *only hope.*"

His eyes light up when he gets my non-offensive *Star Wars* reference, then the bell rings and a more serious expression settles over his face. "All right, Junior Year. Here we come."

This has got to be the dumbest thing our school has ever done. I'm not sure who thought it would be a good idea to crush the entire student body into the auditorium—in *August* with subpar AC—but my nose is already cringing at the clashing odors of cheap body spray and one thousand perspiring teens.

"Let's get out of here," I tell Garrett, who's seated beside me. Immediately, he starts scanning the perimeter with his pale blue eyes in a way that makes me think of a sniper.

Luke sends me a scandalized look. "It's the *first* day."

"So?"

"So I don't want to get in trouble." Luke's been saying this to me since I wanted to steal the classroom gerbils when we were five.

"Well, no one asked you." Garrett glares at him.

Pouting, Luke crosses his arms. "Some teachers are blocking the exits anyway."

I peer over my shoulder. Sadly, he's right.

I'm still looking for a way out when Marissa enters the auditorium, clicking photos with her phone as she walks.

"Hey, Saye!" She smiles, then climbs over my lap to sit next to Garrett, and I guess he was telling the truth because they immediately start making out so hard it looks like they're going to hurt themselves.

More friends file in to join our row, but I'm not sure where Bria is. I keep glancing around the auditorium, and I wince when my eyes land on Abby Whitley, this aggressively Christian girl who was always trying to recruit me into her church back in middle school.

Someone's tapping the mike, so I face the stage. Principal Gardiner, dressed in a crinkled brown suit, clears his throat. "Welcome back, Laurel High School students," he says, and the auditorium goes quiet long enough for him to announce that he's got a real treat for us—an introduction to all the extracurriculars we can join this year.

Fantastic.

A moment later the Thespian Society saunters out. Even their walk is dramatic, like they learned how to do it in a classroom instead of in real life.

I check the exits again. Still blocked.

They perform a ridiculously long skit about avoiding the evils of drugs. We fidget, roll our eyes. Then they reenact the funeral scene from *Steel Magnolias*, and the tough-but-fair crowd starts to boo.

It only goes downhill from there. There's the Glee Club, Chess Club, Computer Club, and with each one, the crowd keeps getting bolder and more Lord of the Flies. When some dude tells a band kid what he can do with his flute, Principal Gardiner stomps back out.

"Faculty." He presses his mouth to the mike. "Please be advised

that you are to write up any student who disrupts today's pro-
ceedings."

The teachers start moving through the aisles like a SWAT
team.

Gardiner spends a few moments staring the audience down
before he waves a beckoning arm toward the wings, and a boy
with chubby cheeks and a head full of bouncing curls rolls a
sheet-covered cart onto the stage. The wheels squeak loudly in
the now-silent auditorium.

"Hello," the kid says in a surprisingly confident voice for someone who looks about twelve. "My name is Evan Zamara, and I'll be
representing the Science Club today."

This should spark a thousand groans, but the crowd's been
frightened into submission.

"The Science Club has some amazing activities planned—
including a viewing party here at school for the meteor shower."
The kid glances around like he's expecting a chorus of gasps, but
it's crickets. "They're predicting a *thousand* meteors an hour—
that's sixteen meteors a minute. Nothing like this will happen
again in our lifetime or the next."

Still nothing from the bored-as-hell crowd.

Undeterred, he points a remote at the giant screen behind him,
and an artist rendering of what the sky is expected to look like is
projected onto the screen.

Luke starts grinning at me like a maniac.

I shake my head for him to cut it out. We were into space stuff
when we were like *ten*, but we're too old for that now. I'm beginning

to think that having a friend who's known you since you wet your pull-ups isn't necessarily a good thing.

Luke pokes out his bottom lip and directs his eyes back to the stage, where the Science Club kid's still talking. "This meteor shower is happening on August nineteenth—just one year from today."

Now the auditorium fills with annoyed murmurs. Why is he even telling us about this? No one's going to remember a meteor shower by then.

I check my phone. We've been stuck in this auditorium for *so long*, but surely things are about to wrap up.

"And now for the experiment," the boy says.

Dear God.

He whips the sheet off his cart, and underneath is a mass of wires and bulbs. He explains his experiment while he's twisting the tiny multicolored cords, and it's boring, so boring.

"If we can just dim the lights . . ." The lights dim a *little*. He flips a switch. "And now . . ."

Only nothing happens.

The boy scratches his dark curls and fiddles with the wires. "Okay, *now*."

Still nothing. If this were the 1920s, someone would be looping a cane around this kid's waist and yanking him off the stage right about now. He keeps on fiddling until I can't take it anymore. It's one thing to miss the first two periods, but this is eating into Homeroom, which is *free time*.

"I think I should go up there and put him out of his misery," I joke under my breath.

Garrett gives me that look—the one that means I'm shocking, but in a good way. "Do it."

Luke shakes his head at me wide-eyed, and now he's just made it irresistible.

I stand up.

Nervous laughter skitters out of my row as I walk down the aisle. I pass a couple of teachers who look like they aren't sure if this is part of the show or not, and I keep taking long strides until I'm center stage, gazing out at a thousand curious faces.

I soak it in.

Then I lower my lips to the mike. "I just want to say how . . . *extraordinary* this has been. I honestly don't know how any of us are going to be able to choose between all these incredible clubs."

The crowd roars with laughter like I'm the best stand-up comedian they've ever heard.

"But I think we need time to process all this, so I'd like to propose that we be dismissed. Immediately."

Thunderous applause races across the auditorium, joined by stomping feet. The curly-haired boy looks up with Bambi eyes, but they quickly shift down to his mound of tangled wires.

Principal Gardiner storms back out and leans into the mike. "All right, Mr. Wayte, thank you for sharing." His put-upon tone just makes the crowd laugh harder. He glances to his old-man watch. "I suppose this has run a little long . . . Very well, people. Dismissed."

"Are you in trouble?" Luke asks when he spots me in the hall a few minutes later.

"What do you think?"

Shaking his head, Luke falls in step beside me. "So what class do you have now?" I show him my schedule, and his blond eyebrows fly up. "You're still taking that class?"

"Apparently."

"But it's so . . . so useless."

"Yeah, yeah, *te futueo et caballum tuum*," I say, and he cracks up with the easy delight of a little kid. I've been teaching him how to curse in Latin and *screw you and the horse you rode in on* just happens to be his favorite.

"But seriously, why don't you just take Spanish or French or something? You're basically fluent now, right? Or actually! Why don't you switch and take art with me?"

"Luke. We have five classes together."

"And . . . ?"

"And you already talked me into using one of my electives on Psychology."

"That's because Ms. Wells is the best. She's our Homeroom teacher too, you know."

"Okay, so that's five classes *and* Homeroom."

"I don't care! Switch into art!"

"I don't think so," I tell him, veering left.

I can't draw to save my life.

When I get to third period, Mr. Rivas closes his newspaper and adjusts his pin-striped bow tie. He looks like a method actor gearing up for a part, only he's doing it all wrong. This is nineteenth-century college professor, not modern-day high school teacher.

"Sayers," he says formally.

"The one and only." I glance around the empty classroom. Looks like I am literally the one-and-only person who registered for Advanced Latin, which is strange, because of all the languages I know, I think Latin might be the most interesting.

"So how was your summer?" Mr. Rivas asks me, in Latin.

"It was all right," I answer, in English. "I went to Paris, but it was boring, then I went to Spain and that was even more boring. How about you?"

"Hmm." He strokes his gray-speckled beard. "My car broke down, so I took the bus to Target a lot. It was fun."

I chuckle. He has a nice, dry sense of humor. "That's funny."

"In Latin."

"Istud ridiculum est."

He corrects my pronunciation, and I argue that it's hard to be certain just what the correct pronunciation is, and he grins as if he's delighted.

"Ready to dive in?" He hands me a new textbook and a syllabus, and soon I'm getting lost in conjugating verbs until my phone—which is bright red like my car—buzzes on the corner of my desk with a series of texts from my father:

Got a new place!

Check it out!

Then a blast of photos.

I scroll through them. They're a total cliché of what bachelors are supposed to want, all modern and silver with lots of windows but no curtains. Through one of the floor-to-ceiling glass walls, something grabs my focus.

I text:

Is that the OCEAN?

And he texts back:

How bout we catch a movie on Sunday, and I'll explain. We can go to the Rialto. I know how much you love their balcony seats.

Yeah. When I was *ten*. My thumbs hover over the screen. I'm not sure I want to see a movie with him. I never have fun when we hang out, plus there are a bunch of back-to-school parties this weekend. But I haven't seen him in over a month.

I'm still trying to decide when I get this I'm-being-watched feeling—and not the good kind. I look up and spot an old man glaring daggers at me from the hall. He huffs and puffs his way into the room with the swagger of a mall cop. The billion keys on his waist are jingling.

"Can I help you, Mr. Elders?" Mr. Rivas asks.

"Is that student s'posed to be usin' his cell phone during class?" he demands.

"I've got things under control," Mr. Rivas says primly. "But thank you."

The old man scowls as he huffs back out.

"Who was that?" I ask.

"Our new assistant principal."

"Doesn't he know who I am?"

"*Sayers.*" Mr. Rivas gives me a mildly disapproving look.

"What?" But then I realize what he's getting at, so this time I ask in Latin: "*Doesn't he know who I am?*"

+ + +

I slip out the back doors before the final bell, beating the after-school crowds, and hop into my convertible. Now that no one's around to complain, I lower the top and race through my town. Over the bridge, past Wayte Library and the Square, and I make it to the wrought-iron gates surrounding my neighborhood in record time.

The guard nods at me through the window in his little booth, then he buzzes me through, and I speed along the winding road to my house. When Luke and I were little, he'd call it my *castle*, and that's probably because the architect modeled it after an actual castle in France. In preschool, Luke would run out of Legos trying to build it. He'd annoy other kids by hoarding all the towers. His version was always a rainbow-colored monstrosity, but in reality Wayte House is all about clean lines.

White stone.

Blue slate roof.

Every window symmetrical, every shrub a neat square or perfect circle.

I press the button on the small remote pinned to my leather visor. The next iron gate parts, so I continue down the tree-lined drive to a parking space, then climb out and stroll down the walkway, passing acres of immaculate green lawn. There's a white gazebo, scattered fountains, an English garden, statues of Greek figures, and at the edge of the property are thick woods. My mom's thrown a lot of events out here, and in just a few weeks it'll be my turn. My mom's even promised to clear out on the night of

Homecoming so I can really be in charge.

Reaching the back door, I brace myself. I'm so ready for a little me-time, but I still have to get past Mrs. Marley, and for a lady pushing seventy, she has incredible hearing.

I cross the black-and-white marble checkered floors of the great room—so far so good—into the long, vaulted hall, and I'm almost to the backstairs when I hear, "Saye, honey? Do you need anything?"

I cringe, embarrassed even though no one's around to witness this. But honestly, no one else my age still has a *nanny*.

"I'm good, Mrs. Marley!" I call over my shoulder.

"Would you like me to bring you up a snack?"

I pause in my steps. I suppose it *does* make her happy to look after me, so I call back, "That would be fine," then I jog up the stairs to my room on the third story. Streams of sunlight are flooding through all my windows, along with the irritating whine of a riding lawn mower. One by one, I snap the shutters closed, then I collapse onto my bed, finally, blissfully alone.

At seven o'clock, I stuff myself into a black suit to attend the fundraiser for some place called Oak Hill that works with troubled horses, or maybe it's troubled kids who ride horses. I can't keep track.

My mother's waiting for me at the bottom of the main staircase wearing a sparkly dress, more sparkly stuff clipped into her blond hair. She lifts her head as I descend, a radiant smile brightening her face.

A secret that will die with me is that when I was eight years old, I bought best friend necklaces for the two of us—that kind where each person gets half a heart. Actually, I guess it's not much of a secret since I wore it to school for weeks until some older boys questioned me about it, then made it clear you can't be best friends with your own mother.

At the moment, my mom's decked out in a strand of dripping emeralds, but to this day, she swears that brass half-a-heart is her favorite piece of jewelry.

"You look so nice!" She draws her phone from her purse as quick as a gunslinger and aims it at me.

Moaning, I hold up a hand, but she ignores me, so I deliberately make monster faces on every click.

"Saye!" Her tone is scolding, but she's laughing too hard to sound very threatening. "Come on—one normal face, just *one*."

"Why? You know they're going to take a million photos at the event."

"I don't care. These are for me. Now stop being such a teenager."

A few media outlets covering the event snap our picture, and before I even have a chance to tell my mom *I told you so*, we're whisked into a crowded ballroom where I'm encircled by legions of her friends and colleagues.

Oh my, so handsome!

Look at that golden hair.

Be careful with this one, Nadine.

All the winks and tones are a lot more suggestive than they

used to be, something Luke would call Seriously Creepy, but my mom doesn't seem to notice.

She nudges me in my side. "Beau Baxter is heading our way—he's a state senator, but word has it he's running for governor next year." She lowers her voice to a whisper, *"Be charming."*

As soon as he reaches us, I hold out a hand. "I hear you're going to be our next governor."

With a big bleach-white smile, he heartily shakes my hand. "I can't confirm or deny anything just yet." Then he leans in like this is just between us. "But that is certainly the plan."

Mom gives me an approving smile before she takes the senator's arm, saying there's someone he just *has* to meet, then they're off to mingle.

I snag a glass of champagne from a passing tray and find a dark corner. Bored, I scroll through my phone, but I look up when a dramatic hush falls over the room.

My grandfather's here, looking like a ruthless sea captain with his blue tailcoat and steely gaze, but his expression softens like it always does when he sees my mother. He wraps her into a warm hug and swoops her around the room, puffed up with pride. They schmooze for a solid hour before we're shown to a dining room dotted in white-cloth-covered tables and votive candles, and I'm all for ambience, but it's so dark I can hardly see.

Increasing the brightness on my phone, I snap a few pics, then post one.

Right away the comments roll in, stuff like: *Where are you??* And of course: *Jealous!*

"Sayers," my grandfather says in the same imperious tone he uses on everyone except my mother. "Why is your phone out at the table?"

Mom sends me an amused look and a wink that says, *We are so not taking him seriously.* Chuckling, I continue scrolling, and my grandfather lets out a weary sigh like arguing with me's not worth the effort.

We're halfway through the main course—grilled salmon with rosemary-butter sauce, and a round cutlet of steak that's too rare even for me—when some guy my mom's age approaches our table.

"Nadine, is that you?"

"Charles!" she gasps. "How *are* you?"

"I'm well, I'm well." The man turns to my grandfather, practically bowing to him like he's a king. "And how are you, sir?"

"Fit as a fiddle," my grandfather answers.

"I was just in Hartview on business, and I couldn't believe how quickly everything was going up. That whole area's booming! Who would've guessed it?" When my grandfather raises one silver eyebrow, the man adds quickly, "Well, other than *you*, of course."

My grandfather's a land developer, and according to everyone, he's supernaturally gifted when it comes to knowing what's going to be worth something one day—and what isn't.

"I'm afraid you'll have to excuse me." My grandfather taps his watch. "There's a call I need to place at nine."

"Of course, of course." And the second my grandfather's gone, the guy aims all his focus on me. "This can't be Sayers!"

"This is Saye," Mom says proudly like she made me herself in a laboratory. "My beautiful boy."

"The last time I saw you, you were in the first grade." He chuckles, then turns back to my mom. "How's Jack?"

My mother's smile freezes in place like she's in shock or in pain, but she recovers quickly. "Jack and I separated." She always says *separated* instead of divorced like that's classier or something.

"Oh . . ." The guy looks embarrassed now. "I'm so sorry to hear that."

"Such is life." Mom waves her hand like she isn't bothered in the slightest, but I know better. I was there the night she found out my dad was cheating on her with not one, but multiple women. The only reason I knew about it was because I used to love eavesdropping on all their conversations, so I overheard her say, "Who is she?" And then Dad was like, "Which one?" And somewhere during the fight he was shouting, "You and your father have to control everything! Maybe I don't want to be absorbed by the Waytes!"

Once my dad left, I snuck out of my hiding place, and Mom wrapped her arms around me. I could feel how much she was shaking, but her voice was calm when she said, "Everything will return to normal, you'll see. He'll be back to apologize—he'll be *begging* to come back."

But that was something he never did.

TWO

I step into the obnoxiously-bright theater and slide a dark pair of sunglasses over my face. I'm still recovering from Braxton's lakehouse party, and even though I only had a few beers, I regret them. It was a dull night, and all drinking does is slow me down and make me feel even more bored. I'd have been better off with coffee.

I spot my father in the refreshment line chatting up a girl who doesn't look much older than me. He's dressed in a tropical shirt, white linen pants, and loafers with no socks, and I hardly recognize him with his new shade of blue-black hair.

Why am I even here? Maybe if I just I turn around slowly . . .

"Well, hello there!" my dad calls out, waving both arms.

Guess there's no backing out now. Sighing, I cross the lobby, and he punches me in the shoulder like we're old college buddies.

"I already got us the tickets, so why don't you treat with some popcorn?" He's talking too loud, too showy, like we're contestants on a gameshow.

"Sure, D—" I'm starting to say, but before I can finish, he tells the girl, "This is my *nephew*, Saye." He gives me a sloppy wink.

"Yeah . . . Hey, *Uncle* Jack."

He smiles like he's never loved me more than he does at this moment, then redirects his attention to the girl. The lobby's packed with lively Sunday-afternoon moviegoers, so I should be able to tune out the nauseating noises of my father in pick-up mode, but it's hard.

When my dad asks the girl if she works out, I can't stop myself from glancing over, and I catch her expression—one that says she's thinking about bolting for a different line. Maybe even a different theater.

I literally face-palm. This is even more awkward than when the women flirt back.

My cell phone buzzes, and I eagerly read the text from Luke:

Where are you?

Movies with my dad, I answer. He's making me call him Uncle Jack so he can woo a college girl.

Creepy, Luke replies, along with a vomiting gif.

He's definitely got his quirks, I text back. But don't we all?

On Monday morning, I'm en route to first period when Garrett nudges me with a sharp elbow. I follow the direction of his sniper gaze all the way to that kid—the chubby-cheeked boy from last week's assembly with the failed science experiment. Today he's dressed in a *Doctor Who* T-shirt that's about two sizes too small around his belly. He's walking delicately, his arms stretched out to both sides as he carries a large, flat wooden box, and he's grinning like a child on his way to show-and-tell.

"Now isn't that the saddest thing you've ever seen?" I joke.

I'm rewarded when Garrett chuckles, then he pastes on his friendliest face. "Hey!" he shouts, startling the boy into nearly tripping over his clown-sized sneakers. "Whatcha got there?"

The curly-haired kid walks toward us with an oblivious smile. "It's a model for Biology. I based it off the old Operation board game."

I peer into the black wooden box, and I could never admit this out loud—but it's extremely cool. I kind of remember the game, a cartoonish guy on his back with cutouts for his organs, but this is a museum-quality sculpture.

I'm not sure what it's made of. Maybe clay? It almost looks like glass with its glazed overlay of flesh, and underneath you can see lifelike muscles, tissues, and veins. There are several open cavities, and inside each one is an incredibly detailed organ.

"You *made* this?" I'm not doing a great job of concealing my awe.

The boy nods, curls bouncing, smile widening. "Yes, and it's fully functional too." He gestures to the red wire attached to a pair of tiny metal clamps.

"Wow," Garrett says. "We'll have to play with you sometime."

I squint over at him. It's hard to tell if he's being serious or not. Probably not, but maybe this genius kid won him over. It's possible. The bell rings, and everyone starts zooming through the halls. Garrett smirks in my direction, almost like he's signaling something, then he swivels to the boy and smacks the sculpture out of his hands.

It lands on the floor, breaking right down the center.

I hold back a startled noise as I look down it, then to the kid, who's staring up at us with giant wounded eyes. He's not even trying to hide how upset he is, like he doesn't know he should, and it's honestly such a pitiful expression I'm about to pat him the way I would Luke, but I'm distracted by a shrill screech.

"HEEEY!!!" A guy, all marionette joints and fiery red hair, is rushing over, wearing overalls with grass stains on the knees like he's a farmer or something. "What happened, Evan?"

"Nothing," Evan mumbles, kneeling to gather up his broken sculpture. Some of the organs have spilled out, and the perfectly constructed heart is in a thousand pieces.

The redhead glares at me and Garrett like he knows *exactly* what happened. He squares his scrawny shoulders as if he's going to tell us off, but what actually comes out is a strangled birdlike squawk of fluctuating octaves. It's such a funny noise that I can't help it—I laugh.

Garrett is less amused. He lunges at Bird Boy, and now the squawk is frightened.

Alarmed, Evan raises his head. "Blair, it's okay. Seriously."

"You boys there!" A teacher is stomping our way.

"Let's go," Garrett tells me, and we disappear into the crowd.

As I slide into my desk, Mr. Rivas gives the analog clock on the wall a pointed look. I'm more than a little late, but at least he doesn't add a sarcastic, *Nice of you to join us* kind of comment. He starts shuffling through the stack of papers on his desk, and then he holds up my quiz. It's marked 100 followed by three oversized exclamation points.

"Oh. Cool." I lean back in my seat.

"This is excellent work, Sayers. *Excellent.* I think you really have a gift for languages."

"Yeah . . ."

"Do you know what this shows me?"

"Hmm?" I take an absent sip of my vanilla latte.

"That you could always do this if you try—and not just in Latin, but in *anything* you put your mind to." And to my dismay, he launches into the you're-smart-but-you-don't-apply-yourself speech, which is a bit much for a Monday.

I continue drinking my coffee, expecting him to wind down, but after a few minutes I realize that's not going to happen. "Mr. Rivas, no disrespect, but what does it matter?"

"What do you mean?"

"Well, this grade, school in general."

Mr. Rivas gapes at me like he's astonished. "High school prepares you for college. If you get good grades, you'll have more options. And college is where you choose your career. That's where you're going to spend most of your life, so certainly it's important."

"But is that how it was for you? I mean, did you really want to be a teacher?"

"Of course I did."

I study his face, trying to decide if he's just saying what he thinks he's supposed to say, or if he really means it. He does seem to genuinely like it here in this little room with its scuffed floors and poor ventilation. He's smiling like there's no other place he'd rather be.

"My grades aren't really an issue," I explain. "I'm going to a good college, and after that I'll work at my family's company. If I want to, I mean. No matter what I do, the money will be there, so I can do something or I can do nothing. It doesn't really matter either way."

Mr. Rivas nods to himself, glancing away for a moment, then back at me, and there's this expression on his face. But I have to be reading him wrong because somehow it looks like *pity*.

I'm starting to think Ms. Wells might be my new favorite teacher. She doesn't force us to endure insulting lectures like Mr. Rivas. She just focuses on the material.

Right now she's in front of our seventh-period Psychology class, juiced up on teaching without a PowerPoint as she tells us about these studies proving how unreliable eyewitnesses are. It turns out humans have notoriously terrible memories—and sometimes we even make our memories up.

She launches into the details of an experiment where these research psychologists had parents tell their adult children about a time they got lost in a shopping mall, something that never actually happened. Soon their kids not only *remembered* the incident, they were adding tons of details like where they went, and how they felt, and even an entirely fictional person who supposedly helped them get back to their family.

Luke's so blown away he's about to fall out of his chair.

"This study demonstrates how easy it can be to implant memories," Ms. Wells says, making me think of a modern-day Snow White with her tiny pale features and short black hair. Luke's hand flies into the air, and she beams at him, cupping her palms like she's about to sing to a forest of cartoon animals. "Yes, Luke?"

"So memories can be implanted . . . but can they be *extracted*?"

Oh God, he's about to ask about aliens, I know it.

Back in grade school when we were both obsessed with all things extraterrestrial, we read tons of books containing supposed firsthand accounts from alien abductees who'd claimed they couldn't remember what happened to them until they underwent hypnosis years later.

It's kind of funny now, but some of those stories were really messed up. Like there was this one guy who swore that a being from another planet took him into a red-lit room on a spacecraft crammed floor-to-ceiling with fish tanks. Only when he got closer, he discovered they weren't fish at all, but the embryos of human-alien hybrids.

For me those stories were fun-scary—I never actually *believed* any of it. Not like Luke.

"Hmm," Ms. Wells muses, and she goes on to tell us about the different types of memory loss like lacunar amnesia and dissociative fugue, and then she's listing all the way our minds can be tricked—syndromes like Capgras and Stockholm and Lima. But why or how this all happens, she says is complicated.

I wonder if there's a disorder that makes you dye your hair slate-blue and pretend you don't have a son. Maybe my dad could be featured in a medical journal.

Ms. Wells keeps talking, and the bottom line seems to be: Our minds are a total mystery.

THREE

"Saye?" Mrs. Marley's knocking on my door.

I bury my face into my pillow. "What?"

"It's after seven."

"I know," I moan, even though I had no idea.

I hear her clucking in disapproval as I grope at my bedside table and locate my phone. Unlocking it, I check the temperature—October 1 and fifty-five degrees. I may even need a light jacket today, which is my favorite kind of weather.

It's too late for a full workout in the gym, so I drop to my floor and get into one of those strict, military push-up positions that Garrett showed me how to do. Slowly, I bend my elbows, lowering my chest till it's below the crooks of my arms, then I rise back up.

I make it to fifty before my biceps begin to burn, but I keep going.

Down, up, fifty-one.

Down, up, fifty-two.

All the way to one hundred.

Feeling accomplished, I hop into the shower, and when I climb out, I give myself a once-over in my bathroom mirror. The workouts are paying off—my arms are definitely getting bigger. I wash my face, frowning a little as my fingers glide across my smooth skin. Still zero signs of facial hair, but of course my dad said he didn't get any real action on his chin till college.

With a sigh, I head downstairs where my mom's directing the staff on where to place the fall foliage decor.

When I was little, I used to beg her to let us turn our place into a haunted house for Halloween, but she said it was tacky and tasteless, so I know that none of these scores of pumpkins will ever be jack-o'-lanterns.

She smiles when she sees me. "What do you think?"

"Nice," I say.

"I actually wanted to speak to you." She's wearing her serious-business face now. "I suppose you heard your father is moving."

I feel myself shutting down. "Yep."

"Do you want to talk about it?"

"Nope."

"Saye—"

"Do *you* want to talk about it?"

She pauses, giving me a look like I'm being difficult. "I'm fine," she says. "But are you?"

"*Mom.*" I rake my fingers through my hair. "It's not a big deal. I hardly ever see him." But she clearly doesn't believe me, and I'm getting annoyed. "I *don't.*" I mean, yeah, it's weird that my dad decided to move to another country—that he even went so far as to buy a house before mentioning it—but I don't care. "It's barely eight a.m. I need caffeine, not a heart-to-heart."

"All right, all right." She throws up her hands. "Changing the subject. I'm heading to Dallas to prep for the gala, and it's going to run late, probably after midnight, so you'll be on your own. But I can ask Mrs. Marley to stay if you want."

"Mom, please don't do that. I'm *sixteen*."

Smiling now, she pats my cheek with a manicured hand. "Yes, I know. All grown up."

I'm sipping my Starbucks, an off-menu mocha, and only sort of listening to the surprisingly respectful discussion on religions of the world. Most of my attention is directed to a text from Bria:

The SGA meeting got canceled. Want to do something after school?

My thumbs fly over the keys:

How about my house? Everyone's going to be gone.

And she replies just as fast:

The Square first? Everybody's meeting there. But after that . . .

And then a winky face.

"Ms. Sims!" All the fantasies forming in my head are instantly doused in cold water by the outraged voice of Abby Whitley.

"Yes?" our teacher says cautiously.

"Listening to this is against my faith. I can't hear about false idols."

A couple more church-kids chime in with their agreement, while Ms. Sims nervously wrings her hands. Leaning back in my seat, I close my eyes. Did Bria's winky face mean what I think it means? She'd said she wanted to wait till Homecoming, but maybe she changed her mind.

"There's a reason people hate Sundays even worse than Mondays," someone grumbles, then another kid shouts, "I'm a Christian too! But that doesn't mean we can't even *talk* about other religions. It's not blasphemous to ask *questions*."

I try to tune the class out and keep picturing Bria, in my house, in my room, in my *bed*. She's wearing a lacy top . . . and now she's taking it off. So I'm taking off my—

"It *is* blaspheming," Abby argues. "Look what happened to Lucifer!"

Okay, I give up. I crack one eye open to find that Abby, dressed in khaki slacks and a white polo like a self-imposed school uniform, is standing. Everyone is watching her, and she's glancing around, almost like she can't believe she has the floor, but she's sure going to make the most of it.

"The Lord our God made Lucifer." Her tone is superior now. "Lucifer was his favorite. But then Lucifer questioned the Lord, and he threw him down to Hell."

A few people aim nervous glances at the ceiling like they're afraid God's about to smite them.

"God made the Devil?" Luke's innocent question sounds like he's making fun of her, but I know he's being genuine.

"*No*," Abby says impatiently. "God made *Lucifer*. Lucifer was an angel, his creation, basically his child. But Lucifer chose to be evil."

Luke seems to be thinking this over. "So Lucifer could leave Hell if he asked for forgiveness?"

"Of course not. Once you're sent to Hell, it's *forever*."

A memory pops into my head. A nanny before Mrs. Marley came into the picture was trying to get me to behave, so she told me God made a list of every bad thing and every good thing you ever did. When you died, he checked your lists, and if the bad was longer than the good, he'd send you to Hell. A place where you'd burn forever. No second chances, no way out.

The whole room's arguing so loudly now I can barely hear it when Ms. Sims starts slapping the bell on her desk. "Class! We're getting off track. Please take your seat, Abby."

Abby's lips turn down in a sad frown, but she does as she's told.

Ms. Sims takes a traumatized breath. "Does anyone *else* have something to share?"

A girl with long braids sticks up her hand. "I do. This makes zero sense." She goes on to declare that the world's a cesspool—starvation, murder, and rape prove God doesn't even exist.

"How can you say that?" Abby looks genuinely hurt. "God *loves* us. He sent his only son, Jesus, to die on the cross for our sins."

"So you really can't ever get out of Hell?" Luke's eyes are wide with anxiety as if he's actually buying all of this. That's the troubling thing about Luke. He'll believe anyone about anything if they speak with enough authority.

"No," Abby insists. "Not ever."

Luke's eyes grow to epic proportions. Abby's freaking him out, and it's actually starting to piss me off. I set down my coffee with a hard thud.

"What kind of father hangs his son on a cross?"

The whole room swivels in my direction.

"He sounds like a dick."

There are a few seconds of stunned silence, then the class bursts into laughter.

"That's love?" I continue.

Abby focuses on me, her eyes cold. "That's *sacrifice*."

When I get to the cafeteria, Luke's alone at our table by the window, his face scrunched up in fear as he struggles to pry open his tiny bag of Cheetos. With a deep sigh, I take the bag and open it for him. He plucks out a single chip and chews on it in the most distraught way a person can chew on a Cheeto.

"Luke, this is ridiculous. Hell doesn't even exist."

"If that's true, then how are people punished for the stuff they do?"

"All right, all right, fine. We'll just pay that fee—what did our teacher call them? *Indulgences?* And we'll get you into Heaven. Sound good?"

"It won't work! You can't buy your way out of Hell!"

"Luke, I'm kidding."

But he's still stress-tapping his orange-stained fingers onto the bag when Lex and Bria join our table, carrying stacks of SGA papers like two ladies coming from a board meeting.

"What are we talking about?" Bria asks.

And I answer, "Hell."

Lex kisses the top of Luke's head, her face disappearing in his blond hair forest. She's wearing a stylish jumpsuit you'd expect to see on a red carpet, while Luke is dressed in high-water jeans and suspenders—the costume people wear when they're *trying* to look like dorks.

"You're not going to Hell, baby," Lex says.

Luke darts an embarrassed glance at me. "I may have voiced my concerns to her via text."

"And why are we talking about this?" Bria wants to know.

"Abby Whitley scared the shit out of him in World History this morning," I tell her.

"But what if she's right?" he whines.

"Luke, *stop*." I shake the bag in his direction, and he plucks out another Cheeto. "Even if Hell did exist, it wouldn't matter. You are the last person who'd go there." Honestly the idea of Luke being condemned to Hell is so preposterous, I can't even fathom it.

"Saye's right," Lex says, two words I never thought I'd hear her utter.

"Hell is so depressing. Can we talk about something more fun?" When no one argues, Bria hands me a square of gold fabric.

Confused, I take it. "Uh, cool?"

Luke chuckles, which is nice because it means he's settling down.

"It's the color swatch for Homecoming!" Bria beams. "Your tie needs to match this."

"Eh, that's all right." I hand the fabric back to her. "The guys are wearing red ties."

Bria's smile vanishes. "Is that really your priority? Color-coordinating with the other boys?"

In lieu of answering, I eat one of Luke's chips, and Bria makes a *baaa*ing noise, calling me a sheep I guess, which is ridiculous since *I'm* the one everyone copies, but I give her my best dazzle-smile. "Every other couple's going to be matching. You know that right? This way you'll upstage all those standard-issue girls."

"Okay, fine! But if I go along with whatever you wear, can we *please* have an elephant at the after-party?"

Lex laughs out loud like she thinks Bria's joking, but she is so not joking.

"Bria, I've told you—the theme is Luxe 1920s, not *circus*. An elephant makes absolutely no sense."

"But it *is* on theme. Remember the movie *Annie*? And the big party at the end where they bring out the elephant? That was the 1920s."

It's pretty obvious Bria's been fantasizing about this since childhood, so I give in. "Okay, you've convinced me. If this is a dream of yours, then why not?"

Squealing, Bria loops her arms around my neck.

Lex looks on stunned. "The Great Gatsby's got nothing on you, Saye."

"Oh, please. Did you even read the book? Gatsby didn't care about his parties—he literally hid in the back the whole time."

"But *you'll* be the center of attention, right?" Lex says.

Bria's arms stiffen around me as she glances from me to Lex, and it's like she's just now picking up on the tension that's been there for months.

"There's nothing wrong with wanting to be seen, is there?" Bria finally says, giving Lex an offended stare.

Lex looks like she wants to argue, but maybe she doesn't have the energy for it today because she starts poking the prongs of her plastic fork into her lettuce-filled bowl. It's a pretty pitiful-looking salad, come to think of it, just some wilty leaves and a lone cherry tomato.

When someone walks by carrying a smelly tray of food, I wince. "I can't wait till we have off-campus lunch next year. Eating in the cafeteria is so . . . degrading."

"I'm surprised someone like you would even go to public school," Lex mumbles, and it should be a compliment, but there's something snide about the way she says it.

"I went to boarding school when I was a freshman."

"Really?" Her perfectly arching eyebrows fly up. "Why'd you leave?"

Before I can speak, Luke answers for me. "Too many rules."

After school, Bria hops into the convertible's passenger seat, and a few minutes later, I'm pulling into a parking garage on the Square. Bria reapplies her glossy red lipstick in the vanity mirror before we hop out. I press my key fob to set the alarm, and it *chirp-chirp*s.

The second we enter the elevator, my pulse accelerates. Bria has a thing for elevators, so now I have a thing for elevators.

With a sly smile, she taps the button for the sixth floor.

As we glide up, I kiss her.

We ride up and down so many times I lose count. We make out against every wall until I'm breathless and about to suggest calling off coffee altogether, but then we reach the ground floor again, and this time, Bria lets the doors slide open.

We continue on to Starbucks, where our friends are already drinking their Maple Pecan Lattes and Pumpkin Spice Frappuccinos. There's Luke and Lex, Garrett and Marissa, and a bunch of uncoupled and formerly-coupled and soon-to-be-coupled.

They cheer when they see us.

Once we've got our drinks, Bria and I join them. Everyone's talking about how great this year's going so far—and next year we'll be seniors—then OMG! College!

Bored, I sip my coffee. I have a feeling college is going to be exactly like this, only in a different zip code.

We've been here for an hour when I catch Bria frowning at her phone. I nudge her, and she shows me the text she just got from her mom:

The sitter didn't show! Bethany's at the house ALONE!!

"I'm sorry, Saye." Bria lets out a sigh. "I guess I can't hang out tonight after all."

I'm more than a little disappointed—I literally never have the whole house to myself—but I stand to go.

"You guys can't leave yet!" Marissa protests. "We didn't even get pictures."

Before I can blink, she's got her phone out, and everyone's squishing their faces into mine for selfies. When Bria's cell buzzes again, she insists that we really have to go now.

Back to the elevator—no making out this time—and soon I'm pulling up in front of her house, where her little sister's sulking on the front porch.

"Do you want to come in?" Bria says. "Help me babysit?"

"Eh . . . I'm not exactly a kid person."

"But it would be good practice. And I'm sure when we have children, you're going to be a great father!"

"When we have *children*?" We haven't even had sex yet. We haven't even finished *high school*.

"We can talk about that later." Bria pecks my cheek and hops out.

By the time I reach my house a few minutes later, the sun's beginning to set. I check my phone—already five hundred likes and counting on the post Marissa just tagged me in.

I grab my now lukewarm coffee from the cup holder and stroll down the back walkway, taking my time as I drink. It's finally starting to cool off for the year, and the trees are changing colors, although it's too dark to really see them at the moment. The fallen leaves look gray, and the statues look like silhouettes with long shadows.

That's strange—one of the statues has been relocated to the tree line.

I wonder who would do that. They're so heavy you need a forklift to move them, so it's not something you could do on a whim.

Squinting, I tilt my head, and then it hits me.

That's not a statue.

At the edge of the woods, a man is watching me.

FOUR

My first thought is he might be a gardener, but that doesn't make sense. He doesn't have any tools, plus it's too dark to do yardwork.

The man begins to close the gap between us.

I take another swallow of coffee.

He's a big, boxy guy with close-cropped hair. I don't recognize him, but he must work for my mom. Maybe this has something to do with the gala.

But why would he be out here when everyone else is in Dallas?

The man marches toward me faster, and I find myself thrusting my hand in my pocket and yanking out my cell phone.

"Hold up!" His deep voice carries across the yard.

I hesitate, my finger poised over the screen.

"I'm the new security guard!"

My eyes narrow. He *is* wearing the standard army-green uniform.

"I didn't mean to alarm you." He's just a few feet from me now.

"You didn't."

He glances to his leather portfolio. "This is the Wayte House, correct?"

"Yes, it is."

"I'm patrolling the area."

"In my yard?"

"Sorry about that. I entered the woods at the back, and this estate is so large, it's hard to tell where your property ends and the rest of the community begins."

"And why are you patrolling? Has there been an issue?"

"No, no, not at all. But I believe it's wise to always be surveilling." He squints around like it's battle conditions, and I take a longing look at my door.

"All right, well, nice meeting you," I say, hoping he'll take the hint.

"Yes, you too."

I show him to the gate, then close it firmly behind him, watching it lock into place. The guard's story really doesn't make sense. Our woods are fenced in too, so I don't know how anyone could claim to have just gotten lost.

I'll have to ask my mom about it—I finish the last gulp of my coffee—if I remember.

FIVE

We're doing bookwork in Homeroom with Ms. Wells's *Tranquil Sounds of Nature* CD playing in the background, something that's supposed to settle us down and help us concentrate, when the overhead speakers come to life for morning announcements.

"Happy Monday, Laurel High School!" a peppy boy says, his voice staticky over the intercom. "The Homecoming dance is *this* Friday! Have you purchased your tickets?" Bria swivels to me with an excited grin. "Your Homeroom teachers will be passing out the ballots for Homecoming Court today. Cast your vote!"

Right on cue, Ms. Wells starts distributing squares of orange paper, and a second later, Bria leaps out of her desk, squealing and shoving her ballot in my face. We've both been nominated, along with Lex, Marissa, and a few others from our group.

The class congratulates us, and Bria does an old-fashioned curtsy, miming the skirt even though she's wearing yoga pants, then she clasps her hands in front of her face. "Please, God. Please let us win!"

As soon as I finish my assignment, I tell Ms. Wells I need to go to the office.

Luke makes his I-know-you're-lying face, which I ignore, and I meet Garrett and Braxton in the hall. Garrett's outfitted in black, while Braxton's wearing a flashy electric-blue leather jacket, his hair spiked up anime-style. He opens his jacket so I can see the bottle of liquor he's got stuffed inside, then we head into the breeze-way—and run smack into Evan Zamara.

The boy's eyes go wide.

"Hey there, *Operation*," Garrett says, making Braxton cackle. "Your boyfriend not with you today?"

Evan's chubby cheeks turn pink over his tan skin. "We aren't boyfriends," he mumbles.

"What was that?" Garrett asks so gently it's kind of scary.

Evan opens his mouth like he's about to answer, then he tries to sidestep us instead, but Garrett blocks him. I sort of wish Bird Boy were here. He's the only one who ever does anything funny. Evan just stands there like a sad second grader whose parents forgot to pick him up after school. At the moment, he's clutching his text-books with his pudgy hands. He still has dimples in his knuckles like a baby, and I'm starting to wonder if he's ever going to go through puberty when a worrying thought hits me.

"Hey, you aren't, like, a prodigy or something, are you?"

Surprise fills Evan's big brown eyes. "Umm, well, I'm in Pre-AP, but I'm a sophomore."

"But did you skip a few grades?" I press, and Braxton cackles again.

The double doors burst open behind us. A grinning Luke bounces into the courtyard, but then he skids to a halt, looking puzzled.

With a bored expression, Garrett takes a deliberate step away from Evan. "All right, you can go."

But the boy doesn't budge like he's afraid Garrett will trip him or something if he tries it.

"Go on." Garrett gives him a gentle pat on top of his curls.

As if galvanized, Evan races off past a confused-faced Luke.

"So what was that earlier?" Luke asks as we're driving to my house after school.

"What was what?"

"You know, in the courtyard. With Evan Zamara." He gives me the look that only he is allowed to give me. "Were you guys picking on that kid?"

"Picking on him? Does anyone actually use that phrase anymore?"

"You know what I mean. What were you guys doing?"

"We weren't *doing* anything. Now when are you and Lex meeting us on Friday?"

"We're not."

"*Seriously*? Why not?"

"Because Garrett makes Lex really uncomfortable."

Now I'm upset. "But we planned this whole limo-ride-to-Homecoming thing together."

"That was before Braxton said *he* had to be the one to rent the limo, and then everyone else got involved."

"So you're going to stop hanging out with your friends just because your girlfriend doesn't like them?"

"If it was only you and Bria, it'd be fine. Lex just thinks you're a spoiled brat—"

"She *said* that?"

46

"Uh, kind of. But it's different with Garrett. She's scared of him."

That makes me pause. I can't picture Lex being scared of anyone. "Why? I know his jokes aren't always the nicest, but he's harmless."

"He's not harmless. He likes hurting people—he gets off on it. It's creepy, dude."

"You think everything's creepy."

For a moment Luke's quiet. Then he says, "Saye . . . can I tell you something?"

"You're going to." At the wounded expression on his face, I moan. "Okay, okay, what?"

Luke's earnest green eyes meet mine. "You never laugh anymore."

"I'm about to start laughing right now."

"I'm serious."

"I know. That's what's funny."

"I'm just worried!" He crosses his arms over his chest. "And you know what? There's a difference between laughing *at* someone and laughing because you're happy. I mean, don't you want anything anymore?"

"Like what?"

"See, that's exactly it. You *don't* want anything. And you don't even *have* to want anything—because other people want for you."

I'm so confused. "What are you even talking about?"

"I'm saying I want things. For you."

"Okay . . ."

"I want you to be interested in things again."

"So you want me to find a hobby?"

"No . . . a purpose."

"A *purpose*? What, are you like a monk or something now?"

His voice softens. "I've been thinking about this a lot. Everyone should have a purpose, Saye."

"Oh yeah? And yours is?"

"Well . . . I don't have one *yet*. But I'm looking for one. We're all trying to figure that out, you know? But lately you've seemed like . . . detached. And I'm not saying it's Garrett's fault per se, but ever since you started hanging out with him last year, you've been . . ."

"I've been what?"

"*Different*. It's like—like Braxton! You used to think he was such an idiot, and—"

"And you used to think he was cute."

Luke squishes up his nose like a rabbit. "*Braxton*? Are you crazy?"

"You did. You gave him that secret admirer card in the fourth grade."

"That was Braxton's brother."

"Oh. Well, they look exactly the same."

"Except his brother isn't a jackass, and you always got that Braxton is, but now he's your friend? And actually, this is my whole point. You never made fun of me for that, but—"

"Why would I?" I get serious now as I turn to him. "I don't care who you like."

"Right, because you're not a bully. But Garrett's—"

"*Luke*." I am officially out of patience. "Will you quit it? I don't need a sermon on how Garrett's the Antichrist who's warping my brain. I make my own choices."

SIX

On Thursday, Garrett and Braxton are trading drags from a cigarette as we lean against my car before school. Tanner—the muscle-bound senior who's taking some boxing class with Garrett—sidles over and bumps his fist into ours. It's nice and crisp out, light-jacket weather, but the smoke smell is bugging me.

Restless, I'm scrolling through my phone when my attention's grabbed by a crazy-loud muffler. A minute later, an ancient red truck with oversized hubcaps rattles its way into a parking space.

"Looks like Bella Swan just moved to Texas," Garrett jokes.

We laugh and watch the driver's side door creak open, waiting for a lip-biting new girl to hop out. Instead, we get Evan Zamara, with his chubby cheeks and springy curls, who happens to be grinning from ear to ear.

I swear, it's like God and Luke teamed up to plant this kid here just to mess with me. Suddenly, I'm stinging all over again from the lecture Luke gave me the other day, and now I'm thinking about what Bria said too—*baaa*ing and basically calling me a sheep.

"Operation's old enough to drive?" Braxton is flabbergasted.

"Nice truck!" Garrett calls out.

Evan's smile vanishes, and he starts speed-walking toward the school.

Garrett stubs the cigarette under his black biker boot, then he and the other guys chase after Evan like missiles. I hesitate—I really do—but why should I lose my sense of humor just because Luke doesn't have one?

So I take off after them.

"Honestly," Tanner says as we catch up to Evan in the hall. "That truck could be a collector's item."

"Thanks," Evan mumbles.

"I didn't know they started letting ten-year-olds drive," Braxton adds.

Evan blushes. "I'm *sixteen*. I just turned sixteen today."

Well, shit. There are rules for messing with people on their birthday. I give Garrett a defeated shrug, but he just quirks up his dark eyebrows and maneuvers himself into Evan's path.

"*Today's* your birthday?" Garrett says.

Evan nods, slowly.

"Well, why didn't you tell us?" Braxton puts on a fake-excited grin. "We would've gotten you a present!"

"But it wouldn't have been as amazingly awesome as that truck," Garrett adds. "How long did it take you to save up for that?"

"My parents got it for me."

"I hate to tell you this, kid . . ." Garrett gives the back of Evan's neck a sympathetic squeeze. "But I don't think they love you very much."

✛ ✛ ✛

In seventh-period Psychology, my phone buzzes on the corner of my desk.

A text from Bria:

Are you still giving me and Marissa a ride home today?

Sure, I reply.

We have a few things we need to do in the gym first to get it ready for tomorrow . . . Last minute Homecoming prep!

I'm about to send a thumbs-up emoji, but I can't think straight over all the pitiful barks and pained yips coming from the overhead speakers.

Ms. Wells is out sick, so her sub's making us watch an old documentary and identify terms on our worksheet as they come up. In said documentary, a 1970s scientist is electro-shocking various 1970s dogs. Half the dogs are able to stop the shocks if they press a lever, but the dogs in the second group can press that lever till their paws fall off—the shocking only stops when the scientist says it does.

"This is so messed up," Luke wails. "Why are we being forced to watch this? Are you *trying* to traumatize us?"

Most of the class starts murmuring in agreement, but the sub just shushes them as the video flickers on the screen. *PART TWO.*

Now the dogs are placed in these contraptions called *shuttle boxes*—that's one of our terms—and all the dogs have to do is leap over this little partition to get out. The scientist guy starts shocking them again to see what'll happen. The Group One Dogs—the ones that could stop the shocks—figure out fast how to escape the shuttle box, but the Group Two Dogs just lie there crying. Luke looks like he's about to cry too.

Okay, I'm done. I tap my phone's screen and scroll through my feeds.

Five minutes before the bell, the sub flips on the light so I snatch Luke's paper off his desk to copy.

"Hey, I'm not finished."

Ignoring him, I scribble down his answers. The last one on Luke's page is blank, so I ask, "What's the answer to number twenty?"

"What's the question?"

"Why don't the dogs in the second group just jump over the wall?"

Luke points to one of the phrases in the word bank, sadly.

Learned Helplessness.

"They've learned that there's nothing they can do to get away." As I write, Luke keeps talking. "It's heartbreaking, you know? Just think of the implications for—"

The bell rings, so I shove his paper at him and take off for the door.

Behind me, he calls out, sarcastic, "You're welcome!"

When I reach the parking lot, Garrett's leaning against my car. He has a very cool, gangster-like lean. We grab coffees and drive around for a while, just killing time, then head back to school to pick up the girls.

Bria texts me as I'm pulling into the nearly deserted lot:

20 more minutes? Unless you guys want to help???

Shuddering at the idea of sticking one toe into that gym full of chipper extracurricular-activities kids, I text back:

We'll wait, then I tell Garrett it might be a while.

"It's already five o'clock," he complains. "Only losers are still at school at five."

"Now that's not entirely true. Bella Swan's still here."

Garrett sniper-scans the lot, and I see the moment he spots Evan Zamara's truck. Breaking into a jagged grin, he says, "What should we do to it?"

"*Do* to it?" I'm not really in the mood to come up with some clever way to mess with Evan's truck, but Garrett's already popping open the passenger door and jumping out. He drags something from his back pocket and executes a quick maneuver with his wrist. When sunlight glances off the blade, I process that it's a knife.

For a second, I'm too startled to say anything, but Garrett's eyes tighten on me.

"*Saye.* Are you coming or not?"

SEVEN

"Today's the day!" Bria's trying to do a happy spin as we're leaving Homeroom, but the mum I had delivered to her house this morning is throwing her balance off.

The mum's way bigger than I thought it would be when I ordered it, covering the entire width of her chest and hanging down to her calves. Bria had to loop it over her neck like a necklace because there's no way she could pin it to her blouse.

Practically every other girl in school is decked out in a Homecoming mum too, all with a bajillion clanging bells, so it sounds like a herd of cows are moving down the halls. A few pain-faced teachers are covering their ears.

"Saye . . . can you?" Bria's voice is strained.

"Oh, sure." I help her lift the mum—it weighs a *ton*—so she can pull out her long hair that's gotten pinned beneath the cord, then I lower it back down, my hands sliding across her neck.

"I love your hands!" Bria says, grabbing them into her hers and rubbing her fingertips over my palms. "They're so soft and *smooth*. I think they're even softer than mine!"

I'm really glad Lex isn't around right now to snicker and make some joke like *That's because Saye is spoiled and he's never done any manual labor.*

"Uh, thanks," I say.

"See you at lunch!" And then Bria's weaving down the hall.

When I get to Latin, Mr. Rivas hands me my assignment, but I don't feel like conjugating verbs today. My eyes drift to the open door. A troop of costumed theater kids are skipping down the hall, excited about whatever theater kids get excited about, and some SGA kids are carrying stacks of flyers and tape, ready to paper the shit out of the school.

"Sayers?" Mr. Rivas says.

I glance up. "Yeah?"

He sets the essay I handed in last week on my desk. It's covered in red corrections and disappointed squiggles.

"You can do so much better than this." He squeezes into a nearby student desk, which is just unseemly for a man his age. "Sayers, do you understand that many people in this school, in this world, well, they struggle?"

"Struggle?"

"Yes. In many aspects of life, they struggle. To survive. But you . . . you have so much to be thankful for. Opportunities most people can only dream of."

"Okay . . . ?"

"What I'm trying to say is having money doesn't mean you should do nothing—it means you can do *anything*."

I flinch. What is it with the lectures lately? "Mr. Rivas . . ."

But before I can go any further, an office aide wearing a Homecoming mum clangs her way into the room and hands him a note.

Glancing down at it, Mr. Rivas lets out a deep sigh. "You're wanted in the principal's office."

When I enter the main office, the receptionist looks up with a friendly smile. Nodding back at her, I continue down the hall toward the interior office, just as Garrett bursts through the door. Eyes flashing like angry streetlights, he crushes a pink slip of paper in his fist.

"You too?" I say.

"That kid's dad came to the school."

"You mean Evan?"

"Yes, *Evan*. Who the hell else would I be talking about?"

"Huh. I didn't think he saw us."

"Well, he told the principal he did. And now Gardiner says I can't do any extracurriculars for six weeks, including Homecoming."

"What is this—*Carrie*?"

"Mr. Wayte?" Principal Gardiner has materialized, Dracula-like, in the threshold of his door. "I'd like to speak with you." He turns to Garrett. "And you need to get to class, young man."

Garrett gives him a dirty look before storming off. I enter the office and take a seat on a pleather sofa, while Gardiner sits behind his desk with a stern expression. There's an oversized Texas flag mounted to the wall behind him like he's the governor or something.

My lips quirk up.

"I'll get straight to the point. Did you vandalize Evan Zamara's vehicle yesterday?"

"No." I lean back in my seat. "I didn't."

"Interesting." Gardiner steeples his hands beneath his chin. "Then why would he say you did?"

I raise one eyebrow in the skeptical way I've seen my grandfather do it. "Are you asking me to tell you what goes on in the mind of someone I've never even had a conversation with?"

"Evan said that too, that you boys have never really spoken. He doesn't know why you're targeting him."

"*Targeting* him? That's a bit melodramatic."

Gardiner's acting like we're hitmen or something.

"If there's one thing I can tell you about Evan Zamara, it's that he's not one for melodrama. But all of this . . . it's making him so anxious he can't cope with it anymore."

Now Gardiner's the one being dramatic. There's no way Evan said that.

"I'm not sure what to tell you. I don't even know him."

"So you didn't touch his truck, you haven't been harassing him in the halls, and you had nothing to do with smashing his project."

"*I* didn't break anything."

"Oh no, not you." Gardiner's voice is suddenly overflowing with sarcasm. "You like to sit back and watch other people do all the breaking."

"You didn't get *anything*?" Garrett's livid as I zip out of the parking lot after the final bell. I don't know why he's so shocked—it's not as if I was the one who scrawled *pussy* in giant block letters onto the side of Evan Zamara's truck.

"Hey, I just kept watch."

"Yeah, nice job with that."

"Are you still coming over or what?"

"Why wouldn't I be? I'm suspended from the dance, not your house."

Ten blocks from school, and he's still boiling.

"Garrett, you don't even want to go to this stupid thing."

"That's not the point, Saye! I already told Marissa I'm taking her. For fuck's sake, I got a tux, and that little bitch shouldn't be able to keep me from going."

We've reached the wrought-iron gate where a few friends' cars are already waiting. I tell the guard they're with me, the gate slides open, and the caravan follows me down the road to my house. Delivery trucks are everywhere, doors wide open as staff unload trays of food, buffet tables, and crates of crystal glasses.

Once we're inside, the guys head down the hall, while I walk around to see how things are coming along. The great room's been totally transformed with strings of beaded lights, a black-and-gold art deco floor, and period-appropriate furniture—luxe loungers, art deco chairs. Three men are hanging a giant black chrome mirror on one wall. Along another wall, someone's setting up the stage for live music.

"Mr. Wayte?" The event planner, a man in tweed, is walking my way. "Everything's right on schedule. The catering bill is a bit more expensive than we initially discussed, but—"

"That's fine."

He scratches something down onto his clipboard. "All right, sir. I've made a note of it."

When I locate the guys in the theater a minute later, Garrett's prowling in front of the screen, partially blocking the view of some show Luke must've chosen because it's about crop circles.

"He told his *dad*," Garrett's saying. "Who does that?"

The guys snicker, agreeing that Evan's pathetic, but this just seems to make Garrett even angrier. "I'm gonna fuck that kid up, I mean it. He doesn't know what's coming, but I'm getting even with him."

"Sounds like you're already even," Luke says around a mouthful of Cheetos.

The room goes silent as Garrett puts all his focus on Luke, who's brushing orange crumbs off his Obi-Wan Kenobi T-shirt.

"What?" Luke raises his eyebrows, confused. "I mean, if you've been tormenting him for weeks, what'd you expect?"

Garrett takes a couple of measured steps in Luke's direction. "And why is this your business?"

"You're telling the whole room! It's not exactly a private conversation."

Garrett's hands curl into giant fists, and I find myself moving to stand in front of him, blocking his path to Luke. "Dude, chill. If you want to go so bad, just go. It's going to be too packed for them to even notice you."

Slowly, his fingers loosen, and his posture relaxes a little. "Yeah, maybe."

"It'll be fine," I say. "What's the worst that can happen?"

EIGHT

I'm slow-dancing with Bria as I wear my golden crown.

"I told you you'd get prince." Bria lifts her head off my shoulder and smiles, wearing a ruby-bedazzled crown of her own. "Didn't I tell you?" She grabs my red tie, tugs me forward, and presses her lips into mine—more than a peck, less than an elevator kiss.

My pulse quickens.

Bria unfastens her mouth. "It's like a fairy tale, isn't it? A princess and her prince, dancing in the clouds."

Except the clouds are cardboard cutouts for the Just Like Heaven theme, and we're in a smelly high school gym surrounded by scowling teacher-chaperones.

But she's so happy, I go with it. "Yep, it's *exactly* like that."

Beaming brighter, she tells me, "I'll be right back." Then she and Marissa link arms as they disappear into the crowd, so I make my way to the opposite end of the gym, where a bunch of the guys are congregating.

Braxton and Garrett are goofing off, but when Braxton notices me, he shouts, "Saye! Did you hear that *other schools* are coming to your party tonight? Like instead of to their *own* Homecoming parties?"

I try to hide the proud smile that's fighting to cover my face. "I guess word's gotten around."

"Gardiner's coming," someone hisses, and we look over to find the principal speed-marching toward us.

Garrett stands his ground, waiting for Gardiner to reach him.

"You are not supposed to be here," the principal tells him sternly.

A few people glance our way, curious, while Garrett fixes his feet to the floor, his eyes glinting like sharp glass. He's taller than the principal, and he uses this to his advantage to stare the older man down.

"All right, let's go." Gardiner wraps a hand around Garrett's bicep.

"Fuck this." Garrett jerks out of his grasp and starts stomping off, but the principal stays right beside him like a police escort, and the whole gym looks on in silence as Garrett's ushered through the gym's double doors.

Garrett's prowling in front of the limo, his face red and sweaty like he's so furious it's starting to impact his cardiovascular system.

"Screw this dance," Braxton says. "I'll leave with you."

"Yeah, that's easy for you to say," Garrett sneers. "You don't have a date."

"I'm ready to go too," I try to diffuse. "I'll get Bria and Marissa."

Heading back into the crowded gym, I find Bria on the dance floor. "Come on," I tell her. "Let's take off."

"What?" Bria's mouth becomes a perfect circle of shock. "Why?"

"Garrett just got thrown out."

"But that doesn't mean *we* have to leave. I'm your girlfriend. The dance is for *us*."

"There's only an hour left anyway. No one stays till the end."

"They do if they're the prince and princess!"

"So what am I supposed to tell Garrett? My girlfriend won't let me leave?"

"You don't have to tell him anything!" Bria narrows her eyes at me. "If Garrett got kicked out, that's on him."

Marissa dances over with a smile, but when she takes in the tension between me and Bria, she says, "What's wrong?"

"Mr. Gardiner made Garrett leave," I explain.

"And the boys want us to leave too," Bria adds, crossing her bare arms.

"Are you serious?" Marissa looks almost as upset as Bria. "We've been planning this dance for months! We can't."

"Wait, so *neither* of you are coming?" Oh God, Garrett's going to be pissed.

"Well, I'm definitely not," Marissa tells me.

And Bria says, "Me either."

"Okay, cool. Stay if you want, but I'm going." I'm expecting Bria to fold, but instead her mouth compresses into a hard line, and she spins around, disappearing into the throng of dancers.

I tell the chauffer to just drive. There are ten of us, and without the girls and the tagalongs, we have plenty of room to stretch out on the limousine benches. The guys pass around the silver bucket of beer, and glass bottles clink together. We take off our jackets, loosen our red ties. I chuck my crown onto the seat beside me.

At a stoplight, Braxton pokes his head out of the sunroof and yells, "Nice ass!" at a lady on the sidewalk. She gives him the finger, and everybody laughs.

The limo speeds ahead.

The guys keep drinking, and soon everyone's loosening up. Well, everyone except Garrett, who's glaring into space like a teenaged gargoyle.

"Relax," I tell him. "The dance'll be over soon. The real event tonight is my party."

But Garrett continues seething, and I guess I can't blame him. He just experienced public humiliation to the nth degree. "Marissa really didn't come . . ." He shakes his head in a shocked kind of fury. "What a *bitch*."

Then he's back to brooding out the window.

Some of the guys start taking shots, and soon they're knocking into each other with inebriated cackles. All of a sudden, I'm highly annoyed. I don't want to spend the next hour smushed into this limo full of dudes. Plus Bria's mad at me, and she's probably going to be in a bad mood all night now. And I'm *bored*.

I nudge Tanner. He always carries an arsenal of pick-me-ups.

Spinning around, his gelled hair falls into his less-than-sober eyes.

"Do you have anything?" I ask.

He fumbles into his pocket and pulls out a baggie.

"What are they?"

"Hydros. They chill you out . . . you know?" Tanner definitely looks chilled, but that's not what I need.

"That's it? Nothing more . . . uplifting?"

He shrugs. "It's all I could get."

I let out a sigh. "Forget it."

As we circle the town, I'm growing more and more restless, but then the limo stops at a red light, and Garrett sits up straight, his eyes on sniper beam.

"What is it?" I ask him, and he nods to the window. Leaning against the brick wall of the Rialto Theater across the street is Evan Zamara, an innocent smile on his face.

Garrett's lips curl at each end. "Maybe things are looking up."

Heads turn my way as I step out of the limo. I'm not sure what's going to happen—I'm not even sure what I *want* to happen—but I take long strides across the pavement toward Evan, who's with a girl. His sister maybe?

No, not with the way he's looking at her. Plus he's wearing a white button-up shirt and khaki pants, while she's got on a plaid skirt and knees socks. *Date* clothes. She's a good three inches taller than Evan, so he has to angle his head back to give her a bashful smile, but then he glances in my direction, and panic twitches over his face.

I force myself to walk slower, and soon I'm standing right in front of him.

"Hello . . ." I pretend to search my memory for his name. "It's Evan, right?"

He nods, wary.

"Could I talk to you for a minute?"

His whole body tenses. It's clear he doesn't want to, but he mumbles to the girl, "I'll be right back." Then he follows me down the wall.

"Listen, Evan," I say, "I just wanted to tell you I'm sorry."

His big brown eyes widen in surprise, and he tilts his head to the side a little.

"We honestly didn't mean to upset you."

"Oh . . ." He looks taken aback. "Well, it's okay. Really."

And I can tell that he *means* it. In an instant, I'm granted total absolution.

It's jolting, but I shake it off. "Let me make it up to you." I walk back over to the girl. "I was just talking with Evan, and if your movie's over, I'd be happy to give you guys a ride home in the limo."

"Oh my gosh!" she gushes. "*Can* we?"

Evan looks hesitant, but he gives me a shy smile. "Okay. Thank you . . . Saye."

"My pleasure."

Together, we head toward the limo. The windows are tinted, but I'm sure Garrett's watching, so I give him a discreet thumbs-up.

"After you," I tell them, opening the door.

And just like that, they climb inside.

Evan and the girl drop onto the empty bench at the back. The guys must've shifted to the side seats to make room. Evan's glancing around the crowded limo, but his eyes go as huge as planets when they land on Garrett, who's actually doing a pretty good job of acting casual.

Garrett holds out a beer like a peace offering. "No hard feelings?"

The kid does that quizzical-head-tilt thing again, then his face relaxes. "Of course not." He accepts the drink, and Garrett clinks his bottle against Evan's.

The boy seems to relax even further as he scoots closer to the girl, who's playing with the buttons along the panel.

"I've never been in a limo before!" she announces.

"No kidding?" one of the guys says, making a few other guys laugh, but she continues to smile like she doesn't know she's being made fun of.

"What's your name?" Garrett asks.

She points a finger toward her heart. "Who, me?"

"Yes, you. I don't think I've seen you before." Garrett's watching her intently, not friendly exactly, but with the face he makes when he's trying to be appealing.

"Oh. That's because I go to Lone Star High. I'm Rebecca."

"Thass a pretty name," Tanner says, slurring his words a little.

"Yes, it is," Garrett agrees.

One of the guys presses the control to open the sunroof. As the wind begins whipping Rebecca's long hair around, she rests her cheek on Evan's shoulder with a serene smile. The vibe's loud and playful until someone shuts the sunroof like a vacuum seal, and it's one of those moments when everyone goes inexplicably silent all at once.

Braxton clears his throat and gives Rebecca a flirtatious grin. "So, you really like *Evan?*"

"Because a girl like you could have anyone," Garrett adds, while watching Evan, and I can tell he likes seeing the flustered look on the younger boy's face.

"Um . . ." Rebecca trails off like she's confused. "Of course I like Evan."

"Lone Star High, huh?" Garrett says. "How'd that happen?"

"Well, we were friends in middle school, but I moved . . ."

"And you stayed in touch," Braxton finishes.

She nods, still looking unsure.

"That's cute. So have you two had sex?"

Rebecca and Evan both start to squirm, and the limo swells with laughter.

"Um . . ." Rebecca mumbles just as Evan speaks up, "It's our *first* date."

"Oh, Evan," Garrett says, his voice sweet, his eyes dark. "This is gonna be one hell of a first date." And then he wraps his hand around Rebecca's knee.

She goes completely still, her eyes locked on Garrett's hand. She's wearing tall socks and a long skirt, so there are only a couple of inches of bare skin, and that's what he's touching.

I feel myself tensing up—this just got weird.

Garrett's eyes are boring into Rebecca with the strangest expression. It's almost like he's forgotten all about trying to mess with Evan, every iota of his focus just on her, and now she's staring back at him, transfixed.

"Ac-actually," she stutters, "we have to get home now. I told my mom—"

"Relax." Like a spell's been broken, Garrett lets her go and falls back against his seat. He loosens the red knot of his tie, undoes the top gold button of his white dress shirt. "We're just having fun."

"Can you stop the car?" Evan says.

But he's not asking us.

His index finger's pressed to the intercom button, and before anyone can contradict him, the driver's pulling toward the curb.

Garrett starts to laugh. "Can you chill out? You don't want to make your date *walk* all the way home, do you?" He presses the intercom button again. "Never mind, driver. We need to go to . . ." He flashes Rebecca a smile. "The driver needs to know where you live."

For a moment, she doesn't speak, but then she says, "1398 Sycamore."

And the limo keeps going.

"You guys are *way* too uptight." Tanner clumsily fishes that baggie of pain pills out of his pocket again. "Want one?"

Evan and Rebecca shake their heads, but they're beginning to look a little embarrassed like they're wondering if maybe they misread things.

A few awkward minutes later, we pull into a suburb.

"This is me." Rebecca points to a house on a cul-de-sac, and as the limo comes to a stop, she says quickly, "Good night, Evan."

"Good night," he tells her, looking simultaneously embarrassed and relieved. But as soon as she's outside, he peers through one of the darkened windows, then scrambles to his feet. "Actually, I think I'll get out here too."

"Seriously?" Garrett's using his most scathing tone. "We *were* gonna invite you to Saye's party. But whatever." Garrett waves a hand like Evan's a gnat in his air. "But first Braxton has to take care of the fee for all of these *unscheduled* stops."

"Right," Braxton agrees, hopping out. "Just give me a second."

"I'm sorry." Evan looks to the floor. "I didn't know it would cost extra to take us home." He's so sincerely apologetic I'm tempted to tell him that Garrett's full of shit, but all of a sudden, the limo lurches forward, and the momentum slams the door closed and knocks Evan back into his seat at the same time.

Slowly, the partition lowers, and Braxton—now wearing the chauffeur's hat—turns to us with a grin. "I'll be your driver for the remainder of the evening."

Everyone laughs, while a strange expression washes over Evan's face. He seems to be realizing two things at once: that he never should've gotten in this limo, and it's too late to do anything about it.

NINE

"Th-thank you." Evan's voice has gone high and frightened. "Thank you for including me, but I have to get home now."

I'm waiting for Garrett to start laughing and say, *Psych!* But instead he takes a slow swig from his beer and keeps staring steadily at Evan. A harsh tension starts thrumming through the limo—or maybe it's just me. Because now that I'm glancing around, the other guys look chill, still drinking, some smirking, all in their white shirts and red ties. Maybe they know something I don't, some plan they came up with while I was outside of the limo.

"Did you hear what I said?" Evan's voice cracks, prompting more loud laughter.

"Come on, Evan, don't be like that." Garrett's tone is mocking. "We're trying to be your friends." He takes another swig from his bottle. "You want to be our friend, right?"

Chest heaving, the boy doesn't speak, his eyes darting from one window to another.

"Evan," Garrett says softly, "when someone asks you a question, you answer them."

Evan gulps and mouths the word *yes*.

It takes him another try to get the word out. "Yes. I . . . I want to be your friend."

Someone opens the door onto a black field on a black night.

"Everyone out," Garrett orders.

The guys stumble onto the grass in varying stages of drunk, but Evan doesn't move. His head stays lowered, those big curls covering his face. I can see the sharp rise and fall of his chest, almost like his heart's beating so hard its shape is visible through his clothes.

"*Evan.*" Garrett's teeth gnash together. "I said *get out.*"

Slowly, Evan looks up . . . and his eyes are shiny with tears.

My stomach gives a sharp twist. I never meant for Evan to get *this* upset.

I turn to Garrett—whatever wrong he thinks Evan committed should be paid in full, all the anger worked out of his system. But if anything, it's *worse.* There's a cold malice itching under the glaze of his eyes and in the sharp line of his mouth, and he looks like he's about two seconds from *dragging* Evan out.

But then Evan climbs to his feet and exits the limo, Garrett right behind him.

Uneasy, I trail them, my eyes following the path of the headlights.

Now I realize where we are. The amphitheater.

The city uses it sometimes for the summer concert series, but it belongs to Braxton's dad. Braxton drove over the grass, practically right onto the stone stage, which faces a semicircle of steps interspersed with grass, like a coliseum that's been abandoned for a century or two.

It's quiet out here, not like in town, and the sky is a scary sort of infinite.

Braxton strolls to a control box and punches a code into the panel. "And let there be light."

A rig comes to life, shooting beams at the stage where most of the guys are forming a loose circle around Evan. His eyes are huge and afraid.

Behind me, Tanner starts hopping up the stone steps. Completely wasted, he drops his bottle, glass shattering everywhere. This startles an even-drunker guy, who asks, "Whus goin' on? I thought we were going to a party."

God, what are we *doing* out here? This is so dumb. Evan's freaked out, and it's not even funny anymore, and I'm ready to get back to civilization, instead of out in the sticks with a bunch of dudes. I'm seriously about to say something when my phone buzzes in my pocket.

Bria's calling, and the second I answer, she's shouting over a cacophony of partygoers, "Everyone's here!"

Or at least, I think that's what she's saying. It's hard to make out her words with the rave beats on her end and the drunk guys on mine, so I walk off from the group and press the phone's speaker against my ear just in time to catch, "You already skipped out on the dance—you're not missing this too!"

"You think *I* want to miss it?" I hiss into the phone. "The whole party was my idea."

"Then what are you doing?"

"Everyone's being stupid. We're in the middle of fricking nowhere."

"Please just get here."

"I will," I tell her, but I don't think she believes me because she hangs up without even saying bye. Now I'm pissed, but I pull myself together and head back over to the group.

They're all being weirdly hushed, almost subdued, and that's when I notice—

"Guys . . . where are Evan and Garrett?"

Everyone's acting fidgety, quiet, guilty. Their eyes stay on the ground until I ask the question again, and finally one of them says, "Garrett took him."

"*Took* him?" I repeat. "Took him where?"

And like a bad comedy, they all point in a totally different direction.

I squint across the field, then spin around to face the wall of trees that backends the stage. I know the woods are there, but it's so dark, all I see is black and more black.

It's been seventeen minutes. I know because I'm watching my phone where Bria's Instagramming the shit out of the party—the band, the fireworks, the *elephant*—showing me what a good time she's having without me.

Lifting my head, I scan the field and the woods again. *Fuck.* What the hell is happening out there? Is Garrett beating Evan up? Forcing him to dig his own grave with his bare hands? All the different possible scenarios are endless, and I'm feeling queasy. But of course Garrett would never actually *hurt* Evan. He's just scaring him.

Around me, the other guys are sobering up, while Braxton happily crashes around, pointing his cell phone at everyone like he's a reporter for TMZ. "What do you think, Tanner? Will Evan Zamara ever be heard from again?"

Tanner looks woozy, but he does his best to shove the phone out of his face. "Stop recording me. I don't even have a problem with Evan."

I check my phone again. *Nineteen minutes.*

"Shit!" Braxton shouts. "My brother just texted me. Someone saw the lights."

"So?" one of the other guys says.

"So my dad said I can't come out here anymore after we fucked it up last time. He told them to send the cops!" Braxton spins toward the trees. "Garrett!"

But there's no movement from the dark.

"Garrett!" he yells again. "Come on—the police are coming!"

Soon all the other guys are yelling for Garrett too, but still nothing.

And then a tall silhouette emerges from the woods in a flash of crisp white and gold buttons.

But I don't see Evan.

I squint into the darkness, waiting, waiting.

And then finally, a small figure appears.

As they near us, I can make out their faces.

Garrett's is calm and collected now. Evan looks dazed.

Dazed, not injured. But instead of relieved, my stomach twists tighter.

Braxton sprints to the driver's seat and starts the engine, while the rest of us climb inside.

Evan has no expression as he takes the back bench exactly as he and Rebecca did earlier, only now he sits alone.

TEN

The instant my alarm goes off on Monday morning, I silence it with a groan. This was a total calamity of a weekend. By the time we finally got to my house on Friday night, everyone except Bria, Luke, and Lex were gone. Bria informed me that the new security guard had shut the party down, and I told her she should've let him know I was on my way. Of course Lex intervened, telling me I had no right to blame Bria since it was my own fault I wasn't there. Then they *left*.

When I got up to my room, the official Homecoming photo of me and Bria was lying on my pillow. I threw it onto my desk, then tried to doze off—something that's usually easy for me—but I tossed and turned all night, and I spent the rest of the weekend holed up in my room.

My alarm's beeping again. Even if I get up right this second, I'm going to be late.

Maybe I should just skip today. It's tempting . . .

But I force myself out of bed.

Shuffling from my car and into the school, I notice that the halls have thinned out, which is kind of nice, but then out of nowhere,

Evan's overall-wearing, red-haired bird friend is rushing me.

"What did you do?" he shouts.

I shrug like I have no idea what he's referring to and keep walking, but instead of dropping it, he chases me around the corner, and then with zero regard for the possibility of teachers or witnesses, he *shoves* me.

I stumble backward, totally appalled. A random guy who was jogging past us halts and gapes. So does a teacher who's hovering in her doorway.

"What did you do to Evan?" he screams again, this time right in my face.

The tardy bell rings, and the teacher steps into the hall. "Boys, get to first period."

"That's what I'm trying to do," I tell her, gesturing helplessly to the crazy-eyed kid. Her class is craning in their desks to see what's going on in the hall, and this is becoming unseemly.

"Listen," I say. "What's your name again?"

"Blair," he snarls.

"Well, Blair, I must say, I have no idea what you're talking about. If you've got a problem, you need to take it up with your friend."

Now he looks like he's going to burst into tears. "Well, I can't ask him, because he's not here. He's not coming back."

What the hell does he mean Evan's not coming back? I get an uncomfortable flash of Evan's dazed expression as he was moving from the woods into the light, but I pretend I'm not rattled.

"That isn't my problem."

The teacher clears her throat. "Settle this later, boys."

Evan's friend keeps staring at me with these intensely sad eyes, then his face twitches with fury. "You *are* the problem! And I swear to God you're going to pay for this!"

By the time I get out of the principal's office, I've missed most of first period. I was forced to endure nearly an hour of grilling, and who knows what Blair's going to say when he gets called in. Honestly, who *yells* at someone that way? *I'll pay for this?* It's like he was putting a curse on me or something.

Stupid Garrett—the whole Evan thing was his idea, yet it's me who's getting hounded by unhinged Bird Boys? It's unbelievable. Then there's the moronic fact that Braxton was filming everything, and he's stupid enough to have sent it to someone or uploaded it somewhere in a drunken stupor.

I pull out my phone. I've got at least twenty new texts.

Bria:

Omg, are you okay??? I heard you got attacked!!!

Luke:

Are you all right? Text me!

And then another one from Luke:

I won't be in second period. About to leave for the art field trip.

A visit to an art gallery sounds amazing right now—much better than spending the day avoiding awkward questions.

Stopping in my tracks, I pivot in the opposite direction.

I've been trailing the school bus for almost an hour, nothing on either side of me but flat green fields. I wish I could plug the address of wherever it is we're going into my GPS, but supposedly following the bus was the compromise for not riding in it with everyone else. It wasn't hard to convince Mr. Rivas to make a case for me to join the art students, but no one mentioned it'd be out in the sticks.

The view's not much to look at, but I'm finally starting to relax. Blair can be mad all he wants, but he obviously doesn't know what happened. And nothing really *did* happen. I'm sure once I get to school tomorrow, this all will have blown over.

When another hour passes, I begin to wonder if I'm being pranked. The roads keep getting narrower and bumpier, and I'm seriously considering turning around, but then the bus veers off onto a spiraling dirt road, and comes to a stop at a colossal wooden gate like the one surrounding Jurassic Park.

I hop out into the nearly empty lot and stretch my legs. It's warmer than it's been in days, so I toss my brown leather jacket into my car, then use my key fob to set the alarm. The bus door folds open, and art students clamber out. I spot Luke in the crowd, looking sleepy and holding Lex's hand, then his face splits into a wide grin.

"Hey!" He dashes over, dragging poor Lex along with him. "What are you doing here? You don't have art."

I wave that off. "I have Latin. It's all connected."

"And you *drove*?"

"Apparently."

"Why didn't you tell me? The bus suuuccckkked!"

"I can imagine."

"I'm riding home with you," Luke says.

"Fine."

"Lex too."

I glance over at Lex, who doesn't look quite as happy to see me as Luke is.

"We heard you were accosted this morning," she says.

"Accosted?"

"Is there a better word?"

Now Luke's studying me with worried-puppy eyes. "Yeah, what happened?"

"Nothing," I say, a little harsher than I mean to. "It was just a misunderstanding."

Luke clearly isn't buying that, but the art teacher's shouting, "All right! This way."

As we head through the gate, Luke slings an arm around Lex's shoulders, grinning at her like they're on their honeymoon. "Look at all the trees. It's so pretty!"

I'm not sure that's how I'd describe it. It reminds me of this place my parents took me to when I was younger, a little community meant to replicate the life of early settlers, and this is like a discount, medieval version of that.

"I saw a flyer back there," Lex says. "In a couple of weeks, it's going to be a haunted theme park."

"Really?" I perk up. "That sounds cool."

Lex rolls her eyes, and Luke tells her, "He's not being sarcastic. He really likes haunted houses."

We stroll down trails, and apart from a couple guys dressed in plastic armor, it's a ghost town—if the ghost town had been sucked dry of anything supernatural, or spooky, or remotely interesting. I'm beginning to think I might've been better off just staying at school. We pass some maidens carrying buckets of milk, then Luke wants to watch this old lady churn butter.

"I'll wait here," I say, leaning against a wooden fence rail.

As Luke and Lex race off, I pull out my phone. I'm holding it in the air to try and get a better signal when there's a snort behind me. Slowly, I turn to face a sullen cow. Looking pissed off about something, it starts stamping its feet into a puddle. I back up—but not fast enough—and foul-smelling mud splashes all over my shirt.

"You've got to be kidding me." Scowling, I stomp onto the trail.

"Where are you going?" Luke calls after me. I stop to let him and Lex catch up, and his green eyes go wide. "What happened?"

"A cow."

Lex snickers, while Luke dives into his backpack. "Don't worry, buddy! I've got you covered." He digs around, then raises his arm in triumph with a wadded-up T-shirt. "Here you go."

I unfurl it in front of me—Luke Skywalker gazing at a binary sunset. Sighing, I strip off my ruined shirt and drop it into a nearby garbage bin, then pull Luke's tee over my head. He grins proudly as if I'm wearing this by choice, and we continue down the trail.

I'm experiencing a level of boredom that should be criminal, but then my eyes are drawn to an L-shaped building with a huge warning sign tacked to its door. I head straight for it to get a closer look. The sign reads: *This exhibit is not suitable for young children or anyone who is particularly sensitive.*

"Sorry, Luke." I pat his back when he approaches. "I guess you'd better turn around."

He gives me a little frown, then straightens his shoulders and bravely walks inside.

Lex and I follow him into a dimly lit entryway where the walls are lined with medieval weaponry and gear. Swords, shields, and this pointy steel helmet that weighs sixty pounds according to the little description card below it.

We make our way down a tight corridor full of strange metal contraptions—ones designed to impale or tear off or remove specific organs and body parts. It's unnerving, the sheer imagination people have when it comes to inventing new ways to hurt each other.

Without speaking, we exit the Museum of Torments and continue down the trail.

In my peripheral vision, I can see Lex and Luke swinging their clasped hands to and fro. A couple minutes later, he stops to pick her a flower.

I really should've stayed at school.

We spend the rest of the afternoon suffering through dull lectures on medieval art, which sucks because it leaves my mind too free to wander about what happened this morning. I just want to go home and relax before I have to deal with school tomorrow, so the second the art teacher dismisses us, I practically run to the parking lot.

Lex and Luke, on the other hand, take their sweet time, and when they finally reach my car, they hesitate like they're not sure who should get in front. Then they both glance to the back.

"Oh no," I say, pressing Home on my GPS. "I'm not your chauffeur."

"It's okay, Lex." Luke dips into a gallant bow. "*You* can have the front."

So she slides into the passenger seat, Luke hops in back, and I peel out of the lot while the other students are still loading onto the bus.

Luke and Lex are chatting about their favorite parts of the day when he falls quiet and points to a decrepit little shack with the words *LIVE BAIT* written on the side in shaky red paint. My GPS tells me to turn right, and on the corner a bunch of men, women, and children are waving hand-drawn signs on pieces of torn cardboard about getting saved before the world ends.

"This is like horror-movie creepy, right?" Luke is shuddering.

"Definitely." Lex is obviously just as disturbed.

My GPS directs me a few more times, and soon we're on a wider road. The bus hasn't caught up with us yet. I glance down at my dash—I'm going eighty, and I didn't even realize it. I guess without any other cars or buildings, it's hard to get a sense of your speed. Luckily, Lex doesn't notice, too focused on stretching her arm behind her so she and Luke don't have to go an entire two hours without touching each other.

After a while, Luke and Lex nod off, and I'm getting sleepy myself just staring into the same empty stretch of nothing. I've got my eyes peeled for a Starbucks when the GPS comes to life and starts zigzagging me around.

"What the hell?" Lex is wide awake now, and I follow her gaze out the window—to a shack with *LIVE BAIT* written on the side in shaky red letters.

Rubbing his eyes, Luke sits up straight, alarmed. "Do you think it's a different one?"

"I don't think so," I say grimly.

We're all paying close attention now as my GPS tells me to turn right, and we pass the same sign-waving crowd from earlier.

"We shouldn't have fallen asleep on the bus." Luke presses his troubled face into the window.

"What about you?" Lex says to me. "You drove here. Does anything look familiar?"

"Saye's never been very good with directions," Luke tells her.

"That's not true. I just couldn't see anything around that giant bus."

My GPS starts giving orders again. Right—right—left—another right—and we're spit back out in front of the exact same bait shop.

"No way, no way," Luke whimpers. "This is some Bermuda Triangle shit."

"Relax," I tell him. "We're two hours from home, not lost at sea."

I press Home on my GPS again, and a robotic voice announces: *This is not a known road. Please continue.*

Suddenly, Luke and Lex burst out laughing.

"How is this funny?" I ask them.

Recalculating. Recalculating.

They laugh harder.

"Guys, it's getting late."

"I know." Luke giggles as if suddenly this is some hilarious adventure instead of the biggest waste of time. He starts clacking away on his phone, then he leans forward and taps the map panel on my dash, spreading his fingers to zoom in. "Saye, your GPS is broken!"

I bristle, offended. "We're in the middle of nowhere, and the roads just aren't mapped properly. My GPS is not *broken*."

"It is, look." He zooms in further. "It's acting like you're still at the park. It's frozen or something."

"It can't be."

"It's probably the GPS antenna," Lex says casually. "I just pulled up the route on my cell. Once we get on the highway, it's simple."

So I keep driving, turning when Lex tells me to turn, and it takes a good hour, but eventually she says, "This is it."

I make a right, and it's not much of a highway, just a wide two-lane road, but it's way more civilized than those backroads we've been on. The trees give way to all that empty green land I saw on the way here, and *finally* things are starting to look familiar.

"How far out are we?" I ask.

"Another fifty miles," Lex says, so I press the gas pedal harder, and suddenly Luke's shouting in my ear, "STOP!"

I slam on the brakes.

"I see a place to eat."

"Are you kidding me? I thought you were having a seizure or something."

"I'm hungry."

"Luke, we're an hour from home. Let's just keep going."

"But that's too long! Please, Saye, I'm starving." He gives me big-pleading-Luke eyes till I fold.

"Ugh, fine." I pull over into the gravel parking lot, and Luke's instantly beaming. "You honestly want to eat here? It doesn't even have a name. It's just called *Restaurant*."

But he's already hopping out and dashing inside.

I tug open the rickety door, and cough on air full of kitchen grease. The packed little diner's a throwback to simpler times with its checkered curtains, mismatched tables, and distressed hardwood floors. Even the white-haired lady who seats us at a wobbly table and gives us a basket of dinner rolls feels like a transplant from another era.

Lex and Luke smile into each other's souls as they butter their bread. Lex catches my squeamish expression, and her mouth clenches into a tight line. "Sorry, Luke. Apparently, Saye's too good for this place."

She's totally misreading the reason for my disgust, but I go with it. "We're all too good for this place. But it does seem to be popular with the locals."

"Speaking of locals, I think one's checking you out right now." Lex nods somewhere behind me.

Shrugging, I flip open my laminated menu while Luke lifts his head and shudders. "*Creepy.* Guy's giving me the heebie-jeebies."

"Not even interested enough to look?" Lex says to me.

"Nope."

"I guess it's all in a day when you're as irresistible as Sayers Wayte."

Luke's stopped paying attention to our bickering, his face buried in his menu now. "Oh my God, everything looks so *good*."

I'm scanning the entrées when my nostrils are ambushed by a perfume cloud.

Our waitress, a round-faced teen with long black hair, has arrived. She's smoothing down the pale blue fabric of her old-fashioned waitress dress, while staring at me like someone thrust her onto a stage without knowing her lines. I wait for her to take our order, but when she just keeps gaping, I say, "Do you serve steak that *hasn't* been deep-fried and breaded?"

"Um . . ." The girl's voice is so quiet I have to strain to hear it. "The only steak we have is the chicken-fried steak."

"I'll take that," Lex says.

"Me too," Luke adds, wearing a happy grin. "And the chocolate cream pie!"

"Hey, is that you on the job board?" Lex points her chin toward a bulletin board nailed to the wall. "My mom's been looking for someone to watch my little brother on Thursdays."

The waitress bobs her head with an eager smile. "I have a little brother too. I can give you my number."

"About my order?" I say. "Can you prepare the steak without the batter? Medium-rare."

The waitress quickly jots it down on her notepad, along with our drink orders, then she's off.

I slide my phone from my pocket. "This place better have Wi-Fi."

Luke and Lex are ignoring me now, interlocking their fingers like those are stand-ins for more private parts, and I wish they'd get a tiny room for their hands. Bored, I post a couple of pics of

Restaurant, and immediately, Bria texts me:

Where ARE you?

I respond with one word:

HELL.

Then I send her a photo of the menu.

Bria's replying with a thousand crying emojis when my nose is assaulted again.

Our waitress is back. "The cook says he can do it," she tells me, out of breath.

"Uh, okay, good." I mean, I assumed as much. I return my attention to my phone, chuckling at Bria's newest text.

"*Saye,*" Lex hisses a few seconds later.

"Yeah?"

"Why are you being so rude? She obviously has a crush on you."

"The waitress?" I have no idea where that came from, but I give Luke a teasing smile. "Have you noticed your girlfriend thinks everyone's obsessed with me? I'm no psychologist, but that sounds like projection."

"Just be nice to her," Lex orders.

"Fine, relax."

But Lex is the opposite of relaxed. "You know she goes to our school, right?"

"She does? Why would someone come way out here to work?"

"I don't know, but she's in choir with me, and she's really sweet, so just—"

Really Sweet Choirgirl has arrived with the drinks, and immediately my nose starts to burn. I think I might actually be allergic to her perfume. Then, like three seconds later, I'm choking again because she's back with more bread.

Fed up, I pull a twenty from my wallet and set it on the table. "Okay, here's the tip—you've got it. So please don't feel the need to stop by every few seconds."

I return to scrolling through my feeds.

And a moment later, I hear, "What the actual fuck?" Lex's voice is hushed and angry, and it's not her normal semi-playful angry either, but like seriously pissed.

"What?"

"What do you mean *what*? That!" Lex points at the bill still on the table.

"What did I do?" I'm genuinely confused. "That was nice."

Lex is apparently speechless because there are a few minutes of no conversation until our waitress, now wearing a guarded expression, arrives with a tray of food. Lex sends her overbright smiles the girl doesn't seem to notice, while I try sawing through my lumpy gray meat.

"This isn't how you prepare steak," I grumble.

"Dude." Luke's already digging in. "Quit acting like a British lord, and just eat it. This stuff's good."

Lex laughs and starts eating too. Annoyed with them both, I push my plate away.

Mouth full, Luke's head snaps up, distressed. "Where's the pie?"

"How can you eat in here? It *stinks*."

Lex glares like she wants to strangle me. "What's the problem now?"

"Besides the charming aroma of fried chicken grease and our

waitress's cheap perfume?"

"You have an issue with her *perfume?*" Lex scoffs. "You're being ridiculous."

"I'm not being ridiculous. It's making me feel sick. Honestly, someone needs to tell her to take a bath before waiting on more tables because—"

A small, shaking hand is reaching out to take my plate. "The cook said he'll fix you another one," the waitress says. "On the house."

Lex looks absolutely horrified, opening her mouth and clapping it shut again.

"No, it's fine," I mumble, a little embarrassed now. "Just forget it." The girl nods, spinning around. "Wait." She turns back. "My friend wants his pie."

She nods again, and then she's off.

Lex stares at Luke, aghast. "Did she hear what he said?"

"I think so." Luke is studying me with this incredibly disappointed expression. "Saye, when she comes back, you need to apologize."

My mouth parts in shock. *"Apologize?"*

"Yes, Saye," he insists, like a stern, alternate-reality version of himself. "You hurt her feelings."

I can't believe this. Since when does Luke reprimand me? And I obviously didn't *mean* for her to hear me. "But she was the one who—"

"I just want to leave," Lex cuts me off, sounding miserable.

I cross my arms over my chest. *"That* we can agree on."

Now some new teen waitress approaches our table carrying an entire chocolate cream pie. "I'll be taking care of you for the rest of your meal," she says, and she might be glaring but it's hard to be certain because she doesn't have any eyebrows.

"We need that to go." I slide my credit card across the table. "And the check too."

"Of course." No Eyebrows smiles.

And then she smashes the pie into my face.

The manager's trying to calm me down, while Lex and Luke laugh their asses off.

"How is this funny?" I throw my hands in the air. "She threw pie at me. Pie! Like we're in some old vaudeville sketch show!"

"It was an accident," Lex says. "*Relax.*"

"That was no accident."

Lex cracks up. "Okay, you're right. It wasn't."

I stand, using a cloth napkin to wipe at the pie that's dripped onto my slacks. Nearby tables are gawking as I only manage to smear the chocolate further.

"Ah, Saye . . ." Luke says cautiously.

"*What?*"

"There's pie in your ear." Luke and Lex look at each other and start cracking up again.

This is when I snatch my keys off the table. "You two enjoy your dinner."

Luke's smile vanishes. "Wait—Saye—how are we supposed to get home?"

"Not my problem."

"Saye!" They're both yelling after me, but I walk faster through the door and hop into my convertible, spitting gravel as I peel out.

I can see Luke and Lex waving their arms in the parking lot as they disappear in my rearview mirror.

I'm barreling down a black road when I realize I have no idea where I am. I wasn't exactly focusing when I raced out of there. Easing up on the accelerator, I try to get my bearings. No one's behind me, so I reduce my speed to practically nothing, and press Home on my GPS.

This is not a known road.

No kidding. There aren't even any streetlamps out here.

I fish around for my cell phone in the console, but it's not there. I pat my pocket. Not there either.

Pulling onto the dirt shoulder, I flip on the overhead light and search under my seat, and in between the seats too, but I can't find it anywhere.

Shit. I must've left it on the table.

For a minute, I just sit here, the shadows of tree branches swaying over my windshield. And then I register—*tree branches.* That's strange. There are towering trees on both sides of the road, but the highway was smack dab in the middle of empty farm fields—I remember that distinctly. And the highway was a lot wider too.

Maybe when I flew out of the parking lot, I turned the wrong way. Maybe this section of the highway is narrower. Easing onto the road, I make a U-turn. Any second now I'm going to see the lights of Restaurant. Part of me wants to stop for my phone, and *maybe* Luke and Lex, but the thought of going back in there after my pie-smacked exit makes me cringe.

Yeah, that's going to suck.

The clock on my dash is beginning to feel ominous. By now the trees should be thinning and the road should be widening, but instead it keeps getting tighter with even *more* trees. The twisting limbs are so huge and sprawling they blot out the sky and collapse the road in like a tunnel. I can hear Luke's voice inside my head: *Creepy!*

I keep on driving super slow, passing little roads with names I don't recognize and ones with no names at all. I'm not even sure what I'm looking for exactly, but I flick my headlights, wishing my car had a higher beam.

The quiet's starting to get to me, so I flip on the stereo.

"REPENT!!!" the speakers scream. *"Yer Holy Father is watchin' you! He is ALWAYS watchin' with love in his heart. But Hell is not full. He's got room for you there—"*

Talk about a mixed message. I flip the channel, but without my iPhone, my choices are fearmongering, static, or country music.

I choose static.

There's a pinging noise, and the gasoline gauge on my display panel lights up. Right above it, there's a flickering *15.*

What is that—a countdown?

I pull over again and search everywhere for my cell. Under the seat, in between the seats, even the glove compartment even though I never put my phone in there.

I give my GPS another shot.

This is not a known road.

This is not a known road.

This is absurd. I can't be lost. I start driving again, shutting off the stereo and the AC—anything that might drain the fuel—and

I'm driving in eerie silence when something in my rearview mirror grabs my attention.

Two tiny headlights in the distance.

For the first time since I left Restaurant, someone else is on the road. I find myself sagging in relief. It almost felt like I was drifting alone in outer space or something, but now there are other humans.

Still on the lookout for something familiar, I continue driving slowly. So slow that the headlights catch up to me—and get right on my ass.

I glare into the rearview mirror. I can't see the driver, just the bulky shape of a redneck pickup truck. I'm quickly rethinking my relief.

"Go around," I mutter, tapping my brakes.

But he doesn't. He just stays right behind me while I tortoise along. The warning light on my dash blinks again, and screw it. This guy can have the whole lane to himself. I flip him off while veering left for a U-turn, and at that exact same moment, the truck decides to pass me. Trying not to smash into him, I jerk my wheel to the right, and I'm swerving off the road at full speed.

ELEVEN

There's a hard, reverberating thud as I crash into a barbed-wire fence. A white echo surrounds my head, my whole body aching like it's been on a dangerous amusement park ride.

Slowly, I take stock of myself. My neck's a little sore—I'll definitely need to pay a visit to my chiropractor—but I'm not injured, not really. Just a little disoriented as I climb out and stare at my convertible. The headlights are streaming across the field at a weird slant, but this car's got technology. I'm half-expecting the tires to reinflate and the grill to bend back up when I hear footsteps behind me.

I look back.

It's the other driver. His headlights are aimed in one direction, mine in the other, so he's just an alien-esque silhouette.

"Are you all right?" he asks in the deep twang you hear when you leave the city.

Suddenly, the tension that's been building up inside me all day bursts out. "No, I'm not all right. You nearly killed me! Look at my car!"

"I'm sorry 'bout that. You spun around so quick I didn't have a chance to—"

"Can I use your phone? I need to be towed. If I can even tell them where the hell we are."

The man steps closer. Between the beams, I can see more of him. Tall and square-shouldered, dressed in a flannel shirt and honest-to-God cowboy boots. That's what he looks like, a guy from some old gritty movie about cowboys. He's maybe around my parents' age, but with deeply bronzed skin like he's never used sunscreen—and he looks worried. He probably thinks I'm going to sue him.

I might.

"I don't have a phone on me," the man says, although it sounds more like: *I don' havuh phone awn me.* "But I can fix you up. Where's your spare?"

"In the trunk, I would imagine." Leaning into my car, I lift the little lever to pop the trunk, but the dumb guy can't figure out the latch, so I stomp to the rear of my car. "It's this button here." I lift the trunk myself. Inside, there's a small tire and a collection of tools that I have no idea how to use.

The big man rolls up his sleeves over his muscular forearms, then grabs the tools and tire all at once. While he goes to work, I climb back into my car, wishing I had my phone or something to entertain myself with, but eventually, there's a tap on my window.

I push the button to lower it. "All set?"

"Well . . ." He sounds regretful. "I hate to tell you this, but one of your other tires busted too. Don't know how I missed it."

"*What?*"

"That crash really did a number."

"Do you have a spare I could use?"

"Normally, but I—"

"Can you just drive me to a phone? This is fucking ridiculous."

He flinches like he's from a time when *fuck* was a shocking word, but he gives me a brusque nod. "I can do that."

The man's truck smells like vinyl, sweat, and some other odor I can't identify. Luckily, the windows are cracked, so once he picks up speed, clean country air rushes in. I can't wait to get home and share my war story with everyone. When they find out I had to hitch a ride from some hill person, they're going to *flip*.

I'm picturing the scene when I get a strange sensation. I turn my head, and the man is watching me. I'm about to ask him what he's staring at, but he shoots me a friendly smile.

"What's your name?"

"Sayers." My answer's automatic, but immediately I regret it. It's been grilled into me since I was three not to tell strangers who I am.

"*Sayers?*" Obviously, the guy doesn't recognize it, which is a relief. "M'name's Caleb." He takes his right hand off the steering wheel and stretches it out toward me. The smart thing to do would be to shake it, but suddenly I'm feeling weird in a way I can't explain. I mean I'm still annoyed, but I'm something else now too.

"I think you'd better keep both hands on the wheel," I finally say.

His arm hovers in the air for a moment, then he grips the steering wheel again.

"How much farther is it?" I ask.

"Not too far. I take it you like *Star Wars*."

"What's that?"

"I noticed your shirt."

"Oh, right." I totally forgot I was wearing it. Luke Skywalker and the binary sun. This guy must have some kind of night vision.

"You a big fan?" he asks.

"Yep, love it."

He smiles, totally missing the sarcasm. "Which one's your favorite?"

I haven't seen a *Star Wars* movie since I started refusing when Luke and I were ten, but I go with, "The first one."

The man nods seriously like this is the correct answer, and I'm starting to think maybe he's just socially inept. It doesn't seem like he's used to being around people. Releasing a breath, my shoulders drop. I just need to endure a few more minutes of small talk, and this total fail of a day can be over.

I direct my gaze to the streaking black sky outside my window.

Then I feel it again.

My eyes flick in the man's direction, and I find him watching me with an expression I can't put my finger on, but it makes all my muscles coil.

"Shouldn't we be near a main highway?" My voice is steady.

"We're getting there." But the road's practically a bike lane at this point, so narrow the trees are scratching the sides of the truck.

"Actually . . ." I stare straight ahead now, tense and on edge. "You can let me out here."

The man releases a doubtful chuckle and keeps on driving.

My hands curl into fists at my sides. I can take this guy if I have to. Definitely. I work out every day in my gym. A hundred push-ups every morning. Fifty pull-ups every night.

"I want you to let me out."

"It's too dark. Can't see nothing out here. Someone could run you over."

My mouth goes dry, and when I try to speak, my words catch onto one another. "It's fine. My phone has my coordinates. And a flashlight."

His eyebrows furrow. "I thought you didn't have a phone."

"I mean . . . I thought I didn't, but . . ."

"We'll be there soon enough."

"I said stop!"

The truck jerks to a halt so fast, I careen forward.

I grab the door handle, but it won't give. I start yanking on it while the man just watches calmly without moving a muscle.

And then he reaches for me.

TWELVE

His arm comes closer, and then it swoops *past* me to jiggle and lift the handle.

My door falls open with a rusty creak.

I'm stunned for a moment, but I get myself together and leap out and slam the door shut.

I have the urge to take off running now, but it feels as if the man is a wild animal, something that won't think to chase me unless I run. So I fight every instinct I have and force myself to *walk* away.

Slowly, the truck eases onto the narrow road. Its red taillights shine across the pavement.

Peeking over my shoulder, I lock eyes with the man in the rearview mirror. The instinct to flee grabs hold of me again, but I force my feet to move at a slow and unhurried pace.

The truck creeps forward.

Just leave me alone. Just go.

And as if it's controlled by my thoughts, the motor guns, spitting out exhaust, and the truck speeds away. I thought it was dark before, but I've never seen darkness like this. I'm not sure how far it is to my car, a few miles at least.

Hands shaking, I pull my keys from my pocket and laugh a little—one of those high-pitched giggles that flies out once you get over the fear, like right after someone jumps out at you in a haunted house.

I press my key fob, hoping to hear that *chirp-chirp*, and I stumble along, trying not to trip over the uneven pavement. All around me it sounds like one of Ms. Wells's relaxation CDs, only it's not soothing at all when you're in the thick of it. Now that I think about it, listening to nature noises to relax is totally illogical. We evolved to *escape* nature. How can we feel at ease when we're surrounded by creatures meant to eat us?

Ears attuned, I keep pressing my key fob, and the longer I walk, the hungrier I feel. I didn't bring anything to eat today, so the last food I had was a child's-sized bag of Cheetos from Luke's sack lunch.

Tired, thirsty, and sweaty, I'm dragging—and then I hear it. A faint *chirp-chirp*. And there they are. Two winking taillights in the distance. Cheering out loud like a student counsel kid on election day, I run the rest of the way to my car, hop inside, and start the engine. I'm just catching my breath when the illuminated gasoline gauge flashes 7, but maybe I have enough fuel to get to the interstate. I'm due for some good luck.

Reversing out of my wire trappings, I'm edging onto the road when I hear a loud metallic grinding noise. I stomp the gas pedal harder. The engine revs, but the car won't budge another inch.

Fantastic.

Throwing the gears into park, I glare at the clock. It's hours from daylight, but what choice do I have other than wait? I don't have a prayer of finding my way out of here in the dark.

I scour my car and come up with a half-filled warm bottle of water. I take a long gulp.

It's getting stuffy in here. There's not much point in trying to save on gas, so I flip on the AC, and cool air rushes in against my cheeks. Sinking into the smooth leather seat, I shut my eyes. My mom is going to *freak* when I tell her about this. I bet she'll even take me on a trip so I can recover from this whole ordeal. I'll get to miss a week of school.

Where do I want to go?

Greece? Italy? Yes, Sperlonga. The mountains and the ocean and . . .

I realize I've nodded off when I'm jolted awake by headlights coming up behind me.

Maybe it's a nice old lady with some sandwiches and a cell phone. I press my hazard lights, but nothing happens. My car must've died while I was sleeping. The way my night's going, the approaching car will speed right past me without even realizing I'm here.

I press the button to lower my windows, forgetting for a second those won't work either, so I open the door and wave my arms.

The approaching vehicle begins to slow. Another rusty pickup. They must *all* be rusty trucks around here. It pulls to a stop and— shit, it's the *same* truck.

I slam my door fast and slap the locks just as the big man climbs out.

Why is he *back*?

He heads to the bed of his truck and hefts a tire into the air, wearing a salt-of-the-earth smile. When I don't move, his eyes narrow like he's concerned for my sanity.

"I felt awful leaving you out here on your own," he explains loudly enough for me to hear him through the thick glass. "This one'll get you a hunnard miles."

And now I get it. He saw my car and he's hoping to collect a reward, and here I am acting scared, which is just embarrassing. So I open my door.

"Great. If you give me your address, my parents will send you a check."

"That's all right." He frowns like I've offended some cowboy code of honor. "Go on and pop the trunk." He moves to the rear of my car and fiddles with the latch.

"You have to press the button," I call out to him, but the yokel still can't figure it out.

Annoyed, I hop onto a road full of nothing but me and the crickets and this guy with the crazy night vision. I feel around for the button and lift up the trunk. No internal lights come on, making it impossible to even see the tools.

"It's so dark," I say.

A hot breath lands on the back of my neck. "Are you scared of the dark?" The man's voice is right behind me, and it sounds strangely . . . hopeful.

I spin around, ready to tell him about a thing called personal space, when I feel my eyes go wide, and his do too. In an instant, I know he's going to do something to me—and he knows that I know.

"This will only hurt for a second," he says.

His hand blurs, and there's a sting in my neck.

I shove at him, but my arms are uncoordinated and heavy. As they move through the night, they leave blurry trails.

"You . . . you . . ." I try to say, but the words are slow and hazy and long.

I stumble backward, watching him through cloudy eyes.

He's holding something—a syringe.

My heart accelerates, a dizzy kind of terror.

I wheel around to the barbed-wire fence. Just beyond it are trees. I can hide there. I *have* to.

Only, my legs aren't working right, and it's like a nightmare where someone's chasing you but you're unable to lift your feet.

I stagger, grasp the fence. Sharp pain in my palms, and the world's a swirling smear.

Blink.

Find myself on the other side of the fence, the tree line so close.

I'm going to make it. I'm going to get away.

Then I feel a hand clasp my shoulder, and the whole world gathers into darkness.

THIRTEEN

There's something I need to remember . . . something important.

Black tunnels fill my head.

A blurry room in a tilted world. A shadow on a string dangles over me.

Everything's quiet, like snowfall at night.

I think I'm still dreaming.

I rise a couple of inches.

Fall down again.

Drag my legs sideways. My bare toes scrape a cold floor.

I stand, sway, the tunnels in my head start to spin.

Now my cheek's resting against the floor. A deep knot in the wood stares back at me like an eye. The ground below me rumbles, and a pair of boots enters my line of vision.

I look up . . . up . . . up to a towering giant.

Is this real?

He bends down close, but I can't make out a face. An arm slides behind my shoulders, another beneath my knees, and I'm hoisted into the air like I'm made of clouds, and carried to a small bed.

No no no—I think the words, but they won't come out.

I try to rise again, but a weight's falling over me.

The giant is still watching me as my eyes fall closed.

I don't feel so good. My alarm hasn't gone off yet, so I've got more time to sleep before school, but I can't make it today. I need Mrs. Marley to bring me some Tylenol. My head's pounding so hard I think I'm going to be sick.

I feel around for my phone. Can't find it. There's an urgent pressure in my bladder, but if I move, I'll throw up. My eyes open—an explosion of light. A model airplane with bright red wings swings above me.

This is not my room.

My heartbeat skyrockets. I look right—a window with drapes so heavy I can't tell if it's day or night. Look left—a sleeping man in a wooden chair. He has black hair, a square jaw, and dark stubble. He's wearing a flannel shirt, blue jeans, dusty cowboy boots, and he has a big leather watch strapped to his wrist.

The memories come in flashes.

The headlights.

The accident.

The *needle*.

It's the man from the truck.

Now my thoughts won't connect, just impulses firing and blinding white like there's a short-circuit in my brain. I'm not sure how much time passes before my mind clears enough to think:

He's asleep. I need to do something and do it NOW.

On the little wooden nightstand beside me there's a lamp with a round, ceramic base. It looks heavy. Heavy enough to knock someone out if you swing hard enough.

I inch toward it, holding back a moan when the movement makes my head pound harder. Slowly, silently, I stretch out my arms. My fingers graze the lamp's base. Just a little farther—the springs let out a loud squeal, and the big man's eyes pop open.

FOURTEEN

The man seems startled for only a moment, but then he smiles at me, and if I've ever been the object of a happier expression, I can't remember it. My heart begins thumping in my ears—a smile from the wrong person is terrifying.

Abruptly, his mouth flips down like he's disappointed. "You don't recognize me."

"Of course I *reckanize* you," I make fun of his accent in an angry panic. "You ran me off the road. You—you—"

I glance wildly around the room. Two doors on the wall behind the man. The one in the left corner's open. Just a bathroom. The other door—has to be the way out—is closed. My eyes flick to the window on my right. It's closer and no one's blocking my path to it, but managing to unlock it and climb through before he could grab—

I hear wood scraping along the floor. The man's got a big hand wrapped over the back of his chair, and he's dragging it closer to the bed.

Quickly, I back away, the sudden action making me wince.

"Are you all right?" His face crinkles in something that looks like concern.

For a moment, I squeeze my eyes tight against the pain. "My head."

"I'm sorry about that." The man stretches out his hand.

"D-don't touch me." I lurch away, but my leg's snagged on something.

I yank off the patchwork quilt and see something so wrong that my brain's not sure how to make sense of it. It's flashing me strange images—a mouse broken under a metal clamp, a leg caught in the teeth of a beartrap. My ankle is chained to an iron footboard.

I start making gasping-gulping noises I can't control.

"It's all right." The man reaches for me again.

I bat him away, but the attempt is neither strong nor coordinated.

"Stop that," he scolds. "You don't need to be afraid of me." He pets my cheek with a warm-rough palm.

"G-get off me."

He drops his hand, studying me for a moment. "You need to eat something."

Standing, he fishes a key ring from his pocket. As his boots thud across the hardwood floor, he shuffles through its many keys, then uses one to unlock the door. He walks out, closing the door behind him.

Immediately, I scoot to the end of the mattress and drag the cuff down, but I can't get it past the knobby bone of my ankle. I claw at it—a round leaden shackle that looks like an antique—but it doesn't give.

There's a short, almost delicate chain linking it to another cuff—that one's clamped to the footboard. I grab the chain and pull, grunting with exertion, but it's a lot sturdier than it looks.

The door swings open.

"Brought you some aspirin," the man says casually, like he doesn't see what I'm doing. He opens his hand to reveal three little white pills.

I'm about to refuse them when my head gives another throb. Releasing the chain, I reach out for the meds. My fingers scrape his palm, making me shudder in revulsion, but I pop the pills into my mouth and swallow.

"You need the bathroom?" he asks.

I nod. My head throbs harder.

He fishes the key ring from his pocket again and uses one of his many keys to unlock the cuff from my ankle.

For a moment, I'm shocked. He's *unlocking* me?

I scramble out of the bed—and nearly topple over.

I'm not strong enough to fight him, not yet. I manage to stumble into the restroom and shut the door firmly behind me. Use one hand to unzip my fly, use the other to prop myself up against the wall. My eyes go foggy as they dart around the tiny, windowless room. I see it in broken pieces:

A shower with no door.

A sink with no mirror hanging over it.

A toilet with no lid.

"You need any help in there?" It sounds like the man has his mouth pressed right against the door.

I zip up, then fumble at the doorknob—no lock. But even if there were, it wouldn't matter. There's nowhere to go. I'm starting to hyperventilate, my breaths coming out in thick, scared gulps, and I feel like I'm leaving my body. Like some higher power is levitating me into a nebulous sky, and I'm watching everything unfold below.

The man opens the bathroom door—and I'm plummeting back down.

Panting hard, I try to shove around him, but my arms are like cotton. Soft. *Useless.*

"Lie down," he says gently. "You're not well enough for this."

The next thing I know, I'm in bed, a billion black dots gathering in front of my eyes.

FIFTEEN

I wake with a start, disoriented and off-kilter, like my body doesn't understand how I'm still here. Experimentally, I try sitting up. I'm queasy, but the movement doesn't make my head pound like it did earlier. With clearer eyes, I study the room.

Not much furniture. Just the little twin bed, a nightstand, and an old bookshelf situated between the bathroom and the door. The cream-colored walls are papered in a repeating scene—two transparent boys flying a blue kite. The shelf is full of books and toys: green army men, action figures, plastic dinosaurs. There must be a kid somewhere in the house, and I'm not sure if that makes me feel better or worse.

Absently, I reach into my pocket for my phone, but it's not there of course.

My breaths speed up, noisy and scattered.

Calm down, I order myself. *Think.* That man wants something because everyone wants something. I just have to figure out what it is . . . then make him think he's going to get it.

And then he'll let me go.

My breaths even out. It's going to be okay. I'll have a little talk with—what was his name?

Something my grandfather once told me pops into my head. Names are important. You win favor by remembering. You diminish someone by forgetting.

I search my brain.

Caleb.

I just need to have a talk with Caleb, and I'll be home in no time. Mom will send the company plane, and she'll take me to Europe to help me recover from this whole ordeal. I'll get to miss a *year* of school. It's okay, it's okay. Everything's going to be okay.

I hear the key rattling its way into the doorknob.

Stay calm, stay in control. You can do this.

The man enters the room, dressed in another flannel shirt that's stretched tight over his big shoulders, but no boots this time, just socked feet. Which makes me wonder—where are *my* shoes? It's creepy imagining him carrying me in here, taking my shoes off while I was sleeping, putting me in the—

"This shouldn't be too hard on your stomach." He hands me a steaming mug. The liquid sloshing around inside has a faintly garlicky odor, and the fact that *he* prepared it fills me with disgust.

"What is it?"

"Broth."

I take a cautious sip. Not great, but it sparks my hunger, reminding me I haven't eaten since—another rush of panic.

I haven't eaten since the field trip, but when was that? How long was I knocked out?

The man leans back in his chair, studying me in silence while I keep sipping the broth. His hands are loose and relaxed over his thighs, unlike mine, which are clenched tight around my warm mug. It's chilly in here, but the man doesn't seem to feel it.

Finishing the last swallow of broth, I say, "This is good . . . Caleb."

When he goes completely still, my stomach clenches. I miscalculated. He must've forgotten he told me his name—you're not supposed to know your kidnapper's name.

But then he smiles, something strangely bittersweet. "That's right. Caleb."

Relieved, I set the mug on the nightstand. As I shift, the springs squeak and I feel the weight on my ankle and nearly panic again, but I squash it.

"Caleb?"

"Yes?" he says eagerly.

"I need you to remove the cuff and bring me a phone." Good—I sounded calm and authoritative, exactly like my grandfather when he's giving an employee some instruction. Caleb's mouth goes slack like he's in total shock, but I continue calmly, civilly, "I guarantee you we can be done with this in less than an hour. I just need to place a call."

"I was afraid . . ." He sounds like he's talking to himself. "I was afraid of this."

"I understand," I say soothingly. He *should* be afraid. "You're in over your head, so why not let me handle it? I have kidnappers insurance, so—"

"*Kidnapper?*" With a dark scowl, he snatches the empty mug off the nightstand. "I think you need more sleep."

And before I can utter another word, he flicks off the overhead light and shuts the door.

For a stunned minute, I just sit here in the ambery glow of the lamplight, but then I collect myself enough to face the window. It's too far to reach in this position, so I flip onto my stomach. My right foot's tethered to the bed, but now my left foot can touch the floor. I stretch, practically doing the splits, but it's no use. The chain doesn't have enough links.

Off-balance and hopping, I propel my body toward the window, trying to drag the bed closer, but it doesn't even *budge*. That's weird—the bed can't be *that* heavy.

I scan the siderail, the footboard, and the legs—which are bolted right into the floor. My heartbeat starts jumping again. Picturing him doing that. Picturing him getting this room ready for me. He must've planned this, not just some spur-of-the-moment thing once he discovered who I am. He must've been faking it when he pretended not to know my name.

But if that's true, why doesn't he want the money? It makes no sense.

And like a shot, the answer hits me, so obvious it's embarrassing. *Blair.*

This can't just be a coincidence. Blair was angry enough to threaten me at school—in front of witnesses. Could he have hired Caleb? Maybe Evan's in on it too. Come to think of it, Blair and Caleb even dress sort of alike. They both have that same backwoods style.

Oh my God, they're probably *family*.

Or Caleb's at least some friend of the family.

I bet there's a camera mounted around here somewhere. I don't see anything attached to the walls, and it's too shadowy to make out the details of what's on the bookshelf, but at the very top of the bookshelf, there's a stuffed owl with big glassy eyes. I remember a news segment about nanny-cam dolls that have cameras in the eyes.

Evan and Blair have probably been watching this whole time. Embarrassment rushes through me, thinking about how scared I've looked, how *stupid*. I bet they're hoping to post a video of me crying on YouTube, those sociopaths.

Well, that's not going to happen.

With an angry smile, I wave at the camera. "I know you're recording this, Blair."

I force myself to appear calm and unafraid as I plan my next conversation with Caleb.

When the overhead lights flip on, I realize I fell asleep again. Whatever Caleb put in that needle must've been strong.

"Brought you a drink." He holds a tall cup into the air. "It's got electrolytes."

Now that I've figured out the truth, the entire situation feels absurd. I mean, this room's obviously staged. Like that haunted psych hospital Luke and I went to with the *abandoned* straitjackets and electroshock machines, only this is Creepy Kid's Room with weirdo '50s wallpaper and vintage toys.

Caleb hands me the cup as he takes a seat in the chair. Obviously, he's been told not to hurt me. Evan and Blair might be stupid, but they're not suicidal. They'd have to realize what would happen to them if they actually harmed me. I'm not exactly sure what sort of hold they have over this man. Caleb could be an uncle or a cousin, but that's fine. Blood may be thicker than water, but money's thicker than both.

"Caleb?"

He scoots to the edge of his seat with an eagerness that borders on mania. "Yes?"

"Do you know who I am?"

A puzzled line appears between his dark brows. "I know exactly who you are."

"So Blair explained to you what kind of resources my family has?"

"Blair?" Caleb's confusion *seems* genuine, but my grandfather told me that people never seem more genuine than when they're lying to your face.

"Oh, come on," I scoff. "He's clearly trying to get back at me. I guess you guys want revenge or something."

"I don't want revenge—"

"But whatever you think you're doing, it has to *stop*." My voice cracks. I take in a calming breath. "Are you aware that this is a felony?"

The big man's jaw starts working up and down. Maybe I shouldn't have said that.

Quickly, I try a different tact. "But no harm's been done. My parents will be thrilled that you helped me. I just need you to bring me a phone."

The man drops his elbows to his thighs and buries his face in his palms.

"Caleb . . ." When he looks up, I hold out my hand. "Bring me a phone."

But he doesn't do it, and I don't understand. Why isn't he *listening* to me? I'm trying to keep my cool, but a horrible and unfamiliar feeling is washing over me. What's that thing Mr. Rivas says sometimes? That hopeless, helpless expression?

I'm at a loss.

Yes, I'm at a loss.

"You're related to Blair or something, right? He hates me, so you do too?"

"I don't hate you," the man says fiercely.

"Then what is this? I can pay you *anything.* I have so much money!"

"I don't want any money!"

"Then what do you want?"

"I want *you.*"

I shrink into the headboard.

"What's wrong?" He sounds genuinely perplexed.

Mouth dry, I don't answer.

"You need the toilet again?"

I nod even though I don't, and he uncuffs me. When I stand, my calf muscles almost give out, and I'm not sure if it's hunger, fear, or a side effect of the drugs. Once I'm shut inside the bathroom, I try to collect my thoughts.

I want you.

I'm not stupid and I'm not naive. I know how that sounds. But I also know Blair and Evan are out for blood. They want to scare me, and what's the scariest thing they could pay some redneck to say? Well, that was it.

With a sudden surge of anger, I slap open the door. They're

trying to trick me—but I'm not falling for it. Caleb's standing with his hands in his pockets, his posture loose. Nothing like frenzied kidnappers in movies, and I guess that's a good thing. Kidnappers do stupid things when they're panicked. Of course, nothing about this feels *good*.

"Caleb?" I do my best to sound casual, even friendly. "I really need to talk to my mom."

There's a pained twinge in his eyes for a moment, then he pulls back the quilt. "It's time for bed."

"Caleb . . ." I summon my grandfather's most imperious tone. "This is enough."

"*Bed*," he repeats, sounding a little amused now, and I don't understand. He should *want* me to call. He should want the money.

I give The Owl Eyes camera another glance. It's humiliating to capitulate, but it would be even more embarrassing to try to fight him and lose, so I climb onto the lumpy mattress and allow him to clamp the cuff around my ankle.

"Want the lamp on?" he asks.

"I don't care."

He makes a face I'm not sure how to interpret, then shuts off the overhead light. Now the room's pitch-black like a cave. No moonlight, no streetlights, no nothing.

"Caleb . . ." I can't control the tremor in my voice. "Where *are* we?"

He doesn't answer.

SIXTEEN

When I wake, the man is watching me from his chair. The over-head lights are on, and the scent of strong coffee's wafting up from his mug.

"Morning," he says, nodding to a cup that's forming a wet ring on the nightstand. I'm hoping for coffee too, but a quick glance shows me it's just broth, something I've already come to despise.

How long have I been here? A few days? A week?

Between the heavy drapes and lack of clock, it's impossible to get any sense of day or night. I'm constantly sitting while Caleb hovers and stares and brings me broth, but never enough to stop me from feeling hungry.

I wonder what my mother's doing right now. I can picture her behind a podium at a televised press conference with my grand-father by her side, demanding my safe return.

But if that's true, then why hasn't a deal been struck by now?

"Anything yet?" Caleb startles me from my thoughts.

"Any what?"

"Anything coming to you?"

"Like what?"

He nods sadly. "The drugs'll be out of your system soon."

"Exactly how much did you give me?"

"Not *those* drugs."

"What does that mean?"

Caleb takes a slow sip of his coffee instead of answering, and I swallow down my frustration. This doesn't make sense. If he doesn't want ransom, then this has to be payback, but he's not acting like a man hell-bent on revenge. He hasn't tried to touch me apart from cuffing and uncuffing me, and he's actually been attentive like a nurse or a nanny.

"Go on," he says. "Drink your broth."

That fairy tale pops into my head, the one about the witch who kept making those little kids eat so she could eat them. Only there's no ravenous evil gleam in Caleb's eyes. Just calm patience. But why is that calm so scary?

All of a sudden, I think I know why. In movies, kidnappers are always on edge for one reason—they're afraid they might get caught.

My hands keep itching for my phone, my fingers absently drumming. I'm hovering somewhere between anxious-hunger and angry-boredom when Caleb enters the room and gives me a plate with an actual sandwich on it.

I lift the corner of perfectly square white bread that looks like something stamped out in a factory to reveal a shiny circle of meat.

"Baloney and cheese," he explains.

With a grimace, I drop the bread.

"Try it."

I take a bite, and it's either a lot better than it looks or I'm so hungry my taste buds are confused because I finish it in under two minutes.

"Can I have another one?" I ask, and immediately my gaze shifts to The Owl Eyes, embarrassed to have been caught asking for more food like I'm Oliver Twist or something.

Caleb chuckles, scratching his cheek where his stubble is on its way to becoming a beard. "I guess that'd be all right."

In minutes, I'm presented with another sandwich. I eat it slower this time, observing the strangeness of the flavors and textures, but it's still so much better than broth.

"Need the toilet?" Caleb asks as soon as I finish.

"Yeah."

He uncuffs me, and when I stand, I feel fine—*more* than fine. Now I'm Oliver Twist from a later scene in the book, energized and aggressive once his captors give him beef after a lifetime of gruel.

But I don't let it show. I use the bathroom, then stumble back out, collapsing into a heap on the bed.

"I'm soooo tired." I'm probably laying it on too thick like the theater kids at my school. Pulling my knees to my chest, I shut my eyes, making myself go heavy as if I'm already falling into a deep sleep. I hear the door clicking shut, and my heart quickens.

Caleb forgot to cuff my foot.

I stay in a tight ball until I'm sure he's not coming right back, then I begin sliding off the bed. If Caleb's in some other room watching me through The Owl Eyes cam, he'll be running in here any second now.

I'm near the edge of the mattress. Almost there—

One of the springs lets out a loud squeal.

I freeze, gaping at the door.

But no Caleb.

Slowly, I continue sliding until both my feet touch the hardwood floor, then I run straight to the window, lift the curtain—and it's like an optical illusion. My eyes flutter a few times as if the shock is blurring my vision.

There's a distorted, patchy square like there *used* to be a window, but now it's gone.

I touch it just to be sure. Hard, cold, filled with whatever walls are made of. That dizzy-levitating feeling is back.

I glance to The Eyes.

Still no Caleb charging in. Maybe he doesn't have access to the feed. Maybe only Evan and Blair have been watching, but maybe they're in school right now, so they don't know what I'm doing. Or maybe . . .

Maybe it's better not to question it.

I creep to the door and twist the knob. *Locked.* Caleb always uses his keys to let himself out after he shuts the door, so it must lock automatically.

On the tips of my toes, I explore the room.

Bathroom: nothing sharp or heavy.

Under the bed: cobwebs and dust.

Bookshelf: just a bunch of ancient toys.

Caleb's chair: too bulky to use as a weapon.

There's nothing useful in this entire room. Except maybe the lamp.

+ + +

I'm crouched behind the door like I'm at a starting line, waiting for the gun. I keep going over what's about to happen in my head. Caleb will come inside, hopefully his hands occupied with a cup and a plate. I stuffed pillows under the quilt like kids do in old TV shows when they want to sneak out, so Caleb will walk right to it. He won't know I'm actually right behind him—not until the lamp crashes into his skull.

Then I'll take his keys and slam the door behind me, locking him in, and then . . .

And then . . .

The rest is hard to picture.

I have no idea what lies beyond this room, or beyond this house for that matter. For all I know, I might not even be in Texas anymore. I could be in the mountains or the woods or somewhere so remote it might take a long time to find help. Which means when I hit him, I'd better do it hard enough to knock him out.

I stand up straight and take a couple of practice swings. It's not as easy as I thought it would be. The lamp's an awkward shape, and the cord whips around and smacks my leg. Wincing, I gather the cord into my fist and try again, swinging a few more times before getting back into position and going over the plan.

I'll hit him in the head.

He'll fall, unconscious.

I'll grab the keys.

I'll find an exit.

My arms are tiring, and sweat's beading along my upper lip. My own smell is starting to get to me. I haven't showered or brushed my teeth since I've been here, and I'm still wearing my pie-stained slacks and Luke's *Star Wars* tee. When Mom sends the plane, the media probably won't be far behind. I'll have to clean up before I'm interviewed.

Again, I go over the plan.

Knock him out.

Grab the keys.

Find a—

The door's swinging open.

I choke back the startled noise I want to make as Caleb enters the room. He goes straight for the bed, exactly like I knew he would.

Holding my breath, I tiptoe out from behind the door.

Right behind him now.

I swing the lamp as hard as I can—just as he whirls around to face me.

SEVENTEEN

The lamp smashes against his forearm, not his head, and now it's lying in harmless pieces on the floor. I'm stunned at how easily he deflected it, at how quickly the timeline I constructed is crumbling.

Shock and anger distort his features as I scuttle through the open door. I try to hurl it closed behind me to lock him inside at least for a moment, but it reverberates off his body. My bare feet pound down a wood-paneled hall, my heart in my ears. I'm scared, the ancient fear all prey feels when something bigger and stronger is chasing it.

I make it to an old-fashioned living room, eyes racing.

Wood wall—wood wall—silver wall—no, that's a *door*.

I run to it.

My hands are closing over the handle when strong fingers clamp down into the muscles of my shoulder.

Caleb spins me around.

It's all instinct when I swing at him with a clenched fist.

He dodges, easily, then he drags me by my wrist through the living room and down the hall. I try to get loose, but my palms are too slick to gain any purchase, and soon he's hurling me back into the little bedroom.

Before I can regain my footing, Caleb slams the door.

He marches to the bed and seizes the cuff. He doesn't look angry anymore, but he does look determined. "Get over here."

I back away, keeping my eyes trained on him as I bend to retrieve one of the larger fragments of broken lamp from the floor.

His eyes widen, alarmed. "Put that down."

I hold it out like a sword, its sharp edges slicing the sensitive skin between my fingers. "O-open this door, Caleb." I've got so much adrenaline now, I bet I'm supernatural-strong like mothers who can lift trucks off children.

Caleb advances in a defensive crab walk, and I make a wild, lunging slash. I'll kill him if I have to. He dodges, then somehow—I don't know how—he's got my back pulled into his chest and my left arm pinned behind my neck, and he's squeezing my right wrist with one hand.

My fingers go numb.

My weapon falls.

I twist around, wrenching my shoulder, and take another swing. This time I hit him square in the eye. Caleb growls, baring his teeth—and then he slaps me. Only it feels unfair to call it that. My neck jerks so hard to the side I think I need to see my chiropractor. I hold my heated cheek, shocked. He's not supposed to do this. He's not supposed to *hurt* me.

Everything's hazy when he tosses me onto the bed. I'm short-circuiting again. There are flashes of grappling-bruising grips and stinking sweat. There are quick thoughts about how it feels when someone touches you without your permission, but it's all stop-motion, and there are too many missing frames to make sense of the scene.

I skip the moment that he takes my ankle, and land on the one where I'm cuffed and kneeling in the center of the bed.

"Goddamnit, I didn't wanna to do that!" Caleb paces while shooting me dark looks. "I don't know what I'm gonna do with you."

"Fuck you," I say, but instead of sounding tough, it comes out weak.

Caleb draws himself up straighter. "I don't want any more of this nonsense, you hear?"

"Fuck. You."

He takes two big steps toward the bed, and I scramble backward. Immediately, I feel a rush of shame. One slap, and I'm already cringing.

He stares me down for a minute, then turns for the door, but before he goes, he says, "I'd think real hard about your attitude. If there's one thing I've learned in life, it's that things can always get worse."

I hold my throbbing cheek in my palm. My wrists are bruised, and there are red blotches up and down my arms. My whole body aches like I've been in an actual fight, and I'm shaking all over as if my adrenaline doesn't know where to go.

I really screwed up. Who knows how long it'll be until I get another chance to run? I'm so furious with myself tears spring to my eyes.

Suddenly, I remember the camera. Were Evan and Blair watching? Are they laughing?

I turn to the un-window so they can't see me, and I stay here for a very long time.

Behind me, the door squeaks open.

"Lemme see that hand," Caleb orders, his voice gruff.

I glance over my shoulder. He's carrying a big bottle of hydrogen peroxide and a washrag. I'm tempted to refuse just on principle, but what good would it do to let my hand get infected?

So I turn around.

Instantly, Caleb's eyes fill with pity. I must look like I've been crying, and this makes me even angrier.

"I'm not doing any of this to hurt you," he says gently. Taking hold of my wrist, he pours the peroxide over my palm. When I wince at the sting, he shushes me. "It's gonna get easier, I promise. You have to trust me."

And then he pets the cheek he hit.

EIGHTEEN

The next time Caleb uncuffs me, his guard is up like an animal trainer with a brand-new lion. I vibrate in anger as he shadows me to the bathroom. Once inside, I slam the door in his face.

I use the toilet—*no mirror, no window, no sharp objects*—then storm back out, and it takes everything I've got to climb in that bed and hold still while he closes the cuff around my ankle.

"Is that all right?" he asks.

"Sure. Love it."

His mouth tightens a little like maybe he actually does understand sarcasm. "I'll get you something to eat."

While he's gone, I quietly seethe. The pain in my cheek has settled to a dull ache, but it's still there, a constant reminder that he *hit* me.

Caleb returns, carrying two plates stacked high with baloney sandwiches. I'm struck with a confusing mixture of gratitude and bitterness as he passes one of the plates to me.

"I know this is hard," he says.

I don't bother responding to that.

Balancing the other plate in his lap, he grabs his sandwich and takes a huge bite. "You gonna eat?"

I want to throw the food at his head.

"You feeling sick?"

"Not hungry."

"At least a coupla bites."

"*No.*"

The thing is, I *am* hungry, but it feels good to refuse. I may not be able to leave this room, but there are still some things I can control.

"You hafta eat." Caleb's tone suggests I'm in danger of dying in the next five minutes, which is ridiculous. But it gives me an idea.

It's almost like Caleb knows what I've been planning because the next time he enters the room, he's got two steaming bowls of what smells like beef stew. My stomach rumbles.

He sets one of the bowls on the nightstand, and the tempting scent wafts up to my nose.

"Go on," he tells me, digging into a bowl of his own.

"I'm good."

"You sure you're feeling all right?"

I stare at the wall straight ahead of me. The two transparent boys flying a kite, over and over.

"So you're gonna starve yourself, is that it?"

I don't even flicker.

"Fine." Caleb takes another bite. "You'll eat when you get hungry enough."

He ignores me ignoring him, just makes slurpy *mmm-mmm*

noises as he finishes his stew, then he takes my untouched bowl from the room.

Alone now, I tap my fingers against the bed. I've gone without a meal before, not intentionally or anything, but sometimes you don't think about it, and then you realize you haven't eaten all day and you feel like you're starving.

But then you simply eat.

I've never wanted food and couldn't have it. It's weirdly hard to stop obsessing about. I remember something Mr. Rivas once told me—you can't think two different thoughts at the same time—so I run through all the ways I know to say hello.

Salve, bonjour, hola, buongiorno.

But against my will my thoughts drift back to food. Five-star restaurants, exotic meals I've had in foreign countries, the crappy cafeteria lunch at school. I can picture my friends gathered around our sunny table, but it quickly becomes a solemn scene. Bria begins to cry, swearing to never love again, and Luke's saying he'll never have another friend.

Annoyed with myself, I shake those thoughts away. That's how people act at funerals, and I'm not dead. I switch gears. Instead of mourning, they're forming a rescue plan. And they aren't even in school—they're searching for me. Actually, there *is* no school. It's been canceled, and it won't be reopened until someone finds me.

Caleb's back with another bowl. The scent fills all the air in the room, so I can't help but breathe it in, and it's like my cells are screaming for it. They can sense protein, carbs, minerals.

He sticks a spoonful in front of my face, and some instinctive part of me quite nearly opens my mouth, but I fight my instincts and continue staring blankly ahead.

"Come on," he pleads, sounding extremely worried now. "You're gonna get sick." When I don't answer, he takes hold of my chin, and I allow him to move my head, but I keep my eyes unfocused. "I can *make* you eat."

My poker face falls away for at least a few seconds, but then I'm back to blank.

He releases my chin and starts to pace. After a couple minutes, he sets the bowl on the nightstand. "I'll leave this here for you."

When I continue pretending to be a statue, he makes a frustrated noise and storms off, slamming the door behind him.

Now I turn to the bowl.

I want to sneak just one bite, but something tells me if I do, he'll know, so I face the wall again.

"I brought you something . . ." I'm expecting more food, but instead Caleb has a lamp with a blue shade tucked under his arm. "What do you think?" he asks as he plugs it in.

I don't answer. It's not really even intentional this time. I'm just tired.

He makes a growling noise, sounding part pickup truck, part grizzly bear, but I'm so out of it that it hardly registers. I'm not sure how long it's been since I've eaten, but I'm hungrier than I've ever been in my entire life.

He sits in his chair and grips my chin with his hand. This time I look at him.

"Caleb . . ." My voice comes out rough. "I'll eat, okay?"

His big shoulders sag, obviously relieved.

"I'll eat if you let me call my mom."

Caleb's eyes flash with disappointment, then he explodes to his feet, his whole face twitching and pulsing like something alive is slithering under his skin. I have a vague and dreamlike thought: *This* is how kidnappers are supposed to act.

He points a shaking finger in my face. "That woman is not your mother."

It's such a strange thing to say that I'm startled into stuttering, "W-what?"

Caleb paces, halts, then paces some more before planting himself on the edge of his chair and blinding me with flashlight eyes. "I need you to listen to me—really listen. Can you do that?"

I nod, a sick-bad feeling in my stomach.

"Those people you think are your parents . . . well, they aren't."

I keep watching him, waiting for the punch line.

"You're not their son. You're mine."

NINETEEN

Hunger does weird things to you. My brain isn't making all the right connections. It's working too slow, like the thoughts are stuck in tar and I'm having to dig them free. I'm trying to figure out Caleb's angle and what I should say next, but nothing's coming. He seems to take my silence as a good thing because his eyes shine even brighter.

"Wait here!" he tells me, as if I have any other choice.

He dashes from the room, then returns with an armful of cardboard boxes. He plunks them on the floor near the bed.

"Just look at all this stuff." He hefts one of the boxes into the air and turns it over at my feet. "They're *yours*." Paperback books. Action figures. A toy spaceship. "And look at these!" He flips over another box, spilling photographs down onto my lap like rain.

Hundreds of images stare back at me of a little boy with blond hair and green eyes like mine.

The sick-bad feeling gets bigger. "Caleb . . ."

"I know you can't remember right now. I didn't wanna push and make it worse, but you're not eating, so I don't have a choice."

He grabs a handful of photos and shoves one in front of my

face—a sulky toddler with white-blond hair and fat cheeks. He shuffles to the next photo—the same boy, a few years older, wearing a blue baseball cap and grinning wide enough to show off a missing tooth. Caleb shuffles again—a group of kids in soccer uniforms. He points to a blond boy in the front row, then drops the handful of pictures onto the bed, insisting, "*Look.*"

I sift through the sea of photographs and pluck one out. The same blond-haired, green-eyed boy is standing by a lake in a puffy maroon vest. I flip the photo over, and scrawled in cursive in the top-left corner is *Daniel—age 8.*

"That's you, Daniel. All of these are you."

The photo slips from my fingers.

Oh God, this is so much worse than I thought.

TWENTY

"Caleb . . ." I say carefully. "This is a mistake. I don't know you."

"You *do*." His voice is pleading. When I don't answer, he darts over to the shelf. "Here—they're your favorites." He piles action figures, army men, and a stuffed blue duck onto the bed.

"These aren't mine."

With a pained noise, he buries his face in his palms. "What did they do to you?"

Reeling in confusion, I watch him. Does he actually believe what he's saying, or is he just trying to mess with my head? I look to the top of the shelf, at the owl with the giant camera eyes. It's interesting that he didn't bring that particular toy over.

Caleb rubs his cheekbones with the heels of his hands. "I'll heat up the food."

"I'm not eating."

"But you told me you would!"

"I said I'd eat if you let me call my mom."

"Didn't you hear a word I just said? She's not your mother!"

"I'm not eating."

"Please," he begs. "Please don't do this. I just got you back."

+ + +

Eventually, Caleb clears everything off the bed, then he sits in his chair, and the conversations go like this:

"Your name is Daniel Emory. You disappeared from a park when you were ten years old."

"No. My name is Sayers. Sayers Wayte."

"*Sayers?* Does that sound like a real name to you?"

I'm tired, hungry, fuzzy, disoriented. "No. Not really. But it's mine."

"It isn't. Your name is Daniel Emory. You disappeared from a park when you were ten years old."

"For fuck's sake, Caleb. Don't you think I'd know if that were true? I can tell you about my whole life with my parents. What I wore on my first day of kindergarten. What I—"

"Those memories aren't real."

"That doesn't make sense."

"Then listen. Why would I lie to you? Look at me—do I look like I'm lying?"

"No . . ."

"That's because I'm telling you the truth. Your name is Daniel Emory. You disappeared from a park when you were ten years old."

"So you're back to not talking to me?"

I don't answer. I feel sick.

"Will you eat? *Please?*"

There's no use fighting it anymore, so I nod. I'll eat.

Obviously relieved, Caleb sets a bowl on my lap.

"What . . . what *is* that?"

"Oatmeal." He sounds disappointed. "You love oatmeal."

Listless, I stare down at something that resembles wet sand with black bug-like specks. "I've never had this before in my life."

"Daniel—"

"Don't call me that."

"Son."

"Don't call me that either."

"But you are my son, and I can't let you go till we fix you. Now, please eat. I put raisins in it just how you like. I know you don't remember right now, but if you just taste it—"

I don't realize I've slapped the bowl away until I see it on the floor. Caleb's gaping down at it, and I'm just as shocked as he seems to be, then he shifts an angry gaze to me.

"Careful, *son*. Don't bite the hand that feeds you."

The oatmeal has dried on the floorboards by the time he returns. He has to use his fingernails to scrape it all off. He blinks in and out of focus. I feel so strange.

"Caleb . . ." The edge of my vision's graying out. "I don't feel so good."

"You need to eat," I hear him say.

My pulse is too fast like I might actually be killing myself. "O-okay."

"You really mean it this time? You'll eat?"

I nod, and the whole room sways.

He's back—I didn't even see him leave—with more oatmeal. It

feels like a lesson. I reach for the spoon, but my arm's so weak, I can't lift it. Caleb closes his hand over mine and guides the spoon into my mouth. I'm hit by a wave of nausea.

"Something feels really wrong . . ."

"You can't go four days without food." He helps me eat another spoonful.

"Four days?"

He pushes my hair off my forehead. I don't even flinch.

I just focus on eating. Bite after bite.

"See?" he says. "It's good, isn't it?"

"Mmm-hmm," I admit. It *is* good.

TWENTY-ONE

Since my hunger strike, I've had two bowls of oatmeal, three cups of broth, and five electrolyte drinks. That strange, otherworldly feeling has finally passed, and now I just feel stupid. Not eating didn't help. All it did was keep me from being clear-headed enough to grasp how ridiculous the man's story is. Like some kind of Greek tragedy or *Star Wars* operetta. *I'm your long-lost father.* So stupid.

Blair and Evan must be laughing their asses off.

Suddenly, I'm struck with a sharp needle of a thought: Why are they letting this go on for so long? Maybe they never intended to take it this far. Maybe they don't know how to end it. I saw a movie once where something like that happened. These guys kidnapped a kid, and it was supposed to be a prank, but then they got scared they'd go to prison.

So they killed him.

Stop it, I order myself. No one's going to kill me.

And besides, there are so many other movies, *better* movies, where the FBI and detectives and a thousand investigators are on the case, and in the final scene after everyone's given up hope— they find him. I'm going to get out of here. I am.

But my anxious heart won't settle.

"Evan? Blair?" I look up into The Eyes. "I get it, okay? You win."

I almost expect the house lights to come up, maybe the walls to slide out like it's all a set.

I keep waiting.

Caleb holds out a towel, a bar of soap, and a folded stack of clothes. I take them without comment and trudge into the bathroom. I toss the clothes onto the sink, then peel off the *Star Wars* tee, my designer slacks, and boxer briefs, then I step into the shower. It's tight like an upright coffin.

When I turn the knob, lukewarm water sputters out in hard bursts before dwindling to barely-there droplets, but it feels so nice against my skin that I linger here longer than I need to before climbing back out. I dry off with a threadbare towel, then sift through the clothes Caleb gave me: a plaid flannel shirt like the ones he always wears, blue jeans—I *hate* jeans—and a sealed package of underwear. I pull those on first. The fabric's scratchy and they're looser than what I'm used to. Next, I drag the jeans up over my hips. They're a size too small and they have a tear on the knee—one that doesn't look like it was stylistically placed either.

Suddenly suspicious, I grab the flannel shirt off the sink and examine it closely. Threadbare in the elbows, a tiny hole in the collar, fabric a little too worn. Oh God, these clothes are *used*.

Skin crawling, I throw the shirt on the floor and rip the jeans back off. I pick up the *Star Wars* tee, and I'm about to pull it on when the sweaty odor in the pits hits me. This shirt really needs to be washed. My slacks do too.

"Daniel?" Caleb lands three hard knocks against the door.

"Just a minute." I grab the jeans and flannel shirt again. They smell like detergent. Like *Caleb's* detergent. But at least they're clean, and I won't have to wear them for long. Boarding up all the thoughts in my head, I dress quickly and exit the bathroom.

Caleb nods like he approves of this ugly ensemble, and when I get back into bed without arguing, he looks like he approves of that too.

Once he cuffs my ankle, he gathers my clothes from the bathroom floor.

"Those pants have to be dry-cleaned," I tell him.

He gives me a faintly stunned look. "You don't need 'em anymore."

"You mean you're not giving them back?" My question comes out a little strangled.

"I'm giving you everything you need," Caleb says, and then he carries them out the door.

Waves of nerves crash through me. Normally, I'd toss those clothes given the sorry state they're in, but it's just . . . they're the only thing here that's mine.

Caleb sits in his chair while I devour a bowl of rainbow-colored cereal. It's sweet and oddly exciting to my senses, easily the best thing I've eaten since I've been here, and I'm so full of sugar my voice is wired when I say, "Can we talk for a minute?"

"Sure we can." He smiles like a friend.

"I know you've been through a lot, and I haven't made things any easier."

His eyes fill with surprised affection.

"But I've been thinking . . . Why don't we get in the truck and drive to my house? If you and my mom could just sit down and talk, I know we could work this out." Caleb's face falls, prompting me to sputter faster. "I—I know you don't want money, but we can hire a fleet of detectives—the best in the world to find the real Daniel."

"But you *are* the real Daniel."

"Will you just listen? My parents can fix things, but only if you let me go. Think about how you felt when Daniel disappeared. That's how my parents must be feeling right now."

"*They* stole you from *me*!"

"But you can't keep me locked in this little room forever. I'll lose my mind!"

Squeezing my eyes shut, I press down the frustration simmering in my gut. I don't know how much longer I can keep doing this. It's exhausting trying to reason with someone who can't be reasoned with.

"You've got a point."

My eyes spring open.

"You've been cooped up for too long. It's bound to make you irritable."

"I'm not irritable. I'm just—"

"Gimme a few minutes, all right?"

And he leaves me alone, wondering what this means. I asked if we could get in the truck, so maybe he's planning to take me for a drive to get some fresh air.

My heart is racing fast now. The hope is like a drug.

The doorknob's turning so I hold my mouth steady to conceal my excitement. Caleb steps into the room and lifts something in the air.

A longer chain.

In an almost-detached haze, I watch as he loops the chain around one of the iron posts in the footboard and brings both ends together in his fist. He unhooks the cuff that's attached to the footboard, slides it through the two end links he has gathered in his hand, and then he snaps the cuff closed. Now my ankle is attached to the chain that is attached to the bed.

With a satisfied smile, Caleb ambles toward the doorway.

A strange, ticking sensation pulses inside my head. A feeling is boiling up—

"See?" Caleb points to the shelf. "Now you can reach all your books and toys."

—and boiling over.

"You fucking psychopath! I am not a little boy!"

Caleb's eyes widen as I leap out of the bed and rush him.

"I'm. Not. *Daniel!*"

The chain pulls short like a leash, and I'm left clawing at the air.

"Let me out!"

"Son, just lis—"

"LET ME OUT!! LET ME OUT!! LET ME OUT!!"

Caleb gives me a sad look, then he turns, closing the door softly behind him.

Enraged, I hurl myself through the room. I throw boxes. I grab the bookshelf, but it's bolted to the wall, so I swipe everything off the shelves. Rip the arms and legs off toy men. Kick over the nightstand with my unchained foot. Drag the mattress to the floor and keep shouting.

Images fill my mind—me running hard enough to yank the bolted bed into the air. Hard enough to crash through the door like a rocket.

I run.

I'm suspended in the air.

And then I plummet to the floor.

For a moment I'm numb, but eventually, all the pain catches up to my brain. My throat, my face, my ribs, my feet.

Whimpering, I roll over. Lying on my back like a snow angel, surrounded by books and action figure limbs, I gaze upward. Tears start streaking down my cheeks, but I don't bother wiping them off my face. I'm pretty sure no one's really watching me. And I don't think anyone ever was.

When Caleb returns, he halts in the doorway, his eyes jumping around the room. All of Daniel's things have been neatly put away. Action figure limbs snapped into place, books on their shelves, nightstand righted, and Daniel's blue duck is in the bed beside me.

"I'm sorry," I say, looking down at my hands. "I'm sorry for throwing my things."

There's the smallest intake of breath. "It's all right. I'll fix you something to eat."

His bootsteps retreat down the hall, but I don't move a muscle. Hot pain encircles my right ankle, and the top of my left foot throbs like a heart . . . but I'm calm.

I understand now.

I know what I need to do.

Nothing I've done has gotten me anywhere, because this is not about ransom, and it's not about revenge—this man is insane. So I'll become the voice inside his head.

TWENTY-TWO

The throbbing ache in my feet keeps building. I need a painkiller. Maybe Tanner's whole bag of hydros. And I need to pee. How much longer will Caleb be? The door's open, so I could shout for him, but the thought of doing that nearly smothers the last bit of dignity I have left.

I glance up at The Eyes that aren't really watching, and it occurs to me that I don't actually have to wait for Caleb to unlock me anymore. In fact, with this new chain, he doesn't *ever* need to unlock me.

Now that's a scary thought. But I shove it down and slide my legs over the side of the bed—and *fuck*. Immediately, my eyes water. God, my feet hurt. They really hurt.

I peer down—afraid to look, afraid *not* to look—but when I do, they throb even harder like my eyes are linked to pain. The area below my left toes is already a blobby-shaped purple from where I kicked the nightstand like a soccer ball. A dark ring is forming around my right ankle under the cuff.

I'm scared to try moving again, but my bladder's about to burst, so I stand, take one stumbling step, and, "Fuck!"

Caleb flies into the room and seems to size things up quickly because he picks me up and sets me onto the bed. Kneeling to examine my feet, his mouth twists like he's sickened.

"Goddamnit, Daniel." He rips the key ring from his pocket and starts removing the cuff. It takes some maneuvering—the cuff's too tight now thanks to the swelling—and Caleb swears again. "You better pray nothing's broken."

My heart trips at the thought. No, they can't be broken. I wouldn't have been able to clean this room if something was broken. But then I remember how this kid at my school played the last quarter of a football game on a fractured femur. With all that adrenaline, he didn't even know he was injured.

Caleb stalks out of the room leaving me uncuffed and the door wide open. Guess I'm no flight risk at the moment. A minute later, he returns with two Ziploc bags of ice, and sets them against my feet.

Wincing, I push them back off. "Too cold."

"Yeah, well, that's what happens when you do something this foolish. Be still." He presses them to my feet again. "What good did that do you, huh?"

I bite my lip and ball my fingers into fists.

"None," he says, answering his own question. "No good at all."

TWENTY-THREE

Without windows there is no light, and without light there is no time.

I don't know how long I've been in this room. Caleb's ordered me to stay off my feet while they're this tender, and I keep asking myself the same question over and over: *What if they're broken?*

But they're not—I know they're not.

Okay, maybe a couple of toes.

And maybe one of the bones on top of the foot, but not a major bone, I know it.

My fingers keep itching for my phone. I just want to check the time, the weather, *something*. My brain's screaming for stimulation, but there's just this bed and this room. And Caleb.

For the past However Long, he's been carrying me to the bathroom, and I have this sense that as long as I live, I'll never get over how it feels to need someone to carry me to the bathroom.

I hate that he has to touch me. I hate that I have to cooperate with being touched, that I have to put an arm over his shoulders like an embrace.

He always sets me down as soon as we near the toilet to give me some privacy, and there are always a few agonizing moments where I have no choice but to put weight on one foot as I tug down my pants before I sit.

I hate peeing sitting down. I hate using the toilet with him standing right outside the door, waiting for me to finish so he can carry me back to bed.

But that's how it always goes, and once I'm under the covers, I'll get painkillers, and then there's nothing to do but sit.

I don't think Caleb means for me to be so miserable. Whenever he leaves the room, he'll hand me one of Daniel's toys. I'll hold on to it, but I always make sure to drop it the moment Caleb reenters the room again as if I'm embarrassed to be caught playing with toys. The embarrassment isn't too hard to fake.

The first time I really processed that they were *Star Wars* action figures, I let out this hysterical laugh, thinking, dear God—Caleb took the wrong blond-haired, green-eyed teen.

I wonder how Luke would cope if he were here instead of me. He gets creeped out by old ladies with cataracts and babies that stare at him. This would *break* him.

Every once in a while instead of a toy, Caleb will give me a book to read, always something a ten-year-old would appreciate. There are novels about kid superheroes, and there's a whole series on animals. I get to learn about the armadillo—it has bony plates of armor like the dinosaurs. The bat—it can hunt in the dark using echolocation.

Written on inside cover of each book is DANIEL EMORY in incredibly neat handwriting for a kid. Sometimes I can even make out a faint pencil line under Daniel's name, as if he used a ruler to get his signature perfectly straight.

In between meals and reading and pretending to play with toys, Caleb will show me photos of Daniel. *Here you are on the first day of third grade. Remember that boy who'd just moved here from Wyoming? Remember how you helped him make friends?*

He'll show me Daniel's team photos: basketball, soccer, Little League. *Remember the time you got three home runs? You were the best player on that whole team.*

According to Caleb, Daniel was smart, polite, and good at everything.

During each story, I'll nod along like I'm hanging on every word, but in my head I'm screaming, *Why can't you leave me ALONE?*

I keep trying to think of something that will win him over, but I don't want to push it, to behave so differently he knows it's an act, so I'm making myself wait.

Patience, patience . . . it'll become one of my virtues.

TWENTY-FOUR

My feet are propped up on a pillow. My right ankle's looking a lot better, enough that Caleb stuck it back in the cuff. The top of my left foot's gone from purple to black and blue to an ugly shade of green, but I still can't put any weight on it without it hurting like hell.

Caleb sweeps an action figure from one of the shelves and sets it on my bed. While he rummages through the box of photos, I give the toy a closer look. The paint on its face is practically gone, but it's clearly Chewbacca. Daniel must've held it constantly.

"He's my favorite," I risk saying, and Caleb's eyes don't light up exactly, it's more subtle than that, but I'm almost positive I'm right.

Caleb lifts a photo into the air—the one of Daniel by the lake—and I'm bracing myself for another Saint Daniel story when he says, "What do you remember?"

"Remember?" I repeat, caught off guard.

"Try, son. Try to remember."

"Well . . . I think we used to go there sometimes."

Caleb's face flickers dark—wrong.

"Or maybe it was the first time we'd been there."

A faint relaxing in his shoulders and eyes—right.

"And I . . ." *Think*, Saye. What was written on the back? "I was eight years old."

Caleb's eyes widen, astonished. "And?"

I study the picture dangling from his fingers. Daniel in a puffy maroon vest. "It was too cold to swim, and . . ." If it were really me, I'd have pestered my mom to let me swim till she gave in, cold or not. "And I kept asking if I could get in the water."

Caleb's face flickers dark again—wrong.

No, Daniel didn't complain. He wasn't like me. He was *good*.

"I mean, I wanted to ask, but I knew it was too cold. I understood."

Now Caleb smiles, but my speeding heart doesn't slow.

"I'll go get us something to eat," he tells me, and a few minutes later he returns with two plates of scrambled eggs and a thermos of coffee under his arm. It smells incredible, *familiar*.

"Can I have some?"

"No." He frowns. "Coffee's for grown-ups." He hands me a freezing glass of apple juice, and I take a sip. My stomach shivers. I really want coffee—hot, sugary, creamy, comforting.

The craving's so painful that I say, "Just a little? I'm cold."

"If you're cold, I can make you a bowl of oatmeal."

I sag into my pillows. "No, that's all right."

He chuckles. "It's funny how you talk now."

"What do you mean?"

"Big city voice."

I've never considered a suburb outside of Dallas to be the big city, but I guess compared to wherever we are, it must be. It scares me—not knowing where *here* is.

Caleb takes a swallow from his thermos. "Anything else coming to you?"

I'm not sure what he means. Do I remember more about that day at the lake? Do I remember more in general?

"Um . . ." I scrunch up my eyes, pretending to be drawing the memories forth. "Sort of. But it's fuzzy."

"That's because of the experiments."

"Right . . ." I nod as if that makes sense.

He rubs the hard line of his jaw, which today is bristle-free. "I wanna know exactly what they did to you, but if I keep on digging, it could be a whole other kind of risk. My thinking is to let it come back naturally. With those drugs out of your system, everything'll come to you."

"How . . . how long do you think that will take?"

He leans in close. "Can you keep a secret?"

Suddenly too aggravated to restrain myself, I make an exaggerated show of looking around the empty room. "I suppose so."

"Well, everything's gonna change. During the big meteor shower, you'll see."

Big meteor shower? Why does that sound familiar?

An image floods my brain. The giant screen in the darkened auditorium on the first day of school. Evan Zamara telling everyone: *Nothing like this will happen again in our lifetime or the next.*

"You mean the one in *August*?"

Caleb's eyes start straight-up gleaming. "You know about that?"

I nod.

"This is a good sign, a very good sign."

I try to choke down my panic. I can't stay here till August. That's almost a year away.

I chew my chewy eggs, drink more juice, shiver.

"Listen, son. I gotta go to work today."

Work. That word conjures images of my grandfather and mother's office—a skyscraper with glass windows overlooking the Dallas skyline and a thousand cars and roads and people.

"I don't like leaving you alone, but I don't have a choice."

"That's . . . that's okay."

"Just wait, I've got something for you." He rushes from the room, then returns pushing a rolling office chair through the door, a brown paper grocery sack in its seat. "You didn't think I'd leave you here all day without a way to get around, now did you?"

"Um, no. This is great."

It's *amazing.* He's going to leave me alone for an entire workday—I'll have *hours* to get loose. I watch as he arranges the items from the sack onto my nightstand: bottled water, crackers, some other nonperishables.

"I'm proud of you, Daniel."

Startled, I look up at him. "You are?"

"Of course I am. I can't even picture how scary all this has gotta be, but you're brave."

He strokes his hand over my hair, and I get the full-body chills. This isn't like when Mom pats me and I get irritated. This feels like an invasion. Like I'm being burglarized. I want to pull away, but I force myself to stay still and pretend I don't mind.

✛ ✛ ✛

The second Caleb's gone, I fall into the office chair and stick out my right heel to drag myself forward. It's slow going thanks to the chain and the pain, but I comb every inch of this room. I run my hands along the floorboards. I peer under the bed. I don't know what I'm looking for exactly. A forgotten paper clip to pick the lock? An escape hatch?

I'm examining each item on the bookshelf when something makes me pause. The Luke Skywalker toy is holding a tiny light-saber.

I slide it from Luke's plastic hand, jam it into my cuff's key-hole—and it actually *fits*.

"Holy shit!"

I bend my ear to the cuff so I can hear the tumblers click, some-thing I've seen criminals do in movies. I'm not sure if what I'm doing is working or not when there's a sharp snap.

I pull the sword back out—which is now a broken stub.

"No, no, no." Next time Caleb unlocks me, his key's not going to fit right, and he's going to figure out what I've done, and all this patience and playing along will have been for nothing.

I shake my leg, trying to dislodge the little piece, but it doesn't work, so I scour the room for another tiny object I could use to dig it out, but there's nothing.

Defeated, I crawl into bed and stare up at the ceiling.

And stare and stare and stare.

When I wake up, I'm still alone in the room. Caleb's been gone a *really* long time.

I shake my ankle for the broken piece. No such luck.

Bored, I eat a few stale crackers. There's nothing to do, so I roll around in the chair, get back into bed, sleep some more, and when I wake again, I'm tired and wired at the same time.

I chew more crackers, stare at the walls—the boys flying kites over and over and over. I shake my ankle in the air—and there it is! The rest of Luke's sword has fallen onto the quilt.

I grin.

But it's a short-lived elation.

What's the half-life of happiness?

In this room it's not long. But what's short and what's long? It feels like Caleb's been gone for fifteen hours, maybe twenty. What if something happened to him? What if he got in a car accident and he can't get here? What would happen to me?

I'd die, the answer comes immediately.

I'd die, chained to this bed.

Now it feels like someone's covering my mouth and my nose—I can't breathe.

My vision grays out. I come back dazed.

I'm still in a strange stupor a hundred hours later when the door swings open, and Caleb strolls in with food and a smile. I'm hit with the usual rush of dread I get every single time he enters this room, but even stronger is my relief.

TWENTY-FIVE

My left knee in the seat of the rolling chair, my right foot on the floor to push, I spin around the room like a fish in a bowl.

I wonder what time it is.

That first day Caleb went to work, he said he'd only been gone a few hours, but it didn't feel like a few hours. It never does. I can't gauge things right, so maybe it's first-period World History and my classmates are fighting about God, or maybe it's seventh-period Psychology and Luke's talking Ms. Wells's ear off.

I remember one depressing Psych class where we learned about the horrors of solitary confinement in prisons. There were a few snide comments, Don't-do-the-crime-if-you-can't-do-the-time kind of stuff, but Ms. Wells shut that down fast. She called it *legalized torture*, I remember that specifically, then she made us watch a documentary about this journalist who agreed to be locked in a prison cell for fourteen days.

The guard who was observing the journalist on a monitor couldn't believe how quickly the guy was acting like a regular inmate. In, like, *hours*, the reporter was pacing, anxious. By day three, he was staring at his concrete wall, and in a week, he was so distraught, they had to end the experiment early.

One of the seniors in class coughed "little bitch" into his fist, which pissed Ms. Wells off.

"We're social creatures," she said. "We need stimulation and human connection. Take that away from us, and we become depressed, even suicidal." Then she showed us MRI photos to prove her point. "See how the brain slows down after just a few days in solitary? Well, longer confinement presents like a head injury."

A head injury.

Maybe I shouldn't be thinking about this right now. And besides—I'm not *always* alone. I've got Caleb. Ha! Luke told me I never laugh anymore, well, the joke's on you, Luke. Look at me—I'm laughing right now. And I'm not in a prison cell, but like the journalist and the inmates, I can't stop pacing. Or in my case, rolling in my office chair.

I roll to the bathroom, to the bookshelf. I pull back the curtains as if *this* time the window will be there, then I climb into bed again and stare at the ceiling, and after a thousand hours, the door swings open, and Caleb strolls into the room, smelling like the outdoors.

I'm bitter and dazed—I hate him—I've missed him.

We eat supper, talk a little, and just as I'm beginning to feel more alert, Caleb says it's time for bed. Panic rushes through me at the thought of spending the next However Many hours alone.

There has to be some way to persuade him to let me outside

where I'd at least have a *chance* of getting away, but I know he's not going to do that unless he's sure I won't run. Somehow I have to convince him I don't *want* to go.

"Good night, son." Caleb hands me Daniel's blue duck, and I roll over, weary and drained, but not as out of it as I'm pretending to be.

"Night, Dad," I say.

My eyes are parted just enough to see his mouth widen into a happy smile.

TWENTY-SIX

It's a lot harder to call Caleb Dad to his face. Half-asleep and mumbled into a pillow wasn't so bad, but now that I have to look him in the eye, my stomach clenches and I'm dizzy in the ears, but I do it. I take the glass of apple juice from his outstretched hand and say, "Thanks, Dad." *Oh, this is sooo much better than coffee.*

I even give him a little-boy smile. But inside I'm boiling, an anger that developed in my sleep. I kept having nightmares, kept waking up remembering stuff—stupid stuff—like the time I asked my dad why we don't have the same last name, and he waved me off, saying it didn't matter, better for me to have the Wayte family name. And my thirteenth birthday, and how my father never showed because he ran off to an island with his hairdresser, so I whined to Luke, "I wish I had a dad who actually gave a shit."

Well, thank you, Universe. You gave me one who wants me so much he chains me inside his house so I can never leave.

"You're welcome," Caleb says, sounding pleased. He hands me a slice of buttered toast.

I clamp the bread between gritted teeth.

Caleb checks the watch strapped to his wrist. "Gotta get to work now." And he's about to pat my head when I yank out of reach. The shock on Caleb's face is almost funny, but then he blinks in astonished disapproval. "Never pull away from me, you understand?"

I laugh—a crazy loud noise I think Luke would appreciate.

Caleb grabs my arm, wrenching me toward him, and I glare right in his face.

"I said, do you understand?"

Rage is still simmering in my gut, but now it's self-directed. *Don't be stupid, Saye.*

Swallowing my pride, I snap, "Yes."

"Yes what?"

"I said yes! I get it." I jerk my arm from his grasp and sarcastically add, "I can say it in twenty fucking languages if that helps. *Sí, ja, etiam*—"

Caleb grabs my bicep again, and this time he squeezes through the meat to the bone. I can't hold back my cry of pain as he pins me with a vicious stare. "Let's get something straight."

I gulp.

"We're not friends."

"W-what?"

"I've been going easy on you, letting you get used to the way things are, but I'm not your friend, I'm your *father*. And this is not how you talk to your father."

That's another ironic thing. This *is* how I talk to my dad when he pisses me off, but Caleb isn't Jack with his Hawaiian tops and goofy loafers. He's a kidnapper.

"When I ask you a question, you say, *Yes, sir.*" Caleb's eyes are less than an inch from mine. "Do. You. Understand?"

My mouth goes dry. "Yes, sir."

He lets me go, and I massage my aching arm.

"I think someone's gonna have to unlearn some bad habits. You never used words like that before."

Right, because Daniel was a saint. The only mistake he ever made was going missing. And just like that, my anger wells up all over again.

"I'm sorry I'm not perfect." Catching the guilt creeping across Caleb's face, I jump on it. "I don't know what you want me to do. You just leave me here by myself every day."

Now a wellspring of sadness floods his eyes. "I'm sorry you're so lonely, son. I really am."

TWENTY-SEVEN

I'm doing everything right. I'm behaving myself, and playing along, and reading Daniel's books, and pretending—but nothing's changed.

Every day, I limp around the room, dragging the chain behind me as I pace the four walls. I'll shuffle through Daniel's boxes. I've organized his photos by age. Daniel as a newborn in the arms of a dark-haired woman who must be his mother. Daniel on his first day of kindergarten. Daniel blowing out ten candles on a birthday cake. I've reorganized the photos by categories. Holidays: Daniel holding an Easter basket full of plastic eggs. Daniel dressed as a T-Rex on Halloween. Sports: Daniel playing T-ball, basketball, soccer.

I'll doze, feel drowsy all day, and sometimes I'll panic, afraid Caleb won't come back. But he always does. It may take a thousand hours, but he comes back. And then we'll eat in my room, and it's worse than being alone, but it's also better than being alone.

Today, Caleb arrives with something called Frito Pie, another one of Daniel's favorites. As I'm crunching my way through it, I have to admit, it tastes better than it looks.

"Um . . . Dad?" I say between bites. "What happened to all my sports equipment?" I practiced that line earlier today, perfecting the exact right tone of causal.

"Nice try." He chuckles. "But if you think I'm letting you play with that stuff in the house, you've got another thing coming."

"Could we go outside and play?"

Caleb's face freezes in a slightly off expression as if someone paused him in an unfortunate moment. "No," he finally says. "It's not safe yet. But I'll tell you what . . ."

He darts out of the room, then returns with a plastic waste bin and a Nerf ball. Grinning, he throws the ball to me, so I climb out of bed, toss it at the bin—and miss by a foot.

We keep playing.

Caleb's making shot after shot, but I'm missing nearly every one. He looks disappointed, and it's not too far off from my actual father's expression the handful of times we've done some sports activity together.

When Caleb's face grows darker, I'm beginning to think it's not disappointment, but something more sinister. Daniel was probably amazing at making baskets.

"The people who took me *hated* sports," I say. "They'd never let me play."

"Is that right?"

"Yes . . . sir."

"What kind of things did you do with him?"

"The man? Uh . . ." I find myself veering toward the truth. "Sometimes we'd see movies."

"But no sports?"

"Not really."

"That doesn't make any sense!" Caleb explodes, squeezing the ball so hard it practically disappears inside his fist. I know I've misfired, but I don't know how to fix it because I don't know why it's wrong. "Why wouldn't he train you?"

I try not to stutter, try not to sound scared. "*Train* me?"

"Yes! They take athletic, dexterous boys and they train them. That's the whole reason they stole you! So why didn't you get the training?"

That's what Caleb thinks? That my parents are part of some scheme to steal athletic kids? For what purpose? It's so bizarre that I just gape at him for a moment, but then I get it together enough to say, "Oh. I *did* train. I thought you were talking about organized sports. H-he didn't put me in those, but we have a gym."

"A gym?" Caleb raises two skeptical eyebrows.

"Yes. I work out every day." I describe my weight-lifting in detail. "And we have a pool—and a track. I'm fast."

"Are you?"

"Yes, I can show you. I—I was always in training. But just not on teams."

He taps two fingers against his stubbled chin. "That actually makes a lotta sense."

I let out a shaky exhale.

"They wouldn't want you getting close to anyone who might help you." Now he drops onto the side of my bed, looking tired and sad. "I'm sorry, Daniel. They were monsters for denying you friends."

My brain's flashing *Crisis Averted* and *Shut Up Now*, but I know

I need to use this while I can. "Sometimes I do miss it. Seeing kids my own age."

He nods, sympathetic.

"It'd be cool to be on a team again. To make friends . . ."

"That's not an option. Not right now."

"Right." I don't want to push it. Watching him carefully, I pitch my voice a little younger, a little nicer, no begging, so polite. "I understand."

TWENTY-EIGHT

A dark voice drifts into my nice dreams, persistently calling *Daniel, Daniel, Daniel.*

I stir under my quilt. Pleasant scents fill my nose—molasses and cinnamon—but then the voice is calling me again. I roll over and find my bedroom door wide open.

"Daniel . . ." Caleb's voice carries down the hall. "Come out here."

Puzzled, I sit up. How the hell am I supposed to do that? But then I notice the distinct lack of weight around my ankle. I throw off my quilt—I'm not chained. Which can only mean Caleb slipped in here and removed the cuff while I was sleeping.

"Daniel!"

Hurrying now, I step onto a floor so cold it stings my feet. My ankle aches as I tread into the empty hallway with a growing sense of dread. The last time I was out here, I was trying to run.

"Hello?" I call out.

No answer.

Cautious, I continue down the hall, reminded of the haunted houses I used to love. The same long, narrow corridors, the same trepidation as I braced myself for a jump scare.

Caleb leaps in my path, wearing a red sweatsuit and a fake white beard. "HO! HO! HO!"

I shriek and grab my heart.

He laughs as he tugs down the beard. "It's me!"

I massage my chest with my fingertips. "I know . . . I just . . ."

He releases the beard, and it snaps back into place. "Come with me."

Still shaky, I follow him into the wood-paneled living room. Against one wall is an artificial tree strung with blinking rainbow lights, piles of wrapped gifts underneath. This isn't possible—it can't be Christmas already. That would mean I've been here for two and a half months, and that isn't fucking possible.

I look up at Caleb. I can tell he's grinning under the fake beard, and he seems to be interpreting my shock as something positive. I have to hide my horror. If I were really Daniel, I'd be excited. I'd say: "Can I open them?"

I hope I sound eager, but I'm scared I just sound scared.

Caleb smiles wryly. "You always did ask to open 'em early."

Hope rushes through me. Maybe it's *really* early. Like six weeks early.

"It's Christmas Eve," he tells me.

My stomach floods with acid. My mom always throws a huge party on Christmas Eve. Tons of people come over. My grandfather, my great-aunt, my mom's favorite cousin Luanne, a bunch of people from the company, and before my dad left, there was his side of the family too.

"Oh, all right," Caleb says. "One."

"W-what?"

"You can open *one*." He smiles, benevolent.

I approach the tree. There are about a dozen gifts in varying sizes. I glance up to find Caleb watching me, intensely. Which one I choose is important. Taking a deep breath, I stretch out both arms, my hands grazing above the tops of the packages like a Geiger counter. Closing my eyes, I try to think like Daniel. If he's alive, I'll read his thoughts. If he's dead, I'll summon his ghost. Tell me, Daniel, what present do you want?

The big one.

The answer pops into my head so clearly, I shiver.

I come to a stop in front of the largest gift. "Can I open this one?"

Caleb smiles. "I suppose."

I kneel, about to tear open the package like an eager ten-year-old, when something halts me. The memory of Daniel's perfect handwriting, the precise ruler marks under his signature. Daniel isn't like regular kids. He's careful. So that means *I'm* careful.

I use my fingernail to peel away the tape. It gives easily, the adhesive leaving a furry dust as I run my hand down the seam. Caleb shakes his head with indulgent affection, and my breath rushes out in relief. I'm doing it right.

The paper falls away revealing a cardboard box with a picture of a khaki tent.

"Are we going camping?" This time, I don't have to fake the excitement.

Caleb doesn't answer, and now I'm afraid I sounded *too* excited.

But then he nods. "We will. Soon as it's warm enough."

"How warm?"

"You're full of questions today." His happy expression vanishes.

I drop my eyes, but he's still observing me closely, I can feel it.

"I—I just love my tent so much. I can't wait to use it."

"I'll tell you what . . ." His voice is gentle enough that I risk looking up again. His Santa beard's down around his neck. "How about we set it up in the living room?"

"Hooray!" I shout.

Do kids say hooray? Does Daniel?

Caleb smiles, so I guess so.

He pulls something from his red sweatpants. A pocketknife like Garrett's. As he slices through the box, my eyes are riveted to the blade, imagining all the things I could do with it. He drags out the tent, presses a mechanism, and it pops open.

"Wow." I crawl inside. "This is sooooo cool."

I zip the tent closed, and now I let myself make whatever face I need to make. Let the tears spring to my eyes and feel the hysteria and imagine my Christmas tree at home.

Did Mom decorate this year? She always hires a company to dress the entire estate. They have fireman-style ladders tall enough to reach the eaves. They hang wreaths and golden lights. My stocking's so huge I could stand in it when I was little.

"Daniel?"

I wish I could lock the zipper.

"What are you doing in there?"

I wish I never had to come out.

But I force a smile and crawl out of the tent.

"Hungry?" Caleb asks.

Not even a little. But I follow him to the round wooden table in the center of the room where food's already laid out. Hash browns, fried eggs, blackened bacon. My stomach turns.

Dragging back a heavy chair with scrolled arms, I take a seat, and suddenly it's like my eyes don't know which way to go. Maybe because I've been staring at the same four walls for weeks, and now there are new things to see.

There aren't any windows in here, but there are doors. On my left, one's open just wide enough for me to see a toilet. To my right, the door's a good seven feet wide and stretches all the way to the ceiling. It doesn't have a knob. Straight ahead of me, behind Caleb, is the silver door I tried to escape through. It looks like a bank vault.

"Daniel."

Caleb's nodding to my plate, so I grab a piece of bacon and chew on it, but I keep studying the room—sparsely furnished, minimally decorated. A braided rug over a hardwood floor, a brown-and-orange paisley sofa, a couple of walnut shelves filled with old books and movies, but no embellishments apart from a globe. The only art is obviously Daniel's, and it's Scotch-taped right to the wall. Dozens of pictures of horses, sailboats, and cities made of crayon and watercolor. Apparently, Daniel's good at drawing too.

I peer over my shoulder where a clunky television with a fish-eye screen sits on the floor, like something you'd see in a museum or an antique shop.

"*Daniel*," Caleb snaps, making me flinch. "Eat."

Turning back to the table, I pick up my fork. Stab it into the eggs, and chew but don't taste. All I can think is: *I have a fork.* And I imagine all the bad things I could do with it.

After the meal, Caleb wipes his mouth with a paper napkin. "You wanna watch TV?"

Right, the television. If I can check out the news or even some local commercial, I'll know where we are.

"Yes," I say, feeling almost giddy.

"Go on then, pick a movie." He nods toward the shelves.

"Is it okay if we watch regular TV?"

"No cable, but we got plenty of tapes."

Trying to mask my disappointment, I go over to the shelf, passing a row of encyclopedias and paperback novels to scan the VHS tapes. Which one would Daniel want to watch? There are some old movies with black-and-white covers, a few sitcoms from the '70s or '80s, and—of course.

I slide the tape from its case, but it takes me a minute to figure out how to slot it into the player. I turn the round knob on the television, and there's a staticky pop.

Soon enough, the *Star Wars* theme music begins.

I glance to Caleb, who's smiling as he reclines on the couch—I chose right.

But then I notice the picture isn't coming in. I'm adjusting the knobs when Caleb says, "The screen's broke." He pats the sofa, so I take the musty cushion on the end, as far from him as I can get.

We face a blank screen.

Luke Skywalker's whining about small-town life when Caleb says, "I guess I coulda got a new TV, but I couldn't bring myself to throw this one away."

"Why not?"

"It was in my house growing up. I guess I'm attached to it."

"But don't you want to be able to see?"

"I barely notice anymore." He sounds lost in thought. "It's funny the things you can get used to."

When the credits start to roll, Caleb tells me the real Santa will be here soon, and I'd better be in bed when he does.

He already wants me to go to bed? I just got up.

What *time* is it? I have the urge to steal the watch off his wrist.

But I don't argue. He follows me to my room and watches me crawl under the covers, then he hands me the blue duck and pats the top of my head. He's still wearing the stupid Santa beard.

"What's that face about?" Caleb asks.

"I'm sad." The words come out before I can stop them. When Caleb stiffens, I add quickly, "Because Christmas Eve is almost over."

Now he gives me a warm smile. "I know what you mean, son. But think about it this way. There'll be another one next year."

TWENTY-NINE

I spend the day after Christmas locked in my room. My family and I always travel before the New Year. We enjoy a week relaxing at some exotic beachfront resort overlooking a friendly sea, and I return to school in January with sun-bleached hair and golden skin.

Today while Caleb's at work, it feels even longer and lonelier than usual. No light—no clock—no time. The walls are even tighter, the same repeating scene, two boys flying a kite over and over and over until my mind goes numb, or maybe off like a computer with two modes. And then after a million hours Caleb's home, and he lets me out into the living room.

Slow and dazed, I find my seat at the table. The vault door's cracked open, not much, but enough for me to hear him preparing dinner in the next room like he's on a bad cooking show. He's banging pots and pans and chopping God knows what, but if there's a kitchen through that door, I bet there's an exit too.

He returns with two plates.

My mind is slowly waking up.

After we eat, Caleb uses one of his many keys to unlock the silver vault door, and he carries the dishes from the room. A moment later he returns and inserts yet another key into the enormous wooden door to my right. It's clearly heavy as he drags it into the wall. A *pocket* door. My mom loves those.

I get a glimpse of a short hall before he shuts the door almost all the way and disappears into some other room.

When he emerges, he has a flat, wilted box in one hand. "Wanna play checkers?"

In my head, I answer *Hell no*, but out loud, I say, "Okay."

Grinning, he sits at the table, lifts the lid, and unfolds a board that smells about fifty years old. Maybe it is, just like the TV.

I take the red checkers. Caleb takes black. I haven't played this game since I was nine or ten, but once Caleb gives me some pointers, it comes back to me.

"You ever do stuff like this with him?" Caleb asks.

Him meaning the man who supposedly abducted me.

A scoffing noise escapes my throat. "No way."

Even when I was really little, my dad and I hardly ever played together, and the few times we did, he'd seem engaged at first, but he would lose interest pretty fast.

I can feel Caleb watching me closely now, and I go still, my stomach flooding with nerves. What if playing board games is like playing basketball—something the kidnapper was supposed to be forcing me to do to improve my mental agility or something?

My mouth twitches, trying to figure out which expression it should form. It seems like my every gesture is examined, studied, cataloged for later, and I want to shout:

Quit staring, and leave me alone!

Slowly, I look up at Caleb . . . who's looking back at me with pity.

I'm relieved—I'm insulted—we keep playing.

Caleb easily wins the first game, but the next one's closer. I may actually have a shot at it. I'm sliding my checker across the board, about to shout *king me*, when over my head there are three short rings that sound like a school bell.

Caleb's handful of checkers clatter to the table. Action-movie quick, he lifts me with one arm encircling my waist, takes two giant steps, and in a fluid move, he slides out a rifle from under the sofa.

My eyes bulge. That was there this whole time?

"What's—"

"Quiet," he orders, head cocked like he's listening, then he sets me back on my feet. "Get to your room and shut the door."

"What's going on?"

Letting out a growl, he scoops me up again and runs down the hall. My face burns at the indignity of it—I'm not a ten-year-old. He sets me down in my room and darts right back out, shutting the door behind him.

Immediately, I try the knob, but it's locked of course.

What the hell is going on? What did that sound mean? Maybe it was a doorbell—which would mean someone's *here*.

I smash my ear to the wood.

Silence.

"Hello?" I punch the door with my fists, then press my ear to the door again.

Footsteps are pounding down the hall.

"HELLO!" I shout at the top of my lungs. "I'm in here!"

The door flies open.

And it's only Caleb.

Forcing a smile, I swallow the disappointment down like a sharp-edged stone. "What was that bell?"

His eyes are cold as he grabs a pair of pajama pants from the piles of clothes on the floor and tosses them at me, a little harder than necessary. "Get ready for bed."

With a sigh, I enter the bathroom to change and brush my teeth, then I climb onto my mattress. As Caleb's closing the cuff around my ankle, I ask again, "What was that?"

"The drive's rigged so I can tell if anybody's coming."

"Someone was here?" My words come out a little breathless.

"Musta just got turned around."

"Oh."

"But it coulda been serious, Daniel." He sits in his chair, leaning forward in a way that makes me lean back. "What if it'd been *them*?"

"I didn't know . . ."

"You didn't know," he repeats, shaking his head with an angry chuckle. "Well, it coulda been, so when I tell you to do something"—he gets right into my face—"you *do* it."

Throat dry, I try to nod.

"Son . . ." His voice is gentle now. "Don't be afraid." He pushes my hair out of my eyes. "I'm making you a promise. I won't *ever* let them find you."

As I pace my room the next day, I can't stop thinking about it. Someone was in the driveway, which means this house can't be *that* remote. If I could just get outside . . .

Maybe after dinner when Caleb turns his back to carry off the dishes, I could grab my chair. But it's so heavy. And then there's the way he moved when that alarm went off. He lifted me like I don't weigh more than a spare tire, and he took hold of the gun, smooth, fast, militarized. I've had this fantasy about my family and friends charging in here to save me, but not only would Caleb hear them coming, he's *armed*.

I'm still thinking about it a million hours later as we're eating supper at the living room table. Cornbread and lentil soup. I hold a useless spoon. My thoughts race. I'm not chained—I'm not drugged—maybe I could catch him off guard, if he turns his head. No, he's too fast, he's too strong.

P-U-S-S-Y. It's as if Garrett's carving that word onto my brain the way he scrawled it into the side of Evan Zamara's truck. Garrett wouldn't put up with this. He wouldn't just *sit* here like a good little boy and play along. He'd *fight*.

Gripping the sides of my chair with both hands, tension's rising all over my body.

"Clear the table," Caleb says.

"What?"

"Go on and clear the table."

Garrett *definitely* wouldn't do that. He'd tell Caleb to fuck off, then he'd slug him and take those keys. But me?

I gather up the bowls and spoons.

Caleb slides back the vault door in an *after you* sort of gesture, and a sudden elation rushes through me. He's never let me in here before. This has to mean something.

We enter a narrow corridor. To the right's a galley kitchen with dingy orange cabinets and a brown linoleum floor. To my left, there's a huge wall covered in cracked and peeling paper, but when

I crane my neck, I can make out an archway to another hall.

"Daniel," Caleb prompts, so I enter the kitchen and set my armful of dishes on the counter.

The air in this room has a stale, waterlogged scent, like maybe the pipes busted at some point and were never fully repaired. Above the sink is a panel of ruffly floral curtains, not a bit of light coming through. Obviously another fake.

I'm jolted by a digital clock on the stove—the first one I've seen since I've been here.

7:09.

Is that the real time?

Caleb's waving a bottle of dish soap and a sponge in my direction.

He wants me to wash them by *hand*? That's disgusting.

But Daniel would do it. So I take the germy sponge, douse it in liquid soap, and start scrubbing. Caleb rinses each dish after I finish washing and sets them in a drying rack, then it's back to the living room again to play games, which is actually kind of fun, or maybe fun is relative. All I know is it's weirdly satisfying to collect a tower of his black checkers.

After the fifth game, Caleb says it's time for bed. I'm about to beg *just one more* like an actual ten-year-old, but I get hold of myself, and without complaint, I walk down the hall, Caleb right behind me. Once I'm in the bed, he adjusts the blankets around me as if I need tucking in, and then he says, "I love you."

I go completely still.

I should say it back—Daniel would. But the words catch in my throat.

I can lie about a lot of things, but not that.

THIRTY

"You wanna be in the living room while I'm at work today?"
Caleb asks.

It takes me a few seconds to process the question.

A whole day with something to look at besides these walls?

"Really? Yeah. Yes, sir."

And even better—there are *doors* out there. There's a *gun*.

He removes the cuff from my ankle, and I hop out of bed, flexing onto my toes. My feet barely hurt anymore, just a slight catch in my ankle if I step too hard. I trail him into the living room, where the vault door's ajar. I try to control my face, *grateful*, but not suspiciously happy.

When Caleb taps my chair, I sit, then he disappears down the hall.

My eyes flick to the open vault door.

Should I run? Is there time?

But a moment later, he's reentering the living room, my chain under his arm.

"Gimme your foot."

"What?" He can't lock me up out here. He's never done that before.

"Your foot."

And that's when I notice the small steel loop drilled into the floor under the table.

With a sinking feeling, I extend my leg, and he rigs the chain to the loop just like he rigs it to the iron post on my bed.

"I'll see you tonight," he says.

"Right . . . see you."

The vault door closes, but I don't move. Just keep on sitting here, not really thinking or doing anything for a long time. But eventually, I stand. The chain thuds to the floor and slides behind me like a metal snake as I'm making a counterclockwise turn to see what I can reach.

Wall One: pocket door—almost, but not quite.

Wall Two: vault door—not even close; couch—nope.

Wall Three: hallway to Daniel's room—barely; bathroom— yes; bookshelves—yes; Daniel's art—yes.

Wall Four: television—yes.

Kneeling in front of the TV, I flip through the channels. *Static—static—static.* Like the static on my car stereo the night I got lost.

I shut the TV off with a click-pop and walk back to the bolt in the floor. How hard could it be to dislodge it? I gather a length of chain into my hands and pull, pull, *pull.*

Not even a quiver from the bolt.

I fall into my chair in another disappointed stupor until I shake myself out of it. Caleb's letting me out into the living room now. This is progress.

Is it? A bitter voice fills my brain. *You're still chained—just chained in a different room.*

I'm not sure how long I've been slumped in my chair when the bells blast over my head.

I sit up straight.

Maybe it's a neighbor.

Or the *police.*

Hope pounds in my chest, and my ears strain. Desperate for a voice to say: *Sayers Wayte, you're safe now!*

But there's only silence until the vault door slides back on its track.

And in walks Caleb. Of course it's just Caleb. Obviously, that bell goes off whenever he drives up, but I was never able to hear it from my bedroom.

"Did you have a good day?" he asks.

I'm wiped, drained, on the verge of tears, but I nod. "Yes, sir."

"Got something for you." He sets a small brown paper sack on the table. "Go on," he tells me when I don't move. I stick my hand into the bag and pull out a package of white printer paper and a forty-eight-count box of crayons.

I'm so confused. Caleb's convinced I'm the Daniel who went missing—the victim of a plot to train dexterous boys to become God knows what. But I'm also supposed to be the Daniel who never left, a boy who never aged, and trying to be both, when I'm neither, hurts my head.

"This . . . this is great." I force a smile.

Caleb beams back at me. "I'm gonna make us some dinner. Go on and draw for a while."

With a nervous stab in my gut, I look to Daniel's wall of art. What will Caleb do when he sees I *can't* draw? Explode like when I couldn't make a basket? Feel sorry for me like when I couldn't remember how to play checkers?

I don't want to risk it, so instead I write over and over in small, neat script:

DANIEL

DANIEL

DANIEL

THIRTY-ONE

Alone in the house I dump out the crayons, roll them around, flick them to the floor, gather them up again. My eyes drift to Daniel's drawings. The horse looks straightforward enough, just a collection of simple shapes, so I slide a brown crayon from the box and start with the body.

A rectangle with soft edges. So far so good.

Now an upright rectangle for the neck and—no. This is awful.

I wish I had a pencil with an eraser, but when I mentioned that to Caleb last night, he told me pencils were too *dangerous*. I wanted to tell him how crazy that is, but I hid my feelings and said, "Okay, Dad," even though it made my gut clench.

Why is Dad so hard to say? It's a simple enough word, just three little letters.

"Dad, Dad, Dad . . ." The more I say it, the more it's just a sound, the bleating noise of a goat. *Daaad*. It's nothing.

Hopping to my feet, I pluck one of Daniel's drawings off the wall and carry it over to the table. I place a clean sheet of paper on top and start tracing, *cheating*, the way I used to cheat off Luke, then I try on my own, and it's so terrible, it's a joke, only I don't feel like laughing.

Maybe I'm just not good at anything.

Well, except possibly languages. Mr. Rivas thought I had a talent for them, but it's a useless thing to be good at when there's no one around to talk to.

Caleb's been gone a really long time.

"Stop it, Saye," I order myself out loud when my heart begins to race. "He's coming back—he always comes back. And per usual, we'll eat dinner and wash the dishes, then we'll play board games, and God help me that will be the best part of my whole shitty day, but that's what we'll do, and I'm not dying today."

I stick an old movie into the VCR just for the noise, and try another horse. It's kind of incredible how difficult it is, that these tiny micro-movements in the wrist are so important, but if a little kid could do this, I can do this.

I draw and draw until—*static.*

The movie's over.

I pop in another one, trace some more, then try on my own. Repeat it a hundred times until finally. It's not perfect like Daniel's, but wow, there it is. An actual horse.

The bells blast over my head.

Leaping up, I tape Daniel's picture back to the wall, and I'm falling into my chair just as the vault door slides open.

"Hey, Daniel."

"Oh, hi, Dad." I pretend to be surprised that he's home. "I'm drawing."

"I can see that." There's a smile in his voice. He starts shuffling through my papers, and then he picks one up—not a tracing, but one I did myself. "This is outstanding, son."

Relief washes over me, but there's something else too. A shy feeling of pride. I worked my ass off for that horse.

THIRTY-TWO

At the table for breakfast, my eyes drift to the wall where dozens of my drawings and watercolors are taped right alongside Daniel's. I'm getting better, even developing my own style. My horses are leaner and jauntier than Daniel's. They're *racehorses*.

I take a bite of Fruity Pebbles, and I'm not sure if it's the colorful cereal or just the sugar, but out of nowhere, I get a crystal-clear memory of dashing across a grassy field with a bunch of other little kids, happily screaming at the top of my lungs.

Suddenly, I want to go outside so bad it hurts.

Caleb turns to me with narrowed eyes. I didn't say anything—didn't even *move*, but it's like he just knows. Like he's been watching me so close for so long that he knows how to read my mind, and sometimes I think if he doesn't stop, I'm going to lose it.

Why can't you just leave me alone?

He takes a slow sip of coffee, then sets his mug on the table and grabs his boots.

Good, just go.

He pulls his boots over his feet.

Yeah. Leave me alone, leave me alone.

He takes his keys out of his pocket.

Leave me alone, leave me alone—please don't leave me here alone.

"Dad?" My voice shakes. "Do you think it might be possible for me to go with you today?"

His forehead crinkles. "Go with me to work?"

"Yes. It's just . . . I don't want . . . I don't want to be by myself again. So can I—?"

"That's not possible, son. It wouldn't be safe."

"Then what if I went outside? Just for a few minutes?"

His mouth becomes a stern line. "No."

"Please?"

"I said *no.*"

And that's it. End of discussion.

I squeeze my eyes shut. Tears build up behind my lids.

Caleb stands, and on autopilot I stand too and start gathering up the dishes.

"We'll wash 'em later," he tells me. "Sit."

So I sit—and yank my legs into the seat.

Caleb looks puzzled. "Gimme your foot."

I tuck my legs tighter beneath me and cross my arms.

"*Daniel.*"

"Why do you have to keep doing this?"

He sighs, checking the watch strapped to his wrist. "All right, let's talk."

My heart skips a hopeful beat.

"What those people did to you . . . they mixed you up in here." He taps the center of my forehead with two fingers. "And it isn't fair of me to expect you not to be confused. You might be for a while. I'm just removing temptation, and once your head's clear, we won't need to do this anymore."

"But my head *is* clear."

He gives me a doubtful look. "Is that right?"

"Yes, sir."

"Okay. Then tell me about the day they took you."

"Well, I remember being at a park . . . and . . ."

"And what?"

Afraid to get caught in a lie, I hesitate, and he nods like he's satisfied.

"But what if I never recover those memories? What if their—their *technology* erased them? I mean, I may not remember everything . . ." I pitch my voice sweeter. "But I know I missed you."

Caleb's whole face softens. "I . . ." He gulps, voice gruff with emotion. "I missed you too." And then he grabs my ankle and pins it to the floor. Before I can wrench it from his grasp, it's in the cuff.

"This isn't fair!" I explode to my feet. "It's like you're punishing me for getting kidnapped, but it wasn't my fault!"

Caleb holds up his hands. "I know it wasn't, son."

"Exactly. It was *your* fault. You let me get stolen because you're a terrible father!"

He reels backward like I slugged him. His entire face is a mask of pain, and then it goes so abruptly cold I shiver. He stares me down in silence, and I'm bracing myself to be grabbed or hit, but instead he snatches his thermos off the table, and storms through the vault door, slamming it so hard that it rattles the wall. All the artwork taped there lifts and flutters.

+ + +

Caleb's still angry with me hours later when we sit down for dinner. We don't talk, our spoons and swallows too loud in the silence. He's mad for sure, but it's also clear that I've hurt him, and for that I feel weirdly guilty.

After we eat, he tells me to go to sleep, not even walking me down the hall to make sure I actually do it. I brush my teeth, dress in pajamas, then sit on the side of my bed, this heavy feeling in my chest. I know it's dumb to be disappointed that we're not going to play some stupid board game or listen to a movie, but it reminds me of the time my parents went out of town when I was four or five, and they left me with a nanny whose name I can't remember.

That used to happen a lot, my mom and dad leaving the country for an adults-only vacation, but this time the nanny thought I was a bad kid. For the most part she ignored me, and I was so *lonely*. Like I had no one in the entire world.

I keep waiting for Caleb to come in or make sure I've shut my door, but it's been a *really* long time. Slipping out of my room, I tiptoe down the hall.

He's still at the table, his face buried in his hands. He must sense my presence because he lifts his head.

"I told you to go to your room." He tries to glare at me, but it's not very convincing since his eyes are red and puffy like he's been crying for hours.

Another rush of guilt pools in my stomach. "I . . . I'm sorry for what I said. I didn't really mean it."

He makes a muffled, choking sound. "C'mere."

I cross the room, and he wraps his arms around me, pulling my head onto his shoulder. He holds me there for a minute, and I'm so relieved it's ridiculous.

"I can't stop thinking tonight," he finally says, letting me go.

"About what?"

"A lotta things. My mother mostly. I wish you coulda known her. When she died, I begged them not to bury her. Did I ever tell you that?"

"No . . ."

"I was just a kid, even younger than you, but my father called me crazy. He said you can't leave a body out. That's what he called her—a *body*." Tears begin rushing over Caleb's cheeks, wetting the dark bristles on his chin. It's an unsettling thing to witness, like seeing a mountain or something that should be indestructible collapse. "I never understood him. How can you *bury* someone you love?"

"I . . . I don't know."

"Well, to my father, what's dead and buried is over and done with. I couldn't even talk about her anymore. Couldn't have her pictures out, nothing." Caleb draws in a quivery breath. "But I grew up, got married, had you." He pushes back my hair. "But then your mother . . . she only got to be with you for a few months, and then she was gone too." Fresh tears pour down over his cheeks. "You know what I used to think?"

I shake my head.

"If I could still see the people I've lost, it wouldn't be so hard. If I could just see their faces, even if they couldn't talk to me, I could survive it. But it was knowing they were underground and I could never look at them again . . . That's the thing I can't take." He wipes his bloodshot eyes. "And when you disappeared, I swear, that was it for me, Daniel. I thought, I'm just gonna make myself sleep. I'll make myself sleep, and when I wake up, we'll be together."

Make yourself sleep? I want to ask and am also afraid to ask.

"But something stopped me. I had this feeling deep inside—this feeling I'd *find* you." He wraps his arms around me again, squeezing tight. "And now I have."

"Daniel?"

Half-asleep, I hear Caleb's voice above me.

"Hmm?"

"I've gotta go to work now." I feel his hand in my hair.

I mumble, "Okay."

"Be good today."

"Okay."

And then he's gone.

I'm not sure how much later it is when I turn over—and I don't feel the chain. Caleb stopped locking my ankle at night a while back, I guess because it's impossible to break out without alerting him, but he always cuffs me before he leaves for work, whether I'm in here or in the living room.

I open my eyes. My door is open.

My door is open and I'm not chained.

Wide awake now, I scramble out of bed. "Dad?"

No answer.

I jog down the hall into the living room, about to call for him again when my voice cuts out.

The bank vault door is open.

Did he really go to work and leave me unlocked? If that's true, he must finally trust me, and after our talk last night, it almost makes sense.

I sprint through the open vault door into that narrow corridor. The kitchen's on my right, the wall of peeling paper's on my left. I head left, and left again through the archway and into a tight hall. In just a couple of steps, it dead-ends and I'm forced to go right. This house has the most disorienting architecture like the kind of place a kid with Legos and a lot of imagination might build.

I keep zigzagging until the corridor dead-ends again into a giant metal door just like the one in the living room. This is the way out, I can feel it.

My heart races, spastic and excited.

I twist the knob. *Locked.*

I throw all my weight against it, over and over in bruising slams, but it's no use. This door's not coming down. I run back through the tangle of halls and peer under the smelly sofa.

The gun is gone.

Hopping back up, I grab the recessed handle of the pocket door. It's locked too. There's a chance I could break it down, but I've never seen Caleb leave the house this way, and if I break it for nothing . . .

But maybe I could pick the lock if I had the right tool.

I race into the kitchen and start tearing open drawers. Spoons, spatulas, some plastic cutlery, but no sharp objects. Even the forks are missing. So maybe Caleb trusts me more than he did, but obviously that trust only goes so far.

I open the cabinets. Boxed pancake mix, boxed potatoes, cereal, canned goods, a lot of plastic dishware and a few pots, but nothing useful . . . until I come across a cast iron skillet.

Grabbing it into my hand, I test its weight, swinging it through the air. It's a lot wieldier than the lamp was, and if I managed to connect with Caleb's head, it'd knock him out, no question.

It's a sickening image actually, hitting someone hard enough to make them lose consciousness. There'd probably be a lot of blood. It makes me think of Luke—he used to faint at the sight of blood.

This is the very first time Caleb's given me this kind of freedom, so I'm sure he'll be on guard today. The smart thing would be to wait a while before trying some kind of sneak attack.

I shove the skillet into the cabinet, and I stand here, at a loss.

I'm gazing at the floral curtains over the useless window when I notice something strange. There's a small space where the drapes don't quite meet, and I should see more plastered wall, but it's *not* plaster.

Lunging forward, I tear back the curtains. There are five planks of wood nailed straight into the wall—and they're covering an actual window.

THIRTY-THREE

My feet lift off the ground as I lean over the counter and press my face up to the wood. Horizontal lines of light shine through, but the boards are too close together for me to see anything. I climb all the way up onto the countertop, grip the end of one of the planks, and pull.

Ouch. I stick my scraped fingertips into my mouth.

The board didn't even budge, but I can do this. *Alis grave nil*— nothing is heavy to those who have wings.

Only now that I'm thinking about it, what does that even mean? When I first learned the phrase, it felt uplifting. Like a battle song. But I *don't* have wings.

Shaking those thoughts away, I hop down again and yank open drawers until it's clear the best tool I'm going to get is a spoon. I flip one around and try to wedge the handle beneath a board, but it's too close to the wall. I try the ladle end, forcing the tip beneath the edge of the board, and the spoon bends in half.

"Damn it!"

In a burst of temper, I punch the boards with my fist. A sharp pain shoots up my wrist, and I yell out again. Watery-eyed, I rest my forehead against the warm wood.

I can feel sunlight on my skin.

I've been at this for hours, digging the spoon into the plaster like I can tunnel my way out of here. Patience, patience, it's one of my virtues. If I can just get three boards down, I'll have enough room to crawl through. Just three boards and nine nails stand between me and freedom.

I'm straightening out the spoon for the billionth time when the bells go off.

My eyes dart to the clock on the oven.

6:00 on the dot.

I toss the spoon back into the drawer and dash into the living room. Just a moment later, Caleb strolls in. I'm hoping he won't notice the scrapes on my fingers and palms, the flush in my cheeks, but his eyes are already narrowing.

"What's wrong with you?" he says.

"Nothing."

"Doesn't look like nothing." He stalks over to the table piled with untouched paper and crayons. "What've you been doing all day?"

"Just . . ." I try to catch my breath. "Exercising."

"Exercising?"

"Yeah."

He gives me a pointed look. *"Yessir?"*

"Yessir. Exercising. I'm used to exercising."

He frowns, and I'm not sure if it's the reference to my *training* or if it's because he knows I'm lying. His gaze drifts off. "They pushed you pretty hard, huh?"

He sounds sympathetic enough that I risk saying, "Yessir. But I like to work out. Being too still isn't good for the body. I bet I can barely run anymore."

He faces me now with a smooth machinelike rotation as if he's switching from human to android. "Why do you need to run?"

For a moment I'm too nervous to answer, but then I stutter out, "I—I don't *need* to. It's just . . . fun."

"Fun," he repeats, and I'm tensing up all over, not sure what to say, but then his eyes fill with sorrow. "I'm sorry, Daniel. What'n the hell am I thinking?" He sits on the couch, his forehead creasing like guilt is drawing the lines deeper into his face. "My only thought was to keep you safe, but I'm not doing right by you. This is no life for a boy your age."

My breath hitches. He's going to let me go. He's going to—

"C'mere." When I sit on the couch beside him, he wraps his arm around my shoulder. "Can you understand why I'm doing this?"

Carefully, I nod.

"And can you give me more time? Can you trust me to know when the right time is?"

"The meteor shower?"

"Yes. After that, everything will be okay, I promise you."

Tears sting my eyes. I can't help it. I can control my expression, but the internal mechanisms like heartbeats and lungs and tear ducts are harder.

I turn away, but he pulls me back by my chin. "What is it?"

"It's just . . . that's a very long time."

I've been at this for days with no tools except willpower. My fingers are bloodied and filled with splinters and my wrist throbs, but I don't care. I'm getting these boards down.

Roaring, I pull with everything I've got—I'm the bronzed lion in front of my school—and I fall off the counter, landing hard on the linoleum floor.

I lie here for a pained beat, fingertips and hips burning.

Then I get back up and do it again. Roaring. Pulling. All my might.

I won't stop till I get them down.

Something gives.

Stunned, I let out a laugh, my eyes glued to the nails shaking in their plaster. With a fresh burst of energy, I yank even harder, and all at once the wooden plank breaks free on one side, three long nails jutting out like teeth.

My heart races like I'm scared. My heart is confused.

There's a two-by-four view of glass, only it's glazed over like something you'd find in a shower and impossible to see through. I grab the top of the next board. It's so much easier to gain purchase now. In just a few minutes, another plank gives, three more nail teeth yanked from the wall. Only one to go, and I'll have enough room to crawl through.

I grip the next board and—the bells are blasting in my ears.

THIRTY-FOUR

No, no, no, I'm so close. I can *see* the glass. I can snake my arm up and feel the window's lock. But I can't fit through the opening yet, and there's not enough time to tear down another board *and* make a run for it.

I lift one of the dangling planks and slot the nails into their holes, but they're looser now, so it wobbles. Long nails are still sticking out of board number two. I drive them back into their slots.

"Stay, please stay." I watch it, *will* it, then run to my room and pretend to be asleep, too rattled to hold a conversation right now.

"Daniel?" Caleb calls out. I can hear him banging pots around in the kitchen, but I keep my eyes closed, facing the unwindow.

A while later, he calls me again, more insistent, so I make my way into the living room, where the table is set with two bowls of chili, sleeves of saltines, and plates of cornbread and green beans.

"Did you have a good day, son?"

"Yessir." My hands shake as I crush crackers into my bowl, but I don't think it's fear anymore. It's *excitement*. As soon as he leaves tomorrow, I'm getting out of here.

"You're quiet tonight."

I'm going to crawl out that window and find a phone and go *home*. I'm going to put on my own clothes and drink coffee and go outside and breathe fresh air. And I'll talk to the police—I'll tell them everything. I wonder what'll happen to Caleb when I do. I guess he'll be arrested. I mean, of course he will be.

A confusing swell of emotions twist around my head before converging into anger.

That's what he deserves.

"*Daniel,* you're not listening to me."

"Sorry . . . I think I'm just tired."

"Well, me too." He sighs. "I'm so damn exhausted, I've been wondering if I should just take tomorrow off."

I tense up. No, he can't do that. He can't—

"But I gotta go in."

"That's a shame," I make myself say, then focus on shoveling chili into my mouth. I don't know how far I'll have to run tomorrow, and I need as much energy as possible. I take a bite of cornbread, a huge bite of green beans.

"Slow down, son." Caleb chuckles. "No one's gonna take it fr—" He halts at the clattering noise coming from the kitchen. "Hurry! Get to your room."

I do as he says, an acid-sick feeling sloshing around the piles of food in my stomach, because I know exactly what that noise was.

I'm pacing when Caleb opens my door, his expression deadly serious. "Daniel?"

"Y-yessir?"

"C'mere."

Doing my best to look curious instead of terrified, I follow him into the kitchen. One of the boards I worked so hard to tear down is dangling on its nails, revealing a tantalizing stretch of window. Caleb points at it as if I need the extra visual cue to know what the problem is.

"Did you do that?"

"No."

He takes a couple steps toward me, and instinctively, I step back. "Tell me the truth."

"I am. I didn't do it."

He nods, slowly, then turns back to the wall and runs his palm across the nail holes. "This drywall coulda come loose . . ." He faces me again and takes more measured steps in my direction. "But I think *you* did it." When I start shaking my head, his hand clamps down onto my shoulder. "Don't you lie to me."

I don't know what to do. If he's positive I did it, maybe telling the truth will make him trust me more. "I—I'm sorry. I was just . . . curious."

"Curious," he repeats, and I'm scanning all his features, but I'm beginning to think I can't read him the way he can read me.

THIRTY-FIVE

My overhead light flicks on, and I blink awake. Caleb's leaning against my wall with a grave expression, his arms crossed over his chest. It makes me think of Principal Gardiner, only I was never actually intimidated by him. That always felt like an act, while this is real.

"I oughtta make you stay in here today after what you pulled," Caleb says.

Turning away from his stern face, I fiddle with a loose patch on my quilt.

"But the truth of the matter is, I understand."

I lift my head. "You do?"

"I was your age once too. It's only natural you'd want to look out."

Yes, only natural. I start nodding rapidly, but then I'm afraid I'm overdoing it, so I quit.

"I thought about it all night, made myself sick over it to tell the truth. I kept that window there for, well, sentimental reasons. My mother made those curtains, and she . . . The point is, I shouldn't have. If it was that easy for you to get those boards loose, just think how easy it'd be for one of *them* to get in." He sounds genuinely disturbed. "It's my job to keep you safe, and I let you down. Again. I'm sorry, Daniel."

"It's . . . it's okay."

Relief washes over his face, loosening up all the muscles there. He crosses my room in two large steps and wraps his arms around me. "All right," he says after a minute. "I gotta get to work."

And then he goes, leaving my door ajar.

For a while, I just sit here. There's no way the vault door won't be shut, and I don't think I can handle seeing that right now.

But eventually, restlessness wins out, so I trek into the living room and skid to a halt.

The vault door *is* open.

Running now, I fly into the kitchen, tear back the curtains—and the window is gone. In its place is a smooth patch of drywall and the strong odor of fresh plaster.

I spend a long time staring at the space where the window should be. As I stare, the disappointment wraps around my eyes like gauze until I can no longer see.

The gauze stays for days.

While Caleb works. While Caleb's home. While I'm locked alone in my room at night.

But slowly it begins to unravel, and little by little I find the clarity to start planning again. I can't get through locked doors, and I can't walk through walls, so I'm going to have to fight. And if I want a prayer of winning, I have to get stronger.

I drop to the floor in push-up position. *Come on, Saye, you've got this.*

Down, up, one.

Down, up, two.

Already, my arms are trembling, and sweat's beading along my upper lip. I can hear my old PE teacher mocking me in my head: *What are you, a girl?*

I swipe his voice away and keep going.

Down, up, three.

Down, up, four.

I've got this. I'm going to get so strong that when I hit Caleb with that frying pan, I'll knock him the fuck out.

Down, up, five.

Suddenly, the image of him slapping away the lamp like it was nothing, like *I* was nothing, flashes in my head.

Down . . . up . . .

I collapse.

Panting, I roll onto my back and stare at a water stain on the ceiling. What's *wrong* with me? I used to be able to do a hundred push-ups easy.

I tell myself to begin again—I've only done five and a half push-ups—but I can't make my body budge. The immense weight of self-doubt is pressing down on me like I've never experienced before. I was so sure once the drugs Caleb gave me wore off, I'd be able to get away, but if anything, I'm *weaker.* And there's a weird thing about memory. The way Caleb moved when those alarm bells sounded—the more I re-see it in my head, the scarier it is. He just keeps getting stronger, faster, unstoppable, unbeatable.

Slowly, the gauze begins to wrap around my eyes again.

When Caleb shakes me awake for breakfast, I mumble, "I'll just stay in here."

What's the point in leaving this bed? Locked here, locked there, what's the difference?

The next time I wake up, Caleb's home, which means I somehow slept through an entire day. It should trouble me, but I can't summon the energy to worry about it.

"You can come out into the living room now," Caleb says.

"That's okay . . ." I burrow my face into my pillow. "I just want to sleep."

THIRTY-SIX

"I have a present for you."

"Huh?" I'm tired, disoriented, unsure if he's leaving for work or just getting home.

He sets something onto the bed that reminds me of an old Polaroid.

"A *camera*?" Caleb might be off his rocker, but he's never been deliberately cruel before, and that's what this is. "What am I supposed to take a picture of?"

"It's not a camera." He laughs. "It's a viewfinder. And this here's the reel." He slides a white, circle-shaped piece of cardboard into a slot, then presses the viewfinder to my face, but I don't see anything. "Look at the light."

I do what he says, and a gasp falls from my mouth.

It's the *sky*.

"I thought you'd like that."

A crisp blue sky, snow-topped mountains in the distance, brilliant yellow-orange wildflowers in the foreground. It's not just a photo, but a 3D image. It looks so *real*.

"Pull that lever on the side," Caleb tells me.

When I do, a new image falls in front of my eyes. A field of wild-flowers that stretches on and on and on. *"Oooh."*

"I'll find you more reels. I've got a box of 'em somewhere . . ." His voice trails off, or maybe I just quit hearing as I keep clicking.

MOUNTAINS.

FORESTS.

FIELDS.

Each image has round black corners, but the depth is so incredible it's like looking through a window.

I lie down, resting the viewfinder against my face. It slips off, so I secure it to my head with a flannel shirt, and then I stare and stare.

As promised, Caleb brings me more reels, and I feel myself light up. It's so nice not to have to fake it like picture day at school, that forced gun-to-your-head grin. So nice that it's easy, and I can mean it when I flash all my teeth.

"These are great, really great. I mean it, I love them."

When he tousles my hair, I find myself leaning in instead of away. I hold my viewfinder in my lap while we eat our meals, and I tie it back to my face while he's gone.

"Daniel?"

I've been in this exact spot since Caleb said goodbye to me this morning, but it felt like no time at all. Dreamily, I slide the viewfinder out from under the shirt and blink up at him.

He's holding a pint of ice cream in the air like an offering.

My arm burns, muscles unwinding as I take it from him and peel off the lid. It's a messy mix of chocolate, almonds, and marshmallows. A very Daniel thing to like.

As I slowly spoon bites into my mouth, Caleb reads me a story about pirates. I'm kind of hearing, mostly just tasting. After a while he pauses, looking at me with a fond smile. "Remember that treasure map you drew? You nearly burned the house down making that thing. Remember what you told the fireman after they put it out?"

I don't say anything, which is fine because he tells me anyway. "You said you *had* to burn the edges to make it look older."

He laughs, a loud barking noise, and it's like a high-speed wind is sweeping the fog from my brain. I'm abruptly alert and clear-eyed for the first time in I don't even know how long.

Caleb continues reminiscing, but all I'm seeing is fire—and a bright red truck full of men with axes.

THIRTY-SEVEN

This is probably a terrible idea.

I know that, but I can't contain my excitement as I hop out of bed the second I wake up.

I'm going to start a fire.

One so huge Caleb will have no choice but to open the doors so we can escape. Obviously, I can't do it when he's home, but I also can't imagine doing it when he's *not* home. He's the only person who can unlock the doors.

An old memory surfaces. First grade. The school library. Sitting cross-legged on a colorful carpet with Luke and a bunch of other kids learning how to survive a house fire.

Stay low to the ground.

If the flames get you—stop, drop, and roll.

If you're upstairs, you'd better have a rope ladder.

And then I'll never forget the haunted expression on the fireman's face when he warned, *But don't get into a closet. You can't hide from fire.*

The thought of being trapped in here is terrifying, so the timing has to be perfect.

As Caleb and I eat breakfast at the living room table, my view-finder on my lap, I clear my throat and try to sound casual. "When will you be home?"

He looks at me over his mug of coffee. "Should be around six."

"But it could be six thirty?"

"No, won't be that late."

"Six fifteen?"

When he frowns, I add quickly, "I thought I'd cook dinner. I want to make sure it's hot."

"*Cook dinner?*" he repeats like the idea's absurd. "No. Don't you be messing with the oven."

"Sorry," I grumble. "I just wanted to do something nice."

Amused, he tousles my hair, then he stands and tugs on his boots. "I'll see you at six."

"Yes, see you."

As soon as I'm sure he's gone, I race into the kitchen. The clock on the stove reads *7:03.*

If this works, instead of another dinner with Caleb, I'll be *home* tonight. I close my eyes, picturing the plane flying toward me. Its door is opening. The stairs are lowering, and my mom, Bria, and Luke are running down the steps. But then something strange happens.

I can see their figures—but I can't make out their faces.

They're like those mannequins with the smooth oval heads.

I concentrate. I know my mom has blue eyes and she curls her lashes and she worries that her nose is too sharp. I know Luke has messy blond hair and green eyes and he worries that his chin is too small. I know Bria has brown hair and hazel eyes and she worries that her upper lip is bigger than her lower lip. I know all their features, but I can't actually *see* them.

It troubles me. A lot.

But I try not to think about it anymore.

I've got eleven hours.

THIRTY-EIGHT

I turn the knob on the gas stove to the right. Two clicks, then a flame. I fish out a torn piece of cardboard from the trash bin. Now all I've got to do is light it, but my hand trembles as a sick torrent of doubts floods my bloodstream.

Maybe I should wait till the bell goes off—just to be safe.

But immediately, I discard that idea. I need time to build a real fire, and if Caleb can stomp it out with his boots, this will all be for nothing.

It's nearly six. I have to do it now.

I press the cardboard into the flame. The corner ignites, but quickly fizzles out, so I stick it back under the burner. This time the spark holds, eating up the corner of the page. I toss it into the bin and move on to lighting another scrap. I wait for it to hold, and once it does, I turn to hurl it into the bin along with the first one, but I stop short.

The bin's already burning in three separate locations as if the fire hopped from one place to another while my back was turned. And now I see it happen with my own eyes—the fire jumps, moving like a living thing. Not spreading, but *leaping*.

"*Shit.*" Fire's devouring the paper in my hand, so I have to toss that too.

Snatching my viewfinder off the counter, I squeeze it to my chest, watching all the separate little fires converge into a single flame. Some animal instinct nearly takes over, one that says run, *hide*.

I check the clock on the stove—6:07, and no warning bell.

He's late.

Not *that* late, but what if this was a horrible mistake? He could be *really* late. He could lose track of time, stop for groceries, get a flat tire. But the fire isn't out of control, not yet. There's still time to undo it.

I reach for the sink hose, but it's way too short. I have to drag the bin closer. I'm kind of scared to go near it, but I snatch up the bin—and pain knocks the air from my lungs. I let go, but not before the searing plastic melts right into my palms.

The bin topples onto its side, and instantly, the fire quadruples in size.

Tripping backward, I watch the towering flame start to bend, shaping itself sideways under the ceiling, then split in two directions.

One flame is licking with ghostlike fingers toward the curtains.

The other travels the ceiling over my head.

My cheeks are hot like they've been singed. I cover my face with my arms. My eyes find the clock.

6:13.

The flames keep on multiplying, cloning themselves over and over.

6:14.

Black ash is sprinkling down like rain.

6:15.

There's so much smoke, I cough hard. He's not coming. He's really not coming.

6:16.

The crackling flames have reached the stove. They melt the clock. And it's too late. Rolling black smoke is all around me, layered like mountain ranges. So massive I can't see the halls or the living room anymore—can't see anything.

There's no way out.

THIRTY-NINE

No thoughts. Just fear. With every inhale, smoke burns my throat and I'm hacking, and I'm going to die. I'm going to die in here alone. I scream, "Help!" even though no one can hear me, and it's too late, it's too—an invisible hand grasps my collar and drags me from the room.

Caleb's just a hazy silhouette, but I pitch forward, so relieved I can hardly stand.

He's here, he's here, thank God, he's here.

"Get down!" He shoves me flat to the ground, then sprints into the smoky living room, completely vanishing from view.

What is he *doing*? He has to let us out of the house. It's the only way.

Frantic, I peer over my shoulder to the wall of smoke blocking the halls. We have to—

Caleb reappears, holding a red object in his hands.

A fire extinguisher.

He pulls the pin at the top, points the nozzle into the kitchen, squeezes the handle.

And in just *minutes*, the fire is out.

Breathing heavily now, he droops in the midst of the smoke-filled room, no sounds but his harsh pants. Eventually, he turns to me. "What'n the hell were you thinking?"

Slow and unsteady, I get to my feet. A bright scream of pain is engulfing my hands, and this awful feeling's taking over me. It's shocking how attached you can become to a plan you only conceived of a day before, but once you feel hope, it can fill every cell in your body until you *are* Hope.

"Answer me, Daniel!"

And now I am Fear. I'd thought about dying, but not about coming up with an explanation as to why I'd destroy our home.

"What'd I tell you!" He grabs me by the arm. Shakes me. "What'd I say I'd do if you ever pulled something like this again?"

But I can't possibly know what he told Daniel.

With a growl, Caleb drags me through the pocket door so fast I lose my footing. I only have a moment to peer down the short corridor before he shoves me into what must be his bedroom. Simple and sparse with more wood paneling. A full-sized bed, shelves of knickknacks, but no windows or weapons that I can see.

He rips open his closet. There's a clacking noise against the back of the door. A row of belts hangs on hooks. He grabs a black leather belt, and folds it in half, tucking the buckle into his fist.

I back away. "No, *wait.*"

But he doesn't wait. He clamps onto my shoulder and twists me to one side and lifts the belt in the air, but somehow I squirm out of his grasp and put some space between us.

"Wait!" I throw up my hands. "Please just listen."

Eyes wild with fury, he reaches out to grab me again, but then he freezes.

"You *burned* yourself?" His voice is shocked and hushed.

He takes my wrists and flips them over, palms up. They look awful, red and shiny with little blisters forming, and they *hurt*, this pain that keeps growing, overwhelming like hysteria. He examines them with the same look of disgust he had when I hurt my ankle, and then he levers one of my hands up and around so that it's half an inch from my eyes.

"That coulda been your *face*, Daniel! That coulda been your whole body!"

I try to loosen myself from his grip, and the simple flexing of muscles hurts so bad—a frantic sort of agony that makes it hard to latch on to any of his words.

Still gripping my wrist, he drags me from his room, and down the hall toward my room.

My stomach's sick with the smell of smoke on my clothes and in my hair, and I'm starting to sweat. Can't think straight. "I . . . I need something for them . . . painkillers or something."

He halts in his steps. "You think you're getting a *painkiller?*" He's gaping down at me in astonished fury. "You did that to yourself. And you're gonna damn well sit with it."

I'd forgotten about the aftershocks. Those shivery-gasping sounds and small shudders your body makes following long and hysterical sobbing. I haven't cried in that particular way since I was very young, some time before clear memory.

While the kitchen was burning, there was so much fear and panic that all my sensors were on high, a staggering kind of stimulation like my brain didn't know how to process it all.

But now, lying facedown on my bed, there's nothing left to feel but pain.

I'm not crying anymore, but I can't stop shivering. I want to run cold water over my hands, but I can't twist the taps, and I want to sleep, but it hurts too much to drift off.

How do people handle things like this? They must be stronger than me.

I stare at the shadows on my wall, and slowly the tremors stop. I keep staring until even my thoughts stop, and all that's left is sore and empty.

When I hear my door open, I turn just my head to find Caleb standing in the threshold, his hands stuffed deep into his pockets. He doesn't speak, just watches me for a long while.

"Are you okay?" he finally asks.

I shake my head.

He sighs and crosses the room to sit in the chair next to my bed. "I didn't wanna leave you like this, Daniel, but you can't go around playing with fire. You coulda killed yourself. You understand that, don't you?" I stay silent, and he looks desperate now. "Well, don't you?"

I can tell he doesn't want me to be angry with him, and this seems like a thing I should use, but I'm too tired to work out any more plans.

"Y-yes." My throat is raw. "I understand."

+ + +

Jostled from a nightmare-filled sleep, I blink to find Caleb standing over me.

"Where do you wanna be today?" he asks.

"Sir?" I go to lever myself up, but when my hands touch the mattress, I whimper and fall over again.

"Here or the front room? You're getting locked up either way."

"Oh . . ." After our talk, I thought we were okay, but apparently, I thought wrong. "Here," I say. I'm hurting. I don't want to move.

With a nod, he starts clamping the cuff around my ankle.

"Dad . . ." My eyes sting with tears. "I'm sorry about the curtains."

I really am—his *mom* made those curtains.

Something flickers in his expression, a slight softening of the eyes, but he just says, "I'll see you tonight." Then he turns to go.

"Dad?"

He turns back.

"How long?" I look to the chain.

"Until I can trust you."

I don't know how much time has passed, but However Long it takes for someone to trust you, that's how long it is before Caleb leaves me alone without locking my foot.

I notice my open door immediately, and it's incredible to walk down the hall, alone and unfettered. The vault door is closed, so no access to the fire-damaged kitchen, but I bet I'll be able to earn that back too. If I'm patient.

Caleb left out my favorite cereal, Fruity Pebbles, and I pour myself a bowl. My hands've finally healed apart from a shiny scar on both palms, so I can do that easily now, then I pop in a VHS tape and fall onto the couch.

While I listen, I gaze up into my viewfinder.

When the tape ends, I put on another one.

I'm in the middle of my third movie and feeling almost serene, when it occurs to me that I need a new plan. Fire failed, so now what? Suddenly, I'm short of breath at just the *thought* of making another mistake. I'm not hurting anymore, but the fear of being hurt is scrambling the circuits in my brain.

Pain fades, but the memory of pain is infinite.

FORTY

I spoon a bite of oatmeal into my mouth. Not my favorite breakfast, but the living room's too cold even with heat blasting from the vents, so hot food helps. I push my hair out of my face and over my ears.

Noticing, Caleb smiles and fondly plucks a lock. "Would you look at that? It's starting to curl up."

I've been here long enough for my hair to curl. For it to grow past my collar.

"C'mon, I'll give you a trim."

Mom's voice appears in my head: *I'd never let anyone but Virginia touch Saye's hair.* As if it were *her* hair, not mine. Caleb returns with a towel, a comb, and a pair of scissors.

Scissors—sharp—weapon.

He drapes the towel over my shoulders, and I close my eyes, imagining the black cape from Virginia's upscale salon. I can practically smell the chemicals. Dye, hairspray, shampoos. I feel the comb, listen to the *snip-snip*.

I blink, but there's no giant mirror to keep me apprised of how it's going, so I shut my eyes again. My hands absently drift to the pockets of my flannel pajama pants, which are sealed shut with wax. I keep forgetting crayons in my pockets, and when Caleb does laundry, they melt in the washing machine.

More combing, more snipping.

"Okay. You're all set." Caleb pulls on his boots and winter coat, then he's gone.

In the silence, I run my fingers through my shortened hair. I wonder how it looks.

But I guess it doesn't really matter. For a moment, I imagine that someone's sitting at the table across from me saying it looks nice.

My mind races with images—a soft hand in my hair, *it looks nice*. The hand drifts lower, under my clothes, touching me, gentle pressure. My hand quickens, and I hold back my gasps as if someone might be listening. But the moment my breathing slows, my mind's back to more innocent thoughts. Company, conversations, someone to play all these board games with. If I just had someone to *talk* to during the day, maybe this wouldn't be so hard.

I get up and pace.

Try the vault door, locked.

Try the pocket door, locked. This hysterical feeling's taking hold of me. I'm not chained. I can walk from the living room to my bedroom. But I can't get out.

I collapse onto my bed and look into my viewfinder. Close-up clouds like what you see through the window of a plane. Maybe I should stop thinking about running away, just surrender to this until the meteor shower. Only I wonder how Caleb's going to react when whatever magical thing he's been waiting on never happens.

My pulse speeds up, wild and hectic.

Something tells me I don't want to be here to find out.

FORTY-ONE

Day after day, I try the doors and I pace, but I can't get my mind right. It's as if I used to live in a grandfather clock, but now I'm set on stopwatch. *Tick tick tick tick tick.* All the colors are too bright and the world's a little tilted, and I keep catching shadow-figures in my periphery, only when I turn, nothing's there.

I prowl and try to come up with a plan, but my thoughts are blurry and too fast to catch. I need to overpower him, but he's too strong, he's too fast. I need to think, plan, but I can't run—I can't fight. I'm a clock and a bomb, and all the thoughts keep swirling faster-faster-faster.

A memory: the medieval torture room with a sixty-pound helmet made of iron. I need one of those to keep all these thoughts inside my head.

The bell's ringing. He's home.

I have to get it together, but my mind's a tornado of crisscrossed black wires and I can't straighten them out.

The locks tumble behind me. The vault door slides open—a terrible, metallic noise scratching my skin—then he's telling me *hello* and something else too, but it's hard to follow, like I'm missing every fifth word.

"I asked you a question."

I blink bright to find that we're sitting at the table, eating dinner. My bowl of chili is filled with crushed saltine crackers.

"Well?" Caleb says.

"Yessir." The answer is automatic, but it doesn't sound like me.

He spears his green beans and brings his fork to his mouth. *Fork, sharp, weapon.*

Can't run—can't fight—can't run—can't fight.

I hold the helmet to keep it on my head.

"What're you doing?"

Can't run—can't fight—can't run—can't fight.

"Daniel!"

An invisible hand tears the helmet away, and my thoughts spray out in bursts. Caleb's telling me to talk right, then he's telling me not to talk at all, so I ball my fingers into fists and throw myself into the wall. Yelling, whining, growling.

A hand grabs hold of my collar and spins me around. "You don't act like this! You're a boy, not a goddamn animal."

But that's exactly what I am. I'm bared fangs and monster-venom, and I pull loose from Caleb's hand, crashing into the television. It falls onto its side. The screen shatters.

Cracked—sharp—glass—*weapon.*

I reach for it.

But before I can grab it, I'm lifted into the air and carried to the pocket door. Caleb turns the key in the lock, jerks the door into the wall. *No no no,* not again.

"Dad, don't! I'm sorry!"

"Not yet you're not."

I let all my weight bring me to the ground, but his hand reaches down to drag me through the hall, *past* his bedroom door. He unlocks the second door on the right to reveal the top of a staircase. It's so dark I can only see the first few steps.

"You're gonna stay there till you learn how to act." He begins guiding me below, and I'm so relieved I don't struggle anymore. I just let him take me down.

FORTY-TWO

Darkness.

I should be afraid, but I'm not. It's almost as if the past However Long has been a dream or I was drunk or high, but now I'm wide-awake and sober. Patches of what happened flicker through my head. I screamed at Caleb. I broke the TV. After all that, his response could've been a lot worse than sending me to the cellar to think about what I did.

Just sitting here, that's nothing.

I blink, unblink. It all stays the same. I can't get any sense of depth as if I could be in a closet or an airplane hangar. Shivering, I wrap my arms around myself and press my cold bare feet into my thighs. Air must be flooding in from outside through a vent—or maybe a *window.*

Suddenly hopeful, I stand and stretch out my arms, stumbling till my fingers hit a stone wall. I lay my palms against it, nice and solid and not as cold as the floor.

I slide along the perimeter. It feels like forever until I reach a corner, then I start on the next wall, halting when the texture changes. Wood, not stone.

A *door.*

But whether it's to the stairs or somewhere else, I don't know.

My hand closes over the knob and twists. Locked.

I keep moving along the wall, and soon find another door. This one opens, so I walk inside. The air's dank and mildewy as I brush against something cold and smooth. My hand sloshes into liquid—it's a *toilet.*

Grimacing, I locate a pair of knobs, relieved there's running water and a cracked sliver of soap. Once I scrub my hands clean, I keep feeling around the little bathroom for something useful, but there's nothing, so I edge back onto the cellar wall. At some point I'm pretty sure I'm covering the same ground.

Shutting my eyes, I try to imagine the layout of the room, but it doesn't matter if my eyes are open or closed. It's the same darkness.

I need to form a plan, but all I can think is that this place smells like it's six hundred feet underground, like a cave, like a *grave.*

I've circled the perimeter of the cellar at least three times, I'm almost sure of that, so I need to figure out what's in the middle. I take a cautious step—it's scary trying to walk when you can't see—counting as I go. *One, two, three*—I trip over a raised bump in the floor. My arms windmill for something to hold on to, but it's all empty air, so I fall. Pain shoots from my elbow to wrist, and out of nowhere, Luke's face appears, just a blur apart from his smile.

If Luke hadn't hitched a ride with me that day.

If Luke hadn't insisted we stop at the restaurant.

If Luke hadn't *laughed* at me.

If it weren't for him, I would've made it home.

His smile fades, and now my mother appears, a faceless silhouette. She's at a nice restaurant, in a nice dress. Someone's patting her hand and telling her how sad it is that I'm gone.

"He was so beautiful," my mother says.

He was. He *was*.

"Fuck you!" My shout wrenches the ribs over my heart. She could've hired the best detectives in the world to find me, but she didn't. If she had, I'd be home by now.

Luke's floating grin reappears. It laughs and laughs.

"Fuck you!" I shout at him. "I hate you! I hate you. I—" My throat squeezes shut. "*Please*. Someone, please find me."

Time is passing. I know this of course, but it's hard to get a sense of how much. I'm starting to feel hungry, and it's wearing down my anger. It's eerie that there's no sight, but even more eerie is the lack of sound. I can hear *myself*—my breaths, my curses, my heart. But other than that, there's nothing.

I'm starting to get a headache. My eyes are closed, but I think my body's urge is to see, even if that means trying to see through my eyelids. I should sleep, just sleep through this.

I lie down, but the ground is like a block of ice, so I switch to my side, only I can't get my arm in the right position to properly cushion my head. I try leaning against the wall. The stone's a little warmer than the floor, so my back feels better, but the rest of me feels frozen.

Waves of trembles begin at the crown of my head and curl down to my stomach, over and over and over.

Bringing my knees to my chest, I rock myself, but the shivers won't stop. I'm exhausted, but also weirdly wired. I remember reading somewhere that being warm makes you feel relaxed and safe, but being cold makes you anxious, because your body can't tell the difference between shaking because you're cold and shaking because you're afraid.

There's a sudden noise—a brushing scrape.

It sounds like a snake.

I sit up straighter. A snake *could* be down here. They like dark places. My heart picks up speed as I picture all the creatures designed to operate in the dark. Bats, insects, rats. *Anything* could be down here.

No. There are no snakes. It's just me. And I'm not scared of the dark.

I'm not scared of the dark.

I'm not scared of the dark.

I'm not scared of the dark.

I wish for a bed. I wish for *my* bed, in my room where the temperature was always perfect. I can see it. Airy rows of shutters flung open to let in the light. A movie screen, a telescope, a model airplane—no, that's not right. That's Daniel's plane, not mine.

I start over. Scan my room in my head. Rise bed, movie screen, blue duck.

No.

I start again, but Daniel's belongings keep showing up, like demons, like invaders, and the more I try to block them from entry, the more our two rooms meld into one.

✦ ✦ ✦

I hear something.

Something that's not me.

Snakes—scorpions—monsters—*light*.

The door to the cellar stairs is open.

Overcome with relief, I scramble to my feet. There are more noises, steps and a crinkling splat as an object's dropped onto the floor.

"Dad?"

No response.

Then the unmistakable sound of the door closing again, and I'm thrust back into darkness.

"Dad, wait!" I shout, crawling toward where I saw the light.

I smack into something. A grocery-sized paper sack. Pushing my hand inside, I feel bottled water. There are two more bags filled with small cardboard boxes. I open one. Cookies. Another box. Crackers.

It's enough food to last for days.

I've stopped crying, but my nose is stuffy, so the food doesn't have much flavor. I dig into the box of cheese crackers, but without my sight, it's hard to guide the food to my mouth.

I take a swig of apple juice, then keep on eating even though I'm not hungry anymore, because it's comforting. I remember reading that too—that food's a primal comfort just like warmth.

I finish off the box, then swallow juice till I hear it sloshing around in my stomach.

I've heard of teeth chattering, but I always thought it was just an expression. Teeth don't chatter in real life. But I'm shaking so hard my jaw trembles and my teeth clack together. This is misery. This is Hell. And Hell is punishment. Caleb could turn the heat on if he wanted to. He could forgive me, let me up. But he wants me to suffer.

The paper sacks are empty. Maybe I ate too quickly.

Or maybe it's been a very long time.

"Hello?" I say just to hear a voice, and I almost expect someone . . . anyone . . . *Daniel* . . . to answer me. "Daniel, are you here? Hello?"

A memory blooms.

A private mountaintop covered in snow. Me, small and cold and wearing so many layers my arms stood out to both sides. I shouted hello, and a moment later, a bigger, deeper *HELLO* answered me. I must've been very young because I remember turning to my mother, my little index finger touching the sky as if to ask, *Who was that?*

And she explained, "It's only an echo."

Because no one was really out there.

I was just hearing my own voice come back to me.

I can see things in the dark. Things that can't be there.

A shark-shaped limousine driving deep into a forest.

An amphitheater.

Young men in black suits with no faces. They wear long red ties. In eerie unison, they slide their ties off, hold them out straight, a red line in their fists.

The boys are weapons.

I see a figure with glass skin, a breakable boy walking out of the woods.

Memories are coming to me, so clear now. Me in a room, an office I think, and a man with blue-black hair sits in a high back leather chair. Behind him are hundreds of fish tanks, stacked floor-to-ceiling, all backlit with red lights, and I'm afraid.

"W-what's in the tanks?" I ask the man.

He smiles with sharp, jagged teeth, but he doesn't answer me.

"Who are you?"

His smile widens. "Don't you know?"

I take in a sharp gulp of air. Yes, I *do* know.

He's Jack.

The man who stole me from a park when I was ten years old.

Hell is not hot—it's cold.

Hell is not bright—it's endless darkness.

What did that girl say a million years ago? In a sunny room surrounded by eyes and light, we talked about God's Favorite Son. That used to be Lucifer. Now it's Jesus. But we're God's children too. Sort of. Not like Jesus. We're not the favorite, so we can't do the things he could do. But God loves us. He'd do anything for us. Unless we disappoint him. Then he sends us down below where there are no second chances and no way out.

My throat is sore. I think I've been screaming.

I cough, wet and hacking. The world's a cold floor.

Then there's something.

A triangle of light. A creaking noise, then steps coming closer, *closer*. My cry shreds my throat, echoes in my ears.

Strong arms surround me, and a voice says, "Daniel, Daniel. My poor Daniel."

Now I'm flying through the dark, lifted into the light.

"Dad?" I raise my face from his warm flannel chest. There's so much brightness glowing all around him as he smiles down at me, benevolent. "I thought we could never get out."

"We?"

"The children . . . they get sent down . . . but they never come back up."

He looks troubled yet loving, as if he can't make sense of my words, but he's trying.

My eyes burn as he carries me to my colorful room with my patchwork quilt. It's warmth, it's bliss, nothing has ever felt as nice as this. He's lowering me to my bed, but I tighten my fist onto the fabric of his shirtfront, afraid to let go.

"You . . . you forgive me?"

"Of course, Daniel. I'll always forgive you. You're my son."

FORTY-THREE

The world's a fire. I float above my body. I'm thrust back in.

My jaw is pried open.

"C'mon, son, we gotta get this fever down."

Pills are pressed onto my tongue, water poured down my throat.

I cough, spraying most of the water back out.

A cold cloth pats my neck and chest.

"Dad?" I blink into his silhouette.

"Yes, son?"

"I . . . I remember it now, the experiments."

The cloth swipes my face.

"I was in his office. The bad man, he had all these fish tanks. But they weren't fish. They were *babies*."

"Shh, shh," he soothes me. "Everything's gonna be okay the second those meteors start falling. The monsters who took you will try anything to make sure we're not together when it comes, but I won't let them."

I float up to the surface of an inky black pool. "What's gonna happen?"

"When the meteors come, time's gonna turn backward, you'll

see. All the way to the day you went missing. It'll be just like it never happened."

If that's true, then everything I am will disappear.

I sink to the bottom of the black pool again.

It's as if I've awoken from a long and terrible dream. I feel clearer— something solid instead of disembodied—but my nose is freezing, my throat burns, and a wet rattling cough hurts my ribs.

I don't think I've ever been this sick before. I hardly ever *was* sick before. I used to take vitamins and minerals. I had regular check-ups. We had a nutritionist and a chef. Mom said you have to be irresponsible to get ill. If you take care of your body, it doesn't happen.

But I guess I've been careless with my body. Or *he* has.

Caleb lays his hand across my forehead. "You're looking better."

I'm feeling better, mentally anyway. Now I know that those visions from the cellar weren't real. Of course Jack's my father, I was hallucinating.

"Daniel, do we have an understanding?"

"Sir?" I cough into my fist. Feel it pull sharp on the muscles in my back.

"Have you learned your lesson?"

I don't remember what the lesson was anymore, but I nod.

"You sure about that?"

"Yessir, I mean it." The cellar—nothing could be worse than the cellar. "I won't ever do anything bad again."

"Good," he says. "That was horrible for me too."

Surprised, I look at him closely. "It was?"

"It was." His voice is solemn. Checking his watch, he stands. "You need more sleep." He crosses my room in his heavy boots and flips off the light.

"Dad!" The word's a strangled gulp of panic.

I hear his shuffling footsteps, then a click on my nightstand. Amber lamplight brightens the room, and I can breathe.

Dad pats the top of my head with a fond smile. "You always were afraid of the dark."

I spend days in my room shivering under quilts and flannel sheets, but Caleb doesn't leave my side, and it's nice. I don't want to be alone when I'm feeling this terrible. We play cards, and I get ice cream which soothes my sore throat, but eventually I ask if I can go out in the living room.

"I'm bored."

Caleb grins. "You must be feeling a lot better."

My whole body still aches, and I feel like . . . what's that expression? *A shadow of myself.* That's kind of how I feel. Like a shadow, an echo, the faint remains of something bigger.

But I nod. "Yessir."

"Come on then." Caleb's smile gets wider. "Bring your blanket."

Wrapping my quilt tight around me, I make my way down the hall and take a seat on the couch, facing the TV. It's the same old television, but it has a brand-new screen. A flicker of nerves makes my skin tingle, but Caleb doesn't comment on it.

"How 'bout a movie?" He pops one into the VCR before

heading off to the kitchen.

I can hear him taking pots and pans from the cabinets as the familiar sounds of *Star Wars: A New Hope* starts up. The scent of tomato soup and butter sizzling on a skillet wafts my way, and I close my eyes, back to bliss.

On a warm couch, in a warm room, there is nothing better than this.

After supper, Caleb brings out a chessboard with a mysterious smile. "You were too young for this before, but I bet you can do it now." And then he shows me the basics.

I keep forgetting which pieces move which way, and I'm not sure if that's because I'm still a little sick or if I just suck at it, but Caleb's patient and seems to enjoy being able to teach me something.

It makes me think about my actual father. My mom was always the one who taught me how to do things. Ride my bike, tie my shoes, write my numbers and letters. Jack would get too bored—nothing like Caleb, who lights up whenever he sees me and is interested in every word I say. But maybe things will be different when I get home. Maybe I'll try harder. Maybe he'll try harder.

Or maybe he's glad I'm gone.

The thought's a bullet with no exit wound. It lodges itself, rusty and hot inside my chest. Without me around, my dad doesn't have to *pretend* to be a childless bachelor anymore.

"Son?" Caleb's hand stills as he's moving a player across the board, his brows knitted in concern. "Are you okay?"

I can't seem to hide anything I'm feeling from him, and for once I don't mind.

+ + +

Caleb has to work today so I grab my viewfinder and quilt, and shuffle to the couch. He hands me a hot mug of chicken-and-stars soup, then he presses play on the VCR.

"I'll see you tonight," he tells me.

"Okay, see you tonight."

Slow and languid, I finish my soup and lie down.

This is nice.

This feels good.

I keep listening, and eventually the tape ends.

No sounds now.

Cozy, drowsy, I don't move.

And the days seem to float.

"You being lazy again today?" Caleb teases when he finds me in my pajamas on the couch after he gets home from work.

I shrug. I haven't felt like drawing or watercoloring in a very long time.

He lays his palm across my forehead. "I hope you're not still sick."

"No . . ." I don't think I'm sick. "I'm just relaxed."

"Hmm . . . go on and find something to read while I fix dinner."

"Okay."

Slow-motion dreamy, I drift to the shelves and scan rows of novels and encyclopedias, coming to a halt on a hardback book I never noticed before.

Languages of the World.

I thumb through its Bible-thin pages. It's an English-to-

Everything book. A thrill races through me. I could learn Portuguese and Greek, and I could get better at Latin and impress Mr. Rivas when—

I'm struck with a startled jolt, that same one you get when you realize you've fallen asleep some place you shouldn't.

How long has it been since I've thought about escaping?

I'm not sure.

My eyes drift over to the television, where my distorted reflection is staring back at me.

FORTY-FOUR

It doesn't take me long to come to the same conclusion I reached months ago. There's no way out. There are two doors. The vault door—I don't have a prayer of getting through that one. It's way too heavy to break down, and the lock's too complicated to pick, so the pocket door's my best bet. There may be something I can use beyond it. A weapon, a phone, an *exit*.

There's no knob, just a shallow recess. There's a tiny keyhole, but no tiny instruments I can fit inside it. Gripping the recess, I give it a tug. It doesn't budge—I knew it wouldn't—but I try once more, and then it's time to pace.

Trekking up and down the hall, a fantasy takes shape in my head. On the day of the field trip instead of dragging myself out of bed, I just stay home.

God why did I go on that stupid field trip? And the answer comes, blunt and heartless:

You wanted to avoid what you did to that boy.

Evan.

The thought slithers around in my stomach like something slimy, so I slide back further in my fantasies. Now I'm in the limo on the night of Homecoming, and there's Evan Zamara, smiling outside the Rialto movie theater. But instead of getting out, I tell the driver to just keep going.

And we keep going.

I continue to pace, and Luke's voice fills my head: *Are you picking on that kid?*

And Mr. Gardiner's saying: *He can't take it anymore.*

Guilt clenches my stomach tight as I picture Evan's face again—and why is *his* face so clear? I try to imagine Luke's face, Bria's face, my *mother's*. Can't.

But I can see Evan perfectly. Can see his big curls and chubby cheeks and the giant brown eyes filled with terror as Garrett ordered him to get out of the limo.

What the hell did Garrett do to him out in the woods?

I pace faster.

I need to focus on the here and now.

Everything's beginning to look like a tool. The screws that hold things in place. If I could get them out, maybe I could do something with them. Or the TV. If I took it apart, there'd be wires I might be able to use to pick the lock.

Only, I'm scared to damage the television. I'd get in trouble, plus I doubt Caleb would replace it this time, and without any movie or shows running in the background, everything would be so *quiet*.

At the moment an old sitcom is playing, and the studio audience is roaring with laughter. Suddenly, I'm remembering the first day of junior year. How I strolled up onto the stage and looked out at all those faces. Everyone was laughing and applauding, for *me*.

But then right before my eyes, the image swirls into an auditorium full of mannequins with cold mocking smiles. Were they laughing *for* me . . . or *at* me?

No, of course it was for me. I was the Homecoming prince—everyone loved me.

But there's this feeling, like needles pricking my insides. *Did they?*

Lex definitely didn't. And neither did Evan's friend, Blair. How many people actually hated me? Lex. Blair. Evan. My father—

I halt, struck by a memory. The time I was five years old and kept begging my dad to play with me, and he said, *Don't bug me*, swatting the air like I was a mosquito. But I kept on till he lost his temper and snatched up his car keys and stormed out of the house. It wasn't really a big deal, but I stood crying at the window, watching him leave like my heart was broken. When you're little, little things hurt.

I rack my brain, but I can't come up with a single time he got angry with me for doing something dangerous, and I did dangerous stuff all the time. I'd climb on the roof, bike without a helmet, speed down highways, get into cars with strangers, and he didn't care—as long as I left him alone.

When Caleb gets home, he falls onto the couch and wraps an arm around my shoulders. I find myself reflexively returning the hug. It's been a miserable day of doing nothing but loop around this house, so being the center of all this affection—it's nice.

"How're you feeling?" he asks.

I'm starting to think he's the only person on this planet who actually cares how I feel.

"I don't know," I answer honestly.

He gives my shoulder another squeeze. "We'll do something fun tonight, all right?"

And true to his word, after dinner, we play games and eat ice cream. He complains a lot during Parcheesi. I've set up a blockade that none of his players can pass, and I'm laughing as I dig into my Rocky Road.

"This ain't right," he complains dramatically, hopping up a little, and I chuckle some more.

His keys jangle in his pocket, and an image floods my head. Me grabbing my chair, swinging it into his skull and taking those keys. It scares me—the sudden violence of my thoughts when I'm still mid-laugh, when my mouth's still full of chocolate.

I know I couldn't actually do something like that. For one thing, he'd stop me before I got anywhere near him. But even if I was capable, the thought of it makes me queasy.

I don't *want* to hurt him.

FORTY-FIVE

I slide a gray crayon from my pocket and sketch the faint outline of a scene. A lonely sailboat on a stormy sea. I wet my brush, dip it into the well of paint, and fill the ocean with choppy strokes. My feet are starting to itch. Time to make my rounds.

I stride down the hall to my bedroom.

Back to the living room, I circle the perimeter. Peer under the couch, along the shelves. I tug at the pocket door—and draw in a sharp breath.

The door *moved*.

It slid right into the wall, and now there's a two-inch peek into the corridor. I've been pulling on this door for God knows how long, so maybe I finally wore down the lock.

Or maybe this is a test.

It's possible Caleb left it unlocked to see what I'd do. If I move it any further, I bet an alarm will go off and he'll come home and I'll be in trouble.

My heart's speeding wildly now. My pain sensors flash. I should leave it alone.

I return to the table, but my hand trembles as I dip my paintbrush into the water. Flipping to a clean sheet of paper, I draw a shaky blue line.

Slowly . . . slowly . . . my pulse begins to even out. Everything's okay, no harm done. I didn't do anything wrong, and when Caleb gets home, he's going to see that I'm doing exactly what I'm supposed to do.

But there's a needling thought. What if it was a mistake? Just a bit of carelessness on Caleb's part? If it really was an accident, I may never get another chance.

I inch back to the door and do an awkward dance of indecision, my arm lifting, then dropping to my side, over and over again.

Just open it, I order myself.

But my hand doesn't obey my head anymore.

Please, Saye. Please try. You can at least try.

My arm trembles.

My fingers quiver.

Then they listen.

They grip the indentation, push right, and the pocket door slides smoothly into the wall. Now I can see the entire corridor, but I don't move any farther. Maybe the alarm won't go off unless someone steps into the hall. Maybe it's rigged just like the driveway.

Or maybe it's not.

Move, Saye.

A suspicious-superstitious feeling falls over me as I cross the forbidden threshold. Bypassing both doors on the right, I head for the one that dead-ends the hall, and order myself to grab the knob.

This time my hand listens right away—only to find that the door is locked.

I give it a little shake. It's flimsier than the other doors in the house. I might even be able to break it down. But some other voice says: *You'd better not.*

All the negatives flood my brain. What if it's just a linen closet or some room with no windows or weapons and Caleb comes home and sees what I've done? No, I've got to be smart. I need to get through, but in a way he won't notice. Just in case.

I examine the door closely.

There's a tiny sliver of space between the door and the frame, so I dash into the living room, and grab a VHS tape from the shelf. I slip off the cardboard case, flatten it, then run to the end of the corridor and wedge the case into the crevice, working it all the way down, while pushing against the door. And just like that—the door opens.

My heart's pounding like crazy now. I'm definitely not supposed to go in there, no question. My ears start tingling like the warning bell just sounded.

But it didn't so I step inside the dark room.

The air is thicker in here, and filled with a strange low hum.

My fingers fumble along the wall to flip on the overhead light.

Just a simple square room with white walls and white floors, completely ordinary apart from the refrigerators that line each wall.

One, two, three . . . nine in all.

It's more than a little weird.

Why does Caleb have so many refrigerators? And why are they locked inside this room?

Apprehension prickles my spine, and my stomach goes strange. Something tells me to get out of here right now—there is nothing that can help me here—but my body ignores my brain, and I approach the nearest humming box.

I grip the scuffed, silver handle and open the door. Cold, smoky vapor fills the air. Chunks of ice cling to its inner walls. They're *freezers*, I realize, not refrigerators.

The smoke clears, and green eyes are staring back at me.

Time is not where I left it.

I'm facing a different wall, and a different freezer door is open, but I'm still staring into green eyes.

They belong to a boy.

He's a little younger than the one before, maybe thirteen or fourteen years old. Frost clings to his blond hair and lashes like they've *become* the frost, like if I were to touch them, they'd break.

My breath rushes out of me.

I shiver as cold air touches my skin.

There are seven more freezers.

My body moves all on its own as if I'm on a conveyer belt, opening door after door until I'm left standing in the center of the room, surrounded by frozen boys. Ones who look like Daniel—who look like *me*.

And I understand.

I'm not the first boy Caleb took. I'm not the first one he thought was Daniel.

You can die of fright, I know that now.

There are some sights your soul can't survive.

I rise up from a dark dream to see that I'm still in the center of the room, surrounded by staring eyes.

A sudden jolt—*no.* We aren't actually here. But my body says different. It's shaking, convulsing, and suddenly bent double and vomiting onto the white tile floor.

I run to my bedroom, drop to my knees in front of the toilet, and throw up again. The frozen boys flash all around me. Dead eyes. Statue eyes. Caleb. He killed them.

"Sayers," a voice says firmly like a soldier in my brain. "You need to hurry."

I shake my head. Dizzy white terror. Can't move.

"You have to," the voice insists. "Or he'll know."

He'll know.

It's so horrifying that it breaks through my panic, and I run back into that room where my vomit is on the floor and all the faces are staring staring staring.

Hurry, the voice says.

I slam every door against every staring eye.

I tear off my shirt, mop up the vomit, then dump my shirt in my bathroom sink, and turn on the faucet. Grab a hand towel. Race into the cold room again, planning to wipe up any remnants when the stench of stomach acid hits me. He's going to smell it—he'll know.

Short circuits. We're not here.

Calm down. Think.

Blurry-eyed, I dash into the living room and smack into the table, knocking over my cup of paint-water, but I don't have time to clean it up. I keep running to my bathroom and grab a bar of soap. Stick that and the towel under the tap, then dart back to the freezer room.

Surrounded by the hum, I scrub the floor with my soapy cloth. Fast and hard—have to get the floor clean. *Hurry.*

It's okay, I have time, the bell hasn't sounded.

Unless . . .

What if it went off while I was at the sink? My bedroom door was open, but would I have heard it over the running water?

I don't know.

Maybe he's already here.

Frames start to skip.

Please calm down. The bell didn't go off. He isn't here yet. Just keep cleaning.

I swipe the soap against the wet rag and scrub, run back to my room for more soap, and find my sink overflowing.

It takes two more shirts to sop up the water from the floor. To the living room again. The pocket door and freezer room door are still wide open. I speed down the hall, shut the freezer room door, and I've got the pocket door half-closed when I hesitate.

Should I make sure the lock catches, or should I leave it like it was in case this was a test?

I don't know.

I don't *know.*

Calm down. Think.

This can't be a test. An accident's the only thing that makes sense so I shut the pocket door all the way, then stand here, panting, clutching my wet knees. It's okay, I just need to change. And hide the wet shirts. There's still time.

The bells start blasting over my head.

My heart trips so fast it hurts, and I'm holding my chest with both hands when I notice something strange. A glowing bar is shining beneath the pocket door.

A voice starts screaming in my ear: *The light! You forgot to turn off the light!*

Tears spill fast over my cheeks making it impossible to see. "Daniel, help me."

I claw at the pocket door, but my hands are shaking so badly, they're useless.

"Please."

And then, oh God, thank you, it gives. The lock must not have caught, or maybe it really is broken, but there's no time to think. I grab the VHS cover, race down the corridor, cram it into the crevice, only this time it doesn't work. It's not depressing the lock.

Dizzy panic.

Caleb's in my head.

He's climbing out of the truck.

He's almost to the door.

I yank the VHS cover back out. The cardboard's torn. No time to grab a new one from the shelf.

Calm down, Sayers. The soldier voice is back. *Focus.*

Turning the cardboard over to the untorn side, I jam it into that little crevice, and this time it works. Bursting into the room, my eyes are dragged to the obvious wet streaks on the floor. My ears throb, listening for the bank vault door. If I hear it open, it's too late.

I rip off my sweats, use them to wipe the floor, listening, *listening*, then I flip off the light and shut the door again.

I'm racing through the corridor when I hear it—the series of clicking locks.

I slam the pocket door closed just as the silver vault door starts sliding open, and I run as fast as I can into my room. Jumping into bed, I bury myself under the covers.

"Daniel?" Caleb's voice calls out

I don't answer, just lie on my side, knees to chest, shaking to the unwindow.

Silence now.

Is he going to his room? Will he smell something strange? The vomit, the soap?

Silence, silence, silence.

And then, "DANIEL, WHAT DID YOU DO?"

He knows he knows he knows he knows.

Heavy boots march down the hall.

Shaking, shaking. *Stop shaking.*

My door smacks hard against the wall. "Daniel!"

I hold the covers over my head, clutching on to them with both fists.

Boots stomp across the floor.

"What'n the hell's all over the floor?" Caleb tears the quilt from my grip. "You know better'n to spill paint and . . . Daniel?" His voice has gone soft. "What's wrong?"

I look up, and he's watching me with nothing but concern.

But he killed them. He killed them. He killed them.

"I feel sick." I heave, and a trash can appears below my face.

There's a warm hand on my cold back.

Why? Why did he kill them?

The hand rubs up and down my spine.

Because . . .

They weren't his real son.

The hand disappears and returns with a wet towel. I use it to wipe off my mouth.

"Oh, Daniel." The mattress sinks beside me. "Poor kiddo."

My eyes blur. "Y-you really are my dad, right?"

"Of course I am. What's gotten into you?"

I crawl over to him, all the way into his lap. He wraps his arms around me, and I break down into heavy sobs. *"Dad."* He rocks me as I cry into his chest. "Please don't let anyone hurt me."

"Never." His arms tighten. "I'd never let anyone hurt you."

And I drift up like a cloud.

A small boat on a gentle sea, growing so calm I could fall asleep.

Of course he'd never hurt me.

I'm his son.

FORTY-SIX

It's almost Christmas. The tree is up and the ornaments are hung and the string of lights are twinkling bright. My gifts for Dad are under the tree. Three watercolors and a board game I made out of flattened cereal boxes. Dad puts on a movie, then takes a seat on the couch. When I scoot closer to him, he lifts his arm so I can rest my head against his chest.

We've had lots of Christmases and Easters and Halloweens, but I've been thinking all day, and my thoughts are bothering me.

"Dad?"

"Hmm?"

"When am I gonna have a birthday?"

He chuckles. "Those presents under the tree aren't enough for you?"

"They are . . ." I fiddle with the pocket on his flannel shirt. "But I never have birthdays."

"Well, I guess that's because they don't really mean much."

"But how old am I?"

"That's not for you to worry about."

Sometimes it's confusing. Dad never told me when the meteors fell, and I thought we were gonna watch together but we didn't, and now I'm wondering if something went wrong. Did I get turned backward or did I keep going?

I sit up so I can look him in the eye. "But am I a kid or a grown-up?"

"You're not a *grown-up*." He laughs. "Not even close. Now stop worrying. I've told you, time's not that simple. It doesn't just go one way."

"But what does—"

"Daniel . . ." He sounds exasperated. "Stop thinking so hard."

With a sigh, I collapse back onto his chest. Maybe it *is* better not to think so much.

Dad wraps his arm around me again. "I love you, Daniel."

My lids go heavy. "I love you too."

I don't wanna fall asleep yet, but my eyes dip closed.

And a woman with golden hair appears.

She smiles and leads me into a golden room with a shiny marble floor that looks like a giant chess board. There's a Christmas tree so tall it touches the sky. The stocking on the mantel's so big it reaches the floor. But the name written on its side . . . it's not right.

It says . . .

"Daniel."

I whimper.

It says . . .

"*Daniel.*"

I blink my eyes open. I'm still on the couch, but the movie is over.

"You were having a bad dream," Dad tells me.

"I was?"

"Mmm-hmm. Come on, let's get you to bed."

He walks me to my room and tucks me in, flipping my lamp on before closing my door, but I don't fall right asleep like I normally do. The woman in the golden room reappears, and I feel a longing so intense it hurts.

I squeeze my eyes shut, and slowly the gold room fills with figures. I know them, they're important to me. I try to remember who they are, but suddenly it feels like I'm dangling half my body off the edge of a mountain. It's windy and snowy and there's ice on my lashes. The memories are right there, entangled in the clouds—I can almost touch them—but if I lean any farther to grasp one, I'll fall.

I spend the day after Christmas trying to play with my presents. Dad got me three new board games, but they're useless without a partner. The Legos are fun, but even they start to seem unremarkable, so I grab my walkie-talkies and speak into the microphone:

"Hello? Over."

Nothing but a static universe on the other end.

I turn both of them on, and they let out a sharp whistle. I look into my viewfinder, aiming it at the lights on the ceiling and watch the clouds until I hear the vault door slide open.

Dashing into the living room, I throw my arms around Dad's waist.

He hugs me back and keeps on squeezing tight. *Too* tight.

"Dad? What's wrong?"

"I hafta go." His voice is strained.

"But you just got here."

"Not now. On Friday."

"But what day is today?"

He makes an impatient noise. "It's *soon*."

"So . . . you don't wanna go to work on Friday?"

"I'm not talking about work. I hafta leave for a few days."

"A few *days*? To go where?"

He falls onto his chair, burying his face into his hands. "Home."

"But you are home."

"I mean my old home. Where I grew up."

"Where is that?"

But he doesn't answer.

Later, after we've finished our supper, I'm holding a bowl of popcorn in my lap as I listen to my favorite movie. The lights are off, and I'm licking salt from my fingertips when a cough-syrup smell tickles my nose. Dad is drinking from a tiny brown bottle.

"Are you sick, Dad?"

"Why're you asking me that?"

"You're taking medicine."

He glances down at the bottle and chuckles, but it's an anxious sound. "Just a nightcap."

"Are you okay?"

"Listen to the movie," he says, so I close my eyes.

An officer of the Imperial Forces is arguing with Darth Vader, and Vader tells him:

I find your lack of faith disturbing.

FORTY-SEVEN

Standing in Dad's doorway, I watch him stuff things into the open suitcase on his bed: three pairs of folded pants, six shirts, a tube of toothpaste, a tie. His gestures are rushed, frenzied. I don't think he wants to leave, but I don't think I can convince him to stay.

"I wish I could go with you," I say.

He swivels his head to me, eyes sharp. "You know you can't leave this house."

"Yessir, I know. I just *wish*."

He hefts his suitcase up by the handle and lugs it into the living room. The table's piled high with sacks of food, all things that don't need to go into the fridge since the vault door's gotta stay locked while he's gone.

Dad gives me a grim look. I guess it's time for him to go.

"This isn't gonna work," he says.

"What won't work?"

"*This*."

"What do you mean?"

"Just go to your room, and let me think," he snaps.

So I hurry to my room and sit on the edge of my bed. I fidget, pulling on the hem of my white T-shirt. A while later he comes in, his hands stuffed deep into his pockets.

"Are you okay now?"

"Daniel . . ." There's this expression on his face, almost like he feels sorry for me. "I've been thinking. While I'm gone, I need you to stay downstairs."

"Downstairs?"

He nods.

"You mean the *cellar*?"

He nods again, and the fear is electric.

"No! Please!" I leap off my bed.

"Daniel, listen to me." He comes toward me, and I press myself into the space between my bed and the wall. "It's the safest place I can put you while I'm gone. It's not a punishment."

"I—I'm not in trouble?"

"I just told you you're not."

"Can I bring my viewfinder?"

"If you want . . ." He comes closer, all the way into the space with me.

"And the TV?"

He hesitates. "There's no electricity down there."

"But if there's no electricity, there's no lights."

Another pause, and then, "I know."

Heart pounding, I scramble over the bed and run out of the room.

"Daniel." He stomps after me. "C'mere."

"No!"

I'm trying to wedge myself under the couch when he grabs me around my waist and hoists me into the air. "Quit telling me no!"

He carries me into the hall and opens the door to the cellar stairs. I grip the doorframe, but he yanks me loose so hard it burns my palms. My arms are grasping at air as he carries me down, down, down, darker with every step.

At the very bottom, he sets me on my feet.

Tears are pouring over my cheeks.

"Please." I grab his shirtfront. "I'm too scared. Please don't. Not if you love me."

"Daniel . . ." The light from above shines around his face, and he looks sadder than I've ever seen him. "You're the only thing left in this entire world that I love."

Then he pushes me inside and locks the door.

My body's in the cellar. My mind's in the sky.

Dad said he'll be home in a few days. A few is more than two, but less than ten. Only time isn't so simple. It can go slow and fast and backward and forward. A few can be forever. Forever can be a few.

My eyes strain. They keep trying to see, doing what eyes are meant to do.

I have sacks of food and water.

I have blankets. I have pillows.

Dad said it's not a punishment, but right before he left, he was angry. Maybe it *wasn't* a punishment, but now it is—it must be.

It's not cold like the last time I was down here, but it's too dark. Bats can see in the dark. They make sounds, vibrations. It's called echolocation.

I try it. *Click-click.* The room stays black.

I want Dad to come home.

I don't want to be alone.

My chest hurts, my head hurts, the dark hurts.

In the cellar I'm always awake and I'm always asleep. You can fall further to one side than the other, but they're not as distinct as you think they should be.

I fall onto the Sleep Side, my mind filled with red-lit fish tanks, but when I return, there aren't any tanks, so maybe I'm nowhere at all.

Lying down on my pillow, I listen to Nothing when suddenly there is Something. A scraping-shuffling sound.

I sit up, panting hard and fast.

"Hello?" My voice is a reverb. HELLO—Hello—hello.

I curl into the wall . . . listening . . . listening . . .

And there it is again.

Something is in here with me. *Breathing.*

An animal maybe? My ears tickle as Something slithers along the floor. It's bigger than a mouse or a snake or anything that could've made it through a vent. It keeps slithering along the floor with a low moan.

Monster.

I shrink away, but it creeps closer—a sliding-scraping-moaning monster. It must be able to see me. I *click-click*, so I can see it too, but it doesn't work. I have to do something before it gets me. I can't run, so I have to fight.

On my hands and knees, I rush the sound.

A scream splits the air.

Not a monster-scream . . . but a girl's.

FORTY-EIGHT

The girl is crying under my fingertips, her long hair tangled in my hands. I scramble backward till I hit the wall.

Hel—ooOOHhh?"

The shaky word is not an echo. Not my own hello returning to me, but *her* hello, but I'm afraid to answer.

"Hello?" she says again.

I wrap my arms around my legs, bringing them to my chest. I hear more crying, and then she begins to whisper—about me and my father and a ghost.

This goes on and on.

Finally I say, "How?"

Her whispers sputter out.

"How did you get in here?"

"Your father. He . . . he said you needed someone to take care of you."

"He did?"

"Yes." She sounds afraid. Strands of her hair still dangle from my fists, and I'm sorry.

"I didn't mean to hurt you. I thought you were a monster."

There's a sudden burst of noise, the overlap of laughing and crying, and then, "What's your name?"

"Daniel."

"Daniel?"

The word travels to my ears and hangs above my head. Words are different in the dark.

I can feel her moving as if the molecules in the air are shifting, her body edging closer to mine. Frightened, I scuttle backward. Her molecules go still.

"Daniel . . ." The word floats to me again. "How old are you?"

"I . . . I don't know."

"How long have you been down here?"

"I don't know."

"Do you know where we are?"

"We're not anywhere."

The girl starts to cry.

"Can we turn on the lights?" she asks sometime later.

"I want to, but they don't work."

"What are you doing?"

"Using clicks."

"Clicks?"

"Yes, for echolocation. If you click the right way, a map appears in your head, and you can see."

"Can you really see?"

"Well . . . not yet."

I hear her moving again. The doorknob rattles.

I tell her, "It's locked."

"Is there another door?"

"A door?"

"Or window? Is there another way out?"

"I'm not supposed to be thinking of ways out. I'm supposed to be thinking of what I did wrong."

"But I didn't do anything wrong. It's okay for you to tell me."

"But there isn't another way. Only Dad has the way."

"Has . . . has he made you stay down here before?"

I'm embarrassed to answer, to talk about the times I've been in trouble.

"Daniel?" She's sniffling again. "Are you all right?"

It's a strange thing for her to ask. I'm not the one who's crying. But the question is kind, and it makes me feel warm.

"Yes. I'm all right."

"Good," she says.

And then it's quiet for a while.

Eventually, her voice returns, in steady and undulating whisper-chants. "Mother . . . now and at the hour . . ." Over and over and over.

"Is that a song?"

"A prayer." She speaks louder, clearer: "Mother Mary, pray for us sinners now and at the hour of our death."

"Is this the Hour of Our Death?"

"No, Daniel," she says. "We're not going to die. We're going to get out of here."

FORTY-NINE

"Get out?"

"Yes."

"You mean away?"

"Yes, out. Away from this house."

"No." I shake my head. "I can't do that."

"Daniel, listen to me." Her voice comes closer.

Afraid, I slide back against the wall.

"I'll help you. We'll do it together."

"No no no." My body starts to quake. "The bad people will get me."

I clap my hands across my mouth. I'm not supposed to talk about the bad people anymore, but my words don't disappear in the dark the way they do in the light. These words hang in the air and repeat.

Bad people.

Bad people.

"What bad people?"

I breathe into my palms.

"Daniel? I can help you get out."

"No! I can't get out and away. No. No. NO!"

She makes a frightened noise. Her molecules fly backward. So do mine.

She starts talking to herself again about Dad and me and the ghost. I don't know who the ghost is. Maybe it's her.

My skin is mountaintop-cold and I shake and shake and shake.

There is a long silence, but it has more depth than most silences.

And then I hear, "Is there a bathroom?"

"Yes," I say, eager to know something useful.

I tell her about the bathroom and how there is soap and a hand towel.

I tell her about the pillows and blankets and sacks of food.

I hear her open and shut the door. I hear her use the toilet, and when she pees, it's quieter than when I pee, then the pipes beat in the walls and water runs and the door squeaks open.

I ask her if ghosts can see in the dark.

She says she doesn't know.

I hear shuffling and more whisper-chants. Her noises are so comforting that I drift closer to the Sleep Side, but then I wake up alone. No sounds. No breaths. A ghost was here but now she's gone. Tears pour over my cheeks.

"Daniel?"

With a gasp, I sit up. "You're here?"

"I'm here."

I cry harder. "I don't like the dark."

"It's okay." Her molecules move toward mine.

This time I stay still, let them get closer, and then I feel it. A hand on my face.

"It's okay," she says again. She has a bright voice, like the color yellow. She guides my head onto her thigh. Her soft hair falls onto my cheek as her fingernails stroke my scalp.

I reach up, touch the long strands. "What color is your hair?"

"Black."

"Like my mother's hair. Are you the ghost?"

"The ghost?"

"The holy ghost?"

"No . . . I'm not a ghost. My name is Penny."

I fall onto the Sleep Side again, and when I wake, I'm right where I was before, my head resting on Penny's stomach. As it rises and falls with her breaths, my head does too.

Her stomach growls.

"Penny, can ghosts get hungry?"

"I'm not a ghost, Daniel."

"You're alive?"

"Yes."

"So you're hungry?"

"Yes."

I sit up, but I'm afraid to be separate from her. I reach out, expecting my hand to fall right through her body, but instead I feel skin. She hasn't vanished, so I crawl to the bags of food and pull out boxes. I tear one open, take out a cookie, then hold it out to her.

"Here," I say.

Her hand closes over mine. I get a cookie for myself and start crunching on it. Chocolate chip. It's very good and sweet.

"Wait," she tells me.

"Why?"

"We need to pray first."

"Why?"

"To say thank you."

"To Dad?"

"To God."

So we say thank you, and then she's crunching. I pass her a bottled water and tell her there are more boxes with all kinds of food, and we keep eating and drinking in silence. She gets full faster than I do, so I continue to eat while she talks.

"Daniel . . . where is your mother?"

"She died when I was a baby."

"I'm sorry."

"Where is *your* mother?"

"She's at home." Her voice breaks on the word home like it hurts her throat to say. "She's with my little brother. Do you have any sisters? Any brothers?"

"No." But the thought does strange things to my brain, because it feels like a lie, as if I do have brothers—maybe a lot of brothers. Or maybe I'm my own brother, like a binary son.

"My brother, Nicolai . . . he's five years old. He's so smart and funny. He's starting kindergarten in the fall."

I keep chewing.

"Daniel, I have to get back to him, to my mom."

"But if you leave, I'll be alone." Now my cookie is dry and tasteless and I can't eat anymore.

✦✦✦

We're on a pillow, under blankets, our faces so close together our breaths mingle. I don't know how long we've been in the cellar. I'm never sure. It's infinity and a blink. But there's lots of talking. She tells me about her mother and Nicolai and her best friend Nina Bishop, and there's lots of sleeping, and dreaming, and praying, and lots of her hands on my hair, and my hands on her hair, and I'm happy.

"Nothing is really forever," I tell Penny when she wants to know how much longer it will be until Dad lets us out. "Time isn't what you think it is."

She tells me more about her family, and she says she hopes I can meet them one day.

"I want to. When it's safe."

"Right," she agrees. "When it's safe."

We're hungry again. She passes me a sleeve of round crackers, and I tear it open, but we have to say thank you first. Penny says it's very important to say thank you. Her molecules move through the air in a sweeping-swiping gesture.

"What are you doing?" I ask.

"Making the sign of the cross."

"How do you do it?"

She takes my wrist, shows me how to move my hand like hers, then I munch on buttery crackers while she eats something soft that smells like applesauce. We wash the food down with warm, pulpy orange juice, and then she's rustling the blankets and lying down.

I put my head on the pillow next to hers.

She breathes out.

I breathe in.

"Penny?"

"Yes?"

"Is Jesus really God's son?"

"Yes."

"Did God make him go on the cross?"

"Men," she says, with a sleepy sigh. "Men put him on the cross."

"But God let them?"

"Yes . . . he did it for us."

"But I didn't want him to do that."

"Do what?"

"Suffer."

"But he did. For us."

"Did God really put Lucifer in Hell because he argued?"

"Lucifer rebelled . . ." She yawns. "Against God."

"Why?"

"He thought he was equal to God. He had too much pride."

"Why don't they make up?"

"I don't know if they can."

"But Lucifer could say he's sorry. Or God could say I forgive you. Why can't they do that?"

"I don't know."

"What if Jesus does something really bad? Will God send him away, and then he'll become the Satan of his own Hell? What if he teams up with Lucifer, and then it would be two against one?"

"Maybe we should get some rest. I think it's late."

"Or maybe it's early. Maybe the sun is out."

"Yes . . . maybe."

But I hear her weariness, so I say, "We can sleep."

Her exhale is heavy. "Good night, Daniel."

"Good night, Penny."

I move my head so that it's touching hers, but I'm afraid to sleep.

What if the Son does something the Father can't forgive?

She says her real name is Penelope, but her brother calls her Penny, and her brother's real name is Nicolai, but she calls him Nickel. She says her mom and dad didn't choose the names on purpose—it just happened that way.

"You have a father?" I say.

"Yes. But . . ."

"What?"

"He died."

I squeeze her soft hand. "I'm sorry."

"Daniel, my mom needs me. She really needs me."

I squeeze her hand tighter, and she tells me a memory. About her first day of middle school and how her mother fixed her hair in a long french braid down her back. She says her mother's an artist at fixing hair.

I smile. "My mom liked to fix my hair too. Mostly she'd take me to someone who'd do it. A lady . . . but I can't think of her name."

"Your mom? But didn't you say . . . ?"

"What?"

"It's just . . . never mind."

+ + +

Penny's favorite weather is Rainy. Her favorite season is Spring. She loves to be Outside.

"I'm not allowed to go outside," I say.

"Not ever?"

"Not ever."

"But, Daniel . . . that's not right."

"He has to keep me hidden."

"Why?"

Now I'm cold cold cold. She holds on to me as I shiver.

"It's not right for him to keep you down here."

She doesn't understand. She thinks bad things about my father that aren't true.

"We have to tell someone."

My teeth start to chatter.

"Daniel, I need you to listen to me." Her fingernails stroke my scalp, and it feels so good my body goes limp. "Your father . . . he came into the restaurant where I work."

"What do you do in the restaurant where you work?"

"I wait tables. Now listen. Your dad came in and—"

"What food did he get?"

"Daniel, *listen*."

I huff. I want to know what he ate.

"So I was waiting on him, and he asked me if I knew of anyone who might be able to watch his son."

"Me."

"Yes. I told him about Nicky and how good I am with kids, and then my shift ended as he was leaving, so we walked out to the parking lot together."

There are knots in my stomach. I whimper. Penny keeps stroking my hair.

"I was giving him my phone number and . . ." Her breath hitches. "He grabbed me. He—he injected me with something."

I shake my head. No. No. No. He's not a bad man.

"Daniel, he kidnapped me, and he's locking you in this room. We have to get out."

"But we can't."

"Yes, we can. When he comes back, we have to do something."

"Something?"

"We have to overpower him."

"How?"

"We wait at the door, and when he opens it . . ."

"We *hurt* him?"

"We have to get away."

I start to cry. "You want me to hurt my father?"

"I just want to go home!"

Ripping my hand from hers, I scuttle deeper into the darkness.

"Daniel, listen to me—"

"No! You *are* a monster."

"Daniel, please."

"NO!"

I pull my helmet over my head.

No thoughts.

No sounds.

Nothing.

Nothing.

Nothing.

In infinity and a blink, I hear rustling bags. I hear the thank-you prayer and crunching and drinking, then Penny says, "Daniel? Are you hungry?"

I don't answer. I'm still angry with her, but I also want to be next to her with my head on her lap and her hand in my hair. I crawl toward her, then crawl away again.

"Daniel . . ."

My body turns in her direction.

"I'm sorry," she says.

I crawl closer.

"I won't talk about that again. Okay, Daniel?"

I touch her arm, and she lets me rest my head on her thigh. She strokes my hair, pushing it off my forehead and down around my ear.

"I'm sorry too." I reach up, touching her face with my fingertips. Her cheeks are wet. "I'm *very* sorry. I don't want you to cry."

"It's okay, we're okay. Friends again?"

"Yes. Friends."

"Good. Now are you hungry?"

When I nod, she presses a cookie into my palm. I take a bite and grimace. It's *oatmeal*. I don't like oatmeal, but I'm hungry so I eat it. Penny keeps petting my hair while I chew, but her fingers go still at the creaking noise over our heads.

"Daniel?" Her voice trembles.

"No," I tell her, sitting up quickly. "It's a *good* noise!"

Bootsteps are descending the stairs.

The door swings open, and there's a blinding triangle of light.

"Come on up," my father's voice calls out.

I help Penny stand, and we ascend the stairs together. My eyes are remembering how to make sense of the light, but I recognize my father's silhouette, and I throw myself into his arms.

"I missed you I missed you I missed you," I say into his shoulder.

He lets out a soft sigh. "I missed you too."

I turn to Penny. We're blinking at one another, *seeing* one another for the very first time. She has long dark hair, brown eyes, and round cheeks.

She's so beautiful.

She's wiping at the moisture beneath her eyes when suddenly they grow wide, and her lips part in a gasp. "*Sayers.*"

FIFTY

I'm at the table with my father and Penny, but I don't know how it happened. I remember standing at the top of the stairs when she said something—something *bad*—and then I was here.

Dad and me are in our usual seats, while Penny's in the rolling desk chair. None of us speak, just quietly chew our food. Hot food, not crackers or cookies, and it tastes good, except my stomach isn't used to this much. My vision's still blurry, but I can't stop watching Penny. In the cellar I could only see her in my imagination, but now she's real.

"Eat, Daniel," Dad orders, sounding sharper than he normally does when I get distracted.

I'm taking a bite when Penny says, "So . . ." Her voice is higher than it was in the cellar. "Now that you're back, I guess it's time for me to go home."

I sit up straight. "You're leaving?"

"No," my father says. "She's not."

Overcome with relief, my breath rushes out. "Good."

Penny studies her plate, her lips move like she's praying, then she lifts her head with a steady, peaceful gaze. "I can come back and watch Daniel any time you want. I wouldn't mind."

Dad stares at her with hard eyes. "Did my son tell you why he can't go out?"

"No."

"My priority is his safety."

"I understand," Penny says. "I want him to be safe too. I'd never do anything to . . ."

"To what?"

"Endanger me," I say.

"That's right." Dad smiles at me, and then he gives Penny a stern look. "You leaving here would *endanger* him."

"But I wouldn't—"

"The answer's no."

As soon as we finish dinner, I ask Dad, "Can I show Penny my room?"

His eyes narrow like he's going to say no, but then he nods, slowly. "I guess that'd be all right."

"Hooray! Come on, Penny."

She follows me to my bedroom, and I head straight to the Lego city I was building before Dad left, but then behind me there's that word again.

"*Sayers.*"

I spin around to face her.

"Sayers—Saye—I can't believe it's you—I can't believe it."

A sick-scared-cold tears down my spine. "N-no. My name is—"

"Your parents, they've been on the news, and your friend Luke—"

"*No.*"

I'm falling from the mountaintop now. I tap my temple with my fist, harder, *harder.*

Penny's eyes go wide. "I'm sorry. Just stop, okay?" She sounds frightened as she glances over her shoulder toward the doorway. "I—I want to see your things. Just show me your things." She grabs something off my shelf. "This! What's this?"

Slowly, I drop my fists from my head. "Window."

"Window?"

"It's *like* a window." I guide the viewfinder to her face. "Can you see it?"

"Yes."

"You can look at other places."

"It's . . . it's pretty."

"Daniel?" Dad's poking his head into my room. "Time for sleep now."

"Okay." I walk to my bed and pull back the covers. "You can have this side, Penny."

"No," Dad snaps in a hard voice. "She can't stay in here."

"Why not? In the cellar we—"

"Stop arguing with me, young man—and stop making that face."

I soften my frown.

"Now say good night, Daniel."

Penny's chest starts moving up and down in quick contractions, but I do as he tells me. "Good night, Penny."

And then I watch her leave with him.

When Dad returns, he drags his chair up to my bed. "So, the girl. Do you like her?"

"Yessir," I answer, cautious.

"That's good. I got her for you."

"Thank you. Where is she?"

"Downstairs."

A gasp falls from my mouth. "Did she do something wrong?"

"I just don't have a good place for her yet."

That doesn't make sense—there's the couch and my bed, and she'll be scared all alone in the cellar. But he's not acting like himself, so I'm afraid to argue.

"Dad . . . did something happen?"

"What d'you mean?"

"When you were gone."

His eyes go empty. "My father died."

"Oh no." Just like Penny's father. "I'm sorry." It's awful that a father can *die*. I don't know what I'd do if anything happened to mine.

"You're the last one," Dad says.

"The last one?"

"The last one with my blood."

I wake up thinking of Penny, and when I get to the living room, she's *there*. Sitting at the table with wet hair and dressed in my clothes. I run to her and sit close enough to smell the soap on her skin.

"Hi, Penny," I say, but she doesn't answer me.

Dad joins us at the table, and I eat waffles with lots of syrup while he drinks coffee, but I don't think Penny is hungry because she doesn't eat at all.

After I finish everything on my plate, Dad stands and grabs his thermos. "You remember what I told you."

"Sir?" But then I follow his gaze to Penny, who's nodding in slow motion.

Dad nods back at her, then pats the top of my head. "Be good today."

"I'm always good."

He humphs with a small smile, then he goes, closing the vault door behind him, and now I'm so excited I bounce on my feet.

"What should we do today, Penny?"

But she still doesn't answer me. I think she must be tired. The chain around her ankle is too short to reach the couch, so I start dragging the couch to her. One of its tiny wooden legs shakes, so I have to move it slowly, inch by fragile inch.

When it's finally near enough, I say, "You can lie down here."

She shuffles to her feet, and collapses onto the sofa. Her eyelids flutter closed the moment her head hits the throw pillow. Yes, she's very tired. I cover her up and listen to two entire movies before she wakes again.

"Are you hungry?" I ask.

Blinking slow, she nods.

Dad left us baloney-and-cheese sandwiches and a bag of Fritos. I fix us a plate and sit on the couch beside her. Penny makes the sign of the cross, so I do it too, then she picks at her lunch, slowly peeling the crust off her bread.

"Once you're feeling better, there are so many things we can do, Penny." I point to my stack of games and my crayons and watercolors and paper. "We'll have fun together, I promise."

"Okay," she says softly, and I'm happier than I've been in as long as I can remember.

It's just perfect, it's just bliss, it's just us.

"Did you move the couch?" Dad asks me the moment he walks through the door.

"Yessir. So Penny could sit with me."

He doesn't look pleased, but he unlocks her foot and lets us read books in my room while he cooks dinner. After we eat, the three of us sit on the couch in front of the TV, me in the middle, and I'm relaxed and happy and not sure whose body to lean on.

Once the movie ends, Dad says it's time for bed.

Fear races across Penny's face, and my stomach contorts into a twisty knot.

"Dad?"

"Hmm?"

"I don't think Penny should have to go back downstairs."

"Oh, is that right?" He scowls at me.

"Um . . . yessir."

Getting to his feet, he towers over me. "Is that for you to decide?"

My gaze flicks to Penny, then back at Dad. "No, sir. I guess not."

"You *guess* not?" He stares me down until I lower my eyes.

"I mean it's not."

Above me, Dad lets out a sigh. "She can sleep on the couch."

"She can? Thank you!" I throw my arms around his waist.

He nods and begins locking up her foot, so I hurry to my room and grab my favorite quilt and pillow, then run back to the living room. "Here, Penny."

She takes them from me, and I'm spreading my arms out wide when Dad grabs my bicep. "What do you think you're doing?"

"I was just gonna hug her—"

"Well, *don't*," he snaps, squeezing tighter.

I look over at Penny. She's watching all of this with big wide eyes. The moment Dad drops my arm, I run to my room and climb into bed. A second later, he storms in after me looking so angry I shrink into the headboard.

"Is this how it's gonna be now? You back-talking me all the time about that girl?"

My thumb drifts up to my mouth.

"Daniel . . ." His voice softens, and he runs a hand over his face. "I just don't want you getting too attached to her, that's all."

"Why not?"

"Because she's not gonna be around when things turn backward."

"I thought they already did turn backward."

"No . . . not yet."

"But what will happen to Penny when they do?"

"That isn't important. The only thing that matters is *me* and *you*."

$$\text{+ + +}$$

Penny is still quiet, so while Dad's at work, I try to think of something that will interest her. I show her my viewfinder and my Legos. I search the shelves for books.

"See this one?" I hold it up. "It's my favorite. *Languages of the World.* I'm learning them all. Do you speak any of these?"

"I . . . I speak Spanish."

"*¿De verdad?*" Excited, I grin at her. "*¡Yo también hablo español!*" I flip through the delicate pages. "The words are like a code. If you memorize this book, you can understand everyone."

"You learned to speak Spanish from that book?"

"Yes. How did you learn?"

"My father was from Guatemala. It's just your accent . . . that's hard to pick up from a book." Penny slowly explores the room, the chain dragging behind her, then she halts, her hand on the globe. "Have you traveled?"

"Traveled where?"

"Anywhere."

"I don't know."

She spins the globe, then stops it with the tip of her finger. "To Argentina?"

"I'm not sure."

She spins again. "To France?"

"Um . . ."

"To Italy?"

A million flashes now like I'm flipping through my viewfinder at warp speed. "Yes."

"What's it like?"

"I didn't *really* go. Only in my imagination."

She studies me with thoughtful eyes, then she spins the globe again. "Did you ever go to Iceland in your imagination?"

Goose bumps race up my arms. "I don't like cold places."

"It's not, not really."

"You've been there?"

"Only in my imagination." Her face is wistful. "My teacher showed us pictures of it in Geography. I used to think it was like Antarctica, but it's so beautiful and green. If we ever get the money, we're going there."

"You and me?"

"Well, I meant my mom and Nickel and me—but you can come too."

"Then I'll have to study! What language do they speak in Iceland?"

"Icelandic."

I laugh. She's teasing me.

"No, really," she insists, so I flip through my book.

"Oh! The letters are fascinating."

"They have a greeting," Penny says. "I don't know how to pronounce it, but in English it's *thanks for the last time.*"

I scan the pages, but I can't find that phrase. "It means hello?"

"Kind of. It's something you say to a friend when you see them again. It's like . . . you're remembering the last time you saw them, and you're saying, *Thank you for the last time we were together.*" Now she smiles at me, something gentle and sweet. "It's nice, isn't it?"

I smile back at her. "It is."

Penny and I sit at the table with piles of crayons and paper. She's drawing a little boy with brown hair and brown eyes. I'm drawing sailboats.

"Daniel?" she says my name without looking up.

"Yes?"

"Do you have a key?"

"A key?"

"To this." She sticks out her foot, rattling the chain and making me shudder. I'd almost forgotten it was there, and I want to pretend we're like the kids in the books with no chains.

"No. I don't have one."

"Do you know where the keys are?"

"Dad has them. Is that Nickel?"

She nods, adding more to the scene. A swimming pool surrounded by palm trees and pink flamingos. "Nicolai loves the water." Her lips lift in a candle flicker of a smile. "He still needs his floaties, but he . . . he's getting really close to jumping off the diving board. Psyching himself up, you know?" Now her eyes are welling up.

"Penny, what's wrong?"

"I have to get home to him."

"But Dad says you can't."

She wipes away the stray tear that's escaped down her cheek.

"Please don't be sad." My arms twitch—I wish I could hug her. "Maybe Dad will change his mind. He might let you go for a little while if it's not too far. Where is your home?"

"Laurel."

"Laurel? But that's not a real place."

"It is a real place. I *know* you. We went to the same school."

"What? No, we—"

"Please just listen. That man kidnapped you, and if we—"

"He didn't kidnap me. He rescued me!"

"And if we just *help* each other, we can get out."

"No!" I stand and cover my ears.

"Saye, please."

Now I'm shivery and queasy and dangling off the edge of a mountain. "Please *stop*!"

I sit on the floor and cry, and she sits at the table and cries.

A long while later I hear the chain sliding along the floor like a metal snake, and then I feel a hand on my head. I reach out just in case she's a ghost, then I jerk my hand away.

"I'm sorry," I say.

"It's okay."

"I'm not supposed to touch you. I'll get in trouble."

"It's okay," she tells me again. "We can have different rules when it's just us."

She sits on the floor beside me and lets me rest on her thigh. She pets my hair, and it's nice, like the cellar.

FIFTY-ONE

Penny tells me she wants to go into the Helping Fields. Those are the jobs where you help other people, like a counselor or a social worker or a doctor or a teacher.

"What do you want to do when you get older?" she asks.

"I'm not going to get older."

"Sa—Daniel, don't say that."

"But it's true." Dad's not home, but I lower my voice to a whisper. "You know how the bad people took me?"

"Yes?"

"Well, it's all gonna go backward."

"What is?"

"*Time.*"

"Time?"

"Yes. Soon I'll be ten years old again." When she gives me a puzzled look, I try to explain. "There are different kinds of time, and I'm in the wrong one. I have to go back to when the bad people took me."

Penny doesn't answer, just takes our lunches from their Ziploc bags and arranges them on paper plates. "Come and eat now."

I can tell she doesn't believe me, and it hurts my feelings, so I turn my back to her and lie on the floor with my viewfinder, aiming it at the ceiling. Sky—forest—ocean—

Penny plucks the viewfinder from my face.

"Come eat," she repeats, and I scowl at her.

"You don't believe me!"

"I just don't understand . . . but if you eat your lunch, you can tell me more about how time really works, okay?"

I'm still upset, but I nod. She gives my viewfinder back to me, and I hold it in my lap while we sit at the table. We make the sign of the cross and say thank you for our peanut butter and jelly sandwiches, and our apple juice and potato chips. After our meal, Penny kneels, so I kneel beside her and listen to her pray.

"Please, God. Please keep us safe. Please make Daniel well again."

"Penny . . . am I sick?"

After a long pause, she says, "Yes, in a way. But you're going to get better."

Penny is drawing her brother. Nicky, Nickel, Nicolai, with dark hair and mischief eyes.

"Can you tell me another funny story?" I ask.

She thinks it over, then she says, "Okay, I've got one."

Smiling, I stuff my crayon into my pocket, ready to listen.

"In Nicolai's preschool class, there's this huge dry-erase board on the wall with a sad side and a happy side. All the kids start out each day with their names on the happy side, but if they act up, the teacher will switch them over to the sad side. And if they're *really* bad, they get checkmarks by their name. So Nicky decided to make a chart for me and my mom. If one of us upset him, he'd put our name on the sad side, and he really thought it would shame us into doing what he wanted. Like if he didn't want to go to bed, he'd pull out his notebook and give us this look like, *Are you sure you want to go through with it?"*

Laughing, I imagine the scene.

"He's so funny. He's always memorizing new jokes and riddles, but he's also just, you know, naturally funny, and sweet and . . ." Her words trail off as tears well up in her eyes.

Penny is lying on the couch, her arms folded across her face.

"Come on, let's do something." I tug her hand.

"Not now. I need to think."

"Think about what?"

"Daniel . . ." She rolls over, away from me. "Why don't you go build something in your room and, when your dad gets home, I can come see it, all right?"

My shoulders slump. "All right."

I trudge to my room and add skyscrapers to my Lego city. Even though Penny's just down the hall, I'm lonely. If she left, this is what it would feel like all the time.

Suddenly overcome with fright, I run into the living room—and she's still here. She hasn't disappeared, she's just sleeping. Lowering myself to the floor, I lean against the side of the couch and wait for her to wake up.

+++

After supper, I ask Dad if we can play checkers.

"*All* of us?" He shoots Penny a dark look. "Checkers is a two-person game."

"I don't have to play," Penny says quickly.

"No, I want you to." I turn to Dad. "What about Parcheesi? Three people can play that game." But he doesn't answer, just stares at Penny who's staring at the floor, and something occurs to me. "Dad . . . don't you like Penny?"

She flinches. Dad does too—but he doesn't answer my question.

While Dad's at work, Penny and I sit on the couch listening to *Star Wars.*

"Daniel?" she says.

"Yes?"

"Why did the bad people take you?"

"To do experiments."

"What kind of experiments?"

"I . . . I'm not sure." Sometimes I try to remember, but it gives me a headache. "They took a lot of kids. For years and years they'd take them. They had plans to use them."

"Use them for what?"

"I . . ." I'm confused again. "It makes more sense when Dad explains it."

"But you thought they were your parents?"

"Yes. They made me think I was Saye."

"Sayers Wayte."

"Right." I laugh. "I can't believe I thought that was a real name."

"Do you remember things about them?"

"It's better if I don't think about it, then when we fall into the real time, it'll be easier."

"I see. But you do, don't you? You remember your house?"

"That wasn't my house."

"I mean the house where you lived."

My stomach gives an anxious twist. "My dad doesn't like me to talk about what happened when I wasn't here. He . . . he used to. He'd ask me questions about what they did to me, but he said it was mixing me up too much. Now he likes it better when we talk about all the good times we'll have when things turn back."

"But you and I have different rules when we're alone, right?"

She's looking into my eyes. I'm looking into hers. A yellow starburst circles each of her pupils like sunflowers.

"You promise not to tell Dad what I say?"

"I promise."

I take a shuddery breath. "I lived in a castle. There were lots of windows."

FIFTY-TWO

"Penny?" Kneeling in the dark beside the couch, I tap her hand.

She awakens instantly and sits up. "Shouldn't you be in your bed?"

"I can't sleep," I confess. "Can I tell you a secret?"

"Yes."

"You know how the bad people took me when I was ten years old?"

"Yes . . . ?"

"And the lady said she was my mom?"

Penny nods.

"Sometimes . . ." Scooting closer, I whisper into Penny's ear, "Sometimes I can remember her from *before* they stole me."

"You can?"

"Yes. I remember her when I was *seven*."

"What do you remember?"

"She'd been out of town, but she was going to pick me up from school when she got home, and I was so excited I could hardly stand it. All day, I wore a necklace. It looked like a broken heart." I draw the jagged line in the air with my index finger. "When school ended, I saw her in the pickup line out front. She was smiling through the window of our car, and I started running to her. There was a big sign in front of the school, but I didn't want to even take the time to run around it, so I tried to duck underneath, and I hit my head. I remember all the blood and the pain, and then the woman jumped out of her car and held me." Now I sigh. "But that isn't real. The bad people have devices. They can implant memories."

Penny squeezes my hand. "But what if it *is* real?"

Dad's at work. I'm drawing sailboats. Penny's drawing Nicolai. Sometimes she signs her drawings at the bottom of the page. *Penelope Valles.*

"You're a good artist, Penny."

She jumps as if she was inside her picture instead of this room, then she says, "Do you want me to draw you?"

The idea makes me feel shy, but I do want her to draw me, so I nod.

"Okay, scoot your chair back."

I do it, and as she draws, she glances from me to her page to me again.

My skin tickles. It's as if her eyes are stroking me, making shivers run down my body, but the shivers feel good. It's nice to be looked at so closely when the eyes are hers.

She switches crayons a few times—yellow, gold, tan, shades of green—and finally she says, "I'm done."

"Can I see?"

Nodding, Penny hands the paper to me, and I stare at it, stunned.

I don't know what I thought I'd look like. Ten years old? One hundred? But in this drawing, I'm somewhere in between. I get a flash of a boy in a dark suit and red tie, and now it's as if someone's pulling the lever on my viewfinder at rapid speed.

Convertibles—crowns—fires—*freezers*.

"No." I thrust the paper away. "That's not me."

When Penny kneels, I kneel beside her. We say thank you for our apple juice and chocolate-chip cookies. We make the sign of the cross.

"Penny, why do we have to kneel?"

"To humble ourselves."

As we continue praying, I imagine what I look like. The boy from her drawing and the one from my memories. Someone who won't exist when things spin backward. My hands will shrink. My body will too. I won't remember the castle with all the windows— and I won't remember Penny.

She prays, "In the name of the Father, and of the Son, and of the Holy Ghost. Amen."

"Penny, is God the Father?"

"And the Son and the Holy Ghost."

"I don't understand."

She closes her eyes for a moment like she's concentrating, and then she focuses her gaze on me. "The most important thing to understand is that God is love, in all different forms. And love is a force nothing can stop."

My hearts swells, imagining love so big that it fills me and Penny and everything.

"Penny, who do you love?"

"A lot of people. My mother . . . my brother . . ."

"Your father?"

"Yes. Very much."

"I don't think it's fair for him to die. It's not fair for such horrible things to happen."

"Bad things happen to everyone, but do you know what I think?"

"What?"

"The bad things are going to change you no matter what, and they can make you angry and bitter—or they can make you *better*."

"How do we know if the bad things will make us better or make us worse?"

She's concentrating again, her sunflower eyes nearly closed. "I think we get to choose."

After I help Dad wash the dishes, I find Penny perched on the edge of my bed, holding a drawing of Nicolai in her hands.

"Penny?"

She doesn't move, doesn't blink.

"Are you okay?"

She doesn't answer, but she's not okay, I know she's not.

And I know what I have to do.

My legs quake as I walk down the hall to where Dad is listening to the TV.

I sit on the couch beside him, and rest my head against his arm.

"Dad, can I ask you for something? It's really important."

"Really important, huh?" There's a smile in his voice. "What is it?"

"Can you let Penny go?"

He drags me up by my shoulders and looks me in the eye. "What'd she do?"

"N-nothing. I just think she should go back to her home now."

"You don't want her anymore? Is that what you're saying?"

"No." That's not true at all. I can't stand to imagine how lonely I'm going to be once she's gone. "It's just that she misses her family."

"Daniel, we *are* her family now."

"But you said when time goes backward, she won't be here."

"I know it's confusing, son." He sighs. "Just go on and get ready for bed."

I sigh too, but I say, "Okay," and trudge to my room, where Penny is still holding her picture of Nicolai.

I shower and put on my pajamas, but when I step out of the bathroom, she isn't there. I go into the living room to say good night, but she's not there either, only Dad, who's setting up the checkerboard.

"Let's play a coupla games before bed," he says.

I sit across from him, watching as he gathers the red checkers and passes them to me.

"Dad?"

"Yes, son?"

"Did you change your mind?"

"About what?"

"Did you let her go?"

He makes a scoffing noise. "Of course not. She's downstairs."

"What—*why*?"

"Is that any of your business?"

"It is if it's my fault."

His eyes snap to mine, and I quickly look away.

"She's not supposed to be talking about those people. If she does it again, you tell me. Understand?"

I don't answer, just tap my red checker into the tabletop in a hard, steady beat.

"*Daniel*."

"I understand."

When Penny is finally let out, her eyes are dazed, and I wonder if that's how I look when I come up from the cellar. We're allowed to play games in my room, but she's quiet, removed, and after a while, she falls asleep.

I get a book from my shelf, then climb into bed and turn the pages extra quiet so I don't bother her. I read some, but mostly watch her. The way her cracked lips keep parting as if she's talking in her sleep. The way her long lashes flutter against her cheeks like scared butterflies.

Eventually, she wakes and blinks up at me. Her eyes are lovely, but vacant.

"Penny . . ." I hold her hand, stroking my thumb against her rough-dry palm. "I'm gonna miss you."

Her lashes flutter again, then something sparks in her irises. "Miss me?"

"Yes. When you go home."

"I'm not going home. He said—"

"I know what he said," I whisper, then sneak a nervous glance at the hall. "We have to keep it a secret . . . but I'm going to help you."

FIFTY-THREE

Penny takes a deep breath, then she joins her palms in front of her face like she's praying.

It's been a long time since I said I'd help her, and whenever we're alone, we think up plans. Penny suggested we find whatever Dad used to incapacitate her, that the drug has to be here somewhere, but I don't believe it actually exists. It sounds like something one of the bad scientists would have, not my father.

I told Penny I could distract him while she slips away, but she said it wouldn't work. We need his keys, and even if by some miracle we got them, Dad would notice too quickly that she was gone. "And besides," Penny said, "we have to go together."

"We'll think of something," I tell her, and she takes in another deep breath.

"Have you ever seen him with a cell phone?" She's asked me this question before.

"No, I don't think so."

"I wish we had our shoes—it would make it so much easier to run."

"Maybe the ground will be smooth."

"But it might be covered in rocks. Are you sure you don't have any idea where we are? Or how close we are to anyone?"

"I don't know."

She's asked me this question before too.

She's beginning to look weary, and although it's not the vacant expression she had before, it's not the glimmery-alive face she had when we first started planning.

"We'll keep thinking," I promise.

I really do wanna help, but I'm afraid. If this all goes wrong, there's a part of me that knows my punishment will be much worse than the cellar. It's a cold thought at the periphery of my mind, like how it feels when you see something out of the corner of your eye, but when you turn, nothing's there.

I shiver just as Penny sits up straight, her eyes alight.

"I have an idea."

FIFTY-FOUR

When we hear the bell, Penny squeezes my hand. The locks tumble and time slows down as the door glides open. My father enters the room, looking hot and out of sorts.

I feel waves of nerves, waves of sorrow.

"Hi, Dad." I hop up from my chair just like Penny and I practiced.

He nods in my direction, and the moment he unlocks Penny's ankle, I collapse to the floor.

"Daniel!" He drops the cuff and rushes to me. "What's wrong?"

"I don't know." Grabbing my skull like it hurts, I tell him, "I think I'm just light-headed."

He holds his fingers to my throat for a moment, then slides an arm under my knees and another under my shoulders, lifting me up and laying me on the couch.

"Rest for a little while." His eyes are full of worry, full of love.

As I'm lying here, I listen to my father and Penny in the kitchen. They never talk to each other, but their sounds are different. Her movements are delicate while his are rough, and the soft and hard motions clash in the soundscape until they're bringing in plates of sandwiches and slices of fruit.

Before we eat, Penny prays in her head and in my head too.

My gaze drifts downward, under the table where the cuff is lying on the floor, still open wide like a hungry mouth and not all that far from my father's foot.

I clench my paper napkin, and then I let it fall. Bending to retrieve it, the top half of my body disappears beneath the table. Time's moving very slow and very fast all at once as I take hold of the cuff and close it around Dad's ankle.

He doesn't even notice. I'm able to slip back into my seat and pick up my sandwich.

I take a slow bite, let the bread soften on my tongue.

Then like an explosion, he surges up so fast his chair clatters to the ground. He stares down in disbelief for a few seconds, then looks back and forth between me and Penny, his face flashing shock—rage—shock—rage.

With a growl, he swoops his hand into his pocket and yanks out the key ring. Penny makes a frightened noise and grabs the chain, hauling him off balance.

The keys slip from his fingers and bounce across the floor.

Penny chases after them.

So does Dad.

But Penny's closer. Grasping them in her hands, she runs to the open vault door, and I'm right behind her when Dad's fist snags my collar.

I let out a wet, choking noise, and Penny spins around. "Sayers!"

She takes my outstretched hands. *Pulls.*

My T-shirt rips down my back, and we're propelled like a sling-shot through the vault door. Dad's bellowing after us as we take a hard left and dash down the tangle of halls. We reach the next metal door. Penny's fingers tremble as she jams one of the keys into the lock.

It doesn't fit.

She tries again.

Doesn't fit.

Again.

I take the key ring from her—my hands are steadier—and I start punching them into the lock one by one. Dad's still roaring, making me and the whole house tremble.

"What if he gets loose?" Penny watches the hall with giant, scared eyes.

"He won't." If he knew some trick to get out, he'd already be out.

I insert another key, and this time, it's a perfect fit.

I go still.

This is it.

All that's left to say is, "Goodbye, Penny."

"What?"

I turn around to face her. "I can't go."

She shakes her head. "Saye, no—you have to come with me—you have to—"

"I can't, Penny. I can't leave him."

"But I—"

"You promise you won't tell anyone? About where we are?"

"But we *both* have to go. We have to—"

A cacophony of noise explodes in the living room, scraping metal and splintering wood, and I'm terrified he's found a way out after all.

"Please, Penny."

She starts to cry, but she's nodding too. "O-okay."

"Go. Hurry." I spin around and race through the halls.

Behind me, I hear the door open.

And then I hear it close.

FIFTY-FIVE

I walk like a zombie.

I'm at a loss.

Tears are falling down my face. I wipe them with my palms as I return to the living room, where Dad is pacing around the broken chair and overturned table. He comes to a sharp halt when he sees me. His whole body goes limp with relief, but then he tenses up all over again.

"Where is she?"

"Gone." The word breaks.

"Daniel." A hushed furious voice. "What have you done?" He charges at me. "What have you *done!*"

I scramble backward, managing to stay just out of reach.

"Daniel . . ." Now his voice is level. "You bring me my keys right this minute, and I'll go easy on you. I know this was her idea."

Slowly, I shake my head.

Jaw dropping, he backs away from me, then he grabs hold of the chain with two hands and pulls. His muscles and veins bulge, and I'm afraid he might be strong enough to yank it from the floor.

But the chain doesn't give, just like it never gave for me.

"I'm sorry, Dad. She misses her family."

"She'll lead those kidnappers right back here!"

"She promised me she wouldn't do that."

"Oh, really? She *promised*?" he snarls, sarcastic, but he's starting to sound more frightened than anything. "If she tells someone . . . Daniel, they'll find you. Is that what you want? Those monsters finding you? Taking you again, doing more experiments?"

"No . . ." I don't want that. The idea is terrifying.

"Then please, son. Give me my keys."

FIFTY-SIX

Dad's yelling behind me as I slink into the kitchen. I toss the key ring onto the countertop and sit crisscross on the floor. Covering my ears, I stare at the stove where the clock used to be.

Penny is somewhere in the Outside Darkness.

Minutes feel like years.

Time is not what it seems.

I'm in a strange stupor when I realize Dad has gone silent.

Climbing to my feet, I peek into the living room. He's still pacing, but his gait is wobbly and sweat's pouring over his face.

"D-Dad?"

He pants, "Water."

I run into the kitchen and grab a bottle. I start to bring it to him, then change my mind and roll it along the floor instead. He gives me a hurt look, but he uncaps it with a shaky hand and chugs it. Now he looks close to tears, and I hate it.

"I'm sorry, Dad."

"They're gonna find you. She'll tell 'em where we are, and they'll find you and make you forget me again."

"She won't."

"You're a stupid, stupid boy to believe that." His feet twitch like he's about to rush me again. "They'll kill me the moment they get here. Do you want to see your father *killed*?"

"No . . ."

"Then unlock me!"

But I don't move, and such a horrible expression of betrayal crosses his face that I can't look at him anymore. As I turn for the kitchen, Dad starts screaming after me—that I've doomed us both, that we're as good as dead.

I put on my helmet and fade away.

When I come back, a thousand years have passed. I climb to my feet on stiff legs and find my father on the living room floor clutching his chest, a ropelike vein bulging under his left eye.

"Dad!" I run to him—and he springs forward and snags my ankle.

Thrown off-balance, I fall to the floor hard, jarring my elbows and spine. Pain knocks the wind out of me, but before I can catch my breath, he drags me to him by my ankle and shoves his hands in my pockets, turning them inside out.

"Where are they?" he shouts.

"W-what?"

He flips me onto my stomach and searches my back pockets, then he flips me over again. "The keys! Where are they?"

I dig my bare feet into the floor and try to scoot away, but he pins me with one hand splayed across my chest, then he lifts his other hand high into the air and brings it down across my face.

A lightning crack of pain under my jaw and into my ear.

"*Dad—*"

He hits me again.

Tasting blood in my mouth, I let out a moan. My ears ring, and my eyes blur, and I'm curling into myself when he grabs my shirt-front and yanks me to a sitting position.

"Get those keys!" he shouts right in my face.

"Please listen. I—"

His palm crashes into my face a third time. "NOW! NOW! NOW!"

I start to cry. "*Okay.*" And I try to move, but he's still gripping onto my torn shirt.

"Promise me if I let you go, that's what you're gonna do. You're going straight to those keys and bringing them to me." When I nod, he shakes me. "*Say* it!"

"I promise!"

He climbs to his feet, lifting me along with him, and he shoves me in the direction of the kitchen. I stumble, nearly trip, but I steady myself.

Sniffing and wiping my eyes, I grab the keys off the counter and edge back into the living room, but then I halt.

What if she needs more time?

"Daniel." His eyes are like magnets, simultaneously drawing me to him and pushing me away. "You promised."

I hesitate a few seconds more.

"Daniel!"

I close the space between us, and he rips the key ring out of my hand. With quick sharp flicks of his wrists, he unlocks himself and flings the cuff onto the ground as if it disgusts him, then he glares at me as if *I* disgust him, and snatches his boots off the floor.

"You're leaving?"

"Of course I'm leaving. I'm going after her. And Daniel?"

"Y-yessir?"

"You'd better pray I find her."

FIFTY-SEVEN

Dad told me to pray he'd find her, but I'm praying he doesn't.

My face throbs, and my spine is aching from when I fell, but I kneel and make the sign of the cross and pray, "Please, God. Let Penny be home with Nicolai and her mother and her best friend. Please please please."

I'm still on my knees when the bells ring over my head.

And I pray.

The locks tumble.

And I pray.

The door scrapes open.

And I pray.

Dad is towering like a mountain. For a moment, he's all I can see. A dark alien-esque silhouette in the threshold of the door. But then he steps inside, with Penny dangling over his shoulder.

I'm crushed, like something stomped under a boot.

She's bruised and unmoving, as if—

"Is she . . . ?"

And then her lips part, and I hear the quietest of breaths.

Thank you.

Thank you.

Thank you.

Relief fills me up like the air in a balloon until Dad's glare deflates me. He adjusts Penny's weight over his shoulder and barks, "Get to your room and shut the door."

But I can't move.

What is he going to do to her?

"I swear to God if you don't listen to me . . ."

Climbing to my feet, I hurry to my room, then press my ear to my door—straining to hear him, to hear her, to hear *anything*—but all my ears can latch on to is silence.

A million years pass before my bedroom door opens.

I blink as if he left me in the dark.

Dad doesn't speak, just curls his hand in a beckoning gesture, and I follow him down the hall, where the table is set for two.

It hurts to walk, it hurts to sit, it hurts to touch the spoon to my lip, but I do all of these things, and I don't complain.

"Dad?" I push my food around on my plate. "I'm really sorry."

He lifts his head in the smooth, indifferent movement of a machine, looking at me in a way he never has before. "Are you?"

"Yes."

"I kept thinking about what you did. Kept thinking about all the times you musta lied to me to plan something like that."

I shake my head, but it's true. I can't deny it.

"I kept going over and over it, and I remembered something. She called you *Sayers*." He looks me dead in the eye. "Did you tell her that was your name?"

"No, I told her I'm not him, but she wouldn't believe I'm Daniel."

"That's because you're not."

My throat closes shut. "W-what?"

"You're not my son."

It's like a punch to the solar plexus. Instantly, my eyes flood with tears. "Dad—"

"Don't call me that."

He's the coldest cold. The darkest dark. If God is love, and love is a force, then this is the absence, the vacuum, the empty.

"Dad, please."

"I said don't call me that! You are *not* my son. You never were."

Burying my face in my hands, I start to cry. "Why are you saying that? Why are you saying that?"

"'Cause I'm finally seeing you for what you really are."

He rises, and coldness takes hold of my arm.

Coldness pulls me from my chair.

Coldness leads me through the pocket door, and a strange series of images fill my head. It's me. No, a circle of me's—and we're all standing like statues in the snow. We can't move, we can't speak, and our eyelashes glitter with ice.

FIFTY-EIGHT

My sobs move me forward in jagged steps, and I crumble to the cellar floor.

Penny's voice appears beside me. "What happened? Are you all right?" Her long hair brushes against my cheeks

"H-he says I'm n-not his son. He says I'm not Daniel."

I feel her breath on my ear. "But you *aren't* Daniel."

For a long time I live in a different kind of darkness. I'm not anyone anymore, and maybe this is how it feels after you die or before you're born. You *used* to exist. Or you're *waiting* to exist. Only I'm less like a soul that needs a vessel, and more like a vessel that needs a soul.

And then there are fragments.

A girl's voice. One that's soft, kind, *good*. And the hollow is beginning to fill up with new memories. Not Daniel's. Not Saye's. But hers. Memories of a lovely life with a mother, and a brother, and a best friend, and a God.

✦✦✦

"Nicolai always carries a pocketful of pennies to the park," the girl's voice is saying. "He likes to toss them in the fountain. As soon as we get close, he lets go of my hand and runs to it. He throws a bunch of pennies right away, but he always saves some so I can watch him and tell him how good he is at throwing."

"What's that expression? *I never met a stranger?* That's Nicolai—he's never met a stranger. We'll go to the mall, and all the managers at all the stores know him. Everyone loves him and . . ."

"We have a big front porch. Mom has it covered in potted plants and flowers. In the springtime the perennials bloom in our garden—those are the flowers that die and come back."

". . . and if it's cold, we get hot chocolate, me and my best friend Nina. We'll spend the whole afternoon just wandering the bookstore. I usually get romance novels, and we'll make fun of the covers. Well, mostly Nina does that. She'll read the descriptions on the back out loud, and I always get so embarrassed. But she says we can't worry about what anyone thinks . . ."

"My dad was so funny. And kind. He was one of those people who can make friends with anyone. He and Nicky would've made such a team. Sometimes I dream of how they'd be together. When we . . ."

". . . go to Mass every Sunday. I always feel better when I leave. Like I'm renewed. But taking walks outside is when I *really* feel

God. It's like I can connect to him more deeply when . . ."

". . . we go to a big movie theater in Dallas. But usually we go to the Rialto in Laurel. I love how it's so old. I like the—"

"Balcony seats."

I hear a sharp intake of breath.

"Yes," she says after a long pause. "They have balcony seats."

Penny presses a cracker against my mouth. "Come on, just a bite?"

But I can't eat.

She holds a plastic bottle to my mouth, pours juice past my lips, and images come to me in broken flashes. A car with no lid. A hazel-eyed girl in the passenger seat. A boy in the back who looks like me. Did I make them up, or did I really know them?

The memories battle out in my head.

Penny wants to hear all my favorites.

Favorite flower?

"Who has a favorite flower?"

Favorite song?

"I don't know any songs."

Favorite day of the week?

"Every day is the same."

Favorite color?

Daniel's is blue. Saye's is red. And mine?

"I don't know."

+ + +

"Okay, now you ask me."

"What?" My voice comes out dazed.

"Ask me my favorites."

I chew a cookie into dust.

"Saye?"

I'm so tired.

But I ask, "What's your favorite flower?"

"Hyacinth. My mom has a garden, and she always cuts the hyacinths for me. Do you know what they smell like?"

"No."

"They smell like *happiness*." After a silence she says, "Ask me another one."

It takes so much energy to think of questions, but I squeeze my eyes shut, and it's like there are bits of strength stored in your cells if you search. "What's your favorite color?"

"Green," she says. "What's yours?"

My mind statics, pulses, blinks.

In the dark, voices have colors, and Penny's is: "Yellow."

I feel her smile. "Keep going."

"Favorite song?"

"I have too many to name them all, but I love old music—you know, like the Supremes, and Simon and Garfunkel, and Cyndi Lauper. I grew up hearing that kind of music with my mom in the car."

After another silence, she taps my arm, so I ask, "Favorite day?"

"Sunday."

"Yeah?" My voice comes out dull. "I heard most people hate

Sundays even worse than Mondays."

"Where did you hear that?"

Another static rush. My mind blurs, and I don't know if I actually heard it or if I just made it up. "I don't want to talk anymore."

More visions. Me behind the wheel of a red car. Only I'm too young to drive. Unless she's right and I really am Saye. She's good and kind and wouldn't lie, so it must be true. I'm Saye with a mother and a house full of windows.

But that would mean Dad is lying, and he wouldn't do that either.

Unless somehow I'm Daniel *and* Saye. Why do I have to be only one?

"We're out of food," Penny says.

"He'll bring us more. If he changes his mind . . . If he lets me be Daniel again."

Penny squeezes my hand. "You're Saye, remember? Sayers Wayte."

"Right."

Unless I'm both.

There's a noise over our heads. Creaking floorboards under the weight of boots, and then a triangle of light as the door swings open.

A tall silhouette fills the threshold.

"Boy," he says. "Come with me."

FIFTY-NINE

I drink in the light and the colors and his face, overcome with relief despite all my fear and all my questions. *Who am I? Who am I now?*

We sit at the table.

His face is dry and cracked like the desert soil that needs rain.

I touch his arm.

He jerks away.

I set my hands in my lap.

After a long silence, he says, "I'm sorry."

My breath catches with hope and love and—

"But I can't keep you."

And now my heart's pounding in a strange, skipping pattern that makes me cough.

"You have to understand. I need to find my real son before it's too late. There isn't much time."

"But I *am* your real son." Now that we're together, I'm almost sure of it.

He looks sick with grief. "I wish that was true."

It is, it *is*. Why won't he believe me? "But even if I wasn't, why couldn't you keep both of us?"

"You mean . . . even after I find Daniel?"

"Yes. We could all live here together."

His face stills as if he's thinking about this.

Then like water doused on electronics—he fizzles out.

I stumble to the cellar sink and drink from cupped hands until the water sloshes around my belly, nearly convincing me I'm full. I splash more water on my flushed cheeks before lying down beside her.

"Are you okay, Penny?"

She nods into my shoulder, but I'm hungry, so I know she must be hungry too. We've already scavenged every discarded box. We licked the crumbs from inside plastic bags, drank the last drops of juice, but I crawl over to the sacks and dig through them again as if there could be a hidden compartment in the bottom of a paper sack.

"He'll bring more food, Penny. I know he will." But I don't really know anything.

I lie down beside her, my face on my arm, and I mouth my skin, not biting really, just chewing to chew, while Penny prays.

"Is that real?"

"Yes." There's a hopeful catch in Penny's voice. "I smell it too."

We crawl toward the scent and smack into bowls. Moments later, our slurping noises are the only sounds as we devour the meaty broth and potatoes. My stomach's stretching to let the food in, and I'm eating so fast I barely taste it when there's a crash of wood against stone—the door's been thrust open so hard it hit the wall.

My bowl is torn from my hands. Penny lets out a startled cry— he took her bowl too. Then the door slams shut, and I can still taste stew on my tongue.

"*Why?* Why did he do that?"

Penny doesn't answer.

We curl together, the scent of stew hanging in the air. My gut burns with unsated hunger.

I'm not sure how much time has passed when Penny lets out a pained whimper.

"Sayers . . . I don't feel so good."

"What's wrong?"

She gags, and there's the wet noise of vomit hitting the floor. The odor of bile fills the air, and now I'm starting to feel queasy too. I pet Penny's back, my heart beating wildly until I have to scramble to my feet.

I make it to the toilet just in time to throw up. My knees crash into concrete and my head throbs like my brain's slamming against my skull. I've never felt pain like this, not ever.

We take turns vomiting into the toilet.

We take turns lying on the floor.

Sometimes one of us is well enough to pet the other and say, "I'm here."

And sometimes we just lie next to each other without saying anything at all.

I'm resting on my right arm and hip, my knees pulled to my chest, sweat cooling on my forehead and upper lip. Penny's beside me, the odor of our bodies unpleasant. Our fingers touch. There have been longer and longer stretches between being sick, and I hope we're getting better.

"The food," she says. "He must've . . . poison."

"No. He wouldn't do that."

But I know she's right, and so I cry again.

It's later when something occurs to me. My body is tired and empty, but somewhere inside there is a spark of hope. "He changed his mind."

"What?" Penny says.

"He took the food away. He didn't *really* want to hurt us. That's good, right? That he changed his mind."

"Yes," Penny agrees, sounding tired. "That's good."

Now that the nausea has finally passed, the hunger returns, a gnawing desperate thing.

"Penny, I'm scared."

"Don't be afraid. We're not alone in here."

I shiver. "Ghosts?"

"No. *God.*"

She pulls me to sit up, facing her. "You can't see him, but you can feel him." She finds my fingers in the dark, and we hold hands where our knees meet. "Can you feel him?"

I press my forehead against Penny's. We're breathing, soft and quiet and close, and it's nice, but . . . "All I feel is you."

I'm awoken by a rustling noise, and then the closing of a door. Edging toward where I heard the sound, I smack into paper sacks.

"Penny! He brought more food."

She doesn't answer, but I know what she's feeling because I feel it too. We're afraid to eat, but we're so hungry we know we're going to try.

We pray before we take our first bite.

We pray before we take one more.

We've eaten entire boxes of crackers, finished whole bottles of water, and our stomachs don't hurt, our heads don't ache. As we start to feel stronger, Penny's memories fill the dark.

"I love school," she's saying. "Well, parts of it anyway. I like it when I have friends in my classes. Who was your all-time favorite teacher?"

"I'm not sure . . ."

"Mine was Ms. Turner, third grade."

"She was nice?"

"Yes, really nice. Do you remember the third grade?"

"I think so. There was a boy . . . on my baseball team. He'd moved here from Wyoming. We . . . we liked planet stuff, and I helped him."

"Helped him how?"

"I . . . I don't know." Is that Daniel's memory or is it mine? "Everything's all mixed up. It's too hard to remember what really happened."

"Okay," she says thoughtfully. "Then let's pretend."

Today, Penny wants to go to Iceland.

"I don't like the cold."

"But it's green," she says. "So green." Penny loves things that are green.

So we imagine we're there. We explore lagoons and emerald cliffs, and at night we stand on black sand beaches and stare up at the aurora borealis.

"Penny, what's that thing they say in Iceland when they see an old friend?"

"Hmm?"

"When they want to remember the last time they were together?"

"Thanks for the last time."

"Right . . . thanks for the last time."

We keep pretending. We visit castles and ruins, we see oceans and rainforests, we planet hop. Penny and I are time travelers and astronauts. We can go anywhere we want.

"Sayers, do you know where I want to go today?"

"Where?"

"Home."

"Home?"

"To Laurel." Penny interlocks her fingers with mine. "Is that okay?"

"Yes." I nod. "That's okay."

"Look, this is my street. Cedar Way. Do you see those two huge trees—how they're wrapped together like they're hugging?"

"Yes, I see them."

"And this is my house." She describes the yellow slats of wood, the cottage-style front porch.

"It's pretty."

"And this is my favorite movie theater."

"The Rialto."

"Yes."

We glide down the red-carpet aisle. The velvet curtain parts, and light from the projector shines against us, flashing our silhouettes into giants onto the screen. We exit the theater, bursting out into the fresh sunny air and stroll down sidewalks.

"This is my school," Penny says.

"What does it look like?"

"Can't you see it?"

"A little . . ."

"It's red brick. There's a statue of the mascot out front. What do you think it is?"

"I don't know."

"Guess, Saye."

I think and think. "A lion?"

"Yes." Penny smiles. "It's a lion."

"Favorite holiday?" Penny asks.

"Christmas. Dad lets me stay up late and listen to movies."

"And when you were Saye?"

When I was Saye? "We'd have huge parties. The house was beautiful. My family would come over and sometimes friends too. Only I can't remember their names."

"Luke Solomon. He's your best friend."

"Right. That's right." But the world outside is a blur. She remembers it better than I do. "What's your favorite holiday, Penny?"

"Mine is Christmas too. I took this picture of Nicolai last year. He was dressed as a lamb for the nativity pageant. I love that photo so much. It's on my phone. I wish you could see it."

"I *can*."

In my mind, I see it perfectly.

Penny loves the rain. She loves raincoats and rain boots and the sound it makes as it hits windows and roofs. She loves going out into it and getting wet, and she loves coming back inside and changing into warm clothes.

"Should we go out, Penny?"

"Yes, for a few minutes. Let's put on our raincoats."

I open the hall closet and pull mine on. It's yellow like Penny's voice.

I ask, "Are you ready?"

"I'm ready." She opens the front door and together we walk outside.

Bright yellow sunlight shines against my eyelids.

"Oh." I breathe out. I feel it. We're really here.

"It smells so good."

"Yes," I agree. "Like springtime. Like hyacinths."

The rain pelts our umbrella. Penny spins it over our heads, she tosses it aside, we get wet. Laughing, we dash inside and change into dry clothes, and we cuddle under all our soft blankets.

We're not down there, we're up here.

We can go anywhere, but for a long time we've been veering toward the familiar. The Rialto with the balcony seats. Penny's house, her front porch and back garden. I taste her mother's coconut cake and homemade bread. I help pick flowers and arrange them in a tall vase in the living room. She shows me her wall of family photos. She loves her family so much.

"I don't think I ever loved anyone," I confess.

"You did. You *do*. You're just confused. This—this is confusing."

"I'm not confused."

"Then you're not remembering it right. Your parents, your friends. I'm sure you loved them."

"Yes . . . I did. But it wasn't the same. It felt like a thing you *have* instead of something you *do*. And I was always so . . . empty."

"Maybe it just seems that way because of how you're feeling now. I learned that in my Psychology class. Like when you're sad, you easily remember all the times you felt sad."

"But that would mean I'm feeling an absence of love in an absence of love."

"What do you mean?"

"I'd view my *before* as lack of love because I feel a lack now, but I don't. I feel more love than I ever have." I grip her hand. It's only now that I notice how small it is, much smaller than mine. "I love you, Penny, I mean it. I really love you."

She exhales a deep exhale and lets me rest my head on her thigh while she cards her fingers through my hair. I'm almost asleep when her hand stills.

A triangle of light is shining across the room.

"D-Dad?" My voice trembles.

But he doesn't answer, and instead of me—he takes Penny.

SIXTY

Alone in the dark, nothing exists but fear.

What will he do?

He might hurt her.

He *did* hurt her. He starved her. He put something in her food. He almost killed her.

The sudden fury is like a gift, feeding and familiar. My skin's hot as I crash into walls, smack my head into stone. Heat's blasting from my soul—I'll eviscerate anything I touch.

This goes on and on until a light glows under the door, and just like that, the fear is back, crushing my anger into nothing.

I hear footsteps.

No, *two* sets of footsteps are coming down the stairs.

The door swings open. Closes.

"Penny?"

"I'm here."

Frantic, I crawl to her, and we wrap our arms around each other. "I was so afraid you weren't coming back." Even though I'm holding onto her, I'm still scared she might dissolve under my hands. "What happened? Did he hurt you?"

"I'm okay, I'm okay." Then she's whispering, "Saye . . . I love you too."

I feel hot tears against my face, hers or mine or both.

I love you, I love you, I love you.

Later I ask Penny, "What did he want?"

For a moment she doesn't answer, and then, "He's mixed up. He's not sure who you are. He wants you to be Daniel."

"But I'm not."

"No."

"I told him if he really loves you, he has to let you go."

My thumbs trace her eyebrows, stroke her cheeks. "I'm sorry, Penny. I'm so sorry I didn't go with you before. If I did—"

"But you didn't. And if you didn't, then you weren't meant to."

"That's what you think? That this was meant to happen?"

"I trust that God is guiding this."

"But how? How can God exist in this?"

"God exists everywhere."

"Even here?"

"*Especially* here."

First we run out of food.

My stomach cramps so intensely that it's impossible to pretend we're anywhere else.

And then nothing will come out of the faucet.

My mouth's dry and sticky. The cellar's a boiling pot with no water, but we keep holding on to each other even though it makes our skin hotter.

"Saye—that picture on my phone, the one of Nicolai." Penny's tone is distraught and frantic in a way I've never heard her sound before. "I need to see it for real. I need to see Nicky's face."

"You're going to see him." Now we're living in the future tense. "You will. I promise."

Her panic-stricken breaths steady as she settles her head onto my shoulder.

And I tell her again, "You will, you will."

I wake from a strange dream. Dad . . . Caleb . . . God . . . was down here with me.

"Son . . ." He pressed a spoon of oatmeal into my mouth. "Eat. You have to eat."

Shivering, I tried to push him away, but my arms were too weak.

"Soon . . ." He poured water and juice down my throat until I coughed. "It's happening soon." He gripped my hands, urgent whispers and flashlight eyes, but I couldn't grip back. "Please, Daniel, you have to focus. This is our last chance. If it doesn't happen tonight—it never will." Then I heard him ascend the steps alone, but before he left, he told me that everything was going to be okay.

But it's not the truth. Nothing's going to be okay.

Penny's labored breaths fill the darkness. "Saye . . . are you all right?"

"I can't do this anymore, Penny. I feel like I'm fading. Like someone's turned the telescope the wrong direction, and everything's getting smaller and smaller."

"Sayers . . ." She pants as if talking is taking too much energy, but her voice is strong as she puts her face against my ear. "You're falling . . . inside of yourself. You have to . . . expand."

When I wake, I reach out my hand. "Penny?"

She doesn't answer.

Sitting up, I call her name again.

No response, only the thick kind of silence that hurts your ears. Panic crawls over me like vines, they wrap around my throat. She must've passed out. She's unconscious somewhere in the cellar. I get to my knees and swipe my arms through the air. I search everywhere.

But Penny's gone.

My cheek rests against the cellar floor. It's just me and Daniel now.

No, it's just me. Just my heart, my breaths.

And I alone have to find her.

Fighting waves of dizziness, I rise to my knees, crawl to the edge of the cellar, and follow the wall with my hands, around and around and around. Suddenly, I'm falling through space as if the wall is missing.

No, the door to the stairs is open.

I need to stand, but just as I know I can't do it, I *can*—almost as if God himself is lifting me to my feet. And now it's like I'm floating, like he's carrying me up the stairs. I can feel his arms around me and hear his soothing noises.

Is God humming?

He sets me back on my feet.

Swaying, I whisper, "Penny?"

No answer, just so much black I can't make out my own fingers in front of my face. My legs quiver as they stagger left, but I keep tripping along until I reach something cold and metal.

The vault door.

It'll be locked, it's always locked.

But it slides back on its track all by itself, like magic.

I keep walking, farther and farther, the walls getting closer together with jagged turns until I hit another metal door, and just like the one before, it slides back. I stumble forward, ready for another hall, another door, they never end. The next room is dizzying in its scale. The air is sweet and clean, and there are gentle buzzing noises. Like crickets.

This is not another room.

I'm *outside*.

I take in a gulp of air. Is this real?

I blink up into the massive vastness of the sky and the brightness of a billion stars. I'm craning my neck, trying to see the entire world all at once, when there's a streak of light. Then another and another.

The meteor shower.

A gasp falls from my lips.

It's *beautiful*, so beautiful I can't take it. The depth of the sky, blue-black, and the stars, so bright they seem close enough to touch, and the strange wonder of the meteors that continue to fall.

I stare and stare and stare—then I hear a shattered voice:

"I don't *understand*. It's not working. We're not going back."

The silhouette of a figure is standing before me. Crying.

"Dad?" I squint into the darkness. "Is that you?"

I blink.

And when I open my eyes again, the figure's gone.

My gaze is lifting back to the night sky when I'm jolted by a loud noise. Somewhere in the distance is an echoing blast like an explosion, like thunder, like the shot of a gun. Confused, I stumble dreamlike through the tall grass toward where I thought I heard the sound.

I trip into something, nearly fall.

And then I see.

"Oh," I say out loud.

"Oh." I say it again.

My father is lying perfectly still. His body too loose, head oddly tilted, face smeared in blood. His eyes are closed, and his arm is outstretched. Hand open as if he dropped the gun that's in the grass beside him. All around us, the meteors keep falling.

I'm here, not here.

I see it, don't see it.

It's real, not real.

Dizzy—spinning—fleeing. Only a few steps before I'm collapsing into the black night grass. I roll onto my back so I can keep watching the universe fall.

SIXTY-ONE

I wake to light bulbs shining hot against my eyelids, and blink into blue.

Mouth dry, I lick my lips, trying to understand what I'm seeing. Something green at the periphery of my vision, wisps of white, an orb of light. Not a bulb, but the *sun*. And over me is a cloud-flecked sky just like my viewfinder, only my viewfinder is a soft-edge square, while this picture stretches to infinity in every direction.

Blinking weakly, I tilt my head to the right. About an acre away is a skinny, tree-lined road. Look left, and there's the house. Just a little beige rectangle I wouldn't even notice if I were to walk past it.

Somehow I got out.

Dad . . . Caleb . . . he was out here too, but—the memories come crashing back. The meteors, the gun, he killed himself, I *saw* him.

Tears wet my eyes, run down my cheeks.

Sniffling, I look up at the sky, the trees, at the green, so much green.

Penny.

She's still inside. I have to get to her.

My fingers dig into the grass. Try to pull myself up. Can't.

Push my bare feet into the ground. Can't stand.

A helpless sob breaks out of me.

My eyes drift back to the hazy road. On the other side of the road's a barbed wire fence, and beyond that an empty pasture, but no houses or buildings anywhere that I can see.

"*Help,*" I try to yell, but it comes out a hoarse whisper, and my body's so tired.

I need to rest . . . just for a minute.

When I blink again, the sun has moved higher. Not pleasant heat anymore, but scalding like every sunbeam's a laser. Sweat's pooling in my shirt, in my hair.

I'm no stronger for sleeping, and I'm *thirsty.* I keep licking my dry lips.

All around me are summer scents, summer sounds. Insects in the grass. Birds chirping in the trees. Sun in my eyes, sweat in my eyes.

I turn another despairing glance to the house. Is Penny okay?

Please get up, Saye.

But again my eyes fall closed.

I'm woken by a rustling noise. The sky's a shade darker, and now comes an awful swell of panic—two men are walking toward me.

Or is it one man, two times? They wear black pants, black shirts, black shoes. They want to steal me and Penny.

I have to run, have to hide.

But all I can do is lie here, weakly kicking at the grass.

"Whoa there," one of the men says in a rough deep voice. "Settle down."

Scared whines crawl out of my throat.

The other man speaks, gentler. "Are you all right, son?"

His shoes, half buried in the grass, step closer, and he kneels in front of me. His eyes are black with yellow flecks like pieces of the universe. In them, I see the cellar and how it never ended and Penny and the frozen Daniels, and his eyes are like mirrors reflecting all the horror back at me.

He stands up straight. A radio crackles, and he asks for an ambulance. He tells them he found a boy. He's *emaciated*, he's *disoriented*.

More cars pull up. More men spill out, and there are too many overlapping words, too many towering bodies. I roll onto my side and stare up into white clouds. They're actually not like my viewfinder at all. These clouds keep changing, little by little.

SIXTY-TWO

Rising up. From anesthesia-nothingness into sunshine-something-ness.

Somewhere soft, somewhere clean, somewhere *good*.

How did we get here, Penny?

"Can you hear me?"

I blink.

A man in a white coat.

Doctor, my brain retrieves the word.

"How do you feel?"

I'm in a bed, in a room with real windows, and there's a needle in my hand.

Penny is not beside me.

I push myself up with my free hand. "Is . . . is she okay?"

The doctor doesn't answer, but his face—it's an expression he can't hide.

And he doesn't have to tell me because I know, I know.

All my muscles snap, and I fall backward as the air rushes from my lungs.

✢ ✢ ✢

I vanish for a long time. Or maybe it's not long at all. Time's not what you think it is. It can speed up and slow down and move in every direction. When I return, a policeman's in my doorway, guarding me from the hall, or maybe guarding the people in the hall from me.

He sees me watching him, then he stands and disappears from view.

A moment later, a doctor, a nurse, and an older woman wearing a fluffy pink sweater file into the room.

"Hello there," the pink-sweater woman says. "I'm Ruth. Can you tell me your name?"

I don't know which name she wants me to give her, so I keep them both to myself and turn away and face the window. The curtains are drawn, but light leaks around all sides of the fabric. The talking continues behind me.

I hear the sounds, but not the words.

I watch the light.

The voices are back, loud and eager. They say they have delicious food for me, and if I don't like what they've brought, there's a whole menu to choose from.

My head aches. I don't want to eat, but a table is wheeled over. A lever is pumped to raise it higher and slide it over my bed. For a moment I feel something that might be hunger, but then someone removes the domed lid from the plate to reveal a slimy slab of meat.

I look away.

"That's all right," a voice says. "Let's go through this menu.

Oh my word, we've got macaroni, and turkey sandwiches, and . . ."

Eventually, the voice goes away again and I do too—until a giant hand closes over my wrist like a cuff.

A strangled shout rips out of my throat. I try to break free, but he's stronger. Tears blur my vision as he presses my fingertips into ink, and I stay curled up into a tight ball even after he lets me go.

Say.

Say.

Say.

The voices again.

What do they want me to say?

I open my eyes, and a woman is beside me. Wisps of golden hair fall over her pale face. She has dry lips, powdery skin, and blue eyes. In them, I see a strange mixture of the deepest sorrow and the greatest joy. I see both at once.

"Saye." She lays her hand on my cheek.

Kidnapper.

Frightened, I jerk away, and the woman begins to cry.

I think I sat up. I think I used the bathroom. But it's all a dreamy blur.

I stretch out my hand, but Penny will never be beside me.

"Saye?" It's the golden-haired woman from a billion micro-memories. I think I know her, only the photo I've had in my head isn't right. She's smaller and older and her colors are dimmer. "Someone would like to see you."

In the doorway is a man in happy, bright colors with blue-black hair and a game-show smile. He crosses the room in jaunty steps and sits in the chair beside my bed just like Dad used to do.

My throat goes dry.

"Can't even say hello?"

I turn my head to the window, but he keeps talking. I don't hear the words, just the lively, cheery tone, then the chair scrapes hard against the floor, and the man grumbles something.

"Please tell me you're joking," the woman says.

"Why would I be joking? I took an eight-hour flight to get here, and he won't even give me the time of day." Her response, muffled, then his voice, raised, "Oh, don't give me that! He's been doing this to me for years. I don't know why I expected anything to be different."

"He's traumatized, Jack. He doesn't know how to—" Now she's pleading, "I can't do this by myself."

"I'm sorry about your father. I really am. But let's be honest, if he were still alive, would you have even called me?"

"Of course I would have. Sayers is your son too!"

And I vanish again.

"Hello, Sayers." The pink-sweater woman is back. Ruth. She steps inside, all the way to my bed. "How are you feeling?"

When I don't respond, she sits in the empty chair next to me. "It's all right, you don't have to talk." She sets some paper and a tiny box of crayons on my tray. "Would you like to draw?"

Slowly, I open the box and slide a green crayon out. Holding it to my nose, I smell the wax, and my chest hitches. I'm not good at people, but I run the crayon along the page, this urge to get her right.

"Who's that?" Ruth asks.

I keep drawing.

"Is that Penny?"

My hand stills. How did she know?

And then Ruth says: "She's improving."

My head lifts, a sharp-shocked tilt.

Ruth gazes back at me, her eyes calm.

But I must be misunderstanding her. The doctor told me . . .

I thought . . . I thought he said . . .

Hope pounds in my chest.

Is Penny *alive*?

SIXTY-THREE

Ruth smiles, nodding like she can hear all my racing thoughts. "She's just down the hall and getting better every day."

My heart starts thudding in my ears.

I need to ask what she means, but no words will come out.

"You eat something, then you can visit her, all right?"

No. If she's telling the truth, I have to see Penny *now.*

I throw my legs over the side of the bed, and Ruth lets out a startled noise. "Saye—" My knees buckle, and she calls out, "Nurse!"

A man in scrubs rushes into the room and puts me back into the bed. Seconds later, the golden-haired woman runs in, asking, "What's wrong?"

But I can't talk so I'm groaning, this hysterical, frustrated feeling.

"He's upset," Ruth says. "He wants to see the girl."

Around me are whispered conversations, then a nurse in bright purple rolls a wheelchair into the room. "I can take him down the hall, just to peek in on her."

Scrubbing my fists into my eyes, I slide from the bed into the wheelchair, and the nurse pushes me out into a cold, bright hall, past unsmiling doctors taking notes on shiny metal clipboards. Scientists—*experimenters*. All the bones in my chest pull tight— what if they're lying to me, tricking me? What if I'm confused?

We keep moving down the hall, then I'm facing a room with an open door.

And there she is.

Eyes closed, black hair fanning around her pillow. An IV is attached to her hand too.

"Penny."

It's as if my brain doesn't know how to fully believe it, to trust that she's real. Around the room are signs of visitors. Stuffed animals. Hand-drawn construction-paper cards. Strange pink flowers that look as if they're made from a multitude of other flowers, all tiny petals in clusters on thick green stalks.

Their scent on the air, I breathe in deep.

"That smell is wonderful, isn't it?" the nurse says in a hushed voice. "Her mother brought them in, but I can't think of what they're called."

Hyacinths. They must be.

It's true—they *do* smell like happiness.

My eyes are tearing up as all that happiness rushes through me.

"What a sweet lady her mother is," the nurse continues. "And that little boy, oh, that child loves his sister. I'm sure they'll be here as soon as he gets out of school."

Nicolai and Penny's mother. I can't wait to meet them in real life.

In some other room, an alarm sounds. "I'll be right back," the nurse tells me before rushing off, and the hospital door taps closed behind her.

For a moment, I just watch Penny from the outer reaches of the room, but then I push the wheels on my chair while gripping the IV stand, propelling myself to her bed.

Looking down at her, my heart catches.

She's so *thin*.

The bones are too sharp in her face, and her skin's waxy and drained of color.

But she's alive.

She's alive, and we're really here. Not just in my imagination, but for real.

I whisper her name again like it's the only word I know how to say. Her lashes twitch against her cheeks. I swallow, so happy I can't stand it.

Her eyes flutter open, a bright sunflower surrounding each of her pupils.

My smile is so huge now it hurts my cheeks. "Hi, Penny."

She blinks like there's a haze obscuring her vision, then she sits up, her hospital gown parting down her back to reveal the bony knobs of her spine.

Her eyes clear—and they balloon in her face, this awful gasping terror like something monstrous is right behind me.

Clenching up, I turn my head, but nothing's there.

I turn back—and Penny's scrambling off the bed like she's trying to flee from whatever it was that she saw, but there is no *it*. There's no one in this room except Penny and me.

"Penny . . . it's all right. It's only me."

But she's still just as afraid. No, *more* afraid.

Her chest starts heaving up and down. Posture unsteady, her legs crumble, collapsing just like I did a few minutes ago, and a loud beep splits the air—she's come disconnected from something.

Panicked, I roll around to the other side of the bed. Her legs, fragile and thin, are pulled to her gulping throat. Her IV is still intact, but now the cord is stretched way too taut. A straining tether from her hand to the IV stand on the opposite side of the bed.

"Penny, be careful." I roll closer.

Eyes huge and scared, her palms push against the white floor, helping her crawl away, and the cord keeps stretching tighter like it's about to tear out of the top of her hand.

"Penny, *stop*." Dropping my IV stand, I reach out for her.

She thrashes against me. Our cords overlap.

"*What are you doing?*" A nurse's shocked voice appears behind me.

"She's going to hurt herself," I try to say, but the nurse talks over me, "Let her go!"

I do it, and instantly, Penny rears back, so hard and fast, she slams the back of her head into the wall. The sickening crack of her skull echoes through the room.

Penny goes still, her face contorted in pain but also confusion.

Slowly, she lifts a hand to her head, then she looks to the blood coating her fingertips.

"Oh no. Penny—"

She begins to scream. More nurses rush into the room, and her screams keep getting louder, but shakier, like her voice is giving out.

"Penny, it's okay," I say. "It's okay, please."

Suddenly, I'm rolling backward. A nurse has caught the handles of my wheelchair, and she's dragging me from the room. A terrible feeling spreads over me, so fast and all-consuming it's as if I've been injected with it. And what did Penny say about pain?

The things that hurt you, change you.

And they can either make you better or make you worse.

SIXTY-FOUR

A nurse pulls the needle from the top of my hand. I'm given discharge papers and business cards with phone numbers for a nutritionist and psychiatrist. I'm given prescriptions for anxiety and for pain.

"I know this is hard, Saye," the golden-haired woman, *mother*, is telling me. "But you have to keep talking."

I have spoken, some. I'm not sure when, but I asked a doctor if Penny was okay. He wouldn't tell me, so I asked if I could see her, and he said, *No, she's calmer now*. But that was the last time I've spoken to anyone.

And sometime, I don't know when, I heard my mother argue with the hospital staff, tell them she wants me out of here—that this place is no good for me.

"Saye, please?" she's saying to me now. "Can you talk to *me*?" And her face is so sad that I want to try.

"You . . ."

"Yes?" She leans forward.

"You don't have black hair."

"Black hair?" she repeats like she's puzzled.

"And no nail polish?"

She makes a noise that might be a laugh. "Yes, well, I've had other things on my mind."

"I—I remember you. Dad said I'd forget."

Now her forehead crinkles in confusion. "Jack told you that?"

"Not *him*. My other dad."

Her face fills with more crinkles, but she sets a black paper sack with ribbon handles from a department store on my bed—brand-new clothes with the tags still on them.

Once I'm dressed, the nurse tells me I have to ride in a wheelchair to the car, and soon I'm in the back seat of a black sedan, a hospital bracelet still loose around my wrist.

I feel like an alien. I can't stop gawking through the window at the endless green fields and blue skies, and the shape of the world, all its bends and curves, and how it expands and expands and expands.

I rest my cheek against the glass and fall onto the Sleep Side. I don't come back until the car stops in front of a white stone castle with more windows than I can count.

My shimmery reflection stares back at me in the polished chessboard marble floor. The odor of cleaning products hangs in the air as if a team of workers just left, but the house feels empty like no one has lived here in a very long time.

"Where is everyone?" I ask.

"I let them go."

"Let them go?"

"Why don't you lie down in your room? I'll bring you something to eat."

But I'm not sure which direction to turn, almost as if I need a map of the house.

She gestures to a grand, winding staircase so I take it up, up, up.

I find my room on the third floor, but it's like a picture drawn from memory where many of the details are wrong. For one thing, it's much larger than I remembered. There's a balcony—I didn't remember a balcony—and an enormous, cinema-style screen on the wall.

I touch the rows of windows with open shutters. I touch a telescope and a collection of objects arranged on built-in shelves, but it's as if none of these things belong to me. I scan the paintings that line one wall. There's a small photo wedged into one of the gilded frames. A pretty girl and boy. He's dressed in a black tailored suit, his hair combed neat and slick.

This is the last image I have of being Saye.

That's him, me, *us*.

Someone's knocking on the partially open door. I wait for it to be pushed open farther, but when it doesn't, I open it myself. My mother is holding a tray, formal and stranger-like. Nothing like Dad, who'd come right on in.

"Thank you." I take the tray from her and set it on a nearby desk.

She looks like she wants to tell me something, but she just nods without speaking, then walks out and shuts the door. Immediately, I tear it back open.

She spins around, her hands swooping like frightened birds to her chest. "What's wrong?"

"N-nothing. I was just . . ." Just checking to see if I was locked in.

"Are you sure?"

I nod, and this time she leaves the door open when she goes. I watch her disappear around a corner, then I grab the plate from the tray and sit on the floor against the giant bed.

Picking up the sandwich, I lift my hand to cross myself, then I let it hover. What good does such a gesture do? Penny and I *said* thank you. I just went along, but Penny really meant it. She prayed and said thank you for every scrap of food and every slice of light, but for what?

I drop the sandwich back onto the plate.

If this food came from God, he can keep it.

SIXTY-FIVE

My mother's knocking on the bedroom door. She never enters without permission.

"It's unlocked," I call out.

And she lets herself inside, glancing around like an invader—*terra incognita*.

She stole me.

The thought's alarming even though I know it's not the truth, and she must sense what I'm feeling because her eyes begin to water. "Are you really so afraid of me?"

"No . . ."

Maybe.

I don't know.

She perches on the edge of the couch. "We used to be so close. We did everything together. We took so many trips, all over the world. You were like my best friend. Don't you remember?"

I do, a little. A brass heart split in two.

But the images are more like dreams than memories.

"I want to help you, Saye."

"I don't think you can."

"Well, then maybe a therapist—"

"I don't think anyone can help me."

"Please don't say that. I just got you back."

"He told me the same thing."

"Who?"

"Dad—Caleb. He said the same thing, that he just got me back."

My eyes are drawn toward the darkening window, and I shiver.

I have a strange new affliction. Every evening as the sun shrinks in the sky, my heart pounds in my chest, and I shake like a pagan, afraid the light will never come back.

"Saye . . ."

My focus shifts back to her.

"Maybe if you went to school. It's almost October, and—"

"October?"

The word sounds foreign and pretty, but October and all months—they're made up. A way to organize something that simply can't be organized. Seconds, hours, days, years, a clock on a wall or in your pocket. You can't contain time.

"I just thought maybe if you were around your friends again."

The word *please* hangs in the air, and there's a sickly desperation on her face—one that's faded like a priceless oil painting someone didn't take care of—and suddenly I feel cruel for doing this to her.

"Okay."

Her eyes widen in hopeful surprise. "Really?"

"Yes. If you want me to go, I'll go."

SIXTY-SIX

My mother's waiting at the bottom of the stairs. "Saye . . . honey, what are you wearing?"

Self-conscious now, I glance down. Loose joggers, a black T-shirt with a screen-print of a galaxy that's so faded the shirt looks inside out.

"That's fine for around the house, but you need to change for school."

I don't see why it matters, but I nod and start back up the stairs.

"And some proper shoes!" she calls after me.

In my room, I pull on an expensive charcoal hoodie to cover the shirt, then I sit on the couch, slip off my sandals, and push my feet into a pair of black lace-up boots.

When I stand, they're like weights.

Downstairs, my mother gives me a once-over. She doesn't look thrilled, but she doesn't say anything else. As we drive, I hold on to the phone she gave me last night. She said it was the latest model, the *best*. I guess no one ever found my old phone with the red case.

"I spoke with Mr. Gardiner," she says.

"Who?"

"Your principal."

"Oh. Right."

"There was really nothing that could be done, so you'll be taking eleventh-grade classes."

"That's okay."

"And I know how much you love Latin, but the man who taught it retired."

"What about Penny?"

She stiffens, and for a moment, she doesn't answer me.

Then she says, "I did look into it. But no, she's not back at school yet."

We pull up to a sprawling red brick two-story, the one Penny and I used to visit in the dark.

"There *is* a lion statue."

"What?" my mother asks.

"Nothing . . ."

She looks worried for a moment, but she forces a bright smile as she gives me a printout of my schedule. "Being at school is going to be *so* good for you, you'll see. Soon you'll be the same old Saye."

SIXTY-SEVEN

Wet leaves squish under my boots as I make my way through the main doors. The crowds are thick and stifling—everyone's so much bigger than me now—and I'm disoriented like someone rearranged the layout of the school.

I scan my schedule.

First period, World History, Room 203.

I'm not even on the right floor.

A bell blasts over my head—Dad's home.

No, stop. It's just the bell for class.

Everyone's hurrying now, and I move with the motion of the crowd, but I stop short at the end of the hall. Plastered to the wall, a giant banner reads: *HOMECOMING.*

It's like I entered a time warp, delivered back to the moment I left, or like I was never gone at all.

Another bell rings.

The hall clears.

But I'm still staring at the banner.

"Where're you s'posed to be?" The booming voice behind me makes me jump. Turning slowly, I come face-to-face with a giant older man who has a key ring attached to his belt.

"I . . . I don't know," I answer honestly.

"You don't *know?*" His face scrunches up into a sneer.

"No, sir."

"Did you hear that *ringing* noise just a minute ago?" he asks, slow and sarcastic.

"Yessir."

"Well, it means you're s'posed to be in first period."

Nodding, I rush past him, around the corner and up a staircase, but by the time I locate room 203, I've already missed twenty minutes. The idea of a late and dramatic entrance feels so awful, I duck into a bathroom stall and hide till the bell rings again.

My next class is only a few doors down, so I'm early. I take a seat in the very back row, and a minute later someone clears their throat. Looking up, I find a guy frowning at me. I think I've stolen his desk. He rolls his eyes and throws himself in a nearby seat. Other than him, no one even glances in my direction.

All around me are stressed-out murmurs. *We have a substitute—and she's mean!*

The bell rings. I shiver.

The substitute's pointy heels click from the hall to the podium. "Before any of you ask," she says, looking out at the room sternly, "the test is *not* being postponed just because Mrs. Mitchell is out sick today." There's a collective groan, but she ignores it and starts taking roll. "Beth Abbott?"

"Here," a girl says.

I'll be last. I was almost always last to be called during the roll. Unless the teacher calls on Daniel Emory. But the *e*'s come and go, and I'm relieved until she passes the *w*'s too, and then a panicky thought strikes me through the temple: *There is no Sayers Wayte.*

"Evan Zamara?"

A vivid memory of a face—brown eyes, chubby cheeks, springy curls. A boy on a stage, a screen full of falling meteors behind him.

Across the room, a tall, slender boy with wide shoulders and shorn hair is raising his hand.

He can't be the same Evan Zamara.

"Put away your things," the substitute says. I don't have anything to put away, so I sit quietly as she passes out thick test booklets and green answer sheets. "You have fifty minutes."

Immediately, exams start rustling, but I'm stuck on the top of the answer sheet.

Name:

Name:

Name:

Daniel—that's what my hand wants to write.

Name:

Name:

Name:

I know my real name, but I haven't written it in so long.

I force my hand to scrawl the letters. S-A-Y-E-R-S.

And then I slump a little in relief. This isn't so hard. Turning to my test booklet, I read the first question. *Beowulf believes that the result of his efforts will be determined by:*

(a) The strength of his body

(b) The strength of his mind

(c) The faith of his people

(d) God and Fate

Another rush of panic—I've never read this book. At least, I don't think I have.

Calm down. Nothing bad will happen if you don't know the answer. Something I once heard floats into my mind: *When in doubt, choose C.*

I almost circle it right onto the test before remembering I'm not supposed to do that.

I locate number one on the . . . Scantron? Is that really what it's called?

Papers are rustling. Almost everyone's flipping to the second page, and I'm still on the first question. Another twinge of nerves, but I remind myself to just bubble in C, and I keep going.

"What are you doing?"

It takes me a moment to realize that the substitute is talking to me.

She marches down the aisle, her brows a bright orange V over her narrowed eyes. She snatches the answer sheet off my desk. "Do you think this is funny?"

I don't understand.

A few curious kids swivel in our direction.

"Eyes on your tests," she orders them before whipping back to me. "How old are you?"

A flurry of answers fills my head.

I'm ten.

No, I'm one hundred.

There is no time, there are no ages.

"This is eleventh-grade English, so I'm sure you know by now that the Scantron machine can only read number two pencils."

Slowly, I look down to my hand. One that is holding a green crayon. I didn't even think about it when I pulled it from my pocket. The substitute sighs, then retrieves a fresh Scantron and pencil from the podium. She sets them firmly on my desk.

"Redo this."

The pencil rolls toward me, sharp like a weapon. I can't touch it, it's not allowed. But that's stupid—of course I can touch it. In fact, I *have* to.

Someone's whispering. Two girls in the next row are watching me. To my right, there's a small click. The boy whose seat I stole is pointing his phone at my face. More murmurs, and now *everyone* is looking my way, and in the crowd of stares I find the Other Evan Zamara.

"Quiet," the teacher orders, but the whispers only spread.

My fingers dig into my thighs.

I want to pull my helmet down over my head.

Can't run—can't fight—can't run—can't fight.

I need Penny. I could do this if Penny were here with me.

The clock on the wall ticks and ticks and ticks.

A loud bell—Dad is home.

NO—stop thinking that. It's just time for my next class. Scrambling out of my seat, I rush into the noisy hall. People are whizzing past me, talking to friends, opening lockers.

One by one, the voices drop off almost in unison as their gazes shift down to their phones.

It's eerie, but I try to shake the feeling as I speed around a corner where more people are gathered at a row of lockers. A girl with long brown hair is squinting at her cell phone. She looks up, then she gapes at me like I'm an illusion. That's exactly what I feel like.

She starts toward me, before coming to an abrupt halt, her eyes flitting from my hair to my shoes. Her face fills with confusion, almost like she thought she recognized me, but now she isn't sure.

"Saye?" Her voice trembles. "You . . . you look . . ."

The tardy bell rings, and perplexed teachers begin poking their heads out of their classrooms. Someone shouts that the media is here, and a bunch of kids dash to the windows.

"Do you want to talk to them?" The girl uses her pinkies to wipe beneath both eyes. "I'll be with you the whole time."

Before I can answer, the crowd is forced to part by two men in black ties. One of them asks me to come with him, and I'm taken down the hall, leaving the girl—*Bria*—behind.

SIXTY-EIGHT

"This is ridiculous." My mother is quietly furious as we sit side by side on a sofa facing the principal's desk. "You swore to me my son's reentrance to school would be confidential."

The principal looks embarrassed. "I can assure you I've only spoken with a few key faculty members about Saye's return."

"Then one of your teachers has a big mouth."

His face twitches. "I apologize, ma'am. The police are out there right now getting rid of those reporters."

"That's not good enough."

"It's not his fault," I say, and they both startle. "A boy in my class took my picture. He must've posted it."

"That shouldn't have happened," the principal says quickly. "I'll make an announcement that anyone who does that will be disciplined." He turns to my mom. "We want this handled as much as you do. It's disruptive to everyone, so—"

"Everyone else isn't my concern."

"Ma'am, if—"

"I need to know my son will be safe!" my mother shouts, shocking me. She *never* shouts, not that I can remember.

The principal's face flickers dark—annoyed? *Angry?*

Stomach clenched, I watch him closely, trying to read him when he gets to his feet. I flinch back—but he's just walking over to the water cooler in the corner of his office. He fills a paper triangle cup, then gives it to my mother.

She takes it from him, her hands visibly shaking.

"Ms. Wayte . . ." His tone's less formal now, more soothing. "It may not seem like it, but we care about Saye's safety very much. He's been through a lot, and it's our goal to make his return to school as unchallenging and painless as possible." He steals a glance at me, and the expression on his face . . . I'm not sure if I'm reading him right, but it looks like pity.

Now that my anonymity's been stripped away, I feel stripped too, and as I'm trying to recall the geography of the school, I keep encountering half-familiar faces. They stare at me openly, and I think I remember how people used to look at me—interested, attracted, envious—but now all I see is horror, shock, and more pity.

I'm met with these same sorts of stares when I slip into my next class.

"Saye?" A teacher with black hair and pale skin is talking to me.

"Ms. White?"

"Ms. *Wells*," she corrects in a gentle voice.

But she looks like Snow White. "I . . . I remember you."

Her chin begins to tremble. "Let's get you settled."

She leads me to an empty desk right up front, then she begins the lesson.

I try to pay attention, but I can feel the eyes of the class on my skin like sharp fingernails. I peek over my shoulder, and a boy with flame-colored hair is watching me—his face so full of hate, I shudder.

As soon as the final bell rings, I escape through the doors and suck in a breath of uncirculated air. My gaze is pulled to the sky, and I spin, neck craning to take it all in.

Today was so much harder than I thought it would be. It'll be nice to get into bed and just *sleep*.

"Saye!" The girl, Bria, is hanging out the back seat of someone's car. I hear, "Come on!" and "We're getting coffee!" and "Get in!" all from different, overlapping voices.

At the same time, my phone buzzes in my pocket—a text from my mother: I'm out front.

I really want to go home, but the voices from the car call me again, so I text my mother: Bria wants me to get coffee.

And right away, she replies: Oh good! Go! Have fun!!!

So I climb inside the packed car, and Bria pulls my hand into her lap. The skin of my palm tickles. My fingers try to remember her fingers.

It seems like she's trying to remember too. Her fingertips keep stuttering over the new marks on my knuckles and palms. She continues holding on to me as we walk into a bright orange coffee shop called Java Shine. I've never been here before, at least I don't think I have. Penny and I never came here, I know that for sure.

Everyone begins placing complicated orders, and then it's my turn, but I'm struck dumb by all the options.

"I—I don't know . . . Uh . . ." Throat dry, I lick my lips. "Um . . .

apple juice—no, coffee."

The lady grabs a pot and pours it into a cup, and hands it to me. It feels like I'm getting away with something. I take a sip. I don't like it. Or maybe I just don't remember coffee.

At the sidebar, I add cream and a packet of sugar. Taste it again. Still bitter, so I pour vanilla powder, more milk, more granules of sugar, then I join the group where they're gathering at a trio of shiny silver tables.

They're all older than me now.

No, they're not.

But they *look* older. Like one year aged them twenty, the boys bigger, their jaw lines more defined, the girls looking like women.

"Don't you love this place?" Bria's beaming. "We were *so* over Starbucks—too corporate."

Nodding, I shift in my hard metal chair. The bells on the door chime—I flinch—turn back and feel something that might be happiness.

It's *Luke*. His blond hair has been combed neatly into submission. He's dressed in a plain white polo instead of a *Star Wars* tee, and I'm down a waterfall of memories.

Luke: five or six years old, grinning like crazy with missing teeth.

Me and Luke: seven or eight, dressed as storm troopers for Halloween.

Me and Luke again: nine or ten, camping out in my theater in front of a screenful of stars.

Penny was right—Luke is real.

These memories haven't been erased—they're here. They're all here.

My vision clears.

Luke's mouth is a tense line as he scans the coffee shop, then his eyes meet mine—and his arms fall to his sides like he's been handed a pair of one-hundred-pound stones.

For a full minute he stands there until I wonder if he's coming over at all. Then he crosses the room and pulls a chair up to the table. Some of the others greet him, sounding shocked to see him, and if I didn't know any better, I'd think he'd been gone for a year too.

But he doesn't say anything to me at all.

"Luke?" I finally say.

"Oh. *Hey.*" He sounds surprised, almost like he sat next to me by accident, like he's only just now noticing that I'm here. His eyes flick over me, before quickly looking away again.

Hurt and confused, I slump in my seat. Around me are threads of hard-to-follow conversations.

"Your hair . . ." a girl is saying. "I've never seen it so long."

I'm not sure if this is good or bad, so I don't know whether to say thank you or say nothing. I consider telling her I wasn't allowed to touch scissors, and even now that I can—I *can't.*

Someone else says brightly, "So what are you going to do now that you're back?"

Now that I'm back? I used to fantasize all the time about getting out. I'd play movies in my head where people are kidnapped, then found, but usually once that happens, the movie's over. There *is* no after.

Everyone's watching me, waiting for an answer.

"He's going to Disneyland," Luke says, and the sarcasm in his tone catches me off guard.

A tense silence takes over until someone else I don't recognize, breaks it. "So are you gonna tell us what happened? Online it said—"

"Shut up, Braxton," Luke cuts him off. "He doesn't have to tell us."

"I'm just asking. Chill."

"Saye doesn't have to tell us anything," Bria agrees. "Unless he wants to . . ."

"Yeah, because we're here for you. To *listen.*"

Now all eyes are on me with a shiny, hungry glow.

My ankles hurt. My boots are squeezing too tight. Would anyone notice if I took them off? Would it really matter if they did notice? I'm bending to loosen my laces when I'm grabbed from behind, and a deep voice rumbles in my ear, "Holy fuck, you're really back."

While I'm catching my breath, a huge guy with heavy black eyebrows drags up a chair. "Everyone thought that little loser killed you."

"Omigod, Garrett's right," Bria says. "The police thought Dillon Blair and his friend . . ."

"Evan Zamara," someone else supplies.

"Evan's practically hot now," a girl says, but when another girl gives a squeamish *"Eww, Marissa,"* she quickly self-corrects, "I mean if he wasn't Evan Zamara. Obviously."

"They figured out Evan didn't have anything to do with it—he had an alibi or something."

"But that red-haired guy, Blair, everyone says his parents went, like, bankrupt, paying for lawyers."

"Well, it serves him right," Bria says. "He *did* threaten to kill you."

And I get a flash from before:

Blair shoving me in the middle of the hall.

Blair screaming, *I swear to God you're going to pay for this!*

"I'm pretty sure that guy hates you now," someone chuckles. "I wouldn't want to run into him in a dark alley if I were you."

There's another silence, and I follow all the glares aimed at . . . what's his name again?

"*Braxton,*" Luke growls.

Right. Braxton.

The whole table frowns at Braxton until Garrett says, "What the fuck's everyone talking about?" He punches my shoulder, snapping my eyes to his. "I mean, dude! You were kidnapped by a serial killer!"

Serial killer.

No one's called Caleb that before—not to me anyway.

It feels wrong. That's not what he is. He's . . . I don't know.

Garrett gives me a fierce look of admiration. "I fucking knew you'd get out." Then he's saying something about how only the strong survive, and more voices chime in, swearing they knew I'd get out too, that I probably had a plan the whole time. Soon they're all talking at once in a hard-to-follow cacophony, but I manage to hear the words:

No one could kill Sayers Wayte.

SIXTY-NINE

When I return to school, all the looks have changed. Instead of discomfort and pity, I'm stared at with open admiration as if I've done the unthinkable. I'm the sole survivor of a long line of victims. I'm not broken or stolen—I'm *elevated*.

I should be grateful my old friends have spun things this way, because when I got online last night for the first time since I've been back, the photo that guy took of me was everywhere.

Over and over I saw a thin, pale face that was mostly eyes. I didn't recognize them. In most of the posts, that picture was right next to my tenth-grade yearbook photo, and I know I don't look the same, but side by side it's alarming.

And the comments . . .

Poor boy, it looks like that monster tortured him.

Now the healing can begin.

Glad he's safe.

He'll never be the same.

"*What* are you wearing?" Bria laughs when she finds me in the hall after fourth period.

I'm puzzled until she strokes her finger down my

red-and-gray-striped sweater.

"Is this going to be your new look?" she asks like it's a big joke, but I like this sweater. It's soft and worn and smells like rain. Ms. Wells dug it out of her lost-and-found box when she saw me shivering. When I don't say anything, Bria laughs again. "Come on, we're going out for lunch."

"I don't think I have off-campus lunch."

"Oh, please." Bria rolls her eyes with a playful grin. "Who's going to stop you?" She grips my hand and leads me out to the parking lot. "Where's your car?"

"My mother dropped me off."

Her lips turn down like she's disappointed, but she says, "It's cool. I can drive." And soon we're pulling up to a fast-food place. Bria kills the engine, then she turns to me, her gaze focused, *intense*.

"W-what is it?" I ask.

"I really missed you . . ." She pushes my hair out of my face on both sides, almost like she's trying to shape it into the way it was before. "The whole time you were gone, I kept thinking about the night of Homecoming. I wish I'd stayed. I wish we'd finally . . . *you know* . . ." She leans in close. "Because I wanted to. I still do."

There's a charged silence.

And then she kisses me.

My hands tighten in my lap. When I try to catch my breath, she slides her tongue between my lips, and my heart starts to race. I think I'm scared.

Bria pulls back. "What's wrong?"

"Nothing."

"*Nothin'?*" she chuckles. "God, your accent is so different."

"It is?" I didn't know that.

"Yeah." She reaches inside her purse and digs out a glossy black tube. "Just a little under-eye brightener." But when she makes no move to apply it, I realize she wants to put the makeup on *me*.

"Oh," I finally say.

"Is that okay?"

"If you want."

She taps the wand to the tip of her little finger, dabbing color onto her skin. "Look up."

I look up.

She presses her finger beneath my eye and starts spreading the makeup.

Now she smiles. "Much better."

But I don't feel much better. My eyes flit around the packed fast-food place where I'm greeted by the same convoy of faces from Java Shine. We order burger combos and sit at tables. I sip my fountain drink, choking on all the carbonation, blood pumping with all the sugar.

"Well, hello, Madam President," someone says to the girl walking our way. She's tall and pretty with rippling mermaid hair and serious eyes. *Lex.*

Her mouth parts as she looks at me, but no sound comes out.

"Saye," she finally says. "How *are* you?"

"I'm . . . okay."

"You look *good*." It's one of those things you tell sick people in hospitals, but I think she means it nicely.

"Thank you. You're the president now?"

A puzzled line appears between her arching brows. "Well . . . of the *SGA*."

"That's nice. Congratulations. Is Luke here too?"

Braxton snorts loudly. "Biwalker's probably off memorizing Bible passages somewhere."

Biwalker? Oh, right. I forgot people used to call Luke that.

Lex glares at Braxton, while Bria nods sadly. "Luke and Abby Whitley are practically inseparable. It's the freakiest thing."

"Seriously," another boy chimes in. "That church has *brainwashed* him."

And now there are too many voices to follow. I know I used to do this all the time, talk in large groups, but for so long there was just one voice, and I don't understand how people navigate all the threads.

When I hear my name, I look up. "Yes?"

A girl jumps a little. "Oh. I was just saying *Daniel.* You know, the son of the guy who . . . Well, he's been a missing person for years, but they just reopened his case."

Now everyone's back to talking at once, throwing out ideas on what they think happened. I catch pieces: "Clearly that psycho killed him"—"If they haven't found him by now"—"Maybe Daniel ran away." And then someone says, "What about you, Saye? What do *you* think happened to Daniel?"

My mind whirls with memories. Caleb insisting to me, then me insisting to him.

You are *the real Daniel.*

I am *the real Daniel.*

SEVENTY

"Hi, Saye!" a girl calls out as I'm walking onto the back steps after school. More people flood outside—talking, energized. Some smile and wave. A guy in a letterman jacket walks up. "Hey! You wanna come to my Halloween party tomorrow night?"

It reminds me of something Bria told me the other day: *I think you get invited to even more parties now than you did before you left.* And then: *We have to throw another party at your house!*

"I'm not sure," I tell the letterman jacket guy. "But maybe."

He grins and hands me a scrap of paper with his address, then takes off.

As the crowds start to thin, I feel my phone buzz in my pocket—a text from my mother saying she's running late—but I don't mind. It's nice being outside, under the wide-open sky.

I set down my leather satchel, and I'm taking a seat on the top step to wait when the door swings open behind me, nearly smacking into me.

I hop to my feet, coming face-to-face with Evan Zamara, who's dressed in blue scrubs like a doctor or a nurse. My viewfinder starts clicking between two frames.

Evan: small and childlike, with big curls and dimpled knuckles.

Evan: tall and slender, with shorn hair and broad shoulders.

It's shocking that he's this tall, that I have to lean my neck way back to look him in the eyes, but as I do, an image fills my head. Evan in the back seat of a limo. His heart beating so hard its shape is visible through his clothes. Only it feels like I've downloaded someone else's memories, and I'm not sure how much is real. Or maybe this is just the way the brain handles things it doesn't want to believe—to see that as a different person altogether. To claim, like the victim of a body snatcher, that wasn't me.

But it *was* me. And I'm overcome with so much regret it hurts.

Evan's brushing past me now to head down the steps, and without thinking, I call after him. "Evan?"

His whole back stiffens, then he turns and looks up. "Yeah?"

So many thoughts are pressing against my lips, but what comes out is: "It's . . . it's weird we're in the same English class now." Not only because he's younger than me, but also because I remember he was really smart. "Weren't you in AP?"

His mouth tightens. "Not anymore."

And now we're both standing strange like we've paused in our footsteps and someone just needs to press play so we can keep going our separate ways.

But instead I say, "Could we go somewhere? Talk?"

"*Talk?*" Hostility's clenching up all the muscles in his face.

A couple kids who are walking to their cars look over at us.

Evan flicks a glance in their direction and lowers his voice. "No. If you want to say something, just say it here."

"Oh, okay. I . . ." I'm thrown by his expression, distrust and plenty of dislike too. "I just wanted to tell you . . . when we messed with you . . . I mean, I just mean . . ."

"We really don't need to do this." Evan adjusts the giant backpack on his shoulder, angling his head toward the parking lot like he can't stand looking at me.

"It's just when we . . . when *I*—"

"I know what you did," he snaps. "I just never knew *why*."

"We thought it was funny." It's only now that I'm saying it out loud that I realize how awful it sounds.

"Why?"

"Well." I rack my brain. "Honestly? Honestly, I don't know."

Evan starts squeezing his backpack straps, body tense, jaw tense, eyes still looking away. "I used to think it would've been easier if I knew *when* you guys were going to do something. The stress of never knowing when it was coming really got to me. I begged my mom to let me be homeschooled."

A rush of guilt pools in my stomach.

"I never understood how you could treat people the way you did and be so popular."

"I guess because we never hurt anyone who mattered."

Oh God, that came out wrong—and now Evan's eyes flip up. And if eyes can pale, his have, and if eyes are windows, his are open too wide. I can see all his feelings and how much what I just said to him *hurt*, and I think maybe he should wear sunglasses for his own protection. It's not safe to walk around with eyes that reveal so much.

"I—I'm sorry, Evan. I didn't mean it that way. That's just how it seemed *back then*. Like there were certain people it was okay to treat like that, so I guess I got away with it."

"And you were charming," he adds with a touch of scorn.

"No . . ."

"It's true. Everyone worshipped you. *I* worshipped you."

"W-what?"

"You were cool and older, and you were *Sayers Wayte*. But you're right—no one cared what you did. It didn't change anything for you. Just for me."

"I—I think I was crazy. I mean, I must've been."

"You're pleading insanity?"

I shake my head helplessly. I don't know anymore.

Another rush of memories. Garrett's teeth gnashing together on Homecoming night, saying, *Get out, Evan*. Garrett was so angry. So yeah, I must've been crazy to just sit back and let him force Evan out of the limo—but I did. And then I walked off.

Why did I do that?

I don't remember.

And what happened after?

I never knew. Maybe Garrett scared him or threatened him.

"What happened when Garrett took you into the woods?"

Evan goes completely still, and for a moment he looks exactly like he did that night, the same shocked-scared eyes, but then his face clenches into stony anger. "Just stay away from me."

"But—"

And in three huge steps, he's up the stairs and towering over me.

Instinctively, I take a nervous step back.

"Listen to me."

Gulping, I nod my head.

"I know we're in the same class," he tells me in a low voice. "And there's nothing I can do about that. But I'm going to pretend you're not there, and you're going to do the same thing. I mean it."

"But I'm sorry, Evan. I really am."

"Yes, I heard you. I just don't believe you."

SEVENTY-ONE

Where am I?

Some place dark and cold—but not the cellar, not outer space, not my room at Caleb's. I keep ruling out everywhere I'm not until I remember where I am: my bed, my house, sometime in November.

I'm waking from another nightmare. Already the details are slipping away. All I can remember is the cold. I grab my phone off my bedside table: *3:00 a.m.*

This keeps happening—I'll fall asleep, but I can't stay asleep.

I tug open the top drawer of my nightstand, fishing around for my anxiety meds. The bottle is empty, but I don't remember taking the last pill. The painkillers are in the drawer too. They have a similar effect so I take one, then hold my phone and watch the minutes tick by.

I'm running late again. I don't mean to, but I keep getting lost.

Luke was right, I have no sense of direction.

The tardy bell rings, so I quicken my steps.

"Who's next?" Ms. Wells is asking as I'm hurrying into the room.

No one raises their hand.

"If I don't get a volunteer, I'll choose someone," she threatens cheerfully while I slide into my seat.

I really hope she doesn't call on me. My classmates have newspaper articles on their desks, ready to share, but I forgot we even had an assignment. Logically, I know getting called on won't kill me, but it's like my body has no levels anymore. It can't decipher between a minor concern and mortal danger.

Did I remember my homework?

Where is my red-and-gray sweater?

When I walked into the building . . . was that man watching me?

"Last chance," Ms. Wells says, and Blair lurches up from his desk, actually taking it with him for a second. A few people snicker as he stumbles to the front of the room. Ms. Wells shushes them, but Blair's face is as red as his hair, and his hands are shaking so hard his papers rattle.

I feel a wave of sympathy.

Then he begins to read: "More details have been released today about the disappearance of Sayers Wayte," and my heart stills. "Investigators have uncovered nine bodies in the freezers of the suspect's home—"

"Blair," Ms. Wells says in a staggered kind of gasp.

Around me, my classmates look on with equal parts horror and fascination.

"They have been identified to be boys between the ages of twelve and nineteen, all with blond hair and green eyes."

It's like being pushed off the mountaintop. When I land, I'm in the cold room. The frozen boys begin flashing all around me. Frost clings to their hair and lashes, and all the faces are staring staring staring.

"Blair, *stop*." Ms. Wells springs to her feet.

But Blair just reads louder. "Investigators haven't indicated whether there was any sexual abuse, but it's been speculated it may have been a component of the—"

Ms. Wells snatches the papers from Blair's hands. "That's enough, do you hear me?"

But he doesn't seem to hear or see anything but me. With an icy smile, his eyes lock onto mine. "So there's this thing called karma . . ."

"Oh my God, Saye! Are you *okay*?" Marissa, Bria, and a bunch of other girls surround me like mother hens in the crowded hall. "We all heard what Blair did to you!"

"But don't worry," Bria adds. "We are so getting him back."

They all nod, and I think they mean it nicely, protective even— but they don't understand.

"It's not his fault," I tell them quickly. "It's mine." His family went *bankrupt* because of me.

But they ignore me as they discuss all the ways they plan to make his life a living hell.

Sweat starts beading along my lip, and my head's pounding like the skin's pulled too tight, and I hear the word *NO* before I realize I've said it out loud, but then I shout it. "No! I just want you to leave him alone!"

The packed hallway goes quiet.

Bria darts a glance at the nearby gawking faces, and Marissa says, voice hushed, "Jesus, Saye. We're just trying to help. This is so not cool."

Now all the girls look at me with distrusting glares like they think I'm a loose cannon.

And I start to cry.

The girls' mouths drop open in shock.

There's part of me, an observer who's witnessing the scene, and he's cringing in shame for the weird guy bawling in the middle of the hall.

"*Saye,*" Bria hisses. "You're embarrassing me."

SEVENTY-TWO

Rain's pelting all my windows. It's tranquil, amniotic.

Is that why Penny loved storms?

Winter break is nearly over, and I don't want to go back to school on Monday, but I also don't like being home. It's lonely—me in my wing and Mom in hers. It seems like she kept to herself the whole time, especially after that phone call with my school counselor. I'm not sure what the man told her, but whatever it was upset her so much, she retreated for days.

I crawl out of my bed and crank open one of the long, narrow panes. The rain's much louder now, and the sky is dark.

Feeling an uptick in my heart, I quickly locate my pain pills. Only three left, and the side of the bottle reads *No Refills Remaining*. If I want more, I'll have to sit in an office with some doctor, so I'd better ration them.

Instead, I pop all three into my mouth, chug some water, and swallow.

I'm only a little bit high. Just enough to tilt the planet sixteen degrees to the right.

I stumble, nearly fall.

Okay, actually, I'm *high as a kite*—that's a funny expression.

Yeah, I'm a *kite*, and someone's holding my string, but they aren't doing a good job down there because I keep crashing into storm clouds.

I never loved the rain like her. Never wanted the water in my body to convert to rainwater. But now I do. Soaking wet, I trip down street after shiny street, all the way to downtown where the lights are twinkly-bright-surreal.

My shoes are too heavy like they're trying to suck me underground. I kick them off and keep walking until I find myself in front of the Rialto Theater, where Penny and I used to go.

I tug on the glass door. *Locked.*

But I want in.

I want to see the red curtain part.

I want to see me and Penny projected against the screen.

I throw myself against the door. It doesn't give, so I try harder, *harder*, and a jagged crack races up the glass like a break in a frozen pond.

Startled, I stumble back.

But the glass doesn't shatter.

The rain's still pouring. My bare arms are chilly like ice, and it's dark and scary and moonless.

Pushing my wet hair out of my face, I walk and walk and walk—until finally, I'm across the street from the tall iron gate surrounding my neighborhood.

I'm tired now, or maybe someone's just pulling my string and dragging me back to the ground.

I start crossing the road, peering at the security booth, but the rain's slashing down too hard to see through its little window. I'm almost there when the security guard pops out of the booth, squinting at me with a cell phone pressed to his ear. "He's here," the guard says into his phone, then he gives me a grim look. "Mr. Wayte, everyone's been looking for you."

Out of nowhere, amusement starts bubbling up inside me.

"Well. . ." I smile and hold out my arms. "You found me."

But he doesn't laugh even though that was hilarious, just shakes his head and presses a button.

The tall gate parts and, oh no—

Inside, there are too many squad cars with flashing lights to count, like the entire government turned up to track me down.

SEVENTY-THREE

I get escorted into my house by three policemen. There are dozens more milling around inside, but they all go quiet when I come in, dripping water everywhere. Near the main stairs, my mom's pacing, but the second she sees me she sags, practically bent in two like a giant stepped on her back.

"Thank God, thank God," she says over and over. And then, "Where were you?"

"Um . . ." There's too much law enforcement eyeing me with suspicion, and I'm still super high and trying to act like I'm not. "On a walk?"

Several officers let out irritated noises. One of them mutters something about wasting their time, and another says, "Do you make a habit of going for walks at three in the morning?"

"Uh . . . not usually." I'm getting tense and stressed, and now my mom's yelling at me.

"Why didn't you bring your phone? And where the hell was that security guard? How did you even leave without him notifying me?"

So I yell back, "What am I? A *prisoner*?"

"Ms. Wayte," a detective-looking guy cuts in. "Your son is clearly fine, so we'll see ourselves out. But my advice would be to keep a better eye on him."

She flinches. I can't tell if she's embarrassed or angry or hurt.

The officers mobilize, a bunch of them shooting me dirty looks on their way out. The front door shuts with an echo and it's quiet till my mom says, "This isn't okay, Sayers. You're going to start telling me what you're doing, at all times."

"Why? You never cared before."

She takes in a harsh breath. "I *did* care. I just never thought . . ." Shaking her head, she says, "You just had too much freedom."

I stare at her for a second.

Then I'm laughing so hard I'm clutching my stomach. "You think I've had too much *freedom*? I've been locked up for a hundred years!" Giggling, I stumble around, dragging one of my legs behind me like it's attached to a chain, but she's not getting the joke at all.

"Saye." Her voice breaks. "That's not what I meant—that's not what I'm saying."

But I keep laughing and laughing, and her eyes go wide. "Why are you acting like this?"

I lift my hand in the air, press down my thumb, and plunge an invisible needle into my neck.

"Are you on drugs right now?"

I'm tearing up. It's just too funny.

"Saye, answer me. Are you high?"

"As a kite!"

"What did you take?"

"Just the pills you got me."

"You mean your *prescriptions*? How many pills did you take?"

"A lot."

Her mouth twitches like she's going to cry. She wipes her nose with the back of her hand. "What were you thinking, Saye? *Anything* could've happened to you in this state. You could've been . . ." But her words trail off like she's scared to say it out loud.

"I could've been what?" I chuckle, but now it's a cold, bitter sound. *"Kidnapped?"*

SEVENTY-FOUR

I flail awake, folded into a weird position on my bed. I don't remember much about what happened last night, but I'm embarrassed by what I do remember. There are mixed-up rainy flashes. Me wandering the streets. Me coming home to the fricking National Guard.

I climb out of bed. My socks are caked with mud, reminding me I kicked my shoes off somewhere. I peel my shirt over my head, get it caught around my face like a blindfold, and another memory springs forth.

Did I try to break into the Rialto?

I think so.

Yeah, that was bad, that was really bad.

Chewing on the side of my thumb, I start to pace, this awful-anxious feeling crawling over me. I wish someone were here with me—I don't want to be alone when I'm feeling like this.

We're never alone.

That's what Penny told me.

I go completely still.

I have to see Penny.

SEVENTY-FIVE

I've found the hugging trees at the bottom of Cedar Way. In a totally flat town, Penny's street slants up. She never told me that. But I guess there's a lot I don't know about her, so much I haven't asked, or forgot to ask, or never got a chance to ask.

Part of me wants to linger here, but the urge to see her drives me up the hill, past a bunch of older homes, the whole road lined in mature trees. I know her street name, but not her street number, so I'm looking close—and then I see a yellow cottage-style house with a big front porch.

And sitting at a picnic table on the porch is a small boy with dark shiny hair, drawing pictures with Magic Markers. It's the face from all Penny's drawings. Little chin, big brown eyes.

Nicolai.

But I'm in no state to talk to a kid right now. I should turn around and go, maybe some other day.

But then the boy looks up.

His eyes grow bigger, this wary expression that has me taking a couple of steps back. I don't want to scare him.

"Hi." I wave at him from the sidewalk.

"Hi," he echoes in a high-pitched voice like a cartoon chipmunk.

"I'm here to see your sister. Penny."

"She's not here." The *r* is missing from *here* so it sounds like *hee-uh.*

"Oh, um, that's okay. Uh . . ." I have no idea how to talk to little kids, no clue. "I can wait." I turn around and lower myself onto the curb, tapping my thumbs against my knees.

A minute later, the boy calls out, "Do you like dogs?"

I twist around. Now he's standing on the top step of his porch.

"Uh. Sure."

"Me too. I want one. Very little so I can hold him like this." He cradles his arms as if he's holding a newborn baby, which is strange because he looks like a baby himself. He's really small for a kindergartner, or maybe I just don't know how big kindergartners should be.

"That sounds . . . nice."

"Penny's not coming back for a long time."

"She's not?"

He shakes his head, and there's a jarring level of sadness on a face so young. "She had too many nightmares." His little brow is knitted as he tries to explain. "She had to go to a doctor-school. It's for if you're very afraid of bad guys and you have to talk about your feelings."

Nerves pool in my gut. Is he trying to describe a psychiatric hospital?

"Do you wanna see my picture?" he asks, and there's something so lonely about his figure, dressed in a little red coat and candy-cane-striped pajama pants, gray sky all around him, that suddenly I'm fighting very hard not to cry.

But I climb the creaking porch steps, and he points to his drawing—a boy with a silver star on his chest the size of his head. "That's me," he says. "I'm gonna be a pweece-man when I grow up. So whoever is lost I can find them."

My throat begins to burn. My eyes do too.

"Sayers?"

Hearing my name, I turn, and a woman with dark hair to her waist is standing in the threshold of the door. Penny's mother. There's a ceramic watering can in her hand as if she was stepping out to feed the flowers, but she sets it down and slides the glasses from her head onto her eyes, getting a better look at me.

Penny's mother can't know about how I was an empty vessel in the cellar that got filled up with Penny's life. That I smelled flowers from her garden, was fed with memories of her food. But it's as if she *does* know, because instead of looking at me like I'm someone she's meeting for the first time, she's looking at me like I'm someone she loves.

"Yes." There's a lump in my throat. "I'm Sayers."

"Do you want to come inside?"

SEVENTY-SIX

The foyer is just like Penny described. Enough plants to fill a greenhouse. Every wall a different color. "I'm sorry for just showing up like this, Mrs. Valles."

"It's okay." Her voice is gentle. "You're welcome here anytime."

My eyes slide off her face and onto the floor. Suddenly, I'm painfully aware of what I'm wearing—a tuxedo shirt over torn joggers. I didn't even think about what I put on before coming over. It's just that almost everything I have is dirty, and clean clothes aren't magically appearing in my closet the way they used to.

"How's your mom doing?" Mrs. Valles asks.

I look up. "My mom?"

"We got to know each other a little when you and Penny were in the hospital."

"Oh. She's . . . okay, I guess."

"I've been thinking of her. Of *both* of you." She takes in a deep breath. "Penny wasn't doing well at home." And I get this feeling she's understating things, by a *lot*, that it's so much worse than what she's saying.

"Nickel said she's in a school?"

Her lips lift into a bittersweet smile. "*Nickel.* Penny's the only one who calls him that." She draws in another big breath. "It's a residential program. Oak Hill. She's able to get treatment and take classes so she doesn't fall further behind."

"Oh. That's good." And I want to say: *Can I see her?* But I'm afraid I'll get the same answer the doctor gave me in the hospital, so instead I ask, "When will she be back?"

"It'll depend on how she's doing. But we're hopeful for the end of June."

The end of *June?* That's so long, that's *months* away.

"I thought . . ." My throat's gone dry. "I thought once she got home, she'd be okay."

"Yes . . . I did too."

"Inside, she was so *strong.*"

Moisture wraps over her eyes. She takes off her glasses, wipes her face. "Penny's doctor told me that's how some people cope. They can hold on during a trauma, but once they're safe . . ."

They fall apart.

C-O-W-A-R-D. It's scrawled into my skull. Rewritten deeper and deeper with every step.

I couldn't do it. Couldn't stay ten minutes before I made up an excuse to Penny's mother, and then to a *five*-year-old, and I got out of there. As I was tearing down the hill, I heard Nicolai's high voice calling after me, "Come back soon!"

But I shouldn't have gone there at all. What was I thinking? Of course Penny's not okay. The last time I saw her . . . It all rushes back.

Penny scrambling off her hospital bed, falling, *bleeding*.

I'm onto another street when I'm struck by an unexpected flicker of anger. How much harder was it in there for Penny because of me? Having to be so soothing all the time, having to take care of me. And even now—God, I was expecting her to do it again. I should've been going to her house to *give* help, not to get it.

But how could *I* help anyone? I'm scared of the dark, I'm scared of everything.

And I never used to be this way. Before, I could function. I knew how to use a Scantron and order coffee and kiss my girlfriend. I was *normal*.

And it's not fucking normal to be crying in the middle of the street like this. Scrubbing my eyes with the heels of my palms, I'm overcome by this enormous feeling I don't know what to do with. I just know it can't be here when Penny gets out of the hospital.

Somehow before the end of June, I'm going to change. I'll get myself together, and by the time Penny's home, I'll be okay, I'll be strong, I'll be what she needs.

SEVENTY-SEVEN

It's morning—things are supposed to look better and brighter in the morning—but I feel even worse. And it doesn't make sense because I *decided*. I was sure. I swore I was getting my shit together. So why don't I feel more together?

There's a frosty glaze covering all my windows. I swipe my palm across the glass, revealing a landscape so white I shudder. Snatching up my cell phone, I check the weather. It dropped thirty degrees overnight, and it's early—an hour before I have to go to school. I need something to do with my hands, so I gather the mountain of laundry that's taking over half my room, along with all the piles of dirty dishes, but instead of hauling everything all the way downstairs, I toss them in the guest room across the hall.

Next, I shower, spend way too long heating my skin under the hot water, then I dress myself in some clothes that smell okay. But when I get to the great room, my mom's not there.

Is she still upset with me?

I peek into her room. She's sleeping, her face slack, and I can't bring myself to wake her.

So now what?

Walk to school?—It's below freezing. The cold makes me nervous.

Skip school?—I'll be alone in my room all day.

Call the car service?—I don't want to get into a car with a stranger.

Drive myself?—Frightening flashes—a broken GPS and a dark road.

There's no choice that isn't scary, but I guess walking is the *least* scary, so I throw on my lost-and-found sweater and some boots that can handle ice, but it's like a fear switch that won't turn off. My nerves are set on frayed.

By the time I'm halfway to school, I'd do anything to make it stop. I wish I had more meds. I wouldn't be stupid and take too many this time. I'd take just enough to calm down. But there's no way my mom's going to get me any more. A sudden hopeful thought—Garrett's boxing buddy from before. He always managed to get ahold of pills. What was his name?

Tanner.

I dig my phone out of my brown leather satchel. There are exactly two numbers plugged into my cell, Mom's and Bria's, so for the first time since I've been back, I open Instagram.

Ignoring the flood of red alerts, I locate Tanner's account and send him a DM, straight to the point: *Hey, man. You have anything?*

I'm walking into the school when he answers: *What do you need?*

My morning's a blur. The counselor—a burly guy in a sweater vest—called me into his office to tell me I failed every subject last semester, then he snapped the rubber band off a thick file folder and spread a whole stack of papers across his desk. My tests, worksheets, quizzes. None of the questions answered, all covered in drawings of horses and sailboats.

My face got hot as he told me I'd have to make those classes up in summer school, and if I didn't start doing better, we might have to make *other arrangements*, but he wouldn't explain what that meant.

Fourth period's my only class that's different from the fall, a one-semester Economics course. I find a seat at the black lacquered table in the very back, and a minute later, Garrett swaggers into the room, somehow even bigger than he was before the break. His arms are practically tree trunks now, and it looks like he's got boulders tied to his wrists.

Braxton, spiky-haired and dressed in a puffy gold coat, is right behind him. They nod in my direction and join me at my table. As soon as everyone has a textbook and syllabus, we're stuck in first-day limbo. There's not enough time for an actual lesson, so the teacher lets us do whatever we want, within reason. I draw sailboats in the margins of my syllabus while Garrett and Braxton compare notes on some New Year's Eve party they went to and how much weight they can lift now.

"Hey—" Garrett's grabbing my shoulder, startling me. "Is it cool if I ask out Bria?"

"W-what?"

"You guys broke up, right?" I must be telegraphing that I have no idea what he's talking about because he adds, "She changed her status."

"Oh."

"She didn't tell you?"

When I shake my head, Braxton laughs. "That's cold."

"So is it all right?" Garrett presses.

"Yeah. I mean, if we're not together . . ."

"Good." He smiles, his teeth edging out from the corner of his lips. "Just checking."

During lunch, the tips of my ears burn as I trudge down a slushy street to meet Tanner at a gas station four blocks from school. As soon as I get there, a tinted window lowers, and a hand waves me over like this is some kind of midnight rendezvous instead of a drug deal in broad daylight. I pry open the passenger door, and then I freeze—I've made a horrible mistake and approached the wrong car.

But no, it's Tanner. He just looks older with his scruffy beard.

He narrows his eyes. "You coming or what?"

When I hesitate for another few seconds, he tenses like he's about to take off, so I scramble inside. While he drives, his gaze keeps flicking from me to the road, to me again.

"Dude, you look so different. Your hair's so *long.*"

He's right, it is, and not in a rock-star-cool type of way either.

Tanner makes me get out a block from the ATM, something about cameras, but as soon as I withdraw the cash, he waves me back to his car. Once I'm inside, he merges onto the road—one hand on the steering wheel, his other hand snaking into the back-seat floorboards—and he comes up with a vacuum-sealed plastic bag that he tosses onto my lap.

It takes me a second to realize what it is. "Weed?" I lift the plastic sack into the air.

"Dude—stick that in your bag."

"No, I need *meds*. I'm out of refills."

"I'm not selling pills anymore."

"But I don't need to get high, I need to relax."

He throws a glance to my bouncing leg. "If you're needing to calm down, this'll do it."

"I don't even have anything to smoke with."

He flips open his glove compartment and fishes out a pipe. "On me."

A button's missing from my lost-and-found sweater. It must've fallen off between lunch and the final bell, so freezing wind's whipping through the gap. Maybe it came loose in Tanner's car. I'll have to message him when I get home and ask if he's seen it.

I cross the bridge that's dripping with icicles and move onto an empty stretch of road. It's so quiet, like the snowfall has softened all sound. I'm readjusting my satchel, crossing it diagonally over my chest when I hear something. A soft engine *vroom*. Faint at first, then more noticeable, like it's closing in.

I look back, and about thirty feet away, a brown sedan with a jutting square nose is idling. Not stopped exactly, but edging along just fast enough to keep pace with my steps.

Someone's following me.

SEVENTY-EIGHT

I'm jumping to conclusions. It's the bad weather—that's why the car's going so slow.

Heart thudding, I sneak another glance over my shoulder. The brown sedan is still trailing behind me like the driver is trying to keep me in sight. Squinting, I take in the misshapen dent on the fender and the Illinois plates. Out-of-towners. Another reason the car might be creeping along. For all I know, they could be lost.

At the intersection, I take a right, and out of the corner of my eye, I can see the sedan turning too.

Following me.

Definitely following me.

I stare straight ahead now, a sick feeling clawing from my stomach up to my chest. Passing an empty playground, I can hear the swings squeaking as they're pushed by the wind. On any other day, the park would be packed with families, but not when it's as cold as this.

The car is still trailing me.

I cut across the playground, stiff icy grass crunching beneath my feet.

As soon as I reach the street, I walk faster, looping around the block, and I've just hit the main road that I was on before when the squeal of halting tires cuts through the air.

Another glance over my shoulder.

The driver's side door is open, and a man with slicked-back hair is climbing out.

The passenger door opens too—another man, bigger, stockier, is getting out—and I run.

Or at least I *try*. But my limbs are slow and clumsy like my body doesn't know how. My boots slide over the slick sidewalk, squelching through puddles, panic in my throat.

The men's feet pound down the sidewalk after me.

"You getting him?" I hear one of them say.

I move faster, and my satchel's swinging up and flipping around my back, and my heart's about to explode when a red truck with oversized hubcaps veers onto the shoulder.

Evan Zamara climbs out, tall and solid like a Roman statue, his brow knitted in what looks like concern. His eyes flick behind me to where the men are chasing me, and an understanding fills his face, followed by this look of total disgust.

I turn now, seeing—a huge camera on the bigger guy's shoulders.

He's filming me.

The guy angles his camera higher. "Sayers! Tell us about Caleb Emory!"

And even though I'm registering that no one's about to steal me, it's like my body doesn't believe it. It's shaking even harder, my knees buckling as I'm panting in cold air, and my eyes aren't seeing things clearly anymore—they're skipping too many frames—and I land on the moment where Evan is standing right in front of me, his mouth tightening across his face.

"Come on, Saye," he says. "I'll take you home."

Evan speeds off down the slushy street. "Were those reporters?"

"I—I'm not sure." Trying to catch my breath, my heart's still racing. "I think more like paparazzi." A nervous laugh skitters out as if to say, *It's funny, right? Absurd that paparazzi are after* me.

"That should be illegal." Evan's eyes lift to the rearview mirror like he's worried we're being followed. When I spin around to check, he tells me, "I think we lost them."

Letting out another shaky laugh, I slump against the seat, searching my brain for something easier to talk about, and come up with: "What's your favorite flower?"

Evan's head swivels to me, his eyes narrowed like he thinks he might've misunderstood the question. "What?"

"Um . . . your favorite flower?"

"Oh. I've never thought about it."

"Then what's your favorite color?"

"Uh, blue. Or maybe silver." But he's looking at me like I'm the strangest person he's ever met, so I switch gears again.

"I . . . I like your clothes. Are they for theater?"

"You mean my scrubs?" When I nod, he says, "I intern at the hospital a few days a week."

"It doesn't bother you?"

"What?"

"Being around sick people."

"No, I want to be a doctor, so that comes with the territory."

"Really? That's cool."

Evan nods stiffly, like maybe he thinks I'm being sarcastic, and it's very possible he still hates me. That he was just being a Good Samaritan by helping me out, and he'd really like for me to shut up now.

But then he says, "So . . . what about you?" in the tone of someone trying to make polite conversation. "What are you going to major in?"

"Me?" The question catches me off guard. "I—I don't know. It's so far away. I'm only . . ." No, I'm *not* only ten years old. "I mean, it feels far away."

"Well, what kind of things do you like to do?"

I like to draw—that's my first thought. But that's not me, that's *Daniel.* Only I *do* like to draw, so maybe it *is* me. Or maybe it's both of us. I search my brain—what would Saye say?

"This is starting to feel like a meeting with my guidance counselor," I try and joke.

"Do you need guidance?" Evan asks, and I can't tell if he's being playful or serious.

"I . . . I guess I like languages."

"Yeah?"

He looks interested now, and it excites me into rambling, "Yeah, it's like a code. And if you know it, you can understand everyone— and I think it's like knowing the secrets of the universe if you can understand everyone."

"I feel that way about biology. Like if I can just understand the body, I could solve anything." Evan smiles, and it's the exact pure smile he wore a hundred years ago when he was showing me that Operation sculpture he made. "Can you speak any other languages?"

"I'm fluent in Spanish and French. And Portuguese and Italian aren't too hard if you can speak those. I also took Latin. Plus I know bits and pieces of a lot of other languages." I start rattling off phrases in French, Icelandic, and Greek, and I'm grinning at the astonished expression on Evan's face.

It's weird, but for the first time since I've been back, things feel almost . . . comfortable.

I'm still smiling when out of the corner of my eye I spot smoke rising from the hood. "What is *that*?"

Evan presses his hazard lights. "It's fine."

But it doesn't look fine at all. It looks like this truck's about to *explode*.

Evan makes it to the shoulder just as the engine sputters out. Before I have a chance to say anything, he's outside and tapping the hood with his gloved hand.

I follow him onto the shoulder, stuffing my freezing fingers into my pockets. "Should we call someone?"

"No, it just overheated." Evan's eyes stay on the engine.

"Cars can overheat in the winter?"

"Afraid so." He looks up for a second. "Go on and wait in the truck. You don't even have a coat."

Now I notice that, unlike me, Evan is dressed properly for the weather in a black knit hat, black gloves, and a gray wool coat over his scrubs. I get in the truck and watch him carry what looks like a plastic milk jug from the trunk to the hood.

My eyes dart around—still no sign of those men.

A couple minutes later, Evan hops back into the driver's seat and turns the key. Thankfully, the motor comes to life, so Evan merges onto the road, but we don't go back to talking like we did before. Things feel off, *tense.*

I flick a glance at Evan—

And now I see it.

He's *embarrassed.* It's written all over his face, and I'm struck with a sharp guilty pain in my gut. Garrett and Braxton and I made fun of him for being too broke to buy a nice car. On his *birth-day.* How could we do that?

I want to tell Evan I'm sorry, but last time I tried, it didn't go over so well.

Before long, we reach the wrought-iron gates surrounding my neighborhood. The guard buzzes us through, and Evan takes the winding road to my house. As he pulls to a stop out front, I'm open-ing my mouth to thank him for the ride, but what comes out is: "Do you want to hang out?"

In the great room, Evan slides off his knit hat. His hair is so short I can see the faint glow of scalp under his bristles. "This place is incredible." Evan's eyes are everywhere—examining the wood carvings on the overdoors, lifting to the mural on the ceiling. "I think I could fit my entire house into this room."

I don't know what to do with the compliment. This doesn't even really feel like my house.

"I can show you around. If you want."

Tours were always something my mother did. A friend or colleague would come over, and she'd gesture here and there, to a painting or sculpture. Some pieces they'd recognize, others from an up-and-coming artist only she was in the know about. She'd tell them where she bought the tiles—imported from Tuscany. The beams—from an old church in England. That lamp—from a Sotheby's auction.

Suddenly, I feel dumb, like I'm showing off. "But we don't have to."

"No, I want to see it," Evan insists.

So I take him to the library, to the solarium, to my mother's room full of porcelain dolls arranged like inhabitants of a miniature city.

"Creepy?" I ask, catching the look on Evan's face.

"Well . . ."

"My best friend, Luke, always said they were."

"*Star Wars* Luke?"

I smile a little. "Yeah, you know him?"

"We've spoken a few times."

"He won't really talk to me anymore." I didn't mean to say that out loud—and I definitely didn't mean to say it in that shaky, almost-crying voice, so I swiftly change the subject. "Do you wanna watch a movie?"

And without any arm-twisting, Evan says, "Okay."

We take the back stairs to my room, and I toss my leather satchel on my desk. "You wanna smoke?" I ask, and I'm not trying to impress him or anything. It's just if I'm going to smoke, it would be rude not to offer.

"No, that's all right."

I shrug as if to say *suit yourself*, then I dig my hand into my satchel and pull out the sealed baggie. I'm fishing around for the pipe Tanner gave me when I catch the startled look on Evan's face.

"You had that in your bag the whole time?"

"Um . . ."

"While you were in my *truck*?" I don't know how to answer. It's obvious that I did, but he already looks really freaked out, and saying yes will probably just make him more upset. "What if we'd gotten pulled over?" Before I can answer, he says, "We would've gotten *arrested*."

"Well, I didn't know you were gonna give me a ride home!" My voice comes out strangled and defensive and way too loud.

"And I didn't know *you* carry around five-pound bags of weed."

And I guess this is it. Three strikes I'm out.

It shouldn't hurt this much, but it does.

"I'm sorry, Evan." I drop my eyes. "It didn't even occur to me. But if we had gotten pulled over, I would've told them it was mine. I wouldn't have let you get arrested."

When he doesn't respond, I lift my head. His face is set in some expression I can't identify, and it's seriously unsettling not to be able to read him.

"So are we going to watch a movie?" he finally says. "You didn't mention you have a literal movie theater in your bedroom." And now I catch the faintly playful lift at the corner of his lips, and my mouth twitches into a happy smile.

"Yeah. Definitely."

Evan takes the couch. I take the bed, then toss him the remote, and watch him scroll through Amazon, past comedies and dramas and documentaries about killers, eventually landing on some sitcom I've never seen before because it just came out last year.

"This okay?" he asks.

"Sure, fine."

He presses play, and the show begins, but for some reason I can't focus. My attention keeps drifting to the row of windows. The sun's going to set in less than an hour, that's inevitable. I start chewing on my thumb, eyeing the bag of weed. If there's even a chance it could calm me down, I want to snatch up my pipe and smoke downstairs, but it'll look weird—like I'm an addict or something. And then maybe when I get back to my room, Evan'll say, *Actually I've gotta go now.* And then it'll be dark, and I'll—

"Are you nervous?"

I remove my thumb from my mouth. "What?"

Evan repeats, "Are you nervous?"

I nod, and Evan's face goes soft. "Does that happen a lot? You getting followed?"

"No." But now I'm even more nervous, because what if it *does* happen a lot, and I just never notice? "I mean, I don't *think* it does. It's just, everyone wants to know about my dad, but he's gone so—"

Evan's eyebrows smoosh together in obvious confusion, and

now I realize what I've said.

"Your *dad*?" he echoes.

But when I don't respond, he says, "Are you seeing a doctor or anything?"

"Doctor?"

"Like a therapist or a psychiatrist?"

If anyone else asked me that, the implication would hurt, but for some reason coming from Evan there's no sting.

"My mom wanted me to see someone."

"But you don't want to?"

"I had a couple of sessions." If I count Ruth at the hospital.

"And?"

"It wasn't for me."

"Why not?"

"The therapist-lady, she made me feel . . . uneasy."

"You have to keep trying till you get someone you feel comfortable with."

"Therapy isn't for everyone," I point out.

"But talking to someone can really help." Evan's looking at me with such intensely earnest eyes, like the nicest eyes I've ever seen, that suddenly I'm overcome with affection.

"I'll think about it."

SEVENTY-NINE

I know I shouldn't smoke before school, that's a no-brainer, but when my alarm goes off, and immediately I'm terrified for no reason—I'm tempted.

Climbing into the shower, I will it to pass.

Calm down, Sayers.

Please calm down.

When I get out, I'm still shivering, from cold, from fear. I don't even know what I'm afraid of, but I'm so past the edge of panic, I can't take it anymore.

Finding my pipe and filling the bowl, I take a hit—hold it for a moment, then release.

I cough, blinking hard. Stand up, stagger, sway.

I study my reflection in the bathroom mirror.

I don't *think* I look high.

I've either got the world's best or the world's worst timing—that's what's running through my mind as we're shepherded out of first period, down halls lined in Valentine's Day hearts, into new rooms for standardized testing.

Turns out Evan and I are in the same room thanks to alphabetical order. I give him a happy wave, but when his eyes narrow, I wonder if maybe I *do* look high.

Sliding into a desk, I try to focus on instructions from the teacher.

Use your pencil to open the seal on the test booklet.

Read the essays carefully.

Don't skip ahead.

You have one hour.

Evan gets right to work. He's got the same focused face he wore a couple weeks ago when he repaired the eighteenth-century clock that stands in my library. He deconstructed it, no book or manual in sight. Then, sitting cross-legged on the floor, he gazed down at the gears and weights and all the pieces of the clock spread out in front of him like they were beautiful—and then he put the clock back together in perfect working order.

Evan looks up from his test and starts twirling his hand at me, a not-so-subtle gesture to get to work.

With a sigh, I focus on my booklet, but the words seem to bend, the *room* seems to bend, and I'm less than halfway through when the teacher calls time.

"Sayers . . ." Evan whispers as we shuffle out of the room for lunch. "You smell like weed."

"I do?" I press my nose into my sleeve.

"Yeah. I think maybe you're smoking too much—"

"It was *one* hit. I'm not even buzzed anymore."

"But these tests are important, you know? You can't graduate unless you pass them." Evan's been pretty appalled about the state of my GPA, and he tutors me every chance he gets. "And you shouldn't smoke before school. What if a teacher notices?"

Sometimes I think if Evan could be in charge of me, he'd give me more rules than my old boarding school. Suddenly the Observer Me shows up, pointing out that the me-from-before would've hated being lectured this way.

But now it feels almost . . . nice. Like it just means he cares.

"I know. You're right, Evan."

And he really is. I'm already a year behind where I should be, so I'm promising to try harder as we turn onto another hall, and that's when I see Bria and Garrett making out against a row of lockers. Her hands tangled in his black hair, his hands squeezing her hips, all definitely against the student code on PDA—and Garett's just caught me watching them.

With a slow smirk, his hands drift down, cupping her butt.

Embarrassed, I look away, locking eyes with Evan, who's obviously just witnessed the whole thing. But we don't talk about it, just head into the crowded cafeteria.

Normally, I'm in B-lunch and have to find some place to hide for forty minutes, so I'm glad the scheduling's been scrambled today. I join Evan in line where we grab trays of Salisbury steak, crinkle-cut fries, and fruit cups.

At the register, Evan flashes a white card that he quickly stuffs back into his pocket.

"I don't have one of those lunch cards," I explain to the cashier lady.

"Are you on free or reduced lunch?" she asks.

"O-oh, um," I stammer, glancing over at Evan, whose cheeks have gone dark red.

"Just pay cash, Sayers," he tells me when I don't move.

I open my wallet and hand the lady a twenty.

Once I collect my change, I follow Evan to a corner table where he introduces me to his group of friends, all guys. I'm not sure what I would've thought of them before—probably nothing good, given the way they're poring over their textbooks while they eat—but that would've been a shame because they're nice, making a real effort to include me in their conversation, and they don't seem put off when I can't think of anything to say back.

I'm tearing open a packet of ketchup when I hear the loud scrape of metal chair legs, and I look up to find Dillon Blair sitting right across from me.

EIGHTY

"Hey," Evan says to Blair, a slight edge to his tone. "What's up?"

"*What's up?*" Blair repeats in a low, outraged voice. "Why is he sitting here?"

"It's okay," Evan says. "I asked him to."

Blair's jaw drops. "So you guys are *friends* now?"

"Listen . . ." Evan's tone is appeasing. "Why don't we just—"

Blair's head swivels to me. "Stop staring at us. No one's talking to you."

Immediately, I drop my eyes.

Around me, I can feel Evan's friends tensing up.

"If you told him to sit here," Blair says to Evan, "then you can tell him to leave."

There's a long tense quiet before Blair snaps, "I don't *get* you, Evan. You used to tell me all the time about the things you'd do to him if you ever got the chance."

Flinching, I lift my head. Is that true?

Evan won't meet my eyes. "Sayers, it's not like that. It's just . . ." But then he turns to Blair and mumbles, "That was before. I mean . . . *look* at him."

Blair gives me a disgusted up-and-down scan. "He's faking it."

I don't understand what he means. "The guy's obviously worked some kind of con if you think he's not the same person he was last year. Sayers Wayte will *never* change."

This settles over me like a prophecy or a curse.

"But all right . . ." Blair lets out a loud, cynical laugh. "Just be careful. We all know what happens if you get on the wrong side of Sayers Wayte, right?" Blair stands up, speaking loudly enough to address the entire cafeteria—and they're listening. It's like everyone has stopped talking, stopped eating so they can give all their attention to what's unfolding. "His psycho grandfather and psycho mom convince the whole town you're a murderer. They get your parents fired too. No one wants a murderer's parents working for them."

A lump's forming in my throat. I didn't know that happened. "Blair . . ."

"Shut. Up." He levels a finger at me.

I look down again, and a moment later I feel a soft hand on my back. One of Evan's friends is patting me, while shooting disapproving scowls at Blair.

Blair flinches like he's been slapped. "Why are you looking at me like *I'm* the bully?" He curls his fingers into his skinny chest.

When no one answers, Blair wilts in place. In his eyes, there's a certain misery I've caught in mirrors, and I have to make this right.

I get to my feet, and the effect this has on the room is startling. An instant flurry of excited murmurs. The word *fight* zips through the cafeteria. Evan surges to his feet too and tries to get to the other side of the table, but so do a lot of other people—ones angling for a better view—and they're blocking his path.

Blair swoops toward me. "You might've fooled some people into thinking you've changed, but I get you! You're still the same arrogant, superior, high and might—"

I sink to my knees.

And everything goes quiet.

My hands to my sides, I lift my head. "I'm sorry, Blair."

There's a collective gasp, then smatters of shocked laughter, but I ignore them and keep my focus on Blair who's gaping down at me.

"W-what are you doing?" he snaps before his gaze darts across the cafeteria like he's mortified.

"I'm sorry," I say again. "Please let me fix this."

"You can't *fix* it. Are you crazy or something?"

Now the cafeteria's roaring with laughter. Blair glances around some more, then he singes me with a glare and whips around, shoving through the crowd of onlookers, so I'm left looking up at nothing.

My eyes drop to the floor, feeling hundreds of stares hot against my cheeks.

I don't understand what I did wrong. I'm *humbling* myself. I thought that was good.

"Sayers?"

I lift my head.

Evan's in the spot where Blair stood a minute ago, his face troubled.

"Come on, Sayers." He holds out his hand. "Stand up."

EIGHTY-ONE

Evan's tiptoeing around my room, but since I'm a light sleeper his subtle noises wake me up anyway. I blink to find him wet-haired from the shower and freakishly perky for a Saturday morning.

When he sees I'm awake, he says, "Are you okay?" Exactly like he did after lunch yesterday, and on the drive home from school, and last night when he was practically tucking me into bed.

Sitting up, I rub my eyes. "Yeah . . . I'm okay."

But he leans against the frame of my door with a gaze that says he's not sure he believes me, like he suspects something might be seriously wrong with me—and maybe there is, because everything that happened yesterday feels like the opposite of getting myself together.

"Evan . . . do you think people can change?"

"Of course," he says without a beat.

That's one of the things I love about Evan. The straightforward answers, no room for doubts.

"How are you so sure?"

"Well, from a biological perspective, we're in a constant state of transformation. The brain is always developing new neural pathways whenever you learn something, and ninety-eight percent of our atoms are replaced every single year."

"Really?" That's comforting.

I imagine every part of myself being replaced with something better.

"So are you going to get ready?"

I look at him blankly.

"To go to the library. There's a book I need for the research paper."

Right. We did talk about that. But at the thought of getting out of bed, I nearly plummet back onto my pillow. "Let's just buy it, okay? I'll order it."

"But it's out of print."

I'm tempted to tell him he can go without me, because seriously, who does homework on the *weekend*? But in all fairness, we are partners on this project, so I drag myself to the side of my bed and start tugging socks over my feet.

Evan grimaces. "Buddy . . ."

I can't even pretend not to know what he's talking about. I've been wearing the same pair for over a week. "I'm out of clothes."

"*Out?*"

"They're all dirty. I need to order more things."

Evan makes a sputtering, laughing noise. "Sayers, just *wash* them."

I don't want to admit I have no idea how to work the washing machine, because it's so cliché it's embarrassing. But the truth is, my only point of reference is movies where well-meaning children try to wash dishes or do laundry and they use the wrong kind of soap and destroy the house.

"Let me see if I can find something," I mumble.

Across the hall, I brace myself to duck into the guest room, which now looks like a city dump minus the flies, and unfortunately, Evan's right behind me.

He stares, apparently speechless.

"Um, do you want me to help you?" he finally asks, and he's being nice—he's always nice—but I don't want him to think he has to keep *helping* me because there's only so much of that kind of thing people can take. And then maybe next time someone tells him to make me leave, he'll listen.

"Sayers, it's fine," Evan says, as if these thoughts are scrolling across my face. "Let's just take care of it."

So under Evan's direction, I sort things into categories. Dirty dishes in one pile, and apparently different-colored clothes must be washed in different loads. Evan complains good-naturedly about needing a hazmat suit or at least rubber gloves, which somehow makes things less embarrassing instead of more embarrassing.

It takes the entire morning, but it's amazing to leave the house wearing underwear instead of basketball shorts under my joggers.

Turns out a used bookstore called Autumn Leaves has a copy of the book, so we go there instead. Inside, it really does smell like leaves, or maybe pressed flowers. Old, but not unpleasant. There are haphazard walkways of pale oak shelves, and wooden signs dangling from the ceiling over various sections: Horror, Fiction, Biographies—*Languages*.

When Evan drops me off a couple hours later, I've got two paper sacks crammed full of books in my arms, and I'm about to head upstairs when I hear: "You look happy."

The smile trips off my face. The words feel like an accusation, but when I turn to my mom, who's stretched out in her nightgown on the sitting room sofa, her expression is sincere.

Things have been tense between us since the night I came home at 3:00 a.m. For the most part, we've been keeping to ourselves, like roommates instead of family, so I'm surprised to see her out here.

"Yeah," I say, cautiously. "I'm all right."

"Where've you been?"

"Out with a friend."

"Good . . . that's good." She nods, and then her eyes drift off, an almost-dazed look on her face.

"Mom?" I step closer to her and set my bags on the floor. "Are you okay?"

"I just got off the phone with Luanne." Mom's favorite cousin. "She's getting remarried."

Right, I think I remember that.

"She still wants me to come to her wedding in March. All the way in *Mexico*." She says this as if it's ridiculous, but I don't know why. She used to take trips like that all the time. At a moment's notice—to Cabo, to Rome, to Paris.

Her shoulders fall, and she starts blinking with slow heavy eyes like she could fall asleep right now if I'd let her, and all at once I realize. She isn't tired—she's *sad*.

With a sudden urgency, I say, "Mom, you should go."

"Oh, no." She sinks deeper into the couch. "It would be so much getting dressed up."

"But you *like* getting dressed up." When she shakes her head, I insist. "You *have* to."

"I do?" A hint of a smile lifts her lips. "You sound so much like your grandfather. He could be so insistent that way . . . He was like that a lot when you were gone. He kept trying to get me to go out and see people, but he was the only person I could stand being around. And once he was gone . . . I couldn't handle being around anyone."

An eerie memory surfaces. Mom without a face in a nice restaurant. Someone telling her what a shame it is that I'm gone.

But of course that wasn't real, just something I imagined when I was locked in the cellar. I shiver, remembering how cold it was, then I focus on my mom.

"Maybe things will feel different now."

"I suppose it could be nice . . . to be out on the water."

"Yes, it would."

"But this isn't a good time to pull you out of school. And you know Luanne, it's going to be a two-week extravaganza."

"I definitely don't need to go."

"I suppose a wedding's not too much fun for a teenage boy, is it?" And her expression is *playful*—for the first time since I can remember.

It makes me so happy I find myself grinning back at her. "Eh, wedding's aren't all bad. I could battle some single ladies for that bouquet."

She lets out an actual laugh. "You really are doing better, aren't you, Saye? Almost . . . almost like your old self?"

EIGHTY-TWO

It's barely light out as I roll Mom's suitcases to the town car waiting out front. I'm lifting the smaller bag into the trunk when the driver rushes out and tries to take it from me.

"Allow me, sir."

"It's fine," I tell him, settling it inside, and then I heft up the larger one with ease. Wow, I've gotten stronger. I bet I could take Caleb now.

The thought nearly makes me drop the suitcase.

I don't want to hurt him—it's too late to hurt him.

Shaken, I climb into the back seat next to Mom. Last night, she told me she wanted to drop me off at school on her way to the airport.

"We'll go on a trip soon," she's saying as I shut my door. "To anywhere you want."

It's hard to picture getting on a plane and going anywhere, but it's a nice thought. One that stays with me all day and is still there when I hop into Evan's truck after school.

As Evan drives, I scroll through my mom's texts.

He nods to my phone. "What's up?"

"My mom's on a trip to Cabo. She sent me some photos."

He tilts his head like he's puzzled. "She went on a trip to Mexico without you?"

"Yeah. Do you always go with your parents on vacation?"

"We don't really go on vacation, actually."

"Oh . . ."

"Well, if you're on your own tonight, then maybe we could have dinner at my house."

"Really?" Evan's never invited me over before. Smiling, I nod. "Yeah, okay."

For a second, something that looks like worry flashes across his face, but before I can be sure, it's gone.

I remember Evan telling me his entire house could fit into my great room. He was exaggerating, but not by much.

We cut through the yard into a little blue house where I'm immediately tackled by two pony-sized dogs who must like meeting new people. They lick my hands and leap into the air, their paws landing on my chest.

Evan pulls them off me, scolding them in such a friendly tone that they whine with joy and curl their bodies around Evan's petting fingers. Laughing, he toes off his sneakers.

I gesture to my shoes. "Should I . . . ?"

He nods, so I follow suit, then trail him into a sunken living room, taking in the cheerful space. Shag carpeting, framed family photos, lots of windows, and mismatched seating. Then I take in the discomfort on Evan's face.

"What's wrong?"

"Nothing," he says too quickly, and I wonder if he thinks I'm judging his house. God, I hope not.

"Evan, is that you?" a woman's voice rings out.

"Yeah, I'm home, Mom," he calls back, and his mother breezes into the room like a fountain of energy, in a red-and-yellow dress and thick black hair coiled on top of her head.

"Hi, honey." Her face lights up on Evan, then she gives me an expectant smile. "And who do we have here?"

"This is my friend." Evan pauses. "Sayers."

Immediately, her mouth stretches into a distorted O. It's the face people make when they get terrible news. She's obviously heard of me—and what she's heard isn't good.

I want to run back out to Evan's truck, but he puts a hand on my shoulder and steers me down a hall to the tiniest bedroom I've ever seen. It's stuffed beyond capacity with two bunk beds, a TV, and just enough space left over for the boys sitting on the floor playing video games.

The older boy's skinny and practically disappearing inside his oversized football jersey. He's probably eleven or so. Evan told me he has a brother in middle school. The younger one, who's maybe seven or eight, has chubby cheeks and big curls just like Evan used to have, and for some reason this makes my chest pull tight.

The little curly-haired boy glances over, then he double-takes like he can't believe his eyes and launches himself into Evan's arms.

Evan beams at him. "Hey, Isaac. This is my friend Sayers."

Isaac ducks his head, shy all of a sudden, almost like he was so starstruck by his big brother's appearance that he literally didn't process my existence until this moment. It's actually really sweet how much he clearly adores Evan.

"And that guy who won't look up from the TV is Jacob."

"Don't distract me!" Jacob keeps stabbing his thumbs into his controller.

Unoffended, Evan shoulders off his backpack and drops it onto one of the beds, and this is when I realize—

"You all *share* this room?"

"Yep. Nice and spacious since my older brothers went to college." I must be making a shocked face, because Evan bursts out laughing. "I'm just kidding. I don't have older brothers."

But the three of them still obviously share this tiny room, which is insane.

Down the hall, I hear the front door open and close, then I make out a deep voice.

"Daddy's home," Isaac announces.

"Yep," Evan agrees, then says to me, "Ready to eat?"

When I nod, Evan carries Isaac on his hip into the living room where Evan's father—paler and blonder than Evan—is standing. He's not a big guy, but his stern expression more than makes up for it. It looks like Evan's mom filled him in.

A memory. Garrett saying: *He told his dad. Who does that?*

It was Evan's father who called the school about the vandalization of Evan's truck, about the weeks of bullying. And now he's glaring at me like he'd happily kick my ass if it weren't illegal.

"Can I speak to you?" he says to Evan, ignoring me completely.

Evan throws me an anxious look. "I'll be right back." Then he follows his father into another room, while I'm left alone, nervous and fidgeting and breathing in whatever's cooking in the kitchen. It smells really good, like lasagna and garlic bread.

A minute later, Evan returns with a closed off expression. "I'll give you a ride home."

It appears I've been uninvited to dinner.

We put our shoes back on and head out to the truck. We don't talk, just drive in silence until Evan says, "Hey, come on, don't do that."

I realize I'm chewing my thumb and tapping the side of my head onto the passenger window like an agitated woodpecker. Wiping my wet thumb on my pants, I force myself to sit up straight. "So your parents hate me?"

He doesn't answer right away.

"I'm sorry about that," he finally says. "I should've told them you were coming. I just thought if they could meet you, they'd feel differently. They're usually very forgiving . . ."

"Are they gonna make you stop hanging out with me?"

Evan gives me what I think is supposed to be a reassuring smile. "They're going to *try.*"

EIGHTY-THREE

But we haven't hung out—not since that afternoon. I do the math, and technically it's only been a few days, but a few can feel like forever when you're stressed and not sleeping and you're out of weed. I was starting to think I didn't even need the weed anymore—I thought I was doing *better.*

But I guess I was wrong because I can't seem to fall asleep without it. I've texted my friend—my dealer?—and he doesn't know when he's getting more, so I'm a wired kind of exhausted, like someone's pumping me full of sedatives but won't let me sleep.

It's Friday night and Mom's still in Mexico and I'm curled up in bed.

I can't remember what I used to do on Friday nights. Almost everything from before still seems like a blur, but I probably hung out with Luke. I keep thinking I'll see Luke in the hall, and he'll be like, "Hey, wanna talk?" Or maybe he'll tackle me with one of those out-of-nowhere octopus hugs like he used to. But whenever I actually do come across him, we don't say anything, and I'm not sure anymore if I'm avoiding him or he's avoiding me.

Lately on Fridays, I've been with Evan. We'll watch movies and order pizza from Sal's, this New York–style pizzeria he likes, and I

426

guess it's kind of pathetic how dependent I've become on him. He's probably relieved his parents won't let him come over. Now he can spend time with his actual friends. Ones who are *normal*. Yeah, good for him. He could use the break. I wish I could take a break from me too.

Again I try to summon the memory—what did I do on Fridays?

Play board games with Caleb.

No, that's not right. Besides, there weren't Fridays with Caleb. There were no days at all, just long stretches with no time, and I was so *lonely*. All I wanted was company, but I'm not sure when my fantasy changed from getting out to having a cellmate.

Disoriented in the half-light, I see a shadow near my bed. "Dad?"

But no one answers. No one's *here*.

And when disappointment falls over me like the heaviest weight, it hits me in a way it hasn't until this moment.

I *miss* him.

Stop it, Saye, you don't miss Caleb. It's crazy, it's evil.

But I do. With the gnawing pain of grief, the way I'd imagine you'd feel if your actual father committed suicide. My eyes fill with tears, they wet my pillowcase.

I wish he was here. He'd comfort me, he'd *hold* me.

But he can't, because I'm never seeing him again.

My throat clamps shut—I already knew that. Of course I knew. But somehow it felt . . . temporary. Because never?

Never.

I lurch out of bed, blind with panic. What is wrong with me? Do I *want* to be back in that house, chained with no windows?

No, no.

I don't know.

I'm sinking.

Into a deep black sea.

At the bottom, I see him in the tall night grass, eyes closed like he's sleeping. I remember it—I was sick and dazed, but I understood. He was never waking up. And I remember how it felt—the crushing permanence of it. No way to undo it. No way to take it back.

Then there was some glitch in my comprehension. Something that said *NO*—there is nothing bad that can't be undone.

But I was wrong.

And now I'm sinking again.

Deeper and deeper.

Until it's just me.

Alone in a dark room.

And I know how to handle the dark.

You stay quiet, and you wait for it to end.

EIGHTY-FOUR

Saaaayeersss...

Sayers . . .

Sayers . . .

I think someone's calling my name, but the voice is distant, too far away to help.

"*Sayers.*"

And now I see him, Evan standing in the middle of my room.

"I let myself in." He's peering at me where I'm standing too. "What are you doing?"

But I can't answer him.

My whole body has turned to ice, and I have to stay perfectly still—or I'll shatter.

I can see it in my mind. First my fingers, ears, and lips, then my limbs and all the rest. The fear is a universe, and I'm falling inside myself again. It goes on and on like the eternity of outer space. We're that deep inside.

"Sayers?"

Evan's voice brings me back to the surface.

"Talk to me."

But I *can't*. If I try, my jaw will splinter into pieces.

"Saye, come on, you're scaring me. I don't know how to help if you don't talk."

And I need help, I do, so I keep my mouth still and hiss, *"Frozen."*

He squints like I'm an equation without an equal sign, then he moves a couple feet to the right, as if he needs to view me from a different angle. "You're cold?"

No, he's not getting it.

I'm panting fast now.

My rib cage is going to snap right through my chest.

"If you're cold, why don't you get into your bed and cover up?" He grips my arm as if to move me, and I let out a panicked yelp. Holding up two hands, he retreats the way you'd back off from a noisy car alarm. "Shit, I'm sorry. Are you hurt?"

Yes, I'm hurt. He understands. The relief makes my eyes water.

But then another shot of panic—what if my tears freeze, and my eyes shatter, and the whole world goes dark? I have to tell him before he leaves me too.

Harsh fast whispers through my teeth: *"F-frozen. If I move—I'll b-break."*

Slowly, his expression changes, dawning awareness like he knows something I don't. "You're frozen like . . ." Then he says, gently, "You're not, Sayers."

I was wrong—he *doesn't* understand. I'm going to die.

"I think this is in your head, Saye." Evan takes hold of my wrist. Ignoring the scared whine coming from my throat, he opens my fist. "Look."

I watch him manipulate my fingers. I feel sick.

Then he touches my arm, which is still in the air from when my body froze mid-stride, and he begins moving it back and forth on its joint like a physical therapist would. "See? See?"

I almost nod, but then remember. *"Neck?"*

He takes my head, nods it up and down.

Moisture clouds my eyes, and again I'm afraid. *"Eyes?"*

He's looking at me with so much sympathy. It's strange how crushing sympathy can be.

"Your eyes are fine, Sayers. You're not frozen."

And it must be true. My jaw isn't shattering, and neither are my ribs. I'm starting to feel prickly as if I'm dethawing. Suddenly my knees crumble—I *am* breaking.

Evan catches me as I pitch forward and helps me lower myself onto the floor.

"Just breathe, all right?" He crouches in front of me.

I grab my thighs—they're not splintering—and I breathe shaky breaths.

"You're okay, you're okay."

I'm okay, I'm okay.

Of course I'm not frozen.

I'm just losing my mind.

How long was I standing there like a statue? It scares me to wonder. Now I can feel the cramps in my limbs, and the dry thirst in my mouth, and I can smell myself. I smell *awful*. Evan has to notice, but he's acting like he doesn't as he stays close to me, his brown eyes just a few inches from mine. Penny's eyes were brown too, only hers were sunflowers while his are amber, like the resin that makes things last forever.

"Evan . . . why are you so nice to me?"

"What do you mean?"

"Why didn't you ever hurt me?"

He startles, and then he smiles—it's the teasing smile you give young children. "I don't enjoy hurting helpless creatures."

But it's not funny. I never cared when *he* was smaller or fragile or helpless.

And just like that, it's back. Blind-white panic. I launch to my feet and pull my helmet over my head, but in an instant, the helmet's too tight. I make noises that aren't words, and I—

Stoppit, Daniel.

I go completely still.

You're a boy, not a goddamn animal.

"Sayers?"

He called me Sayers. He knows I'm not Daniel, he knows.

Can't run—

"What's going on?"

Can't fight—

"*Talk*, Sayers."

"Can't run can't fight can't run can't fight—"

"Look at me, Saye. Please."

I do, and it's Evan, only Evan.

"You *can* run. And you *can* fight." His eyes are on me. "You're not trapped here."

My focus darts around the room. It's like a double exposure or a viewfinder stuck on two frames. Daniel's bedroom right on top of this one. The windows blink in and out of existence. Evan does too. I grab at his shirt, clutching for dear life with scrabbling scared hands.

He takes hold of my hand and leads me from the room—to the top of the cellar stairs.

"No, I'm sorry! Please let me go."

"Calm down, Saye. I'm just trying to—"

"LET ME GO! LET ME GO! LET ME GO!"

The frame blinks out again. The cellar stairs are gone. Now they're mine. Evan's racing ahead, flying down the steps. He pushes the front doors open wide. Green grass and sunshine and a big blue sky. I'm not going underground—I'm getting out.

"Come on," Evan calls up to me.

I stagger down the staircase, across the foyer.

I burst through the doors.

And now it's night.

A billion meteors are streaking across the sky.

"Oh no." I sink into the grass.

Covering my face, I start to sob. Loud racking sounds.

I can't do this. I can't do this again.

There's a hand on my shoulder—and the daylight is back.

Confused, blinking into sunshine, I feel arms surround me, and my face is crushed into Evan's chest. He wraps his hand around my head, pressing my ear into his heart.

"Evan . . ." I continue to cry. "I don't want to fight."

"Okay," he says, soothing. "Then let's run."

EIGHTY-FIVE

I stop to catch my breath in the center of the tree-lined trail. How far was that? Three miles? Four? Evan's the one who always clocks these things, but he's at his little brother's soccer match, so I'm on my own today. We've been going on runs every afternoon for the past month—even if I'm tired, even if I'm not in the mood, we run.

I grip my knees, allowing my heart to slow, breathing in air that's just coming off winter and the green shoots blooming from the trees, and I feel something that might be called peace.

Evan thinks it's all the physical activity that's been helping me, and he's right, I am doing better. He noticed it before I did.

But I don't think it's because of the running—I think it's knowing that I can.

Logically, I've known I wasn't still locked in a house or a cellar. I mean, obviously I knew that. But I think your mind can stay trapped even when your body is free.

An image pops into my head. The shuttle-box dogs. The ones that kept lying there getting electric shocks, even when they could've easily gotten away.

You have to come with me.

Suddenly, I'm remembering Penny begging me to leave with

her. The door was unlocked. We had the key. I could've run.

But I didn't.

Fidgeting now, I pull at the tight chain around my neck. It's actually more of a choker since it was made for a child, but when my mom got back from Cabo, I had the feeling things didn't go well, because she immediately crawled into bed. I wanted to cheer her up, so I let myself into her room and pointed at my throat.

She squinted like she didn't understand. "You're wearing the best friend necklace?" I figured she was surprised I still had it, but then she added, "You're not embarrassed?"

"No," I told her honestly, but she didn't look uplifted the way I thought she'd be.

I'm obviously not very good at helping my mom, and it makes me wonder if I'll be any better with Penny. June is coming up fast, and I'm doing okay, but I want to be more than okay.

I want to be someone she can rely on.

I drop the chain and lean my back against a tree.

Dragging my cell phone from my pocket, I toggle to the website I've browsed a hundred times. Oak Hill, Penny's treatment center. I scroll through high-resolution photos of teens riding horses, canoeing, and walking along the lake like it's a summer camp. Penny told me outside is where she feels God the most. I wonder if she's starting to feel better.

I guess there is a way I could find out.

The last thing Nicolai said to me as I was making my hasty retreat, his baby-chipmunk voice following me up the hill, was "Come back soon!"

That was *months* ago. He probably doesn't even remember me, but here I am, on Penny's front porch and ringing the bell. A few seconds later, the door flies open, and Nicolai is gaping up at me with bright eyes and a megawatt smile.

"Sayers? Sayers!" he cheers like I'm a long-lost friend, and he's hopping up and down and saying my name like *Say-uhs*, so I can't help it if I'm already grinning.

He grabs my hand and pulls me inside. Tugging me to the patio door, he flings it open. In the vivid green yard, Mrs. Valles is bare-foot, a crutch under one arm, and using her free hand to spray the lawn with a watering hose.

"Mommy?" Nicolai calls out, and she turns to us. "He's back!"

I can see the surprise behind her glasses, then with a soft smile, she says to Nicolai, "Should we offer our guest a drink?"

"Yes!" He tugs me into a living room that's covered in flowers. They climb the wallpaper, fill the drapes. He pushes me toward the tulip-upholstered sofa. "Wait here!"

From the couch, I hear crutches flicking over a tile floor, then I hear Nicolai say that *he* wants to be the one to pour the grape juice, and then he's carrying it to me, careful not to spill, while also trying to get it to me as quickly as he can.

"Thank you," I say, taking a sip, and he smiles with all his baby teeth.

His mother shuffles in behind him and carefully lowers herself into a stuffed chair, setting her crutches against the wall.

"Did you hurt your foot?" I ask.

"I just twisted my ankle." She waves her hand like it's nothing.

"I tripped stepping off a curb."

"Oh, I'm sorry. I know it's hard not to be able to walk . . ."

"It's fine, we're getting by."

And I guess they are. Laundry's neatly folded on a bench in the corner, tiny socks and shirts and pants, and the scent of freshly baked bread fills the air. *That's how my mom is,* I remember Penny telling me. *She gets on with things because even when she's hurting, there is work that has to be done.*

Nicolai tugs my sleeve. "Say-uhs? Do you wanna hear a joke?"

"Okay."

"What goes up and down, but doesn't move?"

"I don't know, what?"

"Stairs!"

He watches me expectantly, and the second I smile, he laughs so hard, he nearly topples over.

I find myself laughing too, more at his reaction to his own joke than anything else. My gaze drifts to a wall of family photos that's just like Penny described. There are tons of baby pictures and school photos, then my heart freezes. In one of the photos, there's a giant metal sign over a roadside diner. A word written in all caps: *RESTAURANT.*

And posing in the gravel lot out front is Penny. She's arm in arm with a girl who has wispy white-blond hair and faint blond brows. Both girls are smiling at the camera, eyes sparkling, dressed in pale-blue waitress uniforms.

It's like the breath's been knocked out of me. "Penny worked at Restaurant?"

437

Mrs. Valles follows my gaze. "Yes . . . with her best friend, Nina. The diner belongs to Nina's aunt." Her eyes are quickly filling with concern. "Penny told me they waited on your table. You don't remember?"

"No . . ."

But now I do. Penny was the waitress from the restaurant that night, several lifetimes ago. The one who overheard the mean things I said.

How could I not have recognized her?

"I should really take that picture down," Mrs. Valles says. Her voice has gone up a strained octave. "That's where Penny was . . ."

Abducted. Yes, I know.

"I tried to move it, but Penny got so upset. She told me it makes her think of how things were before . . . But for her to want to keep it up . . . It just didn't make sense to me . . ." She trails off when she notices how closely Nicolai is listening.

And I should ask how Penny is doing now—it's why I came here—but maybe that's not something I should talk about in front of him.

"Mommy?" he says. "Can we go to the park?"

She shakes her head. "Not yet, honey. It's still too hard for me to get over the grass, but we will soon."

His face falls, and I know if Penny were here, she'd do it. Penny told me they were inseparable since the day Nicolai was born. Without really thinking about it, I say, "I could take him."

But right away, I feel stupid. Mrs. Valles won't want me going off somewhere with her son—plus I don't know anything about babysitting little kids.

But before I can take it back, Nicolai's flying into the air like a bird. "Yes, *he* can take me!"

Mrs. Valles looks uncertain. "Are you sure you don't mind? It's just down the street . . ."

And I smile, because helping—even a little—feels really good. "I'm sure."

The second we reach the park, Nicolai takes off at a speed that shouldn't be possible on such short legs. By the time I catch up with him, he's trying to torpedo himself into a weirdly high, circular swing.

"Um, do you need help?" I ask.

He raises his arms, which I interpret as a yes, so I grip him around the waist, awkwardly, like how you'd lift a thirty-pound vase, and I lower him into the leg holsters.

"Push me!" he orders.

I move behind him, but he's so tiny and fragile-looking, I'm worried I'll break his spine or something. Placing my hand on the small of his back, I give him a timid shove that propels him forward about two inches.

Nicky peers over his shoulder, unimpressed. "I wanna go *high!*"

I try incrementally harder shoves until I get the hang of it, and he's happily screaming at the top of his lungs when a trio of moms arrive, pushing strollers in V-shaped formation. They give me dubious stares as they unbuckle their toddlers and stuff them into the swings.

One of the moms says to me, "These swings are intended for babies."

"Oh."

There aren't any other kids waiting, and honestly, I doubt Nicolai weighs more than their children, so I don't see why it matters. When I make no moves to vacate the area, the moms start flashing gymnastic eyebrows at each other.

"Can we slide now?" Nicolai asks, like maybe he senses the tension.

"Sure," I tell him, relieved.

He raises his arms, so I lift him—and the swing lifts right along with him.

Nicolai whimpers loudly. "My legs are stuck!"

The ladies shoot vindicated looks in my direction as I keep pulling, and Nicolai screams like he's in agony. I shouldn't have offered to bring him here. I'm not competent enough to take care of a kid—this is terrible. I'm having visions of the fire department hacksawing the swing apart when his legs pop free.

I set him on the grass, but he keeps making sad noises as we walk toward the slide. I really wish Evan were here. He has little brothers, I bet he knows how to handle crying kids.

"Everything all right?" I finally ask, too formally.

Nicolai nods and rubs his eyes with a small fist, then all of a sudden, his face lights up, and he dashes to a tall stone fountain with three tiers of seashell-shaped basins.

"Do you have any pennies?" he asks once I reach him.

"No, I don't. I'm sorry."

His little shoulders slump. He's not throwing a fit or anything, he's just disappointed, but for some reason, that expression is so horrible to look at I find myself digging into my empty pockets, hoping for a miracle.

Suddenly, he lets out a loud gasp, and I follow his stunned gaze to the grass where a copper coin is glinting in the sun. He races over to it and plucks it up into his hand.

"Do you know what this can *do*?" He holds it in the air with an amazed smile.

"What?"

"You toss it in the fountain, and you can *wish* for things." He closes his eyes, his little face intensely focused like he's praying. "I wish, I wish, I wish."

And somehow I just know. He's wishing for Penny.

EIGHTY-SIX

My nose twitches at the strong scent of incense, waxy candles, and whatever else churches smell like. The Observer Me shows up and points out that the me-from-before would've laughed his ass off at the idea of skipping school to go to church. I should leave.

But I'm almost positive this is something Penny would want me to do, so my feet keep moving all the way to the main office where I ask the lady behind a desk, "Can I talk to a priest?"

"Do you have an appointment?"

"An appointment?" I didn't even think about that. "No, ma'am."

"Just a moment." She disappears down a hall, and a couple minutes later, a white-haired man in a red sweater and a priest square at his collar appears.

"Hello there," he says in a friendly, booming voice. "Come right in." He has an accent I can't place—maybe the northeast? Maybe Maine? He leads me into a cluttered little office dominated by a huge mahogany table. Books, papers, and statues of saints are strewn around the room in a comforting brand of disorder. He picks up a steaming mug from where it's forming a ring on a stack of papers. "Would you like a cup of tea?"

"No, sir, that's okay."

"Have a seat." He gestures to a pair of wingback chairs uphol-stered in green velour.

"Aren't we supposed to go in that little cubicle thing?" I ask as I'm sitting down.

He chuckles. "We don't do that too much, but you don't have to tell me your name unless you'd like to."

"Okay. Thank you, sir."

"Father O'Connor is fine."

Father. The word's an unexpected pain like how it might feel if someone pressed against a particularly sensitive bruise.

"How can I help you, son?"

And that word hurts too. *Father, son, father, son.*

"I'm confused."

His intelligent gray eyes are focused, patient, like he has all the time in the world.

"Do you think it's possible to love someone and hate them too?"

With a wry smile, he takes a drink from his mug. "I'd say that's fairly common. The people we love provoke such strong emotion. But we don't really hate."

"Or maybe we don't really love. "

"Why don't you tell me more specifically what you mean?"

"Well, it's just . . . my father. He . . . Well, I . . ."

Talk, Sayers! Talking helps. I can practically hear Evan screaming this in my head. And then I hear Penny saying it too. She believed in this, in confession.

"It's just . . . my father. I hate him. And I love him."

"Why?"

"I hate him because he did terrible things. And I love him

because . . . I don't know why. I shouldn't. I don't know why I do."

"You do because love is our natural state of being."

No, this is *not* natural. If this man only knew . . .

"Your father did terrible things?"

Tears prickle my eyes. "Yes."

"But he took care of you? Loved you in his own way?"

A couple tears spill over. "Yes."

"Then I'll tell you again—love is our most natural state of being. When we're born, do you think we ask ourselves if our parents deserve our love? Do we ask if they're getting it right or if they have any clue as to what they're doing? No, we simply love them with every fiber of our beings. We come into the world ready to love whoever shows up, good or bad—that's what we do."

Now he sighs, sets down his tea.

"There's plenty of hate out there. We can't deny that, can we?"

I shake my head.

"But if that's true, then is loving this man such an awful thing?"

"Where were you today?" Evan asks, sounding at least twenty years older than he actually is. He seems to think it's his job to keep tabs on me, so there's no point trying to hide it.

"Church," I say, pushing my bedroom door open wider to let him in.

"*Sayers.*"

"I was."

He squints at me like he's trying to decide if I'm telling the truth, and I bristle, offended. I might not tell him everything, but I don't *lie* to him.

"I didn't know you were religious," he finally says, tossing his giant backpack onto the couch.

"I'm not exactly . . . but I'm trying to figure things out." It occurs to me that we've never talked about this kind of stuff before, and I'm curious. "What about you—are you religious?"

"Well . . ." Evan's eyes shift toward the balcony for a moment before training themselves back on me. "My mom's Baptist and my dad grew up Methodist, but I don't believe in God."

"You *don't*?"

It shocks me, probably more than it should. It's just that Evan's so *good* the way Penny is good that I guess I assumed they both believe the same things, that they both have well-loved copies of the Bible, that both their heads are full of saints.

"So you're an atheist?"

Evan screws up his face. "Calling myself that feels weird, like I've taken this official stance against the existence of God."

"Then you're agnostic? You think there could be one?"

"Well, no, I don't."

I must be making a troubled expression, because he adds, "But if someone else does, I'm okay with that. The thing is, I don't really care what people believe—I just care what they *do*."

EIGHTY-SEVEN

I'm sitting on the floor of Autumn Leaves, my back against some shelves as I turn the pages of an old book. Evan's around here somewhere, but we drifted in separate directions not long after we came in. There's a whole section on spirituality I never noticed before, and whenever I'm alone, I've been trying to pray.

The priest said it doesn't need to be formal—you're just talking to God, but so far it feels like I'm talking to myself. A walkie-talkie that only works one way. Yelling *hello* at a mountaintop, and just my echo yelling back.

Except sometimes. It doesn't.

Because sometimes I feel something not-quite-me or higher-than-me, and I know it could just be my unconscious mind or wishful thinking, but it feels like someone's *listening*. Or when I go for runs alone deep in the woods, *I'll* listen. And it's quick, only a glimpse, so maybe it's just the noise of wind moving through the trees, but it feels like God has a language—one I could learn if I keep trying.

"Find anything?" Evan asks, shaking me from my thoughts.

I look up to see that he's got a couple of novels under his arm.

Rising on creaking legs, I nod and gather the dozen or so books I've been piling beside me.

"Is that all?" Evan jokes, and I smile.

Once we make our purchases, we head to my house and into the solarium, where we've moved tables from the library so we can spread out our assignments. Evan's amber eyes are alight, and I kindly avoid teasing him for loving homework so much.

I grab my World History textbook and answer the questions at the back of the chapter. Lately, I've been doing all my assignments and studying for my tests, and I've stopped drawing in class. I'm trying, I really am.

As soon as I finish the questions, I open my English-to-Icelandic book and start jotting down phrases in my journal while Evan does his chemistry. He's smart enough to skip high school altogether if he wanted to.

"Hey, Evan, I'm just curious . . . Why'd you quit AP?"

"I didn't," he answers. But he doesn't elaborate, and it's not like him to be cryptic.

"So what happened?"

"It's, um, well . . ." It's also not like him to be at a loss for words. "I was dismissed from the program."

"Dismissed?"

"Kicked out."

I can't imagine Evan doing something bad enough to get kicked out of anything. "Why?"

Another long, fidgety pause and then, "I cheated on a test."

He looks so deeply ashamed that I find myself laughing. "Evan, that's not a big deal. Everyone does that."

"No, they don't." He sounds scandalized. "I never had before."

"You got caught the very first time you cheated?" I laugh again, but Evan's obviously so devastated about the whole thing that I feel guilty for making light of it. "I'm sorry. I can't believe they kicked you out after one offense. Don't you get a warning?"

"It . . . it wasn't just that. When my teacher caught me, I denied it. It was stupid to lie—he *saw* me do it. But I . . . I just lost it. I went off on him."

Evan's idea of going off on someone is probably very different from mine. "How bad could it have been?"

"Bad enough for him to call the school security officer."

"Shit."

"Yeah."

"Well, he was overreacting."

"How do you know?"

"Because I know you didn't do anything threatening."

"Well, I was yelling, freaking out."

It makes me think of my freak-out in the hall the day Blair read that article. "Sounds like a panic attack to me." And people don't seem to know what to do with that.

Evan starts doing that thing with his pencil, waving it between his thumb and forefinger till it looks like rubber. "I'm not going to make excuses, but I was really stressed out. The workload had never gotten to me that way before."

"This was last year?"

"Yeah."

Around the time Principal Gardiner told me Evan couldn't cope with the bullying anymore.

My stomach clenches.

"I'm just mad at myself," he continues. "Being the valedictorian would've been huge for scholarships."

"You were on track for that?"

"I had the highest GPA in my class freshman year."

"But you still make all A's."

"I do, but it's not the same. Grades are weighted differently for regular classes, so I don't have a chance of competing with everyone in AP."

"Oh . . ."

"It just . . . it sucks. It was one bad choice, but now I'm going to be in debt until I'm fifty." He stills his pencil. It's solid again. "But no excuses."

He resumes his work while I'm lost in thought. For a few minutes, the only sounds are flipping pages and scratching pencils until I say, "Evan?"

"Hmm?"

"I want to pay for your college."

His head snaps up, and I smile at him.

He doesn't smile back.

"What's wrong?"

"Sayers, you can't do things like that."

"But I'm trying to be nice. And it's not even that nice, because it's nothing for me."

Evan's eyebrows fly up. "Do you know how much medical school costs?"

"Around two hundred thousand dollars?"

"That isn't *nothing.*"

"I said it's nothing for *me.*"

"Sayers . . ." Evan looks pained now as he rubs the space between his eyes. "That's five years of my father's salary. Five years of house payments, car payments, electric bills, and food, with no money left over. Do you understand?"

"Yes, I understand." I let out a frustrated noise. "But that's the whole point. If I have it, and I can use it for something *good* . . . I just want to do something good."

Evan's face softens. "I know you do."

EIGHTY-EIGHT

"Hi, Sayers." Penny's mom opens the door with a smile. "Nicky's taking a nap."

"Oh, I'm sorry. I should've texted first."

"Don't worry about it, come in." She opens the door wider, and I step inside. This house always smells nice, like laundry detergent and open windows. "Actually . . ." She lowers her voice to a whisper. "Would you mind staying here while I run to the grocery store? It's so much faster when I go on my own."

"Oh, sure," I say quickly, eager to help.

I sit on the flowery sofa as she throws her purse across one shoulder. "I won't be long."

"No rush."

She gives one last look down the hall where Nicky's sleeping, then she goes.

The house is quiet now, no noise but the hum of the refrigerator and a slow ticking clock. On the wall across from me is the calendar Nicky likes to show me every time I'm here, the pages covered in a rainbow of Magic Marker Xs. He's literally counting the days till Penny gets home.

A vivid memory floods my head. In the cellar with Penny, both of us scared and clinging and crying into each other's hair, saying *I love you, I love you, I love you.*

Blinking slowly, I sink deeper into the soft cushions—and wake up to someone peeling back my eyelid.

Nicky's eyeball is a scant centimeter from mine, and I can see my upside-down reflection inside his pupil. When I jerk backward, he claps his hands over his mouth, cracking up. I begin to untangle from the weird position I fell asleep in, my head *under* the throw pillow instead of on top of it, and the end of my legs dangling across an armrest.

"You're Goldilocks!" he shouts, leaping up onto the couch. "I'm the bear!"

"Are you Baby Bear?" I ask, rubbing a hand over my eyes.

"No," he protests, full of injured six-year-old pride. "I'm Papa Bear!" He growls and pounces on me and pulls my hair. "Only, Goldilocks is not a boy," he adds seriously.

"Then I'll be her brother."

"And my brother!"

"I thought you were a bear."

"Now I'm Brother Bear."

I'm losing the thread of this story.

"We're both brothers, and we *sneaked* in here." He puts a finger to his lips. "WHISPER!"

I don't think Nicky knows what that word means.

"Only now we're superhero brothers." He snaps a plastic toy police badge to his T-shirt, then he grabs my hand and leads me around the house on his tiptoes. "We don't let any bad guys come in. Okay?" He lifts his big brown eyes to me.

"Okay."

"They can't take me or you or Mommy or nobody."

I squeeze his hand. "Okay."

EIGHTY-NINE

Evan and I are studying for finals at a noisy Starbucks. I'm still going to have to make up the classes I failed last fall, but I might even make a couple A's this semester.

I'm flipping open my study guide for English when Garrett walks in. Evan's oblivious since his back is to the door, and I'm kind of hoping Garrett won't notice us, that he'll just grab his coffee and go. But then he sniper-scans the room, and his eyes lock on to mine.

Surprise springs across Garrett's face—and then amusement. Like it's just *hilarious* that he's found me here, hanging out with Evan.

"Hey, Saye." Garrett strolls over to our table with a jack-o'-lantern smile. "I didn't know you two were buddies."

"Hey," I mumble, tensing up.

Garrett's mouth stretches into an even-wider grin. "Hey there—*Operation.*"

For a moment, I'm confused until I remember the nickname Garrett came up with. I aim a guilty glance over at Evan ... who's cowering.

There's no other word for it.

His shoulders hunched, he's obviously afraid, but I don't understand why. It made sense when he was smaller than us and we'd
corner him when he was alone, but now we're in a public place and
Garrett's the one who's outnumbered.

"Stop looking so freaked out, guys." Garrett laughs. "Everything's cool." Then he squeezes Evan in that spot where the neck
and shoulder meet.

Evan's hands tighten around his paper cup, but other than that,
he doesn't move.

A tidal wave of emotions crash through me and against each
other—dread, confusion, anger—because this is *Evan*, who is bigger and smarter and basically better than everyone.

"All right . . . you two have fun." Garrett winks as he gives Evan
one more little squeeze.

Out of the corner of my eye, I watch Garrett buy his drink and
disappear through the glass doors.

Evan returns to doing his homework, and I go back to studying,
but I can't focus anymore.

"You wanna go?" I finally say.

Evan nods, so we gather our things and head to the truck—but
it won't start. He turns the key again, and the engine just lets out
a sputtering whine.

In a sudden fit of anger, Evan slaps the steering wheel. Red-
faced and twitchy, he hurls himself back out of the truck and
wrenches open the hood.

I climb out too and stand beside him, staring helplessly at the
twisting mass of car parts.

"Is everything okay?" I ask.

"No! I just got it fixed." Arms out tense and straight, he grips the fender and leans his head down between his shoulders. The way he's acting is worrisome enough that I lay a hand on his back.

Under my palm, I can feel him take a few deep breaths, then he straightens and goes over to the trunk and digs around inside. A moment later, he's at the hood again with a tool I don't know the name of, making adjustments I don't understand.

"Could you try to start it?" he eventually asks, sounding almost subdued.

"Yeah, of course." I hop into the truck, turn the key, and the engine comes to life. Grinning, I hop back out. "It worked!"

Evan nods and climbs into the driver's seat, seeming calmer now.

On our way home, we pick up a pizza from Sal's, and as soon as we get to my place, we grab plates from the kitchen. I'm trying to brace myself for Study Session Round Two, but then Evan says we can watch TV if I want, so we find a new sci-fi series he heard was good.

When the credits roll on the fourth episode, I check the time—*1:00 a.m.*

"You sleeping over?" I ask.

"Yeah." Looking beat, Evan starts shoving stuff off the couch so he can lie down.

I crawl under my covers, and I'm really tired, but for some reason my body won't relax. "A hit would be nice right now," I find myself admitting out loud, and I'm prepared for Evan to tell me,

You're fine, you don't need a hit.

But instead, he says, "Yeah, sure, okay, if you want."

I'm up and snatching my bong before he can change his mind. I load it, light it, inhale a cloud, then I realize Evan is studying me.

"Do you wanna try?" I ask, even though I'm sure I must be reading him wrong.

But he surprises me by nodding, so I pass the bong over to him.

"What do I do?" he asks. I light it for him and tell him when to inhale. He takes in way too much and starts hacking. "Ah, it burns," he groans through his coughs.

I run to the kitchenette freezer down the hall and grab a cup of ice. When I get back to my room, his eyes are streaming. "Suck on these," I tell him. "It helps."

He crunches the ice, looking so out of it that I risk taking another hit. Loud bubbles fill the room, but he doesn't seem to notice.

Loose and heavy now, I climb back into bed, and it feels so much more welcoming than it did a few minutes ago. Tension's just an idea, an abstract. I'm floating up when the cup falls from Evan's hand. He makes a few uncoordinated attempts to right it before giving up and collapsing onto the couch.

I dim the lights, but the image of Evan looking so small and scared floods my head, and I find myself saying, "I'm sorry about today. It was weird."

After a long pause, he murmurs, "What was?"

"Coffee. Garrett."

"Oh . . . It's okay . . ." He turns to lie on his side, his face in the shadows.

"Evan?"

"Hmm?"

"You don't need to be scared of him. I mean, I know he can be kind of an asshole. But he's harmless."

And I'm starting to drift off when Evan says, "He's one of those people, you know?"

"One of what people?"

"The kind that likes to break things just to see them in pieces."

NINETY

In second-period English, my classmates are losing their minds with happiness. Music's blasting from a girl's cell phone, a boy's dancing a jig in the corner, everyone's talking a mile a minute—typical last-day-of-school delirium, but it doesn't mean much to me since I have to report back here in a few weeks for summer school.

The intercom comes to life over our heads. "Attention, seniors." Principal Gardiner clears his throat. "Please arrive at the auditorium promptly at two o'clock. This is the *final* rehearsal for tomorrow's graduation ceremony."

Evan watches me sideways like he's thinking what I'm thinking—I'm supposed to be with them.

But there's no envy, no heartache. It wasn't meant to be.

It's still May and already scorching, so Nicolai and I have become early birds, at the park by nine to beat the sun. We end up running around for two full hours before he starts losing steam. I check the temperature on my phone—*too hot.*

"Let's get out of here," I say.

"Yeah," Nicky agrees. "Let's get outta here!"

We're nearing the edge of the playground when carnival-style music crowds out the sound of playing kids. A minute later an ice-cream truck brushes against the curb, and Nicky turns to me with Disney eyes.

"Can I have one?"

"Sure."

I never say no to him. If he wants to play at the park for an hour, we'll play for two. *Can you read me a story?* How about three? Whatever he wants, I double it, triple it.

The truck windows are too high, so I lift him up under his armpits and let him examine the pictures taped to the glass. He asks for a Mickey Mouse head on a stick.

I buy it, help him open the package, and in less than a block, it's melting all over his face. Behind us, I can still hear the ice-cream truck. That old-timey music is creepy. Come to think of it, ice-cream trucks are creepy. How hard would it be to buy one and use it to lure little kids? And that mustached salesman was friendly, maybe too friendly.

"Never talk to that guy unless I'm with you," I say, stern enough that Nicolai gives me a concerned look as he slurps on one of Mickey's chocolate ears. "Or *any* strangers."

"Yes, I know."

"You know?"

"Yeah, I know. We don't talk to strangers."

"Good." After another block, I complain, "It's so hot."

"Yeah! It's very, *very* hot!"

I chuckle. Everything I say, Nicky repeats, only he dials it up ten notches.

"Sayers?" He's really getting better with his *r*'s. "Maybe we can go swimming?"

"Sure, I've got a pool. We just need to ask your mom."

He gapes at me, astonished, then he takes off running, ice cream dripping down his arm as he flies up his porch and bursts into his house. I'm just a few steps behind him, and I find Mrs. Valles reading a book on the tulip-covered couch with an amused smile.

"You really don't have to take him swimming," she tells me.

"It's cool. I don't mind."

Nicky dashes into the living room dressed in red swim trunks and floaties. "Does your pool have that slide that goes like this?" He makes a swoopy motion with his hand.

"No, it doesn't have that."

"Hmm . . ." He strokes the air under his chin like he's got a long, invisible beard. "I think we'll go to my pool."

I laugh. "Whatever you want."

Mrs. Valles gives us a ride, saying it's too far to walk in this heat. As she pulls up front, I catch the happy smile on her face. "Call me when you're ready to come home."

I bury my cell phone in Nicolai's Ninja Turtle backpack. "Will do."

And Nicky echoes, "Will do!"

Inside the gates of the public pool, kids are speeding in every direction while adults chase them or recline on lounge chairs. Off to one side, a straw-roofed snack place is selling hot dogs, nachos, fruit drinks, and sodas, and the sweet scent of coconut suntan oil fills the air. The sparkling pool's surrounded by palm trees not native to the area, along with dozens of seven-foot wooden flamingos. I've never been here before, but I'm getting the weirdest sense of déjà vu.

"Come on!" Nicolai grabs my hand, and we leap into the water.

"Ah, too cold," I say.

"WAY TOO COLD!"

But we adjust, splashing around practically shoulder to shoulder with all the other patrons, and Nicky's laughing at the top of his lungs. But then he goes quiet, eyeing the long line of kids at the diving board with awe and a little envy.

"Do you want to jump?" I ask.

He shakes his head no, but a few seconds later he says, "Will you watch me?"

"Of course."

"Then . . . okay."

He paddles to the side, climbs out, and runs to join the line. I swim over to the roped-off area and wave at him. Grinning, he waves back.

About ten other kids jump while I'm treading water and wait-ing, and finally it's his turn.

He tiptoes onto the board, but then he just stands there. Some-thing about how his floaties force his arms out and the way his wet hair's sticking up makes me think of a scared baby duck.

"You can do it, Nicky!" I call out.

"Your little brother?" a woman holding a toddler with wet pig-tails asks me.

I nod, because the real answer's too complicated.

Nicky almost makes it to the end of the diving board before he reverses again, wringing his little hands with nerves—and now I remember. Penny told me Nicolai kept trying to work up the courage to jump off the diving board. He wanted to do it so badly, but he was afraid.

Can this be the same pool?

I glance around at the transplanted palm trees and painted flamingos.

It *is*.

I'm shaken from my thoughts when the woman beside me calls out, "Come on, Nicky! You can do it!" Then she tells her little daughter, "Can you cheer for Nicky? See him on the diving board? See how brave he is?"

A moment later, another lady shouts, "You can do it!"

And the cheer starts to spread, until the whole pool is clapping their hands and chanting, "Go, Nicky, go! Go, Nicky, go!"

Stunned, Nicolai gapes at the crowd.

I hear smatters of kindhearted laughter at his expression, and everyone keeps on chanting.

Nicolai edges to the tip of the diving board, bends his knees— and then he jumps.

Time is not so simple.

Is he underwater too long? Or is it just seconds before he bobs to the top, a shocked smile on his face. As the entire pool applauds, he wipes water from his eyes and nose, then he swims over to me, wrapping his little arms around my neck.

Suddenly, the Observer Me appears, noting that I couldn't do this a few months ago, I couldn't handle being around Nicolai. I thought I didn't have anything to offer, nothing to give. And whatever meager energy I did possess, I had to hide it, save it for a rainy day. And even before that—*before*-before—it was pretty much the same. I wasn't conscious of it, but it was like some part of me believed caring could deplete me. But it's like one of Nicolai's riddles, what is something you get more of every time you give it away?

Love. It makes you bigger. Penny was right—you have to expand.

"Sayers?" Nicolai says. "Did you see that?"

"Yes, I saw."

"I did it."

I kiss the top of his chlorine-scented head. "You did it."

NINETY-ONE

Evan got a job two days into summer break, but when he's not working and I'm not with Nicolai, we've been hanging out at Harvest House Coffee, this place Evan found with exposed bricks and creaky hardwood floors. Evan likes it because it has all these little nooks and quiet alcoves to read in, and I like it because no one from school comes here.

Today, Evan's tired from work and I'm tired from the sun, so we read and drink some kind of tea-fruit fusion until we start to wake back up.

"What do you want to do for your birthday?" he asks, catching me by surprise. I only mentioned my birthday in passing.

"I don't know . . ." I'm getting part of my inheritance and Mom said I should buy myself something nice, but I can't think of anything I want. "Birthdays aren't really that important."

Evan's entire face crinkles up as if I've said something truly awful. "Who says they're not important?"

Caleb—he told me that.

But when I don't answer, Evan tells me, "Well, they *are* important. And eighteen is a big one."

Eighteen.

Sometimes it's as if I skipped seventeen altogether, and I'm not sure what age I actually feel.

Evan's cell phone vibrates on the table. He opens it, then smiles so wide I can see both rows of his white teeth.

"Good news?" I ask.

"Do you want to eat dinner at my house?"

On the drive over, Evan explains that he had to come clean with his parents. "It's too weird being such good friends, and to keep lying about where I'm going."

"They weren't mad?"

He grimaces. "Yeah, they were. But I think they're coming around."

"And they really said I could come over?"

"It was their idea."

I aim my smile out the window, embarrassed to be caught feeling so happy about this. I didn't realize how much I wanted their approval until right now.

A few minutes later, we walk through Evan's front door and toe off our shoes before stepping down into the sunken living room, where Evan's father is waiting in a plaid recliner. His face is so forbidding I'm pretty sure I've been set up.

"Evan, why don't you give us a minute?" he says, and it's not really a question.

"Oh, uh . . ." Evan sounds uncertain, while I send him clear signals with my eyes not to leave me here alone.

"We won't be long," his father adds.

Evan ducks his head in an apologetic gesture, then he's gone.

It's quiet now, just the sound of AC blasting through the window unit on the wall to my left.

I shiver.

"So . . ." his father begins in a stern voice. "Evan tells me you've been spending a lot of time together. While your mother was out of town."

"Yessir." I stuff my hands into my pockets. "But she wasn't gone that long."

"Sayers, please sit."

I place myself in a straight-back wooden chair and study the shag carpet.

"I know some things have happened in the past that were not okay."

"Yessir." That's an understatement.

"But I trust Evan's judgment. If he cares about you . . . then you must be worth caring about."

I'm startled into lifting my head.

"So I'm trusting you."

"O-okay."

"Don't betray that."

I swallow, surprised and touched and weirdly emotional. "I won't."

NINETY-TWO

The first half of my birthday is very official. Mom's lawyers come over with documents for me to sign and contracts to discuss, but after that she takes me out to lunch at a nice restaurant, and we sit on a patio under huge whirling fans.

Mom smiles while she twirls her pasta around her fork, and I don't know if she's happy because we're celebrating today, or if she's really doing better, but I'm smiling back at her.

"This is all right, isn't it?" she says. "Just the two of us?" I must look confused because she adds, "Instead of a big party?"

"Oh. Yeah. This is good."

And I mean it. I didn't even think about having a party but I guess I would have before. Probably something lavish with hundreds of guests.

I lift my hair so the breeze can cool my sweating neck. I'm not sure what's been stopping me from getting my hair cut, especially now that it's summer, because I can touch sharp things now, and I'm free to go to a salon any time I want.

Short hair sounds nice to me.

Like starting over.

+ + +

I'm waiting outside for Evan when he pulls into my driveway. He hops out of his truck, his eyes going wide. "Whoa," he says. "That's drastic." I run my hand over the top of my shorn head, a little self-conscious, then he gives me a wrapped gift and a hug. "Happy birthday."

Smiling, I tear open the paper. It's a book with extremely cool lettering across the cover. I squint at the title. *"Independent People?"*

"That's right." Evan sounds impressed. "It's supposed to be the most acclaimed Icelandic novel ever, and since you love that language so much . . ."

"Thank you, Evan." I glide my fingertip across the raised letters for a moment, then I look up at him. "I want to show you something."

And I lead him around to the lot where a brand-new SUV is waiting, the sun hitting the silver-blue paint so it shimmers like the ocean.

"Wow." Evan's eyes are huge. "You got this for your birthday?"

"Do you like it?"

"Yeah, I love it."

"It's for you."

"What?" He looks so shocked I let out a laugh.

I hold the keys into the air. "I got it for you!"

"Sayers . . ." His eyebrows scrunch up. "I can't take this."

"What?" My mouth starts twitching.

"We've talked about this."

We talked about *medical school*, but that's not the same as a truck.

"It's your birthday, Sayers. You should get something for yourself."

My whole energy's wilting. I know I could buy myself a car, but we have a garage full of nice cars. I could buy something else, but that idea doesn't make me happy either, so maybe this *is* for me—because it felt good to go into that dealership and get this for Evan.

"Please." I put all of my sincerity into that word. "This is the only thing I want."

"Is it weird that I expected to find it surrounded by spectators?" Evan says as we're walking out of Autumn Leaves. "It's just . . . it's really nice."

As he drives back to my house, he's talking fast the whole way about how the brakes work as soon as you press them, and if you barely touch the gas pedal, you *fly*.

But when he parks next to his old red pickup, his smile wobbles.

"What's wrong?"

"I wonder if this will hurt my parents' feelings."

"What do you mean?"

"They were so happy when they gave me my truck. It was a really big deal for us, you know? I don't want them to think I don't appreciate it."

"They'd never think that. They know you."

"Maybe . . ."

We sit here without speaking for a minute until Evan breaks the silence. "I can't believe we're going to be seniors."

"Me either."

"And then next year, college . . ."

"Yeah. Weird."

"This has been a really good summer, hasn't it?"

I have the urge to laugh and remind him summer just started, but instead, I think seriously about what he said. I've had plenty of nice summers, back when summer was a verb. We'd *summer* in Maine, in Aspen, on the Mediterranean in France. But this?

"Yeah." I smile at him. "So far this is the best summer I've ever had."

It's almost midnight when I let myself into my mom's study. I don't know if it's the realization that I'm a literal adult now, or maybe Evan talking about college earlier today—but for the first time *ever*, the idea of going to college actually interests me.

Evan's already taken the SATs. He said he did *fairly well*, which means he probably got a perfect score. I took the pre-SATs last year and never even looked at the results, but I'm sure my mom has the records somewhere.

I try her filing cabinet. Nope.

The antique rolltop desk. Not there either.

Then the middle drawer of her writing desk. *Locked.* But I know where she's hidden the key, so I pluck it from the hidden compartment along the credenza. Fitting the key into the lock, I slide the drawer open, and inside is a phone with a red case.

My phone—the one I left at Restaurant a million years ago.

For some reason, my mother hid it from me.

NINETY-THREE

It feels like bad luck to even touch that phone, like it might suck me back in time or worse, but curiosity drives me to pick it up and tap the screen. It's dead, which makes sense I guess, so I carry it to my bedroom, find a charger, and power it up.

Right away, I understand why my mom kept this from me. A bunch of reporters must've gotten hold of my number because there are dozens of texts asking for interviews, and strangers claiming to have information on my whereabouts.

I'm about to shut the phone back off when something grabs my attention.

A text from Luke.

I run my forefinger across the screen, back and back through all these messages I've never read, and I stop scrolling on one that glares out at me:

About to leave for the art field trip.

The text he sent me the day I left.

And right below it is the one he must've sent after I sped off from Restaurant.

Monday, Oct. 12, 7:30 p.m.
    What the hell dude. Come back.

8:00 p.m.
    This is so messed up.
    What are we supposed to do??????

10:33 p.m.
    We JUST got home, and I had to
    spend 80 bucks on an Uber,
    so thanks for that.

Tuesday, Oct. 13, 9:33 a.m.
    Guess you decided to skip today.

    You should at least say you're sorry.

1:07 p.m.
    Saye, WHERE ARE YOU?? Your mom just
    called me, and she said you never came home
    last night. I keep calling your cell, but it's
    going to voicemail.

    Please call me back.

For a minute, I have to stop reading. I set the phone facedown
and push it away. It's been forever since Luke and I have spoken,

but I can remember that freaked-out quivery voice he used to have whenever he got worried, and he worried a lot. Nothing like me—I never worried at all. I take a deep breath, then grab the phone and move on to the text he sent me the next morning.

Thursday, Oct. 15, 11:06 a.m.
The police are here interviewing everyone.
Your mom and your grandfather were here too.
They gave a press conference asking for information.
All these kids who don't even know you are
answering questions. It's so creepy.

Friday, Oct. 16, 3:30 p.m.
Ms. Wells started crying in class today.
Mr. Rivas came in to comfort her, and they
told us how much they love all their
students, and then I started crying too.

Yes, in front of everyone.
You would've been so embarrassed of me.

Monday, Oct. 19, 11:06 a.m.
Everyone's praying. It was Abby Whitley's idea.
I know you don't like her, but she's not that bad.
She's praying you make it home.

Tuesday, Oct. 20, 2:05 p.m.
The counselor just came into English

and said we can come to her
if we need help "processing."

You would've been proud of me
for real, man. I told her to quit talking
about you like you're dead.

Friday, Oct. 23, 4:45 p.m.
You will not believe this. Maggie Watts is
currently sobbing her eyes out in Spanish Club.
She hardly knew thee. Have you ever even
spoken to her? No, I know you haven't.

She's saying this has put everything in perspective,
how life's too short. Any minute any one of us
could be gone. So basically you disappearing is
making her realize SHE could disappear.
Did I mention I'm eating Cheetos as I text you?

I have the urge to shove Cheetos
up her sniffling nostrils.

Sorry. That's a terrible thing to say.
I would never waste Cheetos like that.

Saturday, Oct. 24, 2:13 a.m.
Your messages aren't saying delivered anymore.
This is gonna sound dumb but every time they'd

say delivered, it felt like you were reading them.

Yes, I know, I said it was dumb.

Tuesday, Oct. 27, 12:06 p.m.
Dillon Blair just got arrested.

Everyone's saying he killed you,
but if you were dead, I'd feel it. I'd know.

Monday, Nov. 10, 9:36 a.m.
I started going to this all-guy group at Abby's church.
We don't just pray. We talk about our problems too.
A lot of the other guys have addiction issues,
and there's this one dude whose mom has cancer.
Then there's me. No addiction, no cancer.
Guess what I do? I make people laugh.

Yep, in a collection of sad misfits, it turns out
I'm ducking hilarious.

Not *ducking.

Ducking

Forget it—my phone won't let me curse.
But I

1:16 p.m.

Sorry. Ms. Sims made me put away my phone.

And his texts keep going, and sometimes I'm laughing, but mostly I'm emotional—because he wrote so *many*. It's like he was sending me every thought that entered his head the whole time I was gone, and so I read every single one. It takes a while, but I get through the fall and winter, and I'm on to spring.

Wednesday, Apr. 7, 11:06 a.m.

Have you heard of God of Gaps?

So the gap is all the stuff we as humans
don't understand, and in the past, the gap
was much bigger. Like . . . what are those
spots of light out in the sky?
When people couldn't explain it,
they'd say it had to be God.

But with more scientific advancement,
the gap started shrinking. We know those
lights are stars, and we know why the days get shorter,
but for the leftover stuff, we still say that's God.

So what if I just THINK God exists because I don't
know any better, or because I just want to believe it?

Tuesday, Apr. 13, 11:30 p.m.

  I don't think I can remember a time before I knew you.
  I'm glad God threw us into that pre-k class together.
  I don't know why you were there. Didn't you have like
  ten nannies? I bet your parents wanted you to socialize.
  Ha! Little did they know you'd befriend ME!

Wednesday, Apr. 14, 12:06 a.m.

  I really wish you'd come home.
  If not for me, for your mom.
  I saw her this afternoon.
  I barely recognized her.

  If you do make it home in one piece,
  please know that I will be taking full credit
  because I'm praying like every second.

  Actually, I'll probably be scared to face you.

Thursday, Apr. 22, 2:30 a.m.

  I've been thinking this same thought lately.
  It's like a video clip, the same few seconds
  over and over. We're driving, and I see the
  restaurant, and I'm telling you to stop,
  and you say: Let's just keep going.

And that keeps repeating over and over.

I'm the one who told you to stop.
You didn't want to, but I begged.

We were an hour from home. That's it.
One hour, and we would've gone to school
the next day and everything would be okay.

I think that hour's gonna kill me.

And that's it, his last text. I scroll back to the beginning, reread
them all, then I find the voicemail he left me two days after that
final message.

I press play.

"Hey. It's me." Luke's voice fills my room. "I went back to the
restaurant and that girl, Penny, was there. Do you remember her?
She was really nice. I'm pretty sure she was just humoring me, but
she helped me look for clues, and we found your phone in a store-
room. I'm looking right at it so I know you can't answer, but I still
thought you would—how crazy is that?" His breaths start making
staticky noises against the speaker. "I just wanted to tell you . . .
you're my best friend, and I love you. Why did we never say that
before? Because we men of Texas do not say such things."

He laughs.

And then he starts to cry.

"I'm sorry, Saye. When you didn't come back, I should've known something was wrong, but I was so pissed off I wasn't thinking straight. I didn't tell your mom, so she didn't even know you were missing till the next morning. If we'd started looking sooner, we would've found you."

For a couple minutes the only sound is Luke's crying, then he says, "I'm *sorry*, Saye. And I'll be sorry for the rest of my life."

The voicemail ends, and I keep staring down at my phone, stunned.

Luke thought it was *his* fault? Is that why he wouldn't talk to me? Because he felt guilty?

I find the last text message he sent, and my thumbs hover over the keys for a long time before I begin typing out my reply:

So . . . I just got your nine billion texts.
I'm sorry it took me so long to write back.

And just for the record.
I love you too.

NINETY-FOUR

Evan's grinning as he walks into my room. I think he must've missed a couple of appointments with his barber because his hair's at an awkward in-between stage, the dark bristles sticking up at different heights like an unkempt lawn.

Suddenly, his smile falls away. "What's wrong?" He says it so gently that I want to find a mirror to see if I look like I've been crying. I shouldn't. I held a cold cloth to my eyes for twenty minutes to bring down the swelling, so I must be telegraphing my emotions in some other way.

I clear my throat. "Nothing. I'm good."

Or at least I should be. Luke's on a college tour with his parents, but as soon as he gets home, I'm going to see him, and it won't be long before Penny's home too. Mostly, I've been feeling hopeful, I really have. But then out of nowhere this morning, I got this urge to hold my viewfinder, and I haven't been able to shake it since.

My hands keep itching, these rising nerves, and I know I'd calm down if I could hold it just for a minute and click through some slides, but it makes no sense. So dumb to need a viewfinder in a room full of windows.

And now I'm wondering if I've really gotten myself together at all, because I thought I was doing okay, but maybe I'm not. Maybe I never will.

Evan's eyes are still probing and concerned. "You sure?"

"Definitely. What kind of pizza did you get?"

And soon we're sitting on my bed shoulder to shoulder watching some family drama he heard was good. It's slow-paced, and I'm distracted and fidgety until the father forces his son to bend over a table so he can whip him with his belt. It's a strange scene for a movie made in this century, directed like the kid is noble for taking his punishment quietly, directed like the father is just doing his duty by beating him.

"This is weird," I say. "Nobody does that to their kids anymore." When Evan makes a noncommittal noise, I turn to him, suspicious. "Did your dad ever do that to you?"

"A couple of times, yeah." He shrugs, like it's not horrible, not traumatic.

"God, I'm sorry, Evan. That's terrible."

He gives me a faintly humored look. "It's really okay."

"No, Evan that's really *not* okay." He has to know that isn't normal. "My dad . . . God, he never hit me with a *belt*."

"Your dad?" Evan tilts his head at me with this quizzical, puzzled expression. The way you look at someone who isn't *together*, and I feel my face getting hot.

"I'm not saying anything crazy."

"I didn't say you were. It's just—"

"Would your dad do that to your mom?"

"Of course not—"

"How about the dogs?"

"Sayers." Evan pauses the movie. "What's going on?

"But a child—his *son*—that's okay?" I'm on my feet now, my hands trembling at my sides. "It's wrong! And if I were you, I'd never speak to him again."

Evan's face goes abruptly cold. "My father is a good man."

"And *that* is Stockholm syndrome."

"*What?*"

"It's when a victim starts feeling affection toward their abuser or capt—"

"Yeah, I know what it means, Sayers."

"What about your little brothers?" I can't catch my breath enough to talk without my words coming out in choppy gasps. "Does that bastard hit them too?"

And now Evan's on his feet. "Don't talk about my dad like that. I don't know what's going on with you, but—"

"He's got you brainwashed!" I start to pace. "He's got you brainwashed, and you don't even see it! I'm not gonna listen to you tell me your dad's hurting you and act like it's okay!"

Evan rakes his fingers across his sprigs of hair, then loosens his shoulders like he's trying to control his temper. "My father isn't *hurting* me. He's punished me twice in my entire life."

"Oh my God, do you hear yourself? *Punished?* It's Stockholm—"

"Stop it, Sayers. I'm not the one with the syndrome."

I halt in my steps. "What's that supposed to mean?"

When he doesn't answer, I press, "You mean me?"

"Yes, *you*. This is about you and Caleb." Evan's studying me, as serious as I've ever seen him. "That man was not your father. He was a serial killer."

Everything goes still as the words echo around the room and in my head.

"N-no. He was my . . ." My eyes start to blur. "He wasn't a—"

"Yes. He was."

I push my fists against my temples. "Sh-shut up. He *wasn't*. He—he—"

"He kidnapped you. He starved you—"

"He *loved* me!"

I swipe my wet eyes with the back of my hand, and when my vision clears, Evan's face has gone soft with pity.

"He *hurt* you, Sayers. I'm so sorry he hurt you." And suddenly . . . I'm empty. Fading off into a dazed quiet as Evan goes on and on, his words just white noise now. They don't mean anything. ". . . but it scares me sometimes. Because he wasn't your dad, and I don't know how you'll ever fully heal if you don't acknowledge that. You have to confront it. You have to—"

I start to laugh.

A sound so cold and mocking, Evan stutters off, a shocked look on his face.

"Evan, who are *you* to tell me anything?" And he might be taller, but I'm looking down on him like he's so far beneath me, I'd have to stoop to find him.

"Saye, I'm just trying—"

"Get out of my house."

Evan lets out a small gasp, and his eyes are showing me every-thing—his confusion, his hurt. But then he shakes his head like he's trying to shake himself out of it, like he's trying to regain control of things.

"Sayers, you don't really want me to go."

Lifting one eyebrow, I smile in a way that seems to shatter him.

"Yeah, Evan. I really do."

NINETY-FIVE

It's the first day of summer school, and weeks since I've talked to Evan or God, and it's like a phone wire that's been cut, like I cut it, or maybe the connection was never there at all.

All my classes are stuffed onto a single hall, and there are way more people here than I thought there'd be.

At the break for lunch, I wonder if I'm hallucinating because I could swear that's *Garrett* sitting on the side of the walkway that cuts through the courtyard. He's making zero effort to hide his bottle of liquor, and I remember being like that—back when there was nothing bad that could happen I couldn't undo.

I cross the courtyard in long strides. "Feel like sharing?"

Garrett looks caught off guard, then pissed for getting caught off guard. "No," he snaps.

I'm tired—I've barely slept in days—so I snap back. "Fuck it. I don't care."

I'm spinning around when Garrett holds the bottle out toward me. His arm's swaying a little, and now I'm noticing his bloodshot corneas and the sheen over his flushed cheeks. Yeah, pretty sure he's wasted. I hesitate for a second before I grab the bottle and sit beside him. I take a swallow—it burns straight down to my stomach—then he pries the drink from my hand.

"So . . ." He's watching me with flinty eyes. "What seven-year-old girl did you steal that from?" He nods to my necklace.

"Fuck you," I say, and he grins like that was the correct response. "What are you even doing here, Garrett?"

"Flunked a couple classes." He shrugs, apathetic.

"Same." I laugh and take the bottle back.

Garrett's face fills with familiar admiration. Winning him over wasn't so hard. In fact, for the first time in forever, something was easy. I haven't drunk enough to be buzzed, but I feel like I am anyway.

I shake the bottle. "This all you've got? Nothing more interesting?"

"Come by Braxton's party tonight. Tanner's hooking us up."

"Sounds good." Sounds *fun*. And is there anything wrong with fun? Why should I literally spend every moment of my day studying or reading or worrying?

"You still friends with Operation? You know, *Evan*?" Garrett says it with a certain emphasis, like Evan's name is a joke.

"No." The word falls out like a stone. "Not anymore."

Garrett relaxes visibly, and he looks at me the way he did when he found out I was taking Latin. Like I'm incomprehensible, but in a good way. "I never got why you were hanging around that little crybaby."

As far as insults go, that one's pretty tame, but it bothers me anyway because it's not true. In my mind, I can still see the Evan from that night. How hard he was breathing, his eyes huge with fear. "But he didn't cry."

"Well, you weren't there the whole time, were you?" Garrett's obviously remembering the same night, and he has a strange glow, like a cruel magician about to perform his greatest trick. "Do you want to know what makes Evan Zamara cry?"

I'm afraid to answer, but slowly I nod.

With a jagged smile, he leans in close. "Giving head."

NINETY-SIX

Garrett starts to laugh. Drunken, reverberating booms inside my brain.

He can't mean what I think he means. That when he took Evan into the woods he—he wouldn't just *say* that, he wouldn't *do* that. Garrett lowers the bottle to his crotch, tipping it over in this sick pantomime and splashing alcohol onto the ground. Then he laughs again and lifts the bottle to take another swig, casual and relaxed like he's already moving on to a new thought, like what he did means nothing.

When the bottle shatters into sharp pieces on the concrete walkway, I realize I've smacked it from his hand. A split second of shock crosses Garrett's face, and the next thing I know, I've got my hands wrapped around his throat, and I'm slamming him into the ground.

Garrett blinks up at me, gasping for air, his fingers clawing at mine. His eyes bulge—then they narrow, and he knocks his boulder-fist into my face.

I careen over onto the grass, seeing stars.

"What the fuck, Saye!" Garrett springs to his feet and shakes out his hand.

There's an echo surrounding my head, and I can taste blood in my mouth. Rolling onto my knees, I spit bright red onto the sidewalk, then I pant up at Garrett, "You didn't do that to him!"

"Fine." He grins down at me. "I didn't."

Roaring, I grab him around the knees and drag him back down.

I swing. He dodges, and my fist smashes into the concrete. My knuckles split, white dust filling the bloody cracks, and I know it should hurt, but for some reason I can't feel anything.

Garrett's swearing at me as he lurches back to his feet.

Suddenly, I'm flung into the air, his biker boot in my ribs.

That I feel.

I make a garbled noise as the air gushes out of me. Leaning to one side, I wretch a dry heave. Garrett lifts his boot to kick me again—

I roll out of reach before his boot can land, and climb to my feet. Sweat is sprouting on Garrett's temple, his big fists shielding his red face, and he shouts, "You thought I was just gonna let him get away with what he did?"

"He didn't do anything to you!"

Garrett lowers his left arm for just a second, and I take another wild swing, only my hand isn't working the way it should so it glances off his chin.

Before I can swing again, Garrett slugs me in the face with perfect boxer's aim.

Blood pours into my eye.

He hits me again.

Again.

And this feeling comes over me, like drums in my head and in my fists. I rush him. Stronger than I should be, I throw him down. Straddle him. He tries to buck me off him, but I'm crazed as I dig my knees into his armpits, and I'm hitting hitting hitting.

NINETY-SEVEN

There's a fresh white cast on my broken hand. My fingers throb a little. My head throbs a lot. My mother's driving me home from the hospital in silence. She spoke to the doctor before we left, made sure the exam was thorough and a follow-up appointment was scheduled, but she won't even look at me.

I can guess why. After a billion hours in the ER, I made the mistake of getting online, and video footage of the fight was already everywhere—from different angles and different phones. It seems like the whole world's weighing in on what happened because everyone has a camera and no context.

"Mom?" I finally say. "Can you talk to me?"

"What were you *thinking*?" Her voice is low and furious. "His family's going to sue us."

"They won't."

"Of course they will. There are witnesses!"

"I know, but—"

"And they're saying you instigated it. That *you* attacked *him*. Of course they'll sue us."

"No. They won't."

She swivels her head to me. "How do you know that?"

"Because Garrett won't want me to tell anyone why I hit him."

I expect her to ask what I mean, but instead she just refocuses on the road. "We were living a fantasy before."

It takes me a moment to connect that she means *before*-before, and it does feel that way. In my memories we all sparkle, invulnerable to the things that can hurt everyone else. Like children of the gods, no blood in our castle.

"It was a fantasy . . ." she says again. "And it had to fall. But who knew things would go *this* bad? I've lost *everyone*. My husband, my father, my son—"

"Your son?" I echo in confusion. "I'm right here."

But she doesn't seem to hear me, her eyes swimming now as she keeps on driving.

And now I think I understand.

To her I'm still gone, because I'm not him. Because I'll never be the Same Old Saye.

"You liked me better before."

She flicks a side glance at me. "Th-that's not true."

"It *is*. Everyone liked me better. My girlfriend, my friends, even strangers. And all this time—this whole time I've been back—I've been trying so hard to get back to that. To who I used to be. But now I don't even know why. I wasn't a good person."

"You *were*. You were beautiful. You were perfect."

"I *wasn't*. You don't know the things I did. Don't you want to know why Blair threatened me that day? It's because I—"

"No! I'm not listening to this. You were sixteen. All teenagers make mistakes!"

"Mom, please." I need to confess this—for her to know the truth and still love me, not just whatever me she's manufactured in her head. "I went along with so much awful shit. I wasn't good, Mom. I—"

"And you think *this* is good?" she shouts, hysterical like I'm shattering everything she has left.

"No," I admit, sinking down into my seat. "But I'm trying."

NINETY-EIGHT

I grab a booth by the window and rub the excess water from my hair. It started pouring on my walk to Harvest House, and it's coming down even harder now. I glance over my shoulder to the empty coffee shop with its dark wood floors and secluded alcoves, then turn back around, shivering as my rain-soaked shirt clings to my skin.

I wrap my hands around my mug—one in a cast, one with taped knuckles—but I hide them under the table just as Evan slides into the booth across from me. It's been less than a month since I've seen him, but his dark curls have taken on a life of their own. Messy and loose, they make him look younger for some reason.

I'm not sure how to start. When I texted to ask if he'd meet me, my plan was to apologize right away, but now the words are stuck.

"Hey," he eventually says.

"Hey."

He zeroes in on my left eye, at the faint bruising around it, and his fingers start tapping the scuffed tabletop, like they're itching for something to take apart and put back together. He settles for grasping the mug of coffee I placed on his side of the booth.

"Thanks," he mumbles.

I nod, and we lapse into silence until Evan breaks it with, "Are you still mad at me?"

For a moment, I gape at him. "Mad at *you*? You're the one who should be mad at me."

His face is soft with regret. "I'm sorry about what I said. I shouldn't have pressured you to talk if you're not ready."

"No, it's okay. Really. You were trying to help, I know that." I fidget, not sure how to explain. "It's just . . . I've never talked about what happened when I was, you know. Gone."

Evan's eyebrows knit together. "You never talked to *anyone* about it?"

"No. I . . . I guess I don't know how. It's just that most of the time it was so . . . so . . ."

"Horrible?"

"*Normal.*" I register the surprise on his face, but I keep going. "I cared about him. I know how that sounds, but I did. It was like he was my dad, and it was just . . . life. We watched TV, we ate dinner. You know, normal. And at some point, all the things he said started making sense to me. I mean, even crazy things."

"Like what?"

"Like—like during the big meteor shower, magical beings were going to turn back time. I'd be ten years old again, and I wouldn't remember my parents. And my parents *weren't* my parents. They were evil scientists who conducted experiments on kids."

Evan's listening, but he doesn't seem to be judging, and if he's not judging me, then I'm not explaining it right.

"Don't you get it? What the hell was wrong with me?"

"Sayers." Evan makes a sputtering noise. "He messed with your head."

"Oh, he didn't just mess with it. He reached in, tore it apart, rewired it—and I let him."

"Come on—"

"Did I tell you I actually believed I was Daniel?"

"No."

"Or that we celebrated Christmas over and over and over, and I fell for it every single time? And it didn't take me *years* to break. In just a few months, I believed everything."

"You believed it because you had to," Evan says like he's stating a fact. "It's incredible what our minds will do to survive."

"But sometimes I'm not sure I *did* survive. I was pretending to be Daniel, and now I'm pretending to be Saye, and I don't know who I am!"

Evan's amber eyes fill with sympathy. So much sympathy that I have to look away.

The rain has slowed to a drizzle, and it's sliding down the window in slow squiggly patterns, almost like it's losing steam, and I'm losing steam too. "Maybe this is what I deserve . . . Karma for the things I've done."

"*Sayers.*" Evan's voice catches. It's a sharp enough sound that halts me into looking at him again, and when I do, his eyes are watering. "You didn't *deserve* that, I promise you didn't."

For a minute, I can't speak. Too overwhelmed, I guess, by the emotion on his face, and because I think I really needed to hear him say that, even if I don't fully believe it. I reach for my mug, which has gone cold, and his eyes widen in alarm as he zooms in on my cast.

"Did Garrett do that to your hand?"

"Ah no, I broke it on his face actually."

But Evan doesn't laugh like I want him to, just looks nervous. "Why were you fighting?"

I'm not going to tell him. Not ever.

But then I realize I don't have to because he can read me too well.

"He . . ." Evan's voice is rough. "He *told* you?"

I hesitate before answering. "Yes."

Evan's face is so stricken that I begin to stammer, "I—I'm sorry, Evan."

He nods, then he nods about fifty more times, and my heart feels like it's splitting. I can't stop myself from picturing it, Evan small and scared and being hurt in the woods. His skin has gone ashen, a sickly shame like it's possible to die from humiliation, and I want to hug him, but a memory springs to mind—one about how you shouldn't touch someone who's sleepwalking, and that's what he makes me think of. Like he's caught in a nightmare, and I need to give him time to wake up.

I wait until I'm sure I won't spook him before saying, "Evan . . . you can talk to me too, you know." When he stays quiet, I say it again. "I mean it, Evan. You can."

"Yeah," he finally says. "Yeah, I know." He studies the tabletop for a minute, then he looks at me. "After . . . after that night, I thought I'd get him back, or do *something*. But I'd see him in the halls and he'd just . . . *smile* at me." Evan's voice breaks. "God, it was humiliating. But I think that was the whole point, you know? To hurt me in a way I couldn't come back from."

And now I'm remembering that conversation I had with Luke when I told him Garrett was harmless, and Luke told me Garrett was cruel.

He's not harmless, Luke said. *He likes hurting people—he gets off on it.*

"I was so afraid he'd find me alone, I stopped going to school. I stopped sleeping. I was jumpy all the time." Evan rakes a hand through his curls. "My parents thought I was losing it. They made me see a therapist."

"Did it help?"

"It took time . . . I didn't click with the first therapist, so I found someone else. But eventually, yeah, it helped."

"Good." I let out a breath. "That's good."

And for a while, we sit here in silence under the weight of these things that have happened, both of us trying to be better, even though these things should make us worse.

"Evan . . . I don't know how you can be around me after everything. But I also don't know what I would've done this past year without you."

"Sometimes I think . . . okay, this'll sound strange." He gives me a flash of a smile. "But it's like I *knew* we were going to be friends. Like déjà vu in reverse or something."

My eyes well up. "You really want to be my friend again?"

"*Sayers.*" His voice is gently scoffing, comfortingly dismissive. "We never stopped being friends."

I smile, something bright and hopeful, but it's hard to hold. "It doesn't make sense."

"What doesn't?"

"Nothing. None of it. All those boys—and Daniel, the *real* Daniel. I don't know if they'll ever find him. But me—I'm here. I'm here, and they're not . . . And then there's Penny. She saved my life in there. I mean literally, she did, but I don't know if she'll ever be the same. And she was so close to her family, you know? They needed her so much. No one *needed* me."

Evan nods, thoughtful, listening. "Well, now they do."

The world's a drippy watercolor. It stopped raining by the time Evan and I said our goodbyes. He offered me a ride home, but I told him I had somewhere to go first and that I wanted to walk. I figured it'd give me a chance to collect my thoughts, but now I wonder if I'm just stalling.

Penny's coming home today.

I sidestep a puddle, nerves in my gut with all my steps. I've been waiting so long for this, but now that it's finally here, I'm more afraid than I've ever been. What if she's not any better? What if she's still just as traumatized as she was the last time I saw her? Or what if she *is* better—until she sees me. And then she panics and falls apart.

And then there's something that's been too painful to face, but now it's a blinking question in my head: *What if she never loved me?*

Maybe she was saying whatever she thought she had to say to survive. How *did* Penny see things? Trapped with a strange boy who thought he was someone else. It must have been unbearable. So she might not want to see me again—not today, not *ever*—and if that's the case, I'll understand. I'll go.

But if there's even a chance she needs me and I could help, I have to try.

So I keep walking. Down wet commercial district streets, through stoplights, past a collection of interconnected storefronts, and onto the smaller, quieter roads where people live.

Pools of rainwater drip from flowers planted in various front yards, and when the breeze picks up, branches shake more rain off the leaves.

My legs are beginning to ache. I've walked clear across town, but I keep going, one step after the other, until finally . . . I've reached the embracing trees on Cedar Way.

Stopping to catch my breath, all the same doubts race through my mind, but I push them aside and start climbing the hill.

Up ahead, I can see Nicolai sitting at the picnic table on his front porch, his little face furrowed in concentration as he draws pictures with Magic Markers, probably making something for Penny. My heart squeezes in my chest.

I glance to the front door. I should go and knock on it, but I'm still hesitating as a car with tinted windows pulls to the curb.

The passenger door opens.

And Penny steps out onto the sidewalk.

Her long dark hair is flowing around her shoulders, her cheeks are fuller, and a green duffel bag dangles from one of her hands. As if she can sense someone watching her, she lifts her head, her brown eyes searching—and then they find me.

But before I have time to worry about what she's thinking, a smile spreads over her face, so brilliant I don't just see it, I *feel* it. It's physically impossible not to smile back. I start up the wet sidewalk again, and Penny glows even brighter—she's a lighthouse, a sunbeam.

A happy shout echoes off the porch. Nicolai's waving at Penny, and under the table, his bare feet are drumming onto the floorboards, he's so excited.

I start to laugh. This moment's a gift, and I don't know how I've gotten so lucky to have been given so many, but I'm grateful. For today and tomorrow and—I falter in my steps.

It's the strangest thing . . . but I feel like I've been here before. Yes, this exact moment. Penny and I have already lived this. It's a scene we envisioned in a dark room. And so I know exactly what's going to happen next. Penny and I will splash through puddles, both of us smiling and smelling the after-rain on our way to her front porch, and once we reach it, we'll hug Nicolai and each other. And then I'll tell her, thank you for the last time.

AUTHOR'S NOTE:

"He'll never be the same."

Sayers came across this comment from a stranger who was speculating about his future. The comment got to him, and this way of thinking used to get to me too. I'd wonder: Can we ever really overcome a serious trauma?

When I was an eighteen-year-old psychology student, I was presented with some pretty bleak statistics. According to the CDC, the more trauma a person experiences before the age of eighteen, the more likely they are to develop serious mental and physical health issues later in life. And with enough trauma, this likelihood can jump by *three-thousand* percent. Dr. Emmy Werner's forty-year longitudinal study resulted in similar findings. She and her colleagues tracked children growing up in extreme adversity, and by adulthood, the majority of these kids had developed mental health issues, drug problems, or were incarcerated.

Reading studies like these, I was terrified, my mind drifting to the little boys I was raising. Months had passed since my nephews moved in, but the four-year-old was still having nightmares. When he woke up in the middle of the night screaming, I would run into his bedroom and he'd fling himself into my arms, gripping my shirt and wrapping his legs around my waist.

He'd never say what the dreams were about, but over time, he'd begun telling me more about the things that had happened to him. What he'd experienced was beyond my comprehension, even though I knew very well what it was like to grow up afraid.

The statistics on recovering from trauma were definitely disturbing, but some deeper part of me said, *no*, these experiences don't have to determine our fate.

I kept studying, eventually earning my undergraduate and master's degrees in mental health. Meanwhile, my family and I got treatment. Sometimes we struggled, but we were also healing. And it was from this place of struggling and healing that I started writing *Dark Room Etiquette*.

The novel began as a thriller—a story about someone who has everything, then loses it all—and in many ways it still is. But the more I wrote, the more I wanted to explore what comes next, the *aftermath* of a traumatic event.

The characters in this book are each doing their best to cope with their individual experiences, but trauma can feel like a dark room. We live in it, or maybe it lives in us, and it can become a place we're not sure we can ever escape.

Ultimately, however, I wanted this story to focus on hope, because there is *so* much hope out there. According to the American Psychological Association, several modalities for trauma recovery are highly effective. There's cognitive behavioral therapy, dialectical behavioral therapy, and Eye Movement Desensitization and Reprocessing.

And over the past few years, I've revisited Dr. Werner's longitudinal study. Yes, there were a lot of difficult outcomes, but amongst the kids who faced the most serious trauma, a third of them went on to thrive.

Dr. Werner called this group *vulnerable but invincible*.

And that's how I see the characters in this book.

It's how I see my nephews.

It's how I'm trying to see myself.

And it's my hope that anyone who is struggling might begin to see themselves this way too. This doesn't mean denying our history, ignoring our pain, or pretending there are no more bad days. On the contrary, for me, it means facing all those things. It means seeking out help when we need it, and trying new treatment methods even after we think we've tried them all. And it means reminding ourselves that no matter what's happened to us, we still have the capacity for so much joy—because there is always a way out of a dark room.

ACKNOWLEDGMENTS

Writing *Dark Room Etiquette* was one of the most challenging things I've ever done, and a theme that arose again and again while I worked on it was gratitude. How important it is to express it. How important it is to feel it. And so I'd like to say thank you to:

My family. My mother Joan Roe, who's always told me with zero doubts: *You can do this.* Joshua Castillo, who inspired so much of Nicolai. And Michael and Braelynn Rose.

My friends. Kate Hawkes and Amber Smith. Our talks mean everything.

My colleagues. My agent Peter Steinberg, who had so much faith in this book. Everyone at HarperTeen: Kristen Pettit, my extremely gifted editor who can somehow see through to the soul of a project and guide you to bring it forth. Clare Vaughn, a warm and kindhearted assistant editor at HarperTeen. And the duo responsible for the cover of *Dark Room Etiquette*, designer Chris Kwon and artist Martine Johanna. This cover is more beautiful than I could have ever hoped for.

My spiritual community. Tracy Brown, Sandra Francis, Veronica Valles, Petra Weldes, and Sherry Woods. These are some of the incredible women I can call when I'm in a crisis.

The book community. All the bloggers, librarians, teachers, and readers who've reached out to me and shared their stories, as well as every single author who's ever shown me kindness.

And my son, Jordan (Joe) Roe. There was a talk we had that I'll never forget, where he helped me map out the entire story of *Dark Room Etiquette*. It was during this talk when he came up with the book's most important twist—the one that made everything else fall into place. And then there were the years upon years of edits, when he read the manuscript over and over, offering detailed, insightful, brilliant feedback, always with compassion and love. So it's no platitude when I say I couldn't have done this without him, but then, there are so many things I couldn't have done without Joe.